The massage was having the desired effect on me. I was aware of Barbara's warm body pressing down on mine as her knowing hands eased the tension from the muscles of my back.

'I can do this better without the towel,' she said, slipping it from my body, so that I was completely nude. I wondered if she was too, and what her big breasts would look like out in the open.

Suddenly she turned me over and those big naked breasts were inches from my face. They looked fabulous...

Also available from Headline Delta

Amour Amour
Amour Encore
The Blue Lantern
Good Vibrations
Groupies
Groupies II
In the Mood
Sex and Mrs Saxon
Sin and Mrs Saxon
Love Italian Style
Ecstasy Italian Style
Rapture Italian Style
Amorous Liaisons
Lustful Liaisons
Reckless Liaisons
Carnal Days
Carnal Nights
The Delicious Daughter
Hidden Rapture
A Lady of Quality
Hot Type
Playtime
The Sensual Mirror
The Secret Diary of Mata Hari

Blue Heavens

Nick Bancroft

HEADLINE DELTA

Copyright © 1994 Nick Bancroft

The right of Nick Bancroft to be identified as the Author of the Work has been asserted by him in accordance with the Copyright, Designs and Patents Act 1988.

First published in 1994
by HEADLINE BOOK PUBLISHING

A HEADLINE DELTA paperback

10 9 8 7 6 5 4 3 2 1

All rights reserved. No part of this publication may be reproduced, stored in a retrieval system, or transmitted, in any form or by any means without the prior written permission of the publisher, nor be otherwise circulated in any form of binding or cover other than that in which it is published and without a similar condition being imposed on the subsequent purchaser.

All characters in this publication are fictitious and any resemblance to real persons, living or dead, is purely coincidental.

ISBN 0 7472 4590 8

Typeset by Keyboard Services, Luton, Beds

Printed and bound in Great Britain by
Cox & Wyman Ltd, Reading, Berks

HEADLINE BOOK PUBLISHING
A division of Hodder Headline PLC
338 Euston Road
London NW1 3BH

Blue Heavens

1. Black and Blue

'So you're off tomorrow, old sport, are you?' Gerry looked up at me over the top of his *Times*. He'd called me in for a final chat, as he called it. I'd been working at his restaurant, the Blue Lantern, these last few months. Gerry was an enigmatic character. I'd always considered him a sort of gangster, though he rarely showed any toughness or roughness to me. He kept himself remote but he was very good to me. He paid me well, even extravagantly, for being not much more than his errand boy.

Being with him over those months had involved me with some delectable young women. They had offered me a lot of sexual favours. I'd lived what most young men would think was an ideal life at that age – in my early twenties. I was well paid, not overworked, and surrounded by luscious ladies who taught me the delights of sex. Gerry's business operation was basically illegal but I convinced myself that most of what I did was not really beyond the law: delivering packages of black market goods, helping Gerry on special missions. It was occasionally a little dangerous but the compensations were a more than adequate recompense – especially with those women.

I had wondered for the last few days why I was giving it all up. I'd always wanted to go to university but I'd found it difficult because all the college places in those years immediately after the war were being given to ex-servicemen. But now I'd been accepted at Manchester. Having waited so long to go, I really didn't feel I could back out of it. So here I was at the Blue Lantern, my bags packed ready to catch the early morning train to Manchester the next day.

'Well, I must say, kiddo, leaving this behind, you've got a lot of spunk,' and he grinned widely. 'I know a few ladies are going to miss that spunk of yours! Still, if it's what you want to do, throwing all of this up.' He gestured with a broad sweep of his arm at that private club of his, where most of the action took place, 'Can't say it'd suit me, sticking your nose in books instead of sticking your dick in these ladies you've got to know so well.'

'I'll certainly miss them,' I confessed.

'Margo's sorry she couldn't come down to say goodbye to you. She's actually a bit upset you haven't been round to see her these last few weeks.' Margo was Gerry's partner in the call-girl side of the business, a stunning woman in her thirties who had given me the benefit of her know-how about pleasing men. I enjoyed her company but I thought she had warned me off so I hadn't been round to her house for a while. 'She forgives you though,' Gerry continued. 'Sent you a going-away present.'

Gerry leaned down and pushed out a large box from under the table. 'She says you'll find this useful when you're up there with those studious women in the provinces. Margo maintains this'll get their minds off their studies.'

I lifted the lid off the box and discovered it was filled with some of the laciest and silkiest pieces of lingerie I'd seen – and I had seen quite a lot of it these last few months as Gerry had contacts in France and had 'imported' it on the black market. Some of the women I knew had modelled slips, panties, bras and garter belts for me. I riffled my fingers through the smooth material, bright with different colours, flimsy, filmy, silky. 'Margo says you'll remember her when you give these out to any women you meet up there.' He grinned again. 'Can't let you just become a mouldy bookworm.'

He reached into his inside pocket and drew out his fat wallet. He pulled out a wad of notes and thrust them at me. 'Here, kid.'

'Oh, no, I couldn't, Gerry. You've already paid me enough.'

'Let's call it a retainer. Consider yourself still on the payroll.'

'But I won't be here.'

'Well, there's lots of stuff going on in Manchester. Let's say you can keep your eyes open for me. I always like to have my fingers in as many pies as possible. I might even ask you to do one or two jobs for me. Nothing complicated. Straightforward stuff.' He insisted that I took the money. Then he went on, 'You got a place to stay yet?'

I shook my head. 'No. That's why I'm going there a few days before term starts, so I'll have time to find myself some place to live.' But the real reason why I was going early was because I'd worked out that if I regretted leaving my job here with Gerry, it would be easier for me to come back. Once term started, I'd find it more difficult. But I didn't tell Gerry that.

He slid a card out of his wallet. 'Here. A friend of mine. Worked for me when she lived here a few years back. A very nice lady.' He smiled. 'Oh, not what you think. Not that she couldn't have worked for Margo on the side. She actually worked as a house agent. She found me some good deals. Good head on her shoulders. She'll know a few places that might suit you, I'm sure. You'll like her. In fact, I'll give her a buzz later to let her know you'll be in town tomorrow.'

I glanced at the card – Barbara Logan. Rentals and Sales. Flats. Houses. Her address and phone number were printed across the bottom of the card. 'Ring her when you get in,' Gerry said. 'I mean it.'

I had made my mind up to make a clean break from Gerry and his associates. I thought that would be the best way so I wouldn't keep being reminded of all the great times I'd spent with Margo, Carmella, Dorothy, Margery and Teresa. I knew it wasn't going to be easy. Another older woman I had met, Mrs Courtney, had told me she was going to visit me for a weekend every now and again. And now Gerry had indicated he wanted me to stay in touch in some way. So as I was going to retain some connection, I thought there'd be no harm in contacting Barbara Logan. After all, though I'd been born and raised in Manchester, I knew very few people there and certainly nobody who would know where I'd find a good deal on a place to live.

I waved the card at Gerry. 'Thanks,' I said, and Gerry stood up, folded his newspaper, tucked it under his arm and put his hand out for me to shake. 'You're a good kid, Nick. Hey, I'd better stop calling you kid, right? I think the ladies made a man of you. Should help you in your 'studies' with those lady students you'll meet. Especially when you hand a few of these things out.' He touched the box Margo had sent with his foot. 'They won't find stuff like this in the library.'

He dropped my hand. 'Well, better leave you to say goodbye to the others. Benny's in the back and I guess you know who's waiting upstairs for you. I'll keep in touch.

And if you find university's not what it's cracked up to be, come on back here. I'll bet there'll be a few more ladies around always ready to make friends with a likely lad like you. So long, old son. Keep your pecker up.'

And with that Gerry sauntered out of the restaurant. I moved into the back. This was Gerry's private club where he ran gambling, private parties, celebrations, all kinds of shenanigans. They all usually involved sexual escapades. Benny, an ex-boxer, bartender, bouncer, was cleaning up behind the bar. He waved at me and raised his thumb to a door at the back of the bar.

'She's waiting for you. She told me to send you straight up. Margo's given her the day off . . . and the night.' He winked.

I walked across to the bar. 'I'm off early in the morning, Benny, so I'd better say goodbye now.' I thrust out my hand and Benny took it, giving me a hard squeeze. I winced a little – Benny never remembered just how powerful his grip was.

'Not goodbye. *Au revoir.*' Benny's French was mangled so at first I didn't know what he was saying. 'You'll be popping in to see us sometimes, I dare say. And you'll be wanting to see Teresa again.'

That was true. Teresa was a young woman I considered almost my steady girl-friend. She was very much a free spirit in sexual matters. She didn't mind too much if I became involved in brief sexual situations with some of the other women who were part of Gerry's operation, though she always expected me to come back to her. I'd asked her to come and live with me in Manchester but she had told me the student life was not for her. 'You can always come and see me on your vac – is that what students call it, "vac"? But I won't come with you. You'll want to be doing your studying and there'll be times when I'll want you to be doing anything but studying. It wouldn't be fair to you.' And then she added, with a mischievously sexy grin, 'Or to me. You writing away and me wanting to see how much lead you've got left in your pencil.'

Teresa had insisted, however, that I spend my last hours with her before leaving. 'I'll get you up in time for your train, I promise.' She gave me her sexy grin again. 'I always get you up, don't I? And I'll make sure you'll be able to sleep like a baby on the train. You'll be so worn out, that three-hour train ride'll pass in a jiffy, with you dead to the world.'

So I was certainly looking forward to spending that last day and night with Teresa. I was a little worried, though, that it would convince me that staying with her would be better than going off to university.

I hugged Benny. 'So long, Benny.' He was a little embarrassed by the hug. He was more used to being held in clinches, his fists pummelling at an opponent's kidneys, so he pulled away quickly and gave me a friendly jab on my shoulder.

'I'll miss seeing you around, Nicky.' He swiped at the bar with a cloth to hide his embarrassment – Benny was not a one for sentiment. 'You'd better get up there to Teresa.'

I went through the door at the back. Gerry had four small flats above his restaurant that he rented out to some of his customers for assignations. When Teresa worked at the club, Gerry let her stay in one of those flats and I often used to meet her there. It was a cosy place, with a big, brass bed and two walls covered with mirrors. I'd spent many an exciting night there with Teresa. I was already primed to enjoy this last encounter with her.

I knocked on the door. 'Come in. It's open,' Teresa

called. She was sitting in an armchair doing something I'd never seen her doing before – reading a book. Her legs were stretched out, her feet on a small stool. She was wearing a black undergraduate gown that draped away, showing the shapeliness of her long legs in their black stockings. She stroked the material of the gown. 'What d'you think? Does this suit me? Not quite the latest fashion, is it? I must say I like my black things with a lot more lace. And I know you do.'

I strolled over to her, leaned down and placed my lips on hers. It was only a brief kiss but it was deliciously soft with promise, moistly sexy. Her free hand reached up and patted my crotch. She could obviously feel that I was getting ready to be with her.

'My! I can feel your mind's not on your studies right now.' She flapped the book she was holding in her other hand. 'I just thought I'd see what you'd be getting up to at university. Are all the books you read there as interesting as this?'

I saw that she had somehow got hold of my copy of *Lady Chatterley's Lover*, a book almost impossible to find in those days. I'd been given a copy by that charming, rather aristocratic lady, Mrs Courtney, who, I discovered, could unleash remarkable, not to say somewhat bizarre sexual energies. I'd worked for her as a gardener for several weeks and she'd been enormously generous in exercising those energies with me among the plants and trees in her conservatory.

'You enjoying it?' I asked her, pointing at the book.

'Parts of it. Somebody's been reading the same pages over and over. The book kept falling open at those places so those are the parts I've been reading. I can see where Mrs Courtney got some of her ideas from. The gardener certainly knew what he was doing. No wonder Mrs C.

gave you the book.' She closed the book. 'But you know me. I'm not a great reader. Actions speak louder than words for me.'

She stood up and wrapped the black gown tightly around her voluptuous figure. 'This was the only student gown I could find. A bit too long. You'd rather see a lot more leg, wouldn't you?' She raised the hem of the gown and pushed a knee out so that the material fell away to reveal her leg's slim curve, her delicate ankle slender in her high-heeled shoe. 'I tried to buy one of those short ones. What do they call them?'

'Bum freezers.'

'That's it. Bum freezers. Show off your bum nicely, they do.'

'They wear that kind only at Oxford and Cambridge.'

'And that's where they give you a blue, isn't it?'

'Yes, if you play on one of the university teams.'

'Well, if I couldn't wear a bum freezer for you, I decided the least I could do was give you your own kind of blue – and we only need a team of two, you and me, to play the kind of sport I have in mind.'

'They don't give out blues at Manchester.'

'All the more reason I should give you one then. And I'm sure you'll like the blue I'm going to give you.' She twirled around, the gown floating out and open so that I could see she was wearing a delectably lacy pair of blue panties. I gazed at her, a bewitching vision in black gown with black stockings held by a black garter belt, covered by the rich blue nylon of her panties. I was sure the female students, whatever sports they might be interested in, would not be walking around chilly, rainy Manchester dressed like that.

'I can see you're all set to get the blue for yourself.' Teresa sidled up to me, one hand coming to my crotch again, the other on the back of my neck, pulling my face to hers, her mouth open on mine, her tongue sliding deeply in, a deep, warm kiss. Her fingers reached around my growing erection.

'I know you're going to be such a hard worker,' she whispered in my ear. 'And I do mean hard.' She gripped my stiff penis, fingers fiddling with my fly buttons. Soon her hand was inside my trousers, then inside my underpants. 'I wonder if you'll be paying as much attention to the lectures as you're paying to me.' Her hand was smoothing softly along my length. 'I can feel something standing very nicely at attention,' she breathed in my ear, then nibbling and sucking at my earlobe.

We stayed like that for a while, her hand busily coaxing me to a fatter and longer attention, my hand under her gown, stroking the silkiness of her panties against the firm curves of her buttocks.

Then she stepped away a little. Smiling at my puzzled expression – Teresa was not a woman who willingly moved away when sexual play was obviously developing – she gripped the top of her gown and slowly lowered it away from her shoulders. She turned slightly away from me as I watched her slide the gown tantalisingly down from her shoulders, down till she let it drop at her feet. While her back was to me, I could still see her breasts reflected in the two wall mirrors where the bed was. Her breasts were not particularly big but they were exquisitely round and firm and already her nipples were pointing out stiffly.

She looked absolutely stunning, with her long black-stockinged legs outlined by the seams, her stiletto heels making her legs seem even longer, her blue panties clinging to the tops of her thighs, a thin silky skin shaping her arse, the lace falling away where the panties had a high slit at each side.

Then she wheeled round to face me. She took a small step towards me, one hand again at the back of my head, the other searching inside my trousers. After a brief flutter of fingers she freed my cock and her fingertips began a sensual flickering touch around the fat head which made me jerk and twitch. She pulled my face down to her breasts till my mouth took in one of those pointy nipples. I licked my tongue round it, then sucked it into my wet mouth.

Teresa murmured, 'That's nice. It's what I call keeping abreast of things.' Her hands were pulling at my clothes, pushing my jacket off, undoing my tie, her fingers expertly unfastening my shirt buttons, sliding it off, her fingers briefly pinching my nipples, licking her fingertips to make them slippery-moist under her caresses.

Then she went to the buckle of my belt, yanked at it, then roughly hauled my trousers down, then my underpants till they lay tangled round my ankles. While she was doing this, my mouth was moistly sliding all over her breasts, leaving trails of wetness from one to the other, licking between her breasts, thinking that I'd like to push my prick there, while she pressed those soft round globes against it. My hands began to explore beneath her panties, one circling round the back, my palms stroking her buttocks, fingers gently probing along the crack of her arse. My other hand was edging very slowly inside her thighs. She shifted a little so that it was easier for me to move my fingers upwards. I touched her groin, felt the soft scratchiness of her pubic hair, letting a finger or two slip down to touch the first sign of juiciness.

She squirmed a little and sighed as I barely skimmed along her clit, along, then onto the wet lips of her quim. I imagined how it would look, enticing in its wet pink, open, taking my fingers into that creamy valley, in, almost not moving, yet probing further in, my fingers inside those slippery walls, Teresa holding my fingers there in a gently throbbing grasp, her mouth wide open, pulling my tongue inside her mouth, her tongue rolling around mine, my cock twitching steadily as one hand worked on me so that it felt as if I would be even bigger and stiffer, her fingers circling the root, her palm smooth on my cock-head. Her other hand was squeezing and massaging my balls, one or two fingers reaching far behind them, tickling at the rim of my arsehole.

I pressed the thin band of nylon of her panties against the slipperiness of her quim-lips. I wanted to feel her panties getting wet, I wanted her to feel them soaked, to remind her of my own juice spurting out of me, into her, slowly seeping down, trickling down, so that when she wore her panties again after I had left her, she would remember how wet my stroking had made her, how eventually jets of my jism had splashed inside her, hot and thick, then dribbled down into her panties. And I hoped that thinking all that whenever she wore the panties, she'd get herself all wet again, would want my fingers to stroke her, want my cock, hard and thick, to knock against that moistness, pushing up to the lips, penetrating, her legs hooking up onto my shoulders to take me in more deeply.

For now both my hands were stroking inside, around the lips, teasing her clit, a finger straying along the inside of her arse-crack.

'It's so wet,' she murmured, 'It's like I'm melting away in a big pool. I'm as wet as the weather in Manchester. A downpour. I'm pelting down. I want to drown your cock in my juices, let it soak in a long drizzle.' Teresa loved to talk when her mouth wasn't busy kissing, sucking and licking. Her mouth now slid away from mine, her tongue licking at my chin, then onto my chest, down – I knew where that delicious mouth was heading and my cock responded by stiffening more, sticking up and out waiting for the warm enfolding mouth to take it in. Soon she was almost kneeling in front of me, her hands still doing their insistent massage, my penis made to feel large in her hands.

As she had now slid down, I could no longer keep stroking her inside her panties so I placed my hands on the back of her head, stroking her soft, black hair, feeling the rhythm of her motions as her mouth began to take in my stiffness.

After a minute or two of that delicious sensation of Teresa's mouth bathing my cock in warm wetness, she looked up at me with her big, dark brown eyes. Then without a word – something that was unusual for Teresa – she held my hard member with almost finicky fingers. Her other hand struggled with the tangled mess of my clothes around my feet. I shifted till she was able to pull them away. Then she stood, still holding me in that enticingly gentle touch, pulling me by my cock so that I shuffled with her to the bed. She turned me and pushed till I was lying on my back on the bed, seeing myself in the mirrors, my cock rigid and straining upwards.

I could also see a reflection of Teresa, looking ravishing in her black stockings and blue panties. She had her thumbs in the elastic at her waist and she began to peel the panties down, smiling down at me as she wiggled her arse, revealing a first glimpse of her pubic mound, then further down till the blue nylon fell to her ankles. She moved slightly as she slipped the panties away from her feet. I could see her curvaceous arse, the thin straps of her garter belt seeming to hold those curves in place, the long black seams of her stockings lining the exquisite shape of her legs.

She was still standing at the side of the bed, the panties hanging down in lacy frills as she held them with just one finger. Her voice came to me in a seductively husky whisper. 'I found out that when you finish and they give you your degree, they put a hood over your head.' She moved her hand so that the panties on her finger were hanging down just about an inch above the tip of my prick. She shook the panties slightly before she went on. 'So these are a blue and a hood. I think I'll give you your degree now. Drop this hood over your head.' Very slowly she lowered the panties. The cool silky nylon felt delicious as it descended onto my cock-head, dropping down till my stiffness was entirely covered in nylon. Teresa's hand started to rub the silkiness up and down my length before she whisked the panties away, throwing them to the foot of the bed.

'But you can't keep your degree just yet. You have to earn it. Same with your blue. We have to play some games before you get your blue.' She clambered onto the bed, snaking her hand out to let her thin fingertips fastidiously touch the rim of skin that had rolled back so that my cock-head was bulging out.

Teresa was a great one for anticipation, for letting things happen almost in slow motion. She kept her fingers on me but hardly moved them though my cock was doing its own moving against her fingers, throbbing with expectation. Her fingers started to play a maddeningly magical game around the rim of my cock-head, fingers straying every now and again to poke at the slit of my cock, flicking it open almost as if she wanted to entice the first drops of juice out.

'You've learned such a lot since you've been here,' she cooed.

I managed to croak out, 'I've had such good teachers. Especially you.'

'Why, thank you, kind sir,' she breathed. 'You've been a very good student. So good, and so big. And hard and fat. And long. And so thick.' Her fingers went on with their magic work, searching out all the sensitive surfaces of my prick, my balls, caressing my scrotum, squeezing, fondling, the whole length of my cock feeling full of come. She was so good at what she was doing that I felt that my cock was straining around a hard steel rod up the centre, a hollow tube that was swelling fatter with come that was threatening to spill out.

It felt as though she had made my cock so thick and long that she could hardly contain it in both her hands. The way she concentrated on playing with it was so delicious that I simply lay back and let her take over. She had worked round so that her buttocks were by my head so soon I began to run my hands up and down her long legs, feeling that satisfaction of touch on her nylon stockings, that strange mixture of smoothness and scratchy graininess. Of course I was letting my hands ride up her thighs to the tops of her stockings, over the tops to sense that lovely warm smoothness of her skin, my fingers playing gently just at the outside of the glossy wet lips of her quim.

She shifted over a little, lifting one leg over my head. Her whispering voice floated up to me. 'You'll be reading all that poetry. Filling your mouth with words. I wonder if the taste of poetry will be as good as this taste,' and she lowered herself down so that I could see the glistening wetness, my fingers sliding gently round, slipping inside a little, reaching to roll her clit between my fingertips, my other fingers straying to push delicately at the neat hole and crack of her arse. She was slowly rotating to help my fingers, and her hands were now more insistently busy on me, one hand stroking in an urgently teasing movement up and down the length of my cock.

I reached up so that the tip of my tongue flicked at her clit. Then I slid my whole tongue along her slit, spreading her sleekness wider with my hands so that my tongue could probe between, in and out as if I had a soft wet cock fucking her. I kept my tongue inside her, opening my lips to suck her lips. She tasted sweet, though not sugary. There was a slight saltiness there, something like the smell of ozone, not as heavy but filtered through that vague sweetness. I couldn't separate that taste from the feel of her velvety skin there – that taste was a part of that glistening liquid that was now full and deliciously oily under my lips.

As if by intuition, as soon as I began my tongue-play, Teresa gave a last, long, lingering stroke up the length of my cock and then I felt the wet warm ooze of her mouth on me. Sucking was then a rare occurrence. Few women would do it and it was usually associated only with the most uninhibited and promiscuous women. But the women I'd got to know through working for Gerry were very obliging in this regard. It was Margo who had first introduced me to the wonders of a warm mouth on my cock but even her wonderful ways paled in comparison to Teresa whose mouth was a veritable treasure of tricks – kisses, licks, deep sucks, little nibbles, lavishly moist slides, flickers of tongue, sloppy caresses, dripping of saliva.

At first she simply took in my shaft deeply as if she wanted to make sure all of it was sloppily moist, sheltering it from the hard touch of her teeth, sliding up and down in steady, smooth strokes. It felt like being immersed in a warm oil that leaked all over my length as her hand pushed around my balls.

And so we gave ourselves up to the lovely flutterings of tongue and lips. Tasting each other, Teresa became like wet velvet under the ministrations of my mouth. My prick beat with ecstatic quivers as she licked the full length, urging me to a fuller hardness, her tongue continually lapping, first at the head, then sliding down to nuzzle at the root, then up to swallow the head, her lips sucking at the rim of skin which now seemed to have rolled even further down to expose more of that hard fat bulge of the head.

I knew I would not be able to last long once Teresa's magic mouth began its work. I kept telling her to slow down. She herself was flowing with a flood of moistness, and would soon want a stiffer penetration than my tongue was giving her. She was obviously enjoying what I was doing. I could hear her quiet growls at the back of her throat mixed with the sloppy slapping noises her mouth was making, together with the gulping guzzles she was engaged in around my cock.

Teresa was nearly always the one who liked to orchestrate our encounters. I was content to let her because she was so adept at guiding me into such trembling excitement without making me spill out. She would take me up to high peaks, keeping me there before she herself was taken up by her own fulfillment. It was then that she began a tumbling, thrashing ride, usually straddled on top of me, writhing down hard on my cock, burying me deep, then pulling up in a long, agonizing stroke, calculated to drive me crazy.

So she moved away from that lovely sucking, switching herself to poise over me, her finger and thumb holding the root of my cock, pointing it upwards to rest just at the very opening of that inviting slit. She then lowered herself onto me, letting the tip of my prick nudge around the clit first. I could tell she enjoyed that as she wriggled and squirmed so that my rod slid along the whole length of her slit outside, returning the stiff, bulging head to rub at her clit. Finally she tucked the head between her moist lips, pushing herself down very slowly.

As my length made its way languorously inside her, Teresa dictated the pace of that entrance. My cock felt like one of those scenes in a nature documentary when a flower is filmed to show it opening its blossom. Pushing deeply inside Teresa, I experienced the quick pulses of her inner muscles, flickering around the head so that it seemed to open out, fuller and fatter, and Teresa kept pushing down till I didn't think I could go any deeper. But she kept pushing and pushing hard and strong till I was sure I was further inside her than I had ever been before.

And she just stayed on me like that, savouring what felt like an enormous length of cock, manipulating that creamy interior with little twitches and flickers till she drew herself leisurely away from me. My cock slid almost gingerly out till the head rested again at her lips, stopping there before she plunged in that effortless slide down on me again.

Teresa made her own rhythms, at first with a deliberate steadiness. When she had taken me as deeply inside her as she possibly could, I raised my pelvis a little as if I wanted my prick to find some deeper core, some inner place that the slit of my cock could reach eventually to pour out jets of come.

This sent Teresa towards her frenzied jostling ride. We began to delve into a faster rhythm, both of us gasping, sighing, Teresa's mouth skimming wetly over my face, my tongue finally reaching inside her mouth, the two of us wet there, the two of us heaving against each other, quickening, Teresa holding my cock-head at her lips, squirming around it, letting it blindly and bluntly bang against her clit, her mouth on mine so that, when she cried out in a deep, strangled voice, I could feel a buzz of hot breath race across my lips. This made me even more excited and I pressed my cock inside and Teresa rampaged against me, up and down in a hectic ride.

We were both teetering on the very edge of a tingling fullness, release building in us till Teresa, sensing the right moment, forced herself way down on my cock, impaling herself on the hardness, straightening up, leaning backwards as if that would give her an even further long reach of cock inside her. She began to shout, 'Oh God! Oh God!' in time to her wriggling ride. I was somehow pushing myself further in, rasping out weird sounds, trying to find some final ecstatic spot inside Teresa that I could deluge with great creamy spouts.

We went on thrashing and groaning. I think we were both surprised how long we managed to carry on riding in this way until I felt a sudden gathering down deep at the root of my cock. I knew there could be no stopping me now. I had no control over that mounting flood inside my balls, rising up the length of my shaft so I let go. Out came a splashing stream of jism. As Teresa felt that hot flood fill her, spraying around her inner muscles, her movements reached to a monumental crisis, faster and faster. We both let out a tremendous yell together, Teresa riding on, unleashing orgasmic quivers one after the other, shuddering and straining to keep going till finally we had to ease down, to lie entwined, my prick still in her till the swelling decreased, and Teresa let my half-limp state slide out of her. But she held me just outside her quim, her fingers on the slipperiness of my cock, touching her own moistness with my floppiness, massaging our mixed juices on both of us.

I was nearly always amazed just how quickly I could recover after such exhausting excitement with Teresa. She was very clever in arousing me again and again. As for the stories I had heard about the prowess of young men, the way some of the men I knew boasted about their devastating skills of recovery I had always believed they were exaggerations. But my experiences these last few months had been such a learning time for me. I was sure my immersion in bouts of exhilarating sex with a variety of women had obviously given me a high degree of potency and stamina. I had come to believe that, the more times I experienced the delights of sex, the more my body was learning to refresh itself in order to fulfill myself time after time.

And yet here I was, giving it all up. After the long hours of rides and gentle embracings running down to languid and lazy fulfillments through that evening and long into the night with Teresa, I had many misgivings. I kept telling myself there'd be other women but I had this nagging doubt that none of them would live up to what I had been through during these last few months. Was I being ridiculous going off to university when I could stay here with Teresa and the other nubile beauties and indulge myself totally?

I was plagued by these doubts through that last night with Teresa. Bleary-eyed, satiated, relaxed beyond belief, I was rolled out of bed by her early the following morning. She helped me to dress, gave me a quick dab of a kiss, and bundled me out of the door when the taxi arrived.

It all happened very quickly. This was, perhaps, the

best way to go, with no lingering farewells. Teresa again dictating the terms. She whispered in my ear, 'See you soon,' and then closed the door firmly. I half turned, thinking I'd knock on the door, tell her I'd changed my mind, but I stumbled down the stairs, went back to my flat to collect my luggage, clutching Margo's gift box as well, then blundered out to the waiting taxi, telling the driver to take me to Euston.

At Euston I staggered on to the train. When I felt the first tug of the engine moving out of the station, I also experienced a tug in my heart, the image of Teresa in her blue panties and her black stockings calling me back, a half-hearted desire surfacing, becoming stronger till I almost thought I'd leap up and dive out of the carriage before we had finally left the station.

But I was too tired. We had been under way only about five minutes before I dropped into a deep sleep, rocked into unconsciousness by the gathering speed of the train. Almost before I knew it, a guard was passing along the corridor, calling out, 'Next stop, London Road, Manchester.'

I shook myself awake, the image of Teresa floating back into my mind. I pulled my bags down from the luggage rack and, as I tucked Margo's box under my arm, I managed a brief smile to myself. Who knew what other delights awaited me once I stepped off the train to begin my three years of study at the university?

2. Coming In Out Of The Rain

As I'd had no breakfast, I decided to have a bite in the station restaurant. The British Railways food did nothing to cheer me up. As I sat munching cold toast and strong stewed tea in the gloomy buffet, my regrets about leaving Teresa came flooding back. I even debated going to check what time the next train left for London. I thought I would go back to pick up that other life again. There in the confines of the station, my thoughts, punctuated by the clank and shuddering groans of trains pulling out with great gushes and hisses of steam, made me feel very lonely and out of place.

The day stretched out in front of me as grey as the weather outside. But I forced myself to move. I pulled out my wallet to pay for the miserable late breakfast I'd had. It was stuffed with the notes Gerry had given me and as I opened it, a card fell out, the card of the house agent, Barbara Logan. I had originally intended to spend that first night in a hotel before looking for a place to live the next day. But now I thought that maybe, if I got under way on that search, it would at least keep my mind off London and Teresa. It might even save me the expense of a hotel if I found a reasonable place and could move in straightaway.

I paid my bill and struggled out of the restaurant with

my two heavy cases and Margo's box jammed under my arm. I suppose I could have let a porter handle my cases but my upbringing had ingrained in me that it would be a waste of money. I was quite capable of carrying my own luggage, I reminded myself, so I swayed and lunged along, banging the cases against my legs, feeling more miserable with every step, finally stopping outside to dump them at the side of a telephone box.

I'd decided I'd call this Barbara Logan just to see if she was in and to let her know I'd arrived. Maybe she'd be available to help me find a place right then. I noticed that she lived in Fallowfield so it would be relatively easy for me to take a bus out there – again, though I'd grown used to taking taxis while I'd been working for Gerry, I told myself I'd better be a little more careful with money now I was a student. I forgot that my wallet was bulging with Gerry's money.

Barabara Logan answered the phone after a couple of rings. 'Logan House Search,' she said in a briskly efficient voice. I was stuck for words for a few seconds.

'Er . . . excuse me. You don't know me but I was given your name.'

'Yes?'

'I'm Nick . . .'

'Nick! Is that you? You're the young man Gerry rang me up about yesterday, aren't you?'

'That's right.'

'He told me you'd be coming in today on the early train.'

'He said it'd be alright for me to ring you when I got here.'

'Sure. Gerry said he'd like me to look after you, finding a place for you to live and all that.'

'Yes.' I paused. I didn't want her to get the impression

that I could afford too luxurious a place. 'You know, comfy but not expensive.'

'I've pulled two or three files out already. They might fit the bill.'

Barbara sounded very friendly and cheerful, her voice both seductive and authoritative. I imagined her as an effective and capable business woman, even though at that time, just a few years after the end of the war, there were not many women around running their own companies.

'I came up a bit early so I could make a start looking as soon as possible,' I told her.

'Of course. We can start immediately if you like. Once Gerry had phoned me, I cleared my appointments so's I'd have the afternoon free for you. I was just sitting here waiting for you to ring.'

'Oh, I didn't mean to ... if you've got other clients ... Tomorrow will do fine.'

'No, no. I'm ready for you.'

'Well, if you're sure that's alright. Just tell me how I can get out there and I'll ...'

'Don't be silly. I'll come and pick you up. Where are you?'

'Oh, I couldn't let you ...'

'Listen. I have my car. I get lots of petrol for my business ... and you know how Gerry makes sure you never run short of anything. It's easy for me to run down there ... wherever you are, that is.'

'I'm still at London Road Station.'

'Wait right there. I'll be there in a jiffy.' She laughed, a sweet but also robust laugh. 'Well, not quite a jiffy. But it shouldn't take me long. Give me half an hour,' and with that she put the phone down before I had a chance to reply.

I waited under a flaking awning outside the station sitting on one of my cases. I stared out at the cars coming up the long ramp to the station to see if I could pick out the one Barbara Logan would be driving. I had no idea what to expect but I was a little surprised when a sleek, dark-red Rover pulled up in front of me and out stepped a tall, black-haired woman in a pair of immaculately creased grey slacks which made her legs look even longer than they were. And she was wearing high heels, something women in slacks were not supposed to do at that time – only tarty females did that.

Barbara Logan was anything but tarty. She was dressed in a shirt buttoned high under a loose-fitting but elegantly draped dark-blue blazer. She gave me a beaming smile as I stood up.

'And you must be Nick.'

'Yes.'

'Pleased to meet you,' she said and without further ado she grabbed one of my cases and began to carry it to the boot of her car.

'Here, let me do that,' I said.

'I can manage. You bring the other.' I lifted the other, forgetting I'd balanced Margo's box on it. It fell to the floor and as I took a step with the case, I gave the box an inadvertent little kick which somehow flipped the lid open. Barbara was watching me as I bent down to close it and pick it up.

'I see you know something about Gerry's business with French lingerie.' I flushed a little as Barbara grinned and went on, 'He still sends me one or two classy items every now and again.'

'Margo gave me these. A going-away present.'

'Looks more like a come-hither present to me,' Barbara grinned again.

She climbed in behind the wheel and I sat next to her. 'That's the thing about Gerry,' she said. 'He never forgets anyone who he thinks has done him a favour. I haven't seen him for at least a couple of years but he still remembers me. Of course I let him know about anything that's happening in Manchester that might interest him and he sends business my way. Like you.'

'I wouldn't say I'm much business for you. I'm only a student.'

'Well, Gerry says I'm to see that you get a reasonable place and he's prepared to help out with the rent if it's a bit beyond your pocket.'

There wasn't much traffic and Barbara was a very confident driver so we moved out of the city centre very quickly. On the way she asked me one or two questions about Gerry's business, wanting to know whether some of the people she knew some years back were still around. I'd already mentioned Margo to her so at one point she said, 'So Margo's still doing it, is she?'

She must have glimpsed the flush that spread across my face and the sly grin I couldn't stop myself from forming. 'Well, I didn't really mean was she still doing that but it looks as if she is. Good for her. A real charmer she was when I knew her, and very attractive – and I can see you agree – but she's tough and organized as well.'

I thought that description might very well be applied to Barbara herself though I didn't say so. What I said was, 'She's the one who gave me that box.'

'That tells me a lot! You must have got on famously with her.' I must have shown a self-satisfied smirk on my face for Barbara turned to me and flashed a wide smile at me. 'Well, Gerry did say you were a special kind of person but I didn't realise you were *that* special. I was the one who bought all those houses for Gerry to set Margo's business up – in my name so he wouldn't be linked to them. Gerry always kept himself in the background but then you know that, don't you?'

I found Barbara easy to talk to – I even thought, after a few minutes, that we were getting along famously, as she'd said I had with Margo. As I'd had such a great time in bed with Margo I began to wonder if Barbara was the same kind of person. But I kept all that to myself. After all, I hardly knew her.

But she told me more about herself as we drove. She was like me – she had been born and raised in Manchester, then had moved to London. And like me, she had moved back to live here.

'I don't know how much you remember about the city but I thought what I'd do was I'd take you to this one house I have for rent. It's not in a great district. Moss Side, near the infirmary. Nice old house. Just like those houses Gerry has. Used for the same thing too.' She grinned again. 'The ground floor's vacant right now so you might as well stay there till I get you fixed. Better than spending a night in a hotel. I hope you don't mind a bit of noise. Oh, Daisy's pretty good, so I'm told. She's the one who lives upstairs. You just might hear her clattering up and down stairs with her clients. Well, maybe every now and again – Daisy's very choosy, not your average run-of-the-mill...' She left the sentence unfinished.

Soon we were driving past the Royal Infirmary. Then we turned left just beyond Whitworth Park and soon pulled up by a large house with wide bay windows.

'Here we are.'

We carried the cases in and I flopped into a large plush armchair. The place was on the gaudy side, red wallpaper with gilt-flocked patterns, a very soft, velvety sofa and chairs, heavy plum-coloured curtains and a variety of lamps, most with long silk tassles.

'Looks a bit like a brothel, I'm afraid,' Barbara said. 'But basically that's what the lady used it for, though she was very discreet.' Then she pulled some files from her briefcase. 'There's three places we can look at this afternoon,' she went on, waving the files in the air. 'In your price range probably. Why don't you do a bit of unpacking while I go out and make a few phone calls to set things up? Don't unpack too much. You won't be staying here long, I don't think.'

She was back inside half an hour. She told me she had picked up keys from her office so she was ready to show me around. 'They're quite close actually. That makes them handy for the university. You're in luck, coming early. There'll be a rush for decent and cheapish places once the students start to arrive. And at this point we might be able to dicker the price down a little.' She paused. 'I actually know a place that's free but I don't normally recommend it.'

'Free? I'm a bit worried about expenses so if...'

'Well, I said free but there's a few catches, it seems to me. Depends what you mean by 'free'. It's a bit of a free-for-all over there, I sometimes think. Maybe they go in for free love as well – who knows?'

'It doesn't sound so bad to me.'

'Maybe you shouldn't ask me. I'm not very sympathetic to the idea. You get what you pay for, I always say.'

'But it's free, you said. You don't have to pay.'

'No. But there's other rules. Tell you what, later I'll

introduce you to a young woman I managed to get in there. Her name's Lorna. Gerry asked me to help her out.'

One of Gerry's young ladies – this sounded interesting, I thought. Again Barbara must have seen the look on my face because she went on, 'A really nice lady, Lorna is. And I bet you'd get along famously with her.' There was that phrase again. 'And she seems happy in the place.'

'So what's the problem?'

'I'm not sure quite how it works. This man, Stanley Milton his name is, he has a group of houses, a sort of self-contained estate, and he operates it on a barter system. There's a big central notice board and anything you want to get rid of, you put up a notice about and if someone wants it, then you exchange it for something of theirs that they don't want.'

'Sounds alright to me.'

'The catch is, once you move in, anything you bring in stays there. Some idea about all belongings being really communal, so all your furniture and stuff belongs to them. I begin to wonder what else they expect you to share! You have to pay a fairly big deposit when you move in so, if anyone moves out, I suspect all the residents pick over what they've left and then sell it to pay the rates. I think Milton is a broker so he invests in high-interest properties. Goodness only knows what he gets up to.'

'Are the houses nice?'

'Pretty good. But I always have the feeling something very shady is going on there. Like it's a cover operation for something else. And that Milton always gives me vague answers when I ask him anything. Never looks me straight in the eyes. Still, Lorna says she's had no problems but it's just too good to be true. Something's not on the up and up. I call it Paradise Lost.'

'Doesn't sound so lost to me.'

'Well, it's not quite the Garden of Eden, though the people who live there think it is. And what with the owner's name being Milton, the name seems to fit. He's a kind of creepy man – looks like he might be into the white slave racket.'

'Oh, come on, Barbara.'

'When I told Gerry about it, he told me to find out about it but it's pretty difficult to get anything out of Milton. And I sometimes think Gerry's put Lorna in there, you know, as a sort of spy. Anyhow, maybe Paradise Lost is not the place for you so let's go and see these.' She waved the files at me again.

The second place she showed me seemed just right. I was ready to close the deal then and there. Barbara said we should look at a few more the next day but I'd pretty well decided. It was the ground floor of a large old house in Victoria Park, on a tree-lined street I could look out on from a big bay window. It had a living room, a small dining area, a kitchen, a huge bedroom, a bathroom and a small study, all tastefully decorated. At first I couldn't believe I'd be able to afford it but Barbara assured me the rent wouldn't be outrageous – I discovered later that Gerry had arranged to pay half of it.

I was delighted to think I'd be able to live in such a great place and for the first time since I'd arrived I lost all those feelings of self-pity and regret I'd been wallowing in.

And being with Barbara helped – she was so cheerful. I enjoyed her company while she was showing me around the houses and she seemed to enjoy herself, laughing, making a few sly jokes, some on the risqué side. Once, as we were in the large bedroom of one place, she patted the mattress and leaned over to me to say impishly, 'Plenty of room for action here. Those things Margo gave you will come in handy.' She nudged me and laughed. 'I mean, being a student doesn't mean you have to live like a hermit.'

When we'd finished our house-hunting, I suggested I take her out for dinner in return for all the trouble she'd gone to. 'That's very sweet of you, Nick,' she replied. 'But I have a couple coming in tonight to sign a lease.'

'How about tomorrow then, after we've seen some more houses?'

'Tell you what,' she said. 'Let's see which one you want to rent. Then we can draw up the lease and you can sign it. You'll probably be able to move in by the end of the week. So you can come round for the lease tomorrow night at my place and I'll make dinner.'

'I couldn't put you to all that trouble.'

'No trouble. I love to cook. What d'you say?'

I put my hand out. 'It's a deal,' I said. She took my hand. Hers felt soft even though her grip was firm. I thought I detected a playful touch as she slid it out of mine. And she also had that cheeky grin on her face. I wasn't quite sure what to make of that and maybe I was imagining it because most of the women I'd known through Gerry often gave me enticing looks which nearly always led on to other enticing things. After all, Barbara was in one sense a woman who had been part of Gerry's operation two or three years back.

'Of course I can't promise it'll be quite like those high old times you had in London. But you'll find we still know how to have a good time up here in Manchester.' And that sounded promising.

That first evening I did a little more unpacking, then

decided to read. But I couldn't settle to it so, by about eight o'clock, I was back in my state of regret and self-pity. I thought maybe a couple of beers might cheer me up.

It was one of those Manchester evenings I remembered detesting when I lived there – a damp breeze blowing, chilly as well. The streets were deserted, the occasional bright lights shining through the curtains of houses. They gave out a little colour but emphasized my feeling of being left out of things.

The pub I eventually found did nothing to change my mood. The few people in the bar paid no attention to me. I drank two pints and contemplated whether I should continue drinking. At least I wouldn't keep brooding if I could get myself plastered. But if I woke with a hangover the next morning, I'd feel even worse.

Just as I was downing the last of my beer, a plump woman came in, shaking her umbrella, saying to no one in particular, 'It's raining cats and dogs out there.' Then she walked to the bar, unfastening her tightly belted raincoat. She was big-breasted under a flouncy blouse. She said to the bartender, 'Give us a gin and orange, Alf.'

Then she noticed me. 'Hello, love,' she said in a smarmy voice, smiling with her large red mouth. I nodded at her and finished off my pint, plonking the glass down on the bar and getting off my bar-stool.

'What's the rush, ducky? You'll get soaked out there. Have another drink. Stay a bit. I could do with some company.' And she winked, settling onto her stool, crossing her legs – not bad but a little heavy.

She noticed me looking at her legs so smiled at me again. I began to shrug myself into my mackintosh and as I did, she reached out to pat my arm. 'Teeming down it is.' I tried to move off but her hand gripped my arm. 'Hold on. Nice lad like you. Bet you'd like a bit of company. I can give you a really good time.' She moved her hand away and placed it under one of her large breasts. 'Look there. Nice jiggy-jig.'

In my mood I was sort of tempted. She was not unattractive in her rather vulgar way and I tried to tell myself she was the kind of woman who'd be just right to pull me out of my miserable state of mind.

'My place is just around the corner. Only two quid.'

But I thought of Teresa – and I'd be seeing Barbara the next day so this woman seemed a little too unappetizing. 'Sorry,' I said. 'Don't have the time.'

'You can always make time for the old fucky-fuck.' The way she was talking was putting me off – I like dirty talk but not quite like that. She went on, 'Tell you what. You stay and buy me another gin and I'll make it thirty bob. Go on, love. Treat yourself. Thirty bob, can't beat it.'

But I belted my raincoat, turned and went out into the night. It was sheeting down and I was soon drenched. That didn't do anything for my mood. I started to run, splashing through puddles, passing a woman standing under an umbrella who called to me but I ignored her.

Then I saw another woman lounging in a doorway. As I came towards her, she swung her coat open – she had a very trim figure. She spread her coat wide and said, 'Keep you nice and warm in here, sonny.' She stroked her hand along her upper thigh.

Seeing these women made me feel very ambiguous. I had left a life full of sexual encounters and I didn't know what to expect in my new life as a student. So I was almost tempted again but, feeling so sorry for myself, I was not really attracted, so simply rejected the idea.

When I got back, I got out of my clothes quickly and jumped into a hot bath, soaking in it for some time. I put on pyjamas and dressing gown, took a book from the shelf where I'd placed my small supply and started to read, hoping that I'd be able to concentrate.

After a few minutes I heard the front door open, then the flapping of an umbrella being roughly shaken, a hissed 'Damn and blast!' and then the sharp ring of high heels on the stairs. Obviously it was the woman who lived upstairs – Daisy, was that the name Barbara had mentioned?

After about a half hour of spasmodic reading, I was surprised to hear a sharp knock on my door. I had a fleeting thought that it might be Barbara knowing I'd be feeling lonely. When I opened the door, however, I saw a petite brunette standing there, dressed becomingly in a new-look dress in a muted floral pattern. Her face was lit up with a bright smile and her large blue eyes positively twinkled. She was altogether a bewitching figure to find on one's doorstep.

She was holding a tin-opener in her raised hand. 'D'you know how to work one of these damn things? I nearly cut my hands to pieces trying to open a tin of beans.'

'Well, I think so.'

'Good.' We stood there for several seconds, staring at each other without speaking till she said, 'I'm Daisy. From upstairs. Barbara mentioned she was probably going to put you up here for a few days. Nick, isn't it? Hello.' She waved her other hand at me. 'What a godsend! I don't know what I'd have done without you being here.' She paused. 'About the beans, I mean.'

'The beans,' I repeated. 'So where are they?'

She smacked her hand against her head and laughed, a delicious, almost provocative laugh. 'I'm a dunce. Just a dunce. Wait there just a sec. I'll go and get it.' She turned and moved to the stairs. Then she turned back to look at me. 'Better still. It'd save time if you came up to do it. Mind you, my place is in a real tip.'

'I'm hardly dressed to go visiting. Just a minute. I'll change.'

'What the heck,' she said. 'Doesn't bother me.' She beckoned to me. 'Come on.' And with that she began to move up the stairs, looking back at me when she was a few stairs up. She reminded me a little of Teresa, who always went up stairs in front of me to give me a good view of her legs. The way Daisy was swaying up the stairs made me suspect that she was swirling her skirt so I could see her legs, which were well worth showing off.

I wondered why she had dressed herself in this form-fitting dress with a full skirt after she'd come in from the rain. Maybe she was expecting a visitor, one of her select clients. But then she wouldn't be inviting me upstairs if she was.

'Come on in,' she said at her door, stepping inside and stooping to pick up what looked like a white lacy slip from the floor. 'Oops! I was in such a hurry to get my things off, I just flung them anywhere. Take a pew,' and she waved me to a plush sofa.

I glanced around the room quickly. It was a little like the place I was staying in below but a little more tastefully done in blues and greens.

She sat opposite me in a straight-backed armchair, quite large so that she seemed to be even smaller than she was. In the process her dress had ridden up just above her knees as she crossed her legs.

'Well, here we are!' She looked directly at me, very provocatively and so openly that I lowered my eyes. She laughed again. 'It's alright. You can have a good sken. I don't mind.' She pushed her skirt a little higher above her knees. 'You're a leg-man, right?'

I blushed as I nodded. 'I can usually tell,' she continued. With her virtual invitation I just sat and stared – her ankles were trimly shaped by her high heels and her legs had just the right curve to them. She uncrossed her legs but in such a way that her skirt still folded above her knees.

'It's very flattering, the way you keep on looking. Does a girl's heart good.'

I glanced away and said, 'The beans.'

'Oh, God, yes, the beans. I'll go and get them.' She stood up, swung around, her skirt flying around a little as she walked slowly towards what I presumed was the kitchen. She stopped at the door, leaned against the frame and stretched out a leg, pulling her skirt up to mid-thigh. 'Forget about the blasted beans. Look, I'll come clean.' She began to walk seductively back towards me. 'To tell you the truth, I don't really like beans. I'd be surprised if I had a tin in there.' She was still carrying the tin-opener so she put it down on a sidetable. Then she perched on the arm of her chair. 'It was such a miserable night, what with all the rain. And when I came in, I was hoping you'd be in too. I saw your light on, so I thought I'd be a good neighbour and say hello.'

'Very nice of you.'

'Stupid to dream up that stuff about the beans.' She stood up again and stepped towards the sideboard. 'A drink's better than beans. I called at the off-licence on the way back.' She opened the sideboard door and pointed to a bottle. 'Sherry – that's for me, and I didn't think I'd go far wrong if I got beer for you.'

'Fine for me.'

She poured the drinks and then sat back in her chair. As she sipped her sherry, she talked. I was surprised how frank she was. 'I suppose Barbara told you what I do.' She sipped her sherry and gazed at me with her big eyes over the rim of the glass. 'I don't mind her knowing. After all, she found this place for me.'

She went on to tell me she had built up a small but steady clientele, 'Most of them are successful business men who like to live it up when they're in town. That's how I got a phone – one of 'em has some pull with the GPO. So he can always reach me when he's in town. And that's how I knew you were moving in today.'

'How's that?'

'Barbara phoned me yesterday. I have a spare key and it saved her having to go to the landlord. And the way Barbara talked about you, this important young man coming in from London was how she put it, well, I was intrigued. She made you sound like a very interesting person,' She raised her glass to me and smiled. 'So, here's to you, Nick.'

I found Daisy was easy to talk to though she did most of the talking. She explained how she'd set herself up in her 'business'. 'I didn't want to slave away in an office for very little money. You can earn a lot more, and more quickly, in this game. And I only go with special blokes. Nice respectable gents. Makes it so's I don't have to go out in all weathers, standing about. And you never know what's out there. Course, I go out every now and then – like tonight. Bit of extra pocket money, I thought, then it starts raining. Didn't get too wet. I was wearing my new plastic mac. Have you seen them? Rain rolls right off. It's like being wrapped in cellophane.'

Daisy babbled on and plied me with more beer. I had a sneaking suspicion she was trying to get me a bit drunk so I might offer to stay with her. Later I decided I was being unfair to her. She was genuinely friendly.

She told me she was only going to stay in the game for just another two years or so. 'I'm giving up when I'm twenty-five. I should have saved a nice little nest egg by then and I'll be still young enough to enjoy spending it. Find myself a nice feller and we can have a good time together.'

'Don't you do that now?'

'What? Go out with a boy friend? Oh, no. I didn't want to involve anyone else in this. If I was going to be in the game, I was going to be right in it. The only way. So I never give it away for free. Maybe that sounds a bit cold but it's a business. I'm not saying I don't enjoy myself sometimes when I feel like it. I mean, some of my businessmen, they want to be serious about me. And though I do say it myself, I'm a cut above your ordinary, run-of-the-mill tart. And I cost more. Five pounds. But I know I'm good value for money.'

'I'm sure you are,' I told her and she nodded her head vigorously. 'You see, it's my old dad. He always said it wasn't right to cheat people out of what was rightfully theirs. He had a corner tobacconist's, always paid his bills. Mind you, he was a soft touch – I'm not like him that way, I don't think! But I saw the way he let people have things on tick and I'm sure he never got paid by some of them. Took advantage of him, they did. So I made up my mind, nothing on tick for anybody. Everything on the up-and-up. That way everyone gets what they pay for. All fair and square.'

She stopped to pour herself another sherry — I think it had loosened her tongue. 'You must think I'm a right gasbag.'

'No. It's very interesting.'

'Go on with you!' She paused. 'And what about you, Nick? What have you been doing with your life?'

I told her a little about my life in London. I must confess that, while I didn't emphasize the illegal side, I laid it on a bit thick about the delights I'd been indulging in with several of the ladies. 'You sound a bit like them, Daisy,' I told her, 'though they weren't at all scrupulous about the money side.'

'Ah, well, they weren't into it like me, were they, love? I mean, that Gerry sounds as if he took good care of them. I'm on my own but I wouldn't mind working for a man like Gerry.'

'I can put you in touch with him if you like. And Barbara knows him.'

She shook her head. 'I'm doing alright on my own for now. And I like being independent. And it's only two more years for me.' She stopped for a moment. 'And I do enjoy it most of the time. You'd be surprised what you learn doing this.' Then she laughed. 'Like with my raincoat, for instance.'

'What d'you mean?'

'It's clear plastic and the last few times I've worn it, it's pulled the men up short. I mean, you can see right through it. The way they look at me, you'd think they were seeing right through all the other clothing as well! Makes me feel like I've got nothing on except the mackintosh. Here, let me show you.'

She stood up and went to a small cupboard. She unhooked her mac, put it on, belting it tightly around her small waist. Then she pushed up her umbrella which she had left open on the floor to dry, and balanced it on her shoulder. She started to parade around the room. 'What d'you think?' she said.

'Very nice.'

She turned and walked seductively towards me. 'You seeing through my dress as well? Thinking how I'd look without a dress on? Go on. Don't be shy. You can tell me.' She leaned over me. 'See my underwear? Thinking what I'm like in my underwear? Or even without my underwear.'

This was beginning to get to me and I wondered what Daisy was up to, acting so provocatively even though she told me how she kept everything very business-like. So I wasn't sure how I was meant to react. But I said, 'You'd look great whatever you're wearing ... or not wearing.'

'You'll turn my head, you will.' She strutted away from me so I got a full view of her legs, her snug waist, her firmly round bum. She knew what she was doing because she turned round with a mischievous smile on her face and said, 'Fancy a bit?'

I sat still and didn't answer. She had made it clear she didn't offer herself free. Then she went on, 'Most men jump at the chance when I say that to them, even when I tell them it's five pounds.' She strolled across to another door, opened it slightly but enough so that I could see it was her bedroom. 'How about it, Nick? Like a cosy cuddle?'

'Five pounds, right?'

She nodded. 'That's the rule. No exception ... I mean, I'd like to. I'd put you first in the queue if it was free.'

I shrugged and shook my head a little. She relaxed from her sexy pose. 'That's the way it goes. And I should have known, after you'd told me about all your London birds, you wouldn't really see the need to give out five pounds.' She put down her umbrella and began to undo her mac with just a hint of sexy striptease about it. I thought for a moment I was going to be lucky, that Daisy was going to relent, that she would go on and take off her dress and...

No such luck. She took off her raincoat, went over to her easy chair, picked up her sherry and came to sit next to me. 'So much for that. Got that out of the way.' She raised her glass. 'Cheers, anyway.'

I wondered whether she had noticed how much her short performance with the raincoat had had its effect on me. While I wasn't fully aroused, I was pleasantly and warmly stiffened a little inside my pyjama trousers.

'Funny how it takes some men,' she said.

'What?'

'That business with the mac. I mean, while they like to see naked ladies, I find most men really like the idea of something being partly covered.' She smiled and briefly patted my knee. 'I don't mean you like it all wrapped up in a thick blanket. I mean just having something on that shows a bit of what's underneath.'

She'd hit on something that appealed to me. It was what I liked about lingerie, though a plastic mac was not in the same class.

'I thought you might be a man like that.' As I nodded, she went on, 'Well, it takes all kinds. That's something I've learned – how different men can be. I suppose you've heard a lot about what women like us do, all kinds of things, and you think it's us that thinks these things up. Men just have the one thing on their minds, isn't that what they say? You know the old joke: who cares about the mantelpiece when you're poking the fire?'

She glanced at me with a slightly puzzled expression, trying to judge just what my response to what she was saying was. 'That's one of the problems. Think about the woman. Even someone like me. Oh, it's a business, yes, but it's still nice to be treated special. Sometimes that puts us in a good mood and so it works out the man gets a better deal then.' She was resting her hand on my knee and her fingers were moving ever so slowly. My warm feeling was increasing.

'I mean, how would you like it if every woman you went with paid no attention to you and what you wanted? Just got on with what she wanted. I've been doing this long enough now to know it's best to give the man something he thinks is what he really wants. Initiate things a bit. In this business it's too easy not to bother. Just get on with it and get it over with, pocket the money and that's that. Well, I don't think my men would keep coming back if I did it that way.' Her fingers were now splayed wide along my thigh. 'After all, he's the one who's paying, so I try to go along with him, try to figure out what he really wants. You know, it's funny, a lot of men, even when they're right into it, they're shy about saying what they want. So you have to try and work it out for yourself. Like with me, I can tell sometimes when you first touch a man.' As she said that, her hand moved almost imperceptibly up my thigh and I felt a hardening twitch in my erection. I was definitely getting fatter and thicker.

'I try to make it special that first time I put my hands on him. I like to make him feel that I really want to put my hands right where he wants them, as if I can't wait to get my hands on him – and sometimes that's true. It can be a sort of...' she hesitated as if she was searching for the right word. 'Well, I guess it's a magic moment. I know it is for me, that first time of touching ... and the first time he touches me.'

Her hand slid down and off my leg and I was disappointed. The conversation seemed to be leading somewhere interesting and now Daisy looked as if she was backing away. She picked up her glass of sherry and held it in both hands as she sipped. Her eyes gazed over it with a soft but penetrating look, still with that bright twinkle in them. I was being thrown for a loop, not quite sure what to do after all she'd told me about keeping things strictly as a business. I wasn't sure whether she was just teasing and flirting with me or whether she was trying to get five pounds out of me.

She put her glass down but kept her eyes on me. 'Take you, for example. I bet you're feeling right now as if you'd like to lean over and touch me up a bit, right? But you're a bit scared. Don't quite know how I'm going to take it.' She slid a little closer to me on the couch. 'Well, in spite of me being in the business, it's the same with me. I just don't know with most men.' She took one of my hands in hers. 'Nice hand. Smooth. You can tell a lot from a hand.' She began to stroke my hand, her fingers gently skittering across my palm in what seemed almost like an invitation to proceed. 'You've got lovely, soft skin. Mmmm!' Her head was slightly back as if she was drifting into a lazy kind of acceptance so I tried to move my hand out of hers – I had the idea of putting my arm around her but she shook her head quickly and dropped my hand. 'Can't break the rules ... however nice it might be.'

She was sitting quite primly now, both hands in her lap. 'You'd be surprised what kind of tricks men get up to at the beginning to get you to touch them, even though we both know what's going to happen. I mean, when they're with me, they know that.'

'I wouldn't have thought it would be that difficult. I'd be sure to let you know pretty quickly.'

'I've discovered most men are shy. Even with someone like me. And I like that. It's nice. Makes it as if we're not just together because of the money.' She was still staring directly at me, then she lowered her gaze quite deliberately to my crotch. I blushed a little. 'You see,' she said, and laughed. 'Like you. You don't know quite what to make of me, do you? And I like that. I'm just having a bit of ... sexy fun. You don't mind? Maybe it's the mood I'm in tonight.'

She put a hand firmly on my thigh and let it stay there without moving. I didn't know whether she wanted me to proceed and I was certainly ready. My cock was stiff and straining inside my pyjama trousers but she had issued a warning that she was still in the business.

'Don't look so worried, Nick. It's alright. Really!' She gripped my thigh and went on. 'Most men would be leaping all over me by now if I was talking to them like this, if I was touching them like this.' Her hand now began a slow circle on the top of my thigh. 'And if they do that, I don't mind. That's what they're with me for and I try to ... accommodate them.

'Mind you, there's some men who go for it straight-away. Take hold of my hand and plop it down on them. Just like that.' Then she raised her hand from my thigh and left it suspended above me, almost as if she was going to illustrate what she had just said. I half imagined that her hand would drop slowly onto my crotch.

But it didn't, so I reached over and took it into my hand. Then she looked at me with a brilliant smile, her head tilted to one side as if she was asking me a question. Or maybe she was wondering if I'd decided to fork out five pounds. I'm sure it would have been a splendid evening with her but somehow I just wanted to see how she would go on. I pulled her hand downward a little. I met no resistance – her hand felt soft and warm and light in mine. I held it just above me where my cock was standing up inside my trousers and I'm sure she had seen what state I was in. I held her hand there a few seconds and she didn't try to pull it away so I gently exerted a little pressure till it was almost touching the tip of my stand. Quickly I pulled my hand away and her hand fell onto my cock.

She rested her hand there without attempting to do anything more though she whispered, 'There. That was very nice, the way you did that. Most men are rougher than that. Yours was a nice gentleman's touch. I like that. Maybe you'd like a gentle lady's touch.' Her fingers folded round my length and squeezed. That squeeze encouraged me even further for my cock sprang up as if it wanted to fit itself inside Daisy's hand. She didn't reach in so I was still covered by my pyjamas.

'Didn't I say it was like magic, that first time? And it does something for a woman, you know. Makes her think she's something – a man getting like that just for her.' And still I didn't know what to make of Daisy, for she was just letting her hand fold round my cock without moving. I didn't want to make a move in case I ruined that magic that she'd been talking about. If anything was to come of this, I was determined that she'd be the one to take the initiative. It was excruciating to have her hand there without her stroking me. She must have been feeling something herself, with a full, hot handful. I was tempted to move so that somehow I'd be poking out of my pyjamas. Perhaps that might help to set things going. But I didn't want to move in case I spoiled things.

Daisy leaned closer to me, her other hand now on my other thigh but still just placed on my pyjamas. Then she crooned in my ear, 'Those men who do this to me, put my hand there, they sort of twitch and then they push at me and it's obvious they want me to start wanking them immediately.' Her warm breath in my ear and what she was saying made my cock twitch and she must have felt it. 'Like this,' she murmured.

The hand on my thigh folded back my dressing gown, then slid up to my waist to unfasten the cord of my pyjama trousers. Her fingers pulled at the waist and she lowered them and I carefully shifted my arse so that she could pull them right down. Her other hand was still on my cock but as I shifted, my cock seemed to leap and bang and poke inside her hand. And that had the effect of starting her to stroke me quite vigorously, increasing her pace steadily.

Her words in my ear were both enticing and softly commanding. 'Why they want it so fast, I'll never understand. Some of them let go after a minute or two of this.' I knew if she kept on, that would soon happen to me, whether I wanted to or not. But her hand began to slow down. 'I don't think you're like that. You like to take your time. Like this.'

Her strokes slowed down, making leisurely and lingering touches as her other hand now moved up to take my balls in her fingers. 'And now we're like this, I don't want you to spill just yet. I'll be careful.' And surprisingly after a few seconds she lifted her hands away though left them hovering very close, flickering her fingers slowly.

'Some men like a very gentle touch, almost as if you're not doing anything. Like this.' Her fingers fell so that her fingertips played a very delicate scale along the length, almost not touching, maddening my prick into quick twitches as her fingers made delicious circles round the skin. She pulled away from the fat, red head, skimming, plucking, one finger strumming at the thin band of flesh stretched tight across the rolled-back skin. Her other hand was silky smooth on my balls. Then two fingers skidded delicately at the slit of my cock, opening and closing it as the other fingers played around the head.

'Some like my fingers to go round and round. Like this.' She suited her actions to her words and I felt one smooth fingertip with a tiny scratch of her nail circling round my cock-head and the rolled-back skin while her other hand was now rougher, grasping the base of my cock hard.

'Some like to push themselves right into my palm.' Her hand cupped the whole of my cock-head, the fingers trailing and trickling down my length.

'Some like it wet.' For one moment I thought she would bring her mouth down on me but she licked her palm and fingers till they were very moistly slippery and it was exquisite to feel that wet smoothness on me. 'Oh, look what's happening.' She spotted a pearl of spunk emerging from the slit. 'I'll just have to make sure you don't spill out any more. I'll take care of that.' I watched as she extended a finger and very delicately lifted that drop of come onto her fingertip and then smoothed it around the head.

'And once I've been doing this for a while, most of them just lie back and take whatever I want to do.' Quickly she raised her hands, turned me, pushed my shoulders so that I was lying full-length on the very long couch we were sitting on. Then I felt her hands wandering all over my cock and balls, pushing and pulling, gentle then hard, squeezing then flicking, then flickering till soon Daisy was insistently gripping me, stroking me, one hand wet from her mouth, palming the head of my cock and coaxing out droplets of jism. Soon I was pushing my pelvis up, trying to bury my cock deeply in her hands, feeling myself wanting to gush out.

Her hands were now thoroughly moist with her saliva and my come and her hands were moving in long strokes up and down the length of my cock. 'Then I let them slide into me,' she sighed out. 'I can make myself very wet doing this. Think about sliding into me.' I thought she was going to relent but her hands kept on, reducing me to a shivering tingle till I could feel a great surge rising up my cock and then an increasing throb of delight as I released.

As the creamy liquid shot out, her fingers played at the slit as the come gushed and showered out so I flooded all over her hands. They were now oily and slippery and she rubbed them round my cock-head and down the length, my movements thrashing up and down as my cock thrust between the creamy wetness of her hands, squirming, the massage making me tremble and shiver till I was fully spent.

Daisy kept her fingers twined round my prick, let it slip and slide around while she teased my balls as well. She let it squirm between her two hands until it lost some of its hardness but her soft touches kept it from going completely limp. She snuggled her head on my chest and I could hear her dreamily murmuring, 'It's lovely to feel that first gush, all hot and sticky, and then so slippery.' She stayed like that for a few minutes, me going a little limper though she kept her hands slowly stroking me.

She eventually sat up, her hands clasped in her lap, making no effort to clean her hands or wipe me. She bent low over my diminishing cock, took a deep breath and said, 'I like the smell as well,' then coyly looking up at me, her eyes wide and innocent-looking, she said wickedly, 'and the taste.' She soon returned to her matter-of-fact recital of the whims and quirks of the men she knew. 'That squirt's delicious. Sometimes I like to have a man spill all over me, all squelchy on my breasts and I love to try to catch it in my hands. Or a stream of it spilling onto my thighs. It's lovely. Of course, I make 'em wear a French letter if they want to spill inside me and that spoils it a bit because I like to feel the splash inside as well. Like hot cream.'

She smiled at me. 'And you. Who'd have guessed you had such a big gusher? There! That's only about a quid's worth. Think what you'll get for a fiver.'

We talked a little longer as I finished off my beer and Daisy had another sherry. Eventually I stood up, ready to go back downstairs. I had to be up early to go to university the following morning and then I was off to see more houses with Barbara.

As I stood at the door, I gave Daisy a big hug. She had been a great companion for the evening, getting me wet rather than venturing out into the rain which was still coming down. 'I wish you'd have broken the rules tonight,' I said.

'Well, I did just a teeny bit, didn't I? And in any case, only two years and a few months to go, then there'll be no more rules.'

'It'd be a nice way to celebrate your twenty-fifth birthday.'

'I'll hold you to that,' she answered, though I thought that she was just carrying on with her teasing. Her mischievous grin came back as she continued, 'But you don't have to wait two years – even if you hang on to your five pounds. We can still keep in touch, Nick.' And she laughed, then reached her hand up to stroke my face and I caught a faint whiff of myself on her hand. 'Drink a little beer and sherry. Wet our whistles ... and maybe wet other things as well!'

She stood on tiptoe and quickly kissed my nose. 'I'm glad I didn't have any beans! But it was nice to be neighbourly. Even though you'll be moving in a few days, don't forget the first neighbour you met!'

I went down to my place. I could still hear the rain pattering on the windows but that made no difference. I wasn't going to sink back into that sad mood again. I'd had a pleasant rainy night as it turned out, getting myself soaked, then soaking myself in the delectably efficient hands of Daisy. I was glad the rain had driven her inside and I was feeling more reconciled to spending my time here. With someone like Daisy around, the next three years didn't seem to look as bleak as they had done earlier that evening. In spite of the rain, the evening forecast a clearing trend.

3. Naughty Sweetie

Next morning, I found my way up to the English Department office to report for my timetable. I had to wait a while as the student before me was obviously taking his time, trying to chat up a secretary, a pert young blonde. The student was a little older than the usual run; he spoke with a very cultured upper-class accent. He cut a rather dashing figure – he was already wearing a long university scarf which he had slung round his neck so that it fell down his back, the other end dangling down at the front.

The blonde secretary looked flattered by the student's flirtatious attention. She was giggling and blushing, scattering papers across her desk, dropping some on the floor, scrabbling to pick them up. While she was bent down, the student turned to me and winked. The secretary kept on protesting but it was obvious she was enjoying every minute of it.

'Go on with you!' she said.

'No. Really. I didn't know they had such pretty girls in Manchester.' She giggled. 'But maybe you're the only pretty one around here.' He leaned over her desk and whispered, 'Better than that old sourpuss out there,' he said nodding towards the door.

'Miss Pogson? She's ever so nice.'

'Well, I bet you'd be "ever so nice" to any young feller

you took a fancy to.' Then he reached for her left hand and took it in his own. 'Look there! I don't understand it.'

'What?'

'No ring. I'm surprised no one's snapped you up. Just give me half a chance.'

'You're just having me on,' she said between giggles.

'No, I'm not. You'd better watch out. I'm going to be looking out for you. I'm glad I signed up with the English Department.' He picked up a small sheaf of papers he'd put on the secretary's desk, then turned to me. 'Sorry, old boy. Got a bit carried away talking to this young lady. Excuse me.'

He reminded me a little of Gerry, one of those hearty upper-class men, oozing confidence. With my background, I always mistrusted that kind of person. Gerry sometimes made me feel uneasy but he'd always treated me fairly and certainly he was a good boss, though I knew he'd be very difficult to deal with if I stepped out of line.

This young man was a little older than me, looking rather raffish and debonair in an untidy way, wearing a corduroy jacket, his tie loose on his shirt, a big smile, a shock of thick brown wavy hair. He thrust out his hand. 'I'm Ron Burns,' he said. I took his hand. He had a very firm grip and he pumped my hand very enthusiastically as I told him my name.

'You studying English?' he asked. I nodded. 'We'll be in the same classes then.' He flicked his head towards the secretary. 'Look what they've laid on for us. Not bad, eh? But hands off. I saw her first.' He said this in a low voice, nicely calculated so that the secretary could hear. She giggled again.

Burns looked down at his timetable. 'Doesn't look too tough. I can cope, though I don't like the sound of this

Anglo-Saxon stuff.' Then he nudged me. 'At least we might learn a few more four-letter words, what?' He turned to the secretary. 'Give the man his papers – and no flirting with him.' That set the secretary off into a series of giggles again. Then she gave me a wad of papers.

Burns threw his arm round my shoulder. 'Glad I ran into you. Not too many people around yet. I came up early. Spent a miserable night in some fleabag of a hotel. Got to find myself a decent place. You busy right now? I'll give you a lift downtown if you like. I'm going to pick up a few books.'

So that's how I found myself sitting next to Ron Burns in his sporty Morris. He told me his father ran his own company and finagled extra petrol coupons. 'I couldn't do without the old jalopy. Very useful. It impresses girls no end if you've got a car.'

He went on in this breezy manner and, in spite of my initial mistrust, I found him very likeable. He seemed sincere and friendly despite his breeziness. He told me he'd stayed on in the army for a few years after the war. 'I didn't like it all that much but I got a better pay-off when I was demobbed. I hated the army as a matter of fact. Glad to be out of it and ready to raise a little hell.'

Later, after we'd bought a few books we were sitting in a Kardomah café drinking tea, I told him something of my life in London. He was inordinately interested. 'Maybe I could drive you down some week-end and you could introduce me to some of those ladies.' He paused. 'I wonder what the bints'll be like at the university. I hope they're not all innocent schoolgirls. Mind you, I'm just up to corrupting a few. And that secretary wasn't half bad, eh? Thick as a brick, probably but she looks a bit of alright. Still, I like my ladies to have some brains – they can think up a few different ways to interest me then.'

He rambled on about his tastes in women and his experiences in the army. He was sort of overwhelming but he was so genuinely full of life, so cheerful, I couldn't find it in myself to dislike him. He was generous and amiable and while he told me a little boastfully about some of his affairs, it wasn't all swagger because he also told me about some of his failures and disasters with women. I liked a man who could laugh at his own mistakes.

'I got in yesterday evening. Bloody teeming down so I drove to the nearest hotel. Christ! It was awful. Worse than living in barracks. I'm off this afternoon to find a nice place to rent. I'm looking forward to holing up on my own till I can find a nice young lady to invite over for a bite to eat ... and a bite at anything else that's going!'

I told him I was going house-hunting with Barbara. I was sure she would be able to help him out. I gave him her number saying I'd be finished by mid-afternoon so maybe Barbara would be free then. 'She has a few listings and she knows about a place that sounds interesting though she doesn't want to show it to me.'

'Why not?'

'Because it's free.'

'Free, as in no rent to pay?'

'That's right.' Then I told him what little I knew about Paradise Lost. 'I don't believe it,' he said. 'There must be some snags. After all, army barracks are free and I know what they're like.'

'I don't think it's like that at all. Anyhow I'll let you know if I find out anything else about it.'

'And I'll phone this Barbara Logan sometime today to see if she can take me on after she's finished with you.'

I was actually finished with Barbara about two that afternoon. I'd told her about Ron Burns and how he wanted her to find him a place. She was very effusive in her thanks. 'It gets to be a real scramble when the students all descend on you. That'll happen in a few days so if I can lease out these few places I have before then, that'll earn me a nice lot of commission without rushing around. Then I can take it easy.'

We hadn't taken it easy that afternoon. She whizzed me around four other houses. All were well kept and well appointed but none of them came up to what I had found in the second one she had shown me the previous afternoon. At one point I said she could have brought Ron Burns with us and that would have saved her some time, but she shook her head. 'Oh, no,' she said. 'I don't like doing that. Sometimes causes arguments when both your clients like the same place. Besides,' she said, giving me a big smile, 'I wanted to just take you with me. Gerry said I was to look after you well. And that's what I intend to do. I know how Gerry expects his friends to be treated.'

While Barbara was not what I would call beautiful, she was very attractive. Even during this business afternoon she was fun to be with. She was a tall woman in her late twenties, I guessed, looking good in her slim black skirt and a plain white blouse. Her dark hair was loosely waved and her face was lit up by a pair of intensely brown eyes.

She also seemed to know her business, being adept at pointing out the advantages of a house but also making sure I knew the drawbacks. She accomplished all this in her fulsomely gregarious manner – indeed, occasionally I wondered if she was becoming a little more than gregarious. In one place, she was showing me the bathroom, standing by the door while I poked around in it. When I moved to come out, she stayed at the door and I had to sidle past her. As I did, I had a vague notion that she leaned slightly into me so that her breasts pressed briefly against me. I glanced at her and again I wasn't sure if an almost teasing smile hovered around her mouth.

In another place I was about to enter one of the rooms but she stopped me by grasping my lower arm. 'This one's locked,' she said and drew her hand from me to search in her purse for the key. But it was the way her hand had moved on me that intrigued me. For a brief moment her long fingers seemed to caress my wrist before she pulled them away, Again I caught a glimpse of that sly smile.

In the final house we looked at, there was a loft which could be climbed into by means of a ladder that folded down from a trapdoor. She had to stretch up to pull it down and that raised her skirt high on her legs. I noticed just how splendid her legs were. Then she began to climb up it, holding her skirt above her knees as it was too tight for her to climb easily. She left me standing at the foot of the ladder and of course I made sure I had a good look at her legs. She was wearing expensive seamed nylons and I figured that she was probably wearing a garter belt to hold them in place. I also saw her white underskirt, very fancy with lace. She looked down at me with that smile again, a mixture of the mischievous and the lascivious, I thought. Then she stepped down. 'Maybe you'd better go up to have a look. I have no head for heights.'

Then when I backed down the ladder and reached the last two rungs, just for a few seconds I felt the whole length of her body pressed against my back before she stepped back. 'Just steadying the ladder,' she breathed. 'You never know just how safe these things are. It wouldn't do my reputation any good if one of my clients got injured while I was showing him around.'

Those three little incidents, together with her remark about action in the bedroom when she'd shown me round the first place the day before, gave me pause. Just what kind of a woman was she? She had worked for Gerry and I knew what most of Gerry's women were like – most of them free with their favours, enjoying life, not worrying about strict behaviour, often exciting, always enticing. And here was Barbara, clearly a dynamite business woman but perhaps sending out intriguing, if mysterious hints. Or was I misreading or exaggerating them?

I finally dismissed them. She was a woman settled in her work and I had appeared out of nowhere. There could be no reason why she should be interested in me beyond being a client. Besides, I was only a student, younger than her by several years. It was all probably part of her outgoing nature, I told myself.

While I dismissed it at the time, some other thoughts surfaced after I had left her. Was she really suggesting anything? I hated being rebuffed by a woman when I had been mistaken about her intentions so I didn't want to attempt anything with Barbara and make a fool of myself. After all, she lived her life here, and probably knew plenty of men. Why on earth would she be bothered with a mere student?

When I told Barbara I still wanted to rent the second house I had seen, she said, 'Well, it's a deal then. I'll make the lease out, go over it with you, checking with the landlord first. He'll sign it and I'll have it ready for you to sign tonight. Are we still on for that? Dinner at my place. At seven.'

'Fine.' I said. 'And maybe you'll tell me a little more about that free place, what's it called ... Paradise Lost?'

'I'm sure that's not the place for you, Nick.'

'It can't be all that bad.'

'I'm not sold on it. It's too good to be true, I think. I'll probably give you the worst impression of the place. You should talk to the woman I got in there, Lorna. You'll like to meet her. You have a connection in any case.'

'How?'

'She does an occasional job for Gerry here.'

That sounded interesting. I thought of the women who did occasional jobs for Gerry, those I had met in London, and they had turned out to be particularly friendly. If this Lorna was like them, I was certain I would like to meet her.

'She'll give you the lowdown on the place, show you around, tell you what she thinks about it.'

I had a vague doubt in my mind – was Barbara just being the eager business woman? Perhaps she wasn't letting me see Paradise Lost because she probably didn't get as much commission when she placed someone there? But my doubts disappeared when she added, 'Don't worry. I'll write the lease so you can break it without any problem if you want to go to live somewhere else. Though I should warn you, it's not so easy to get into Paradise Lost. There aren't always many places available there. So let's just settle you in at this place you want.' Then one more time she gave me that entrancing smile. 'And let's not turn the dinner into just a business meeting tonight, right? It's all settled so we can relax and have a little fun together.'

It wasn't the Barbara I'd expected who opened the door to me just after seven. She was wearing a short apron over the slim black skirt she'd had on in the afternoon – I wondered if she was still wearing that frilly underskirt. She had changed her plain white blouse for something more dazzling – a white background with dizzy and bold slashes of black, zigzagging and squiggling over the whole blouse.

'Come on in,' she said. 'I'm a little behind.' She walked in front of me leading me in and I felt I'd like to say she had not just a little behind but a very fetching one. But I kept my mouth shut. 'I haven't really had time to change,' she went on.

'Well, I like the blouse. Very jazzy.'

'Why d'you say that?' She turned to look at me.

'I don't know. It just struck me, you know, snazzy, lots of flair, that's jazzy to me.'

'I'm not complaining. It's just that ... jazzy ... it's not a word I hear much these days. Brings back some memories.' She brushed a stray lock of hair out of her eyes. For a moment I thought she was brushing away a tear.

'Sorry,' I said.

'No, really. It's alright. The memories are ... sort of nice and sad at the same time.' She patted her hair, straightened her apron. 'Look at me. A mess. Still cooking, I'm afraid. Why don't you come into the kitchen with me?'

I followed her into her small kitchen, cool and white. 'I thought we'd have seafood,' she said. 'I hope you like seafood.'

'Fine with me. Though I brought red wine.' I gave her the bottle I'd brought.

'Who cares? As long as we like it, we can do what we

damn well please.' She put the bottle on the counter. 'Help yourself to the wine in the fridge. I got started before you came.' She held up her glass of white wine and I poured myself some, raising my glass, saying, 'Cheers!'

'Cheers! Here's looking forward to ... what? Friendship. Good times.'

'Home cooking,' I added.

'And I love to cook, especially if whoever I'm cooking for appreciates home cooking. So I'll drink to that. Home cooking together!' And she swigged her glass and stretched her hand out with her glass in it. 'More please, Nick.'

I was beginning to think that maybe she had been at the wine for some time but the bottle was still half full. I poured some for her and she went on, 'I'm doing oysters to begin with. Then it's difficult to know exactly what can come after oysters.' And that mischievous smile appeared again. 'Well, it's salmon. Grilled salmon. But I don't have to do that right now. Just pop the stuffing in the oysters. Why don't you sit down and keep me company while I do it.'

As usual, I found Barbara very easy to talk to. She asked me about Gerry and Margo and before long she was telling me about how she got to know them. 'I was a very quiet girl, believe it or not. I came out of grammar school and didn't know quite what I wanted to do with my life. I got a job with a building society, learned something about houses, mortgages, that sort of thing. I was still young and in those days they didn't promote women to good positions even though there were openings with all the men being off to the war.'

She stopped what she was doing at the counter. 'There! They're done. Only take ten minutes to cook.

D'you want to eat now or should we sit and drink wine and talk for a bit?'

'I'm easy. Whatever you want to do.'

She took off her apron. 'Maybe I should freshen myself up.'

'You look fresh enough to me.'

'Well, it depends how fresh you want me to be,' she said with a laugh.

'You look good enough to eat,' I said, wondering what the effect would be.

'You young men. Always ready with the flattery.'

'It's true. Very tasty ... and jazzy.'

'Well, true or not, it's good to hear.' She moved out of the kitchen when she took another bottle of wine out of the fridge. 'Bring the opener. It's on the counter.' I found the opener and took it with me, following her into a small living room, almost under-furnished but comfortable, with a large fireplace.

She gestured with her arms flung out. 'Can't stand clutter. Just like everything clear so everyone knows where they are. And this place is really not big enough for me to have a lot of things.'

She perched on a small buffet near the fireplace. I sat near her on a soft, tweedy armchair, opened the wine and poured us each a large glassful. 'Maybe I'll light the fire later. I love to have a log fire.' She drank and neither of us said anything for a while. She leaned forward, elbows on her knees, one hand propped under her chin, and looked directly at me. 'I'm sorry.' Then she glanced down.

'Sorry? What for?'

'I wasn't ready for you.'

'That's alright.'

'Well, I did want things to go well tonight. I've really

been looking forward to it. Sort of reminds me of old times, when I was in London ... and all that.' She drank again. 'Excuse me. Tell me if I'm getting maudlin.'

'Everything's fine.'

'In a way it's your fault, my being not ready for you.'

'What d'you mean?'

'That friend of yours, Ron Burns. What a character! He kept me talking on the phone this afternoon, tried to get me to show him houses right away but I had this lease of yours to deal with. But he was very persistent. It was ... well, almost as if he was dying to meet me, like he wanted a date with me. Made me feel ... this'll sound silly ... desirable.'

'Nothing wrong with that.' Then I ventured again. 'After all, you are.'

'What?'

'Desirable.'

'There you go with the compliments again!' I shook my head and she gave me a look that almost held a kind of scorching quality in it. 'Anyhow, he'd given my number to three others and two of them phoned me as well.' She kept gazing at me. 'That was nice of you, sending business my way like that.' She raised her glass. 'So I've got a busy day tomorrow, dealing with all three of them. All the more reason to relax tonight.'

I poured more wine for her but she told me to give her just a little. 'I tend to do a few crazy things if I tank up too much.' She paused. 'But then sometimes I can go a little crazy without wine as well ... when the mood takes me.' She fingered her blouse, then added, 'Jazzy, eh?'

'Yes.' Again we didn't speak for a minute or so though

we both looked at each other, I stole glances at her legs which she had stretched out in front of her. Then I reminded her that she had been telling me how she had met Gerry.

'It's a long story. Maybe you'll find it boring.' She took a long breath. 'I was working at that building society, still young, nineteen, and then I met Bill.' She stopped for a long moment, then shook her head. 'Sorry. It's a little difficult for me to talk about this even after all these years.'

'If you don't want to...'

'No, no. It'll do me good.' She swept her hand across her forehead. 'My God! Believe it or not, I don't know how to say this. A grown woman of twenty-seven and I'm embarrassed.'

I didn't know what to say so I covered the silence by pouring myself more wine. I offered some to Barbara but she refused. I told myself that I must watch how much I drank. I didn't want to appear foolish with this charming woman who seemed in the mood to be confessional about something.

'D'you mind if I'm blunt?' I shook my head. 'Bill was only three years older than me but years ahead of me in lots of ways. He introduced me to a whole new world.' She sipped some wine. 'Sex!' She shook her head, almost in bewilderment. 'After all these years, I find it incomprehensible that I'd got to the age of nineteen without the faintest inkling of that. It's...' She seemed to be groping for words. 'I mean, now we're ... grown up ... what we've been through.' She was gesturing as if to include me in what she was saying but I didn't want to tell her that I was older than her before the world of sex had opened for me. The life I'd led in London had begun less than a year ago.

'I'd really no idea but Bill ... so gentle with me. Just fantastic. It got so's I couldn't think of anything else. Nothing else mattered.' She paused. 'Bliss, I suppose it was. Sheer bliss. For months and months. He'd had a deferment to go to university but when he got his degree, well, he had to go in the forces. The navy. He was posted down to Plymouth and I went with him. I couldn't do without him.'

She held her glass out. 'Just a touch please.' She sipped, then continued, 'He was put on convoy duty. Some bloody old corvette. We had three days to ourselves before he went on the Murmansk run. We lived it up in London. God! Those three days. What we packed in. And that's why you threw me when you called my blouse jazzy.' She fingered one of the buttons on her blouse. 'Reminded me of Bill.'

She was silent for several seconds. 'We went to a jazz club every night, drank wine, went back to the hotel to make love the rest of the night, slept through the day, made love again, then went out to eat and back to the jazz club. It was the best three days of my life.' She swept her hair back in that same gesture – it seemed to be some kind of nervous reaction.

'Gerry owned one of the clubs we went to.' She was acting a little uneasy now. 'Then Bill went on his convoy. Torpedoed. Drowned.' She put her glass down, stared about the room. I stood up to give her more wine but she surprised me by standing up and throwing her arms around me. 'I went mad. I went the rounds of those clubs I'd been to with Bill, picked up anyone, slept with a lot of them. I suppose I was looking for someone like Bill. No one was. Then of course Gerry saved me.'

She pulled away from me. 'Sorry,' she said, then sat

down again. 'There's not much more to tell. Gerry saw me in the club one night – he'd seen me there before, he told me later, saw what I was doing. Well, he offered me a job when he found out I'd worked at the building society. Set up a house agency for me and he asked me to work out leases for him on some houses. Made them out in my name. I guess I was pretty naïve. I mean, he was using me. But you know Gerry. Won't let you down if you do something for him. So he treated me very well. That's how I got started on my own.' She paused. 'And he paid for me to learn something else – "something to fall back on if the house thing goes kaput," he said. I suppose he meant if I didn't make a go of it after I'd done the leases for him. As Bill had introduced me to the delights of massage, I decided I wanted to do that. So Gerry paid for me to train as a massage therapist.'

'Really?'

'And I still keep it up. Makes a change from the rental business.' She stood up. 'I must be boring you with all this. Just sat you down and you had to listen.'

'It's alright. Nice sitting here with you. Nice room as well.'

'It's only a small place but I like it. D'you want to see the rest of it? If you're not fed up of looking round houses, that is.'

'No. I'd like to.'

'Well, I'll give you a quick guided tour. Then I'll put the oysters in and we can eat.' She took my hand and led me out of the living room. 'As I said, it's only small so it'll only take a jiffy. Across the hall there's the dining room.' Then we arrived at the foot of the stairs. 'Up there's my bedroom ... and there's another small bedroom that I've converted so I can do my massage in there. I have another tiny room, more of a cubbyhole really and I use that as an office. And the bathroom's upstairs. And that's it.'

As she'd been telling me this, she had started to climb the stairs, pulling me up with her. As she'd already described what was upstairs, I was surprised she was taking me up to look but she seemed determined to show me. She even threw open the door to her bedroom. It was immaculately neat, a fluffy comforter covering the bed, pale yellow sheets, neatly folded back, frilly pillows in the same yellow, a dressing table filled with creams and powders and along the back of it was a three-part mirror. She also had a wardrobe with sliding doors. It looked snug and cosy and for a moment I thought it was all posed and planned. Again I was wondering just what kind of woman Barbara was, especially after her confession. I remembered those strange incidents during the afternoon.

She moved along the small hallway to open another door. 'And this is the massage room.' It was rather spartan – a low divan covered by a coverlet, a full-length wall mirror, an open closet with towels and bathrobes, all dark blue. 'Silly of me, I suppose,' Barbara said, 'but I keep everything blue. Blue for the navy.' Then she moved to the end of the hallway to another door and opened it. 'My office.' She closed the door. 'But we don't want anything to do with business tonight.' And she walked past me, brushing slightly against me in the narrow hallway – was it another hint or was she not offering hints at all?

She waited for me at the top of the stairs and as I joined her, I said, 'It's curious, this mixture of house rentals and massage.'

'Not really curious. Massage goes with anything.

Business is always stressful and massage gets rid of the stress.'

'Does it work for you? I mean, you're giving the massage.'

'Oh, it makes me move and exercise when I'm doing it.'

'Does it really work?'

'Have you never had a massage?' I shook my head. 'Well, what better time than now after we've been working hard this afternoon?' Again she brushed past me to go the door of the massage room. She opened the door. 'Come on in.' She invited me in as she stood at the door. 'That is, if you want one. You're a prime candidate for a massage – leaving London and all that hectic life you had working for Gerry, settling down in a new place, wondering what your courses are going to be like. I'll bet you're all wound up.' She raised her hands and waggled her fingers. 'Barbara's magic fingers will do the trick.'

When she said that I was reminded of Daisy the previous night, saying how magic it was for her to touch someone for the first time. There was Barbara offering her own magic, even if it was a very different massage than the one I'd had from Daisy. She was giving me one of her teasing looks. What did I have to lose? She went on, 'I love doing massage. It relaxes me as well. Do us both good, if you're game.'

I tried to sound as nonchalant as I could. 'I don't mind trying it.'

'Good. In you go. There's a clean robe there. I just have to get some things. I'll be back in a minute.' And off she went.

While I was undressing and putting on my robe, I mulled over what I might expect. Would Barbara arrive undressed? Maybe just in that frilly underskirt? Would she be that obvious? Or would it be nothing like that at all? Whatever she appeared in, I couldn't rid my head of these interesting ideas. Under the robe, I was already in a state of semi-arousal.

Barbara arrived dressed as a professional masseuse and I must confess my heart sank a little. She was wearing a light blue cotton coat, slightly starched so she looked crisp and efficient. She pulled a small table on wheels to the side of the divan. 'Lie down,' she said briskly. 'We start by giving the back a complete rub-down.'

I clambered onto the divan and lay down on my stomach, keeping my robe wrapped round me so she couldn't see any sign of a bulge. This looked as if it was going to be a genuine massage.

'You need your robe off,' she said quite sternly and threw me a towel. 'You can drape yourself in this if you want.' In fact, when I was lying down, Barbara put the towel across my buttocks. Then I felt a slight pressure at one side of the divan, and then the other side. Obviously, Barbara was straddled across my legs.

'I can get more pressure this way,' she said. 'I hope you don't mind.' I grunted no into the pillow my head had sunk into. Her hands gripped my shoulders, kneading the flesh. 'Relax,' she said quietly. 'These muscles are all tensed up.' I felt a little warm liquid spread across my shoulders. 'Nothing to worry about,' she crooned in a soothing, almost sing-song voice as her hands smoothed my flesh slowly and deliberately, shaping my shoulders, her hands drawn down my arms as well, then up, across my shoulders, then lower down to the bottom of my shoulder blades.

After two or three minutes I sensed that her hands

were covering a little more flesh, moving down under my shoulder blades towards my waist. She was pushing along the length of my backbone, up and down, stopping twice for a little more lotion. Her hands opened and pushed from my backbone out to the sides, then down to my waist, in, then up the backbone. She kept this same motion up for a few minutes, her hands very firm but, in a strange way, they felt as if they were also caressing me. Sometimes she gave me little shocks by brief pummels with the sides of her hands, sometimes she would gather flesh into her hands and squeeze it, letting it drop and spreading a smooth hand across it.

This massage was having the desired effect. I was falling into a relaxed, almost dozy state. I was still aware of this woman's warm body next to me, on top of my legs. I could feel her body warmth so I was very much at ease. My cock was now in a pleasantly erect state, pressed into the divan. Its stiffness was warm against my stomach.

Her hands were now moving a little below my waist so the towel shifted down, then further down as her hands explored the first swelling of my buttocks just below my waist. She said something so quietly, I didn't hear.

'What?'

'I can do this better if you remove the towel.' I reached back and slid the towel away. 'Thanks,' she said and her hands began to grip the flesh of my buttocks. Then she was smoothing them, round and round, dropping her hands further down to almost fondle the cheeks, the roundness below.

She stayed doing this for awhile, all the time humming a tune which was vaguely familiar to me.

'What's that song you're humming?'

'Relax.' She interrupted her humming. 'Just fall into

it.' Her hands had fallen into a kind of intense yet soothing pressure on my buttocks, straying occasionally to the top of my thighs, insinuating fingers to the inside. And she started humming again.

'I can almost recognize that song,' I tried again.

'Maybe.' Then she went on humming and massaging. Her hands were almost teasing now, still seeming to concentrate on kneading my buttocks and the end of my backbone but letting her fingers gently nudge into the crack of my arse, slide inside my thighs. 'It's an old jazz song. Bill's favourite as a matter of fact. The band played it on our last night together. And I've collected a few different versions of it on records. I don't often play them now. Makes me feel a bit sad, though not when I sing it, if you can stand my croaky voice. It's quite a snappy tune.' Her hands were definitely smoothing along my arse-crack, her thumbs pressing so that it opened a little as her hands slid away, then down to the backs of my thighs.

'How d'you like this?' she asked.

'Very nice,' I mumbled into the pillow. That was an inadequate reply. Her hands were moving me into a very steamy feeling even though I was somehow floating. She had moved her legs so that they were now touching my own. I was feeling warm all over and my cock was making its presence felt in no uncertain terms. And yet somehow I thought this really was a proper therapeutic massage. It was as if Barbara didn't really do this massage to arouse; it was simply the way the massage worked, covering each part of the back of my body equally.

By now she had edged towards the foot of the divan, her hands starting at my buttocks. Slowly, but with careful pressure that relaxed into a soft smoothness, she moved them right down my legs, thighs, calves, ankles, toes. 'Relax,' she whispered. 'Feel all that tension flow out of your feet.'

She continued to work on my legs, then said, 'Blues My Naughty Sweetie Gave To Me.'

'What?'

'That's the name of the song.'

'Right. I thought I recognized it.'

With what seemed like a final squeeze of my ankles and toes, her hands lifted away. I thought this was probably the end. I didn't know whether she would expect me to roll over. I didn't know what she would make of seeing my cock in its full fat state. Then, maybe, it happened to all the people she massaged and it didn't mean anything to her. Or maybe she would only massage my back.

'Hot work, this,' she murmured. 'You're very knotted up, but we're getting there.' With that, her hands returned to my toes and ankles and slowly began to move up my calves, behind my knees, onto my thighs, shifting her weight as she moved a little up the divan on her knees. As she moved up, I felt just a touch of warmth, a slight brushing sensation against my legs. At first I couldn't figure out what it was – her hands were massaging the tops of my thighs pliantly, yet something small and flexible was on my calves, swaying in rhythm with her hands. She was pushing down with her hands and hovering over me closely so I thought it must be her body touching me. But it didn't feel as if it was the cotton of her coat. Then I remembered she had stopped for a moment to complain it was hot work. Had she taken her coat off? I couldn't turn my head round to see but I was almost certain she was brushing her nipples against me.

And still I didn't know quite what to do. Again maybe part of the massage was this nudity. After all, I was naked so maybe I was to make nothing of this though my shaft was making a lot of it! She was still pressing and pushing with her hands and I felt that extra touch pressing on my legs.

My thoughts were beginning to race along with my cock. I wondered if she had not only taken her jacket off but also her skirt. Was she in fact as naked as I was?

Barbara obviously felt me squirming a little as I tried to turn my head to check on her so she stopped humming and said, 'Relax. Don't worry about a thing. Let it just float along.' And I was relaxed into that floating feeling, though I was very firmly anchored by my full stand. It seemed to grow even thicker as her fingers began to slide further inside my thighs. It was almost as if her fingers were searching to find what was pressed hotly and stiffly into the divan. Then she pulled them back, delved right inside till a finger or two briefly flicked my scrotum, sliding up my arse-crack, then widening out along my buttocks, slowly down, then round to search out the space between my body and the divan again.

But still she was not making it obvious just what her interest was. It could still be construed as a genuine massage though more and more I was imagining that this was developing into something else. Still I was unsure enough that I didn't want to take any initiative. I played a waiting game and Barbara seemed content with that.

Her fingers kept returning to those sensual parts, the pace quickening somewhat – or was it that she was returning to those parts more quickly and lingering there a little longer? And that made it all the more tantalising for me. Her humming had continued but now it was broken into by some of the words. More often than not, she seemed to sing just 'Naughty sweetie' and I began to see a pattern – as she sang 'Naughty sweetie' each time her fingers returned more maddeningly to flick quickly at my scrotum, even sliding under more.

Then she stopped. Her hands no longer touched me and the humming had stopped. I half expected her to hand me my robe while she put her jacket back on so we'd both be where we were at the beginning, But she said, 'Roll over. Time to do the front now.'

I was in a dilemma. Her hands had been suggestive but not enough to warrant my reading too much into those touches. When I rolled over, my hard-on would be straining up at her – maybe that was what she had intended or maybe it was only to be expected from the massage, nothing more. Maybe she'd be offended that I had presumed she knew what she was doing. As she had told me, she was a grown woman and her confession indicated that she had been through a lot of sexual experiences. She was certainly not an innocent; nor was I now after my life in London.

And I certainly wanted to roll over because that would give me a chance to see if she was fully naked. If not, I'd be able to see her breasts. But I still couldn't get rid of the idea that this was a Swedish massage. There was enough in the air in those days about the Swedes and how they took nakedness in their stride without it amounting to very much. So I remained dubious.

'Come on, Nick. Roll over. If you liked the back massage, the front will feel even better.' And she began humming again, the words 'naughty sweetie' breaking into the humming.

She had placed the towel next to me on the divan so as I rolled over, I put the towel across my middle though not very successfully – it was scrunched up and my cock poked up under it. But Barbara settled things for me. She shook her head and laughed, looking directly down on me, her full and firm breasts close to me. She was quite naked.

'I can see the massage has worked for you.'

'Well, maybe, though you don't seem to have managed to get the tension and stiffness entirely out of me.'

'I'm sure I'll be able to do that,' she said, whisking the towel away. 'My! What a naughty sweetie!'

'You're the naughty sweetie,' I told her.

'Two naughty sweeties together. That'll make even a better song. I wondered whether you were a naughty sweetie this afternoon. You seemed a bit slow on the uptake, especially coming out of Gerry's stable of young stallions. I was surprised. You didn't try anything – even when you could have.'

So she had been giving me hints that afternoon – except that I'd disregarded them. Still, she was giving me more than hints now.

She clambered onto the divan to straddle me again. She leaned down over me and her hands started on my shoulders. 'We're still doing the massage,' she whispered down to me, Her hands travelled down my arms, then up to my shoulders again. In the process the outer side of her little fingers tantalisingly brushed against the tip of my cock. She pressed down onto my shoulders and her breasts came down so close to my face that I couldn't resist licking first one nipple, then the other.

'Naughty, naughty,' she cooed as she wriggled herself further down. Her stomach slid tauntingly across my cock. 'Naughty, naughty,' I said in return.

Her face above me had that provocative smile on it as she continued to squiggle slowly around the end of my straining erection. I was now devoting more effort to licking and sucking round Barbara's breasts. The humming of her song became more erratic as she broke it up with little sighs and moans and sung 'naughty sweeties'.

She was enjoying moving herself across my cock, sliding down so she could press my hardness onto her pubic mound. I mumbled from between her breasts, 'Am I allowed to return the massage?' for I wanted to bring my hands up to her breasts which were now thoroughly slippery from my mouth. She was still pressing on my shoulders so I couldn't raise my hands to stroke her. Barbara seemed almost oblivious. I wasn't sure she had heard me, as she had become dreamily entranced with my kissing and sucking and nibbling at her nipples. This, in turn, was making me feel as if I wanted more than her teasing my cock with her body. I wanted to probe inside her so I was trying to thrust my prick further against her. I managed to slide it between her thighs and I felt a smooth and mossy wetness against its length.

As she felt me prodding there, Barbara's singing became almost tuneless, a monotonous throaty drone. I repeated my request to massage her as my mouth travelled across her deep cleavage.

'Only especially naughty sweeties do that,' she murmured teasingly. I redoubled my thrusting at her thighs, wishing I could grasp her buttocks to drive her down on me. This brought a more strangled note to her droning and I tried to dribble more saliva onto her breasts to make them even more slippery.

'Naughty, naughty, naughty,' she breathed out in time with my thrusts.

'Especially naughty?' I asked.

'Yes, oh, yes,' and she released her hands from my shoulders so I could place my hands gently on her moist breasts, feeling the hard nipples, the beautifully firm weight of each. Barbara pushed the lower half of her body down on top of me, full length against me, her legs closed around my cock. I was still not inside her but she was very creamy so my cock slid easily there with each thrust.

'I know a massage that will bring you to your knees.' She pressed her legs even more tightly together, pushing down onto me so that her breasts were squashed against my chest. Then she slowly began to slide down the whole length of my body, her breasts at my cock, her hands squeezing them so that my length sank between them before she held each nipple at my cock-head. Then further down she went, and very slowly her tongue licked down the whole length, onto my balls, below my balls, down along my inner thighs till she dribbled a little along my toes before standing at the foot of the bed.

'Turn over,' she said. I was disappointed – I thought we were heading towards more enticing massages, not those little hints on my back. But I rolled over just the same. 'Now slide down. Come on, further. Right to the end. That's it, knees just at the edge. Now up on your knees. Yes, That's right. Kneel.'

I felt a little foolish, perched precariously on my knees right at the end of the divan, my balls hanging exposed, my cock stiffly stretching out. Barbara's hands came to my buttocks to steady me, then she slid them across to the inside of my thighs, brushing at my balls as her fingers reached through to grab my prick.

I must have flinched when I first felt her hands gripping my cock quite harshly so she pulled one hand back, placing it back on my buttock to steady me again. 'It's alright,' she said. 'Just be careful. Try to relax.'

'How can I relax when you're doing this to me?'

That one hand still had a firm grip on my cock, stroking it evenly, pulling on it as if she wanted to make it longer. It was a unique sensation because as my prick thickened a little, straining out and up, Barbara was pulling it down and back as if she was trying to make it point straight down at the divan. It was slightly painful because she was so insistently hard and firm and strong, forcing my cock down in that way. Yet it was an intense pleasure and that cancelled out the slight pain. It was as if her stroking was inducing a kind of ache right inside the length of my cock and also smoothing the ache away.

'There, there!' she murmured. 'Don't you like being brought to your knees this way?' And indeed I found it both excruciating and exhilarating. The pressure she exerted downwards on my cock had the effect of making me feel drawn out very long, my prick like a lithe, stiff snake ready to strike. Barbara was taming it and coaxing it to grow longer and stiffer. Her other hand was busy on my balls. Somehow she was softly fondling them, mixing in a tight squeeze every now and again, mostly when her other hand was increasing its push downward on my cock.

'This is very naughty of you,' I managed to gasp out.

'Wait. You haven't begun to see how naughty I can be.' And then she exerted hard pressure so that I literally thought she might break my prick right off. I let out a half-sob, half-sigh.

'Don't worry. See, you like it.' Her finger had found a sticky drop of jism leaking out of the slit. As she pulled down, her finger took that stickiness and let it trail around that tender skin rolled back from my cock-head.

It felt marvellous, blotting out the ache in my prick. I shuddered and that signalled Barbara to take me further into this paradoxical world of sensual ache and delight.

Her hand floated lingeringly away from my balls, tickling deliciously along the crack of my arse till one finger began to trace slow circles round the rim of my hole, her other fingers lightly splayed across my buttocks. Her hand on my cock was still firm, holding it down, though her hands were now slippery with come which was slowly dropping out of my cock, little warm drops that oiled the cock in her hand.

Then the finger circling my arse-hole was edging a little inside. I must have clenched a little for Barbara pushed herself against me to whisper soothingly in my ear: 'It's going to be alright. I'm just relaxing you. Loosening you.' And her finger became relentless in its tantalising circles round and round, pressing in a little, then out to circle again. I could feel a slight sharpness from her nail so the sensation was the same as the one surrounding my prick – a little jolt of achiness, not really painful, that was massaged away and that made the stroking seem all the more delectable.

'There! Didn't I tell you you'd like it?' she whispered very low as her finger was slowly probing inside. It was exquisite. With a kind of soft pinch I felt her nail, my arse tight against her finger moving in till I felt as if the end of her finger was somehow pressing at the root of my cock from the inside. I expected her finger to poke right up inside my cock to make it thicker and stronger and stiffer as her other hand still insistently pulled it downwards further, stroking and teasing and tickling.

I had never been stroked and probed in this way before. Teresa had first made me aware of the area between the underpart of my scrotum and my arse-crack, a secret place she loved to finger and nudge but now Barbara was extending that pleasure, her finger pushing my cock out, heavy and rigid and long, as if it was completely massaged inside and out by her hands.

'You are an especially naughty sweetie,' she almost hummed, 'so you deserve an especially naughty treat.' With a final yank and probe, she pulled away from me so that I nearly fell off the divan. I looked round and saw her leaving the room so I scrambled after her. She waited at the door and as I approached, she turned her back and spread her buttocks so that my prick slid easily between her legs. Again she gripped me, not so tightly this time. My arms encircled her so my hands grasped her still wet breasts and I stroked and squeezed. We did a slow march glued together that way out of the room, along the hallway and into her bedroom, a deliciously sensual march, precise steps together.

She quickly threw the bedcovers back, then turning back to me, she enveloped my cock in both hands. Slowly stroking and pulling me to the bed, she said, 'He's such a lovely, naughty sweetie, he deserves another special massage.' She shoved me down on my back.

Moving her hands all over my body, she deliberately avoided touching my cock. She was expert in approaching it closely, making me feel each time that her hands would grasp me. But still the teasing continued. She must have noticed how my cock was twitching frantically, waiting for that moment.

When it came, it was the most delicate touch: fluttering fingers, little flicks skimming along the surface of my full length, gentle pressings, almost as if she was not touching, a smooth rolling-back till it seemed my cock-head was swollen enormously. Her fingers played an almost imperceptible rhythm around it, then moved down to flicker at my balls.

'He's such a lovely sweetie,' she said huskily. 'I bet he tastes delicious. And I'm going to taste him.' But her fingers continued their tiptoeing dance as I waited for her mouth to descend on me. Again I had to wait but it was an agony of sweetness. Her hands were so attentive to my prick but eventually, as the soft pads of her fingertips trickled around the head and a hard, thin fingernail probed delicately at my slit, I felt the tip of her tongue lick at the slit held open by that nail. Her fingers slid in slow motion down the length followed by her mouth. The inside of her lips were softly wet and it was all I could do to lie still. I wanted to push myself deep inside her mouth, feel my cock filling her mouth, the end nestling right at the back of her throat.

My cock-head pushed past her teeth, lying along her tongue, her lips now at the rim of skin, exerting gentle pressure to roll the skin back further. My cock was bathed in warm liquid openness. I could have sworn her mouth was full of a warm thin syrup, this juice that was bathing the sharpness away from her teeth as her mouth went further and further down.

For a few moments she was still, letting my cock rest in that juiciness. Then she repeated that slow journey up the length, sucking up the skin, feeling the slippery inner lips trail over the head till her tongue searched out my slit again. Once more the whole process started again, down the length, then a rest, then up again.

I gave myself up to this wonderful sucking, her mouth on my cock, her hands busy at the root, following her mouth up and down, fingers searching to the back of my scrotum, balls fondled in the palm of her hand. I would have liked to slide my fingers inside her but she was so intently engaged on this mouth-massage I didn't want to disturb her. I was certain that as she seemed so thoroughly immersed, her quim must have become a slippery ooze of delight. Soon she would want me to return the favour.

Eventually her mouth lingeringly left my cock. It was glistening wet Her vivid dark eyes sparkled, inviting me to stare at her. 'He's such a sweetie.' Then in a little girl's voice she added, 'A tasty lollipop.' She gave a childish giggle and began to sing "On The Good Ship Lollipop" but Shirley Temple never gave it such a voluptuously lecherous interpretation.

As she was singing she knelt on the bed, putting one knee on one side of my chest. She plumped some pillows under my head so I could gaze directly into the neatly curled hair of her pubic mound. Then she stopped singing and muttered, 'Some naughty boy might try to dip his fingers into the sugar bowl.'

Who was I to resist such an invitation? She was half-sitting, half-crouching on my lower chest. One of her hands was on her pubic hair, pulling upwards to give me easier access. Her other hand, as she leaned back a little, was doing its gently provocative touches and squeezes on my stand which was now as stiff and hard as it possibly could be.

Her attitude suggested she wanted me to get an eyeful first. The lips were pink and shiny and I could almost see the liquid slowly oozing around, the bud of her clitoris looking erect and moist. 'Sticky honeypot,' she whispered. 'Getting ready for your sugarcane,' and she gave my cock a hard squeeze, tempering it immediately with a teasing, glancing dance of fingertips.

I raised a hand and covered her quim with it on the outside. Barbara shuddered (that was Daisy's magic first-time touch). Then I drew my hand back and began a fingertip glide along one of her lips, down, round, up the other lip, slowly across her clit, then down the lip again, round and round, at a leisurely pace but insistent, each time lingering a little more on her clit, pressing, rolling it, tweaking it between two fingers, then onto the lips again, my finger pushing in, just at the edges, then slowly deeper but not too far, making her wait for me to probe right inside. Her juice was flowing freely and I could hear that slight suck-and-slap sound my fingers were making as they flitted around and just inside her quim.

Her hand on my cock was beginning to fit a rhythm to the movement of my hand on her. Her breathing was a mix of little yelps and sighs. An occasional moan broke out, especially when I let a finger sink a little deeper. I was relentlessly taking my time, my two hands now busy on her, one circling the lips and clit, the other sliding further in. I slid another finger inside her, the two of them perhaps reminding her what a thick prick would feel like there. That seemed to reach her for the juices became a sweet stream.

She was moving her pelvis on my fingers and it came to me that I should take my cue from the way she had given me her special massage. I let my two fingers stay inside her while my other arm looped round, smoothing across her arse, seeking her crack. Barbara sensed what I was doing for she reached behind her with both hands and again began the special mixture of roughness and tenderness on my cock and balls.

I found the rim of her arse-hole. 'Relax, sweetie,' I mimicked what she had told me as I let my finger slide inside. I had come to the idea of pushing deep into her, two fingers now revolving back and forth inside the rich cream of her quim, the slippery inside getting more slippery, more creamy. My other finger moved inside her at the back as if it was trying to reach through and touch my other two fingers working deeply from the front. But I moved both fingers, front and back, and Barbara relished the feel of them moving inside her. Her fingers coaxed more length out of me, more come spewed out, not in full orgasmic spilling but now not just drops, a steady leak that I felt would never stop flowing and I would still have enough to come to climax as well. That gluey cream from me was bathing her hands and she was slopping it all over my cock.

It was remarkable how long we were able to last with this mutual massage, we were both on the verge of letting go. But Barbara let me know it was time to press on even further. In some kind of acrobatic move she changed her position. Her legs switched, her quim juicily poised over my mouth as her mouth again came down on my cock.

That mutual licking and sucking and probing was exquisite. I lay back to let her mouth swallow my thickness. Her pelvis sank down so that my tongue could flutter on her clit, my hands pulling her slit wider so my open mouth could suck at her lips. We were both slavering, making sucking noises as we nibbled and licked and lingered wetly on each other.

It was obvious to both of us that we couldn't last much longer. She was shivering and gasping, her pelvic motion becoming quicker, her mouth a steady dynamo pumping up and down my cock so that it felt like a rod filled with hotness ready to gush out. She must have felt the pulse throbbing towards its climax for she stopped, turned round to lie full length on her side. My fingers were still working on her and her hands were rubbing the moistness from her mouth. I was reminded of that moment when, for the first time, I would slide my cock into the juicy warmth of a quim. And that's what I was ready for now.

Then, and this came as a complete surprise to me, she gave me a tender, deep-tongued kiss. I was surprised, even though I was so taken in by the rhythms of our strokings, because this was the first time we had kissed. It occurred to me that this was completely natural, more erotically sensual perhaps than the touchings we were indulging in. Normally the kissing comes first, that slow merging of lips, both mouths opening like flowers, tongues darting in. This is what happened with our kisses now, more sensual because we were tasting each other more deeply. The warm juices of quim and cock – some spunky drops had been drawn out of me by Barbara's mouth – were on our lips, tongues, in our mouths mixed with our salivas and we were savouring them. That in turn was making me concentrate even more on the silky warmth of Barbara's quim as I imagined Barbara was remembering the hot muscular throb of my fat cock.

Our voices, as we kissed, were growling in our throats. It was now certain that in that high state of excitement, we had to reach up to the higher plateau to release ourselves. I rolled her over. She held my cock delicately in her fingers and pulled it to the opening of her quim, circling it round the lips, letting it push at her clit, as my tongue and fingers had done. I began to feel her body shudder, her legs kicking up high, closing together so that my cock slid onto a tight, oozy wetness. I pushed in and I could feel jism beginning to rise.

I wanted to burst out yet at the same time hold back that flood of jism at its peak. I sensed that Barbara wanted to let herself go yet also wanted to hover right on the verge, letting the surge reach a fullness, a gigantic wave at the moment when it is curling over before it breaks into a long, flowing dash of white.

And as I thought of that, I thought of my come edging to the top of my cock, as if it was the foam spreading along the crest of that enormous wave. Barbara and I had been through such a long, involving series of touches, of strokes that brought us to such trembling awareness of each other that I knew that only a few pounding thrusts deep into her would release a great splashing shower of spunk inside her and that, in turn, would break her apart, the hot gushes spilling in her driving her over the edge.

So I thrust and thrust till it was automatic, unstoppable. I was taken over by that rhythmic insistence and Barbara squirmed and thrashed, her legs drumming on my shoulders as she tried to pull me deeper and deeper inside her, as much hard fatness as she could take, to feel filled up tight. And yet there was room still for the hot stream to erupt and bathe us both in a velvet cream of heat as I broke open, flooding, Barbara moaning in a high, piercing voice that slid down a whole scale.

The after-play with her was deliciously gentle. She was affectionately teasing with me, making jokes but always showing how much she had enjoyed our encounter. And I even told her I thanked Bill with all my heart for introducing her so magnificently into this stunning world of sexual pleasure she had obviously cultivated. I covered her body with small, quick kisses, tasting her salty sweat, licking it, then transferring it to her mouth. That simple action reminded me how we had exchanged other juices so I began to wonder if we should start all over again.

But Barbara rolled away from me. 'Naughty, naughty,' she said, laughing briefly. 'It's a lovely sweetie,' she went on, 'but let's save it as a sweet after dinner.' She moved out of the bedroom. 'Let me put the oysters in the oven. Just think. Oysters and salmon. That should perk you up no end. And we'll be more than ready for a sweet after that.' She came back to the bed, licked her fingers, let my semi-erect cock squirm in their wetness, still with a thin skin of jism on it. Barbara licked her fingers again. 'Yum, yum. I'm looking forward to my just dessert.'

4. Blues With Barbara

That dinner date with Barbara was a turning point. It reconciled me to my new life, reminding me that what I had left in London – a life I had been regretful about leaving – could be duplicated. Barbara's involvement with Gerry also convinced me that I hadn't lost touch with the London connection. I knew that Barbara was similar to women I had known there and, through her, I thought I might meet others. After all, she had been talking about my meeting Lorna, another woman who did some work for Gerry.

The evening developed into a wholly delectable event. After she had left me in the bedroom, she went downstairs to cook. When I went into the kitchen, the sight of her there told me how fortunate I had been to meet her.

She was standing at the stove; she had put her small apron on, though her back was to me, I could see the bow she had tied at her waist. But that back view was sensational. She was wearing black stockings, garter belt and high heels. She had also put on a pair of filmy black panties that clung to her buttocks but flared with lace at her thighs. She still had on her jazzy blouse which was hanging loosely from her shoulders.

She turned to me when she heard me. She had not fastened her blouse so she was showing her cleavage and the roundness of her full breasts. She untied her apron; the panties were simply a black veil so I could see the neat triangle of her pubic hair. I went to her, kissed her, my hand snaking inside her blouse to fondle her breasts. Her hand reached down to find the gap in my robe and gave me a very friendly fondle.

Our dinner developed in the same way. We ate the oysters and the salmon but we often put down our knives and forks to indulge in petting, holding each other, kissing, licking, fondling until we were ready to partake of our 'dessert' upstairs.

Late in the evening Barbara lit the fire and snuggled with me in front of it. She sat between my legs, her hair silky against my cock, my hands inside her blouse. She got into her confessional mood again.

'You know, on the way to pick you up yesterday, I was already thinking in sort of randy terms about you.'

'I'm flattered but I don't understand why.'

'It's Gerry, I suppose. I knew what kind of life you must have been leading and it reminded me of when I first knew Gerry and how it was with Bill, so I was getting myself in a very sexual frame of mind. And then tonight – well, I didn't quite know what I was going to do but I suppose I'd decided to try something...'

'I'm glad you did. I didn't realise just what jackpot I was hitting when I said your blouse looked jazzy.'

'That was another thing.' She turned her head round, her hair swishing over my cock. She gave my half-erect stand a wet kiss right at the tip which fluttered me to being more than half-erect. 'And so I was ready for almost anything this evening. I've not been living the life of a nun but I have slowed down... till tonight. You certainly picked up the pace for me. You were just the right kind of naughty sweetie!'

'It's nice to think that, because I like jazz, and it worked in this terrific way with you. Now I know you like it as well, perhaps you can show me around the clubs here ... all kinds of things might come of it!'

'We can do it right now.'

I looked at my watch. 'It's one o'clock in the morning and you've done your best to wear me out.'

She gave me her lascivious look. 'A big strong lad like you ... Surely you're not going to stay like a wet lettuce leaf, are you?'

'Look here.' I pointed down to show her that my prick was beginning to look more like a celery stalk than a lettuce leaf. She patted my cock gently, leaving her fingers on it for a few seconds.

'That's what I like to see.' She got up from her sitting position and strolled over to a gramophone and soon was playing a record, soft, insinuating. 'Listen to these words here.' A sultry voice was singing about wanting a little boy – it was very sexy so it was obvious she wanted anything but a *little* boy. Barbara was adding her own seductive voice to the music.

She kept singing along till the record finished. She had come back to sit in front of me, facing me, her hands again doing a smooth massage of my cock and balls.

'Bill used to sing that to me,' she said huskily.

Her hands were stroking me up to a fierce, hot, hard stand. Then she stood up again, holding her arms out to me. 'Dance?' I held her and we waltzed over to the gramophone and she put more music on. We danced very close, my cock rammed against her filmy panties, one of her hands low on my buttocks holding me in place tightly. As we danced she muttered in my ear. 'Bill and I used to play a little game with tunes. We'd try to remember the names of tunes with the word "dance" in them. And change them – used the word "fuck" every time the word "dance" was used. "Dance, dance, dance, little lady" became "Fuck, fuck, fuck, little lady". That was one of my favourites, and so was "Let's Face The Music and Fuck".'

'How about "Dancing on the Ceiling"?'

'Fucking on the ceiling! It'd be difficult.'

'And "Mad About Dancing".'

'Mad about fucking. I don't know that song.'

'Neither do I. I made it up. Because that's how I feel with you. Mad about fucking.'

She reached down and grabbed my cock and rubbed it against her hard. 'You're the naughtiest sweetie I know!'

'And you're the fuckiest sweetie,' I told her softly and worked my prick inside her panties and we stayed like that, dancing, a kind of fucking, till the music stopped.

'Damn!' she said. She walked over to the gramophone and put on another record, came back to me, held me, carefully tucking my cock inside her panties again. I longed for the day someone invents a record that plays longer than three minutes. 'Think what might happen if the music went on for twenty minutes,' I said. 'It wouldn't just be lyrics – and the dancing would turn into fucking.'

But we didn't need the music. Soon we were walking upstairs, me naked, Barbara sloughing her blouse, me pulling her panties down as she climbed the stairs ahead of me, shaking the panties from her ankles, turning to lead me into the bedroom.

It was only at 4:30 a.m. that I signed the lease for my new place and Barbara demanded that I take her to bed one more time to seal the deal.

That was the beginning of my seeing Barbara on a

regular basis during the whole of my time at the university, usually once a week, sometimes more than that, sometimes stretching out to ten-day intervals. She was seeing two or three other men and I got to know a few other women. During the time I knew her, I sent her students looking for a place to live and she was always grateful for the business and showed it in the most delectable ways.

The other women I met in my first few weeks were all attractive but none of them had indulged in the free-and-easy lifestyle that I had grown accustomed to. Of course I was always pleased to see Barbara. Most of the students I met were straight out of grammar school, eighteen or nineteen, fresh-faced, clean-living, but with little experience beyond some fumbling in the back seats of cinemas.

Barbara was always ready with new twists so I never knew quite what to expect. Once I remember how she undid my fly buttons in the cinema and stroked me all through the film, keeping me on a nervous edge, manipulating me but not to the point of making me shoot off into her hands. As the film came to an end, she seemed to be having difficulty stuffing my cock inside my trousers. Her hand was still holding it when the lights came up.

'Barbara!'

'Cover it with your mac,' she whispered, laughing, as she managed to drape her own raincoat there as well as she linked me, but still keeping her other hand holding my cock.

'What's the matter?'

'I can't tell,' she spluttered out – she was still laughing. 'I think the chain of my bracelet is caught on one of your buttons.'

'Get it off!'

'I'm trying.'

It didn't feel as if she was trying – it felt as if she was still enjoying stroking my cock under the raincoats. We were moving along the seats to the aisle, her hand still busy. Soon we were in the aisle, jammed in a crush of people. As we slowly walked up the aisle she very deliberately wanked me off, the jism splattering into the raincoats.

By the time we got into the foyer, we were disentangled. She took her raincoat away and flapped it out. There was a big dark wet patch on the back. She held it up and said loudly, 'Just look at that, Nick. You must have spilled your ice cream on it.' Several people nearby sniggered. 'Still,' Barbara went on, 'you enjoy it so much, I don't mind, though I wish you had given me a lick.'

I really liked seeing Barbara. She was fun and she was enormously sexy. I suspect Bill had unleashed in her a lot of pent-up sexual energy and she was still making the most of it – I happened to be in the right place at the right time.

After that first time with Barbara I got back to my place about five-thirty in the morning. I soon fell into a deep sleep, wakened by a hammering on my door. I shambled out of bed, struggling into my dressing gown, yawning as I opened the door. It was Daisy. She looked at me and laughed. 'It must have been a very rough night,' she said.

'Well, if it isn't fresh-as-a-Daisy,' I mumbled. And she did look fresh in a light cotton dress, little make-up, hair a little frizzy but tumbled provocatively around her face from which her eyes twinkled. I invited her in but she declined. 'One of my regulars is in town. Coming round this afternoon.'

She dug into a small pocket at the front of her dress and

pulled out a piece of paper which she gave to me. 'From someone called Lorna. She said you'd know who it was. She's inviting you over for tea tomorrow afternoon. La-di-da! I suppose Barbara gave her my phone number so I could pass the message on. Sounded as if she's really interested in seeing you.' She laughed and winked. 'First time I've heard it called Saturday afternoon tea.'

I looked at the scrawl on the paper. 'Is this her address?' Daisy nodded. 'And this phone number? Is it hers? Do I have to phone her?'

'No, silly. She's expecting you around four. And that's my phone number so you can keep in touch with me when you move. You don't know when you'll need my number.' She smiled. 'Though from the looks of you it looks as if someone's got your number! Kept you busy all night, did she? I heard you come in. Dirty stop-out! You've been a very naughty boy!'

I couldn't help laughing when she said this but I didn't tell her I'd been Barbara's naughty sweetie. Still, Daisy obviously knew something had been happening. 'So you have been naughty all night!'

I waved the paper at Daisy. 'Thanks for this.' I made to close the door but Daisy stopped it with her foot. 'Don't lose my number,' she said. 'You never know when you'll have some spare cash. And in any case it's only just over two and half years to go.'

'Two and half years to what?'

'Don't you remember? My birthday. I invited you ... but if you go on like this maybe you'll lose your memory altogether.'

She seemed serious about her birthday but I somehow didn't think I would really be a part of her birthday celebration. It was a long way away but I said, 'Thanks. And of course I'll remember.'

'And phone me to let me know how you're getting on. I'd like to hear from you.' She smiled. 'Might get together some time. Maybe you'll need a little more instruction from Daisy's mine of information!'

I promised I would keep in touch and in fact I did, every now and again over the next two years or so. I met her sometimes for lunch but we never got into the kind of situation we got into on my first night in town. And I did get in touch with Lorna that Saturday afternoon.

I didn't quite know what to expect when I rang the doorbell at Lorna's. She lived on the rambling ground floor of a big Victorian house in solid brick, with large windows arched at the top with stained glass designs. It was on a semi-circular drive with other Victorian houses, each with an immaculate lawn and trim bushes along the front. This was the Paradise Lost complex.

I had no idea what kind of a woman Lorna would be. She had apparently known Gerry and she now knew Barbara so my first thought was that she might be used to living in a free-and-easy style. On the other hand, she might be a very independent woman. She had stood up to Barbara about going to live at Paradise Lost, a place Barbara was uneasy about. In a way, I expected to meet a self-assured, self-confident woman. Beyond that I couldn't guess.

Nothing could have prepared me for the woman who opened the door to me. She was the most stunningly beautiful woman I had ever met, so beautiful she was intimidating. There was no way I felt that I could ever be close to her – her beauty was so ravishing it made me feel an absolute dolt.

The first thing that struck me was her face, skin like cool alabaster, almost translucent, with make-up applied meticulously to give the appropriate touches of colour to emphasize the high cheekbones. Her eyes were big and lustrously brown. Her hair, dark brown, was quite short but shaped so that it fell forward with an almost peek-a-boo look.

'You must be Nick,' she purred in a voice as coolly attractive as her looks. Then her smile – even, gleaming teeth framed by lips shaped by a bright lipstick. 'Come in.'

She walked ahead of me so I got a chance to admire her figure – very slim and elegant. When she turned to show me to a chair to sit in, I could see her breasts were small but perfectly rounded under her green silk shirt. She sat herself down opposite me and her full white skirt fell in a swoop and swirl across her legs, her ankles finely boned, shown off to advantage in her shoes, not quite high heels but obviously chosen to complement her skirt and blouse in the same colours.

So far I had said nothing – I was literally dumbfounded. Her fragility was exquisite, wonderfully compelling. In a sense she was one of those women, frail and so ravishing, whose appearance was a protection. Most men in her presence would find her incredibly erotic, would want to fulfill all kinds of sexual fantasies. They would leap into their heads at the mere sight of her. But she was so immaculate that men might be scared off, afraid to approach her, as if such a delicate being could never have anything in the least like sexual desires. She was not remote, she simply created an aura around herself. It kept her from being damaged, as if she would never lose hold of her composure. Of course a thought flitted through my head – what would she be like if you once undid that elegant composure: would an exceptional passion break out of her, as superb as her appearance?

But she seemed so calm and self-possessed I almost felt guilty for having sexual thoughts about her.

Even though I felt so overwhelmed, we got on very well together. She immediately put me at my ease when she started to talk about our mutual connections. It turned out that she had never actually met Gerry. Her brother had worked for him. 'I wonder if you ever met him.'

'I rarely met any other men who worked for Gerry. He didn't want us to fraternise in case we found out too much about his business.'

'No, I suppose not. Ken, my brother, never told me much about what he did but he did indicate a few things.' Here she smiled, a devastatingly innocent smile that then seemed to take on a knowing irony as she continued, 'The men were always welcome to . . . fraternise with the women who worked for Gerry.'

'So how did you come to work for Gerry?' I asked her.

'Ken mentioned he had a sister living here and as he usually had some shipments coming up the Ship Canal. He thought I'd be the person to sign for them and clear them through.'

That was a very shrewd move on Gerry's part. Lorna, because of her almost ethereal looks would never raise the least suspicion in any officials she had to deal with. I bet Ken had shown Gerry a photograph of his sister and that would have been enough for Gerry to decide to make use of Lorna.

'I sometimes deliver a few packages as well. Nothing very spectacular though Gerry seems to think so for he pays me very well. Sometimes he sends me the most marvellous presents.'

I wondered if those presents were lingerie. I tried to imagine what she was wearing under her skirt and blouse and how she would behave when she had got rid of her outer clothes. She broke into my thoughts by saying, 'Tea?'

Her tea service was as elegant as she was, fragile bone china, delicately rimmed with gold. Her long slim fingers handled the cups and saucers with a finicky grace. As we sat and sipped tea, I was terribly afraid I would look clumsy. I became even more nervous, though Lorna made every effort to make me feel comfortable.

Her portion of the house was filled with exquisite pieces – tables with inlay on fine spindly legs, chairs with intricately tapestried upholstery, lamps with charmingly frail shades, curtains with lace swathed in velvet folds.

'Barbara told me you wanted some information about this place.'

'Yes. It seems such a good deal, I can't understand how it can work.'

'That's what I thought and Barbara is still sceptical about it – in fact, she is really not quite sane about it and I admit that the man who runs it, Milton, is a very odd character. Even so, the place runs along nicely. And of course it's not really free. You have to make a hefty deposit – three hundred pounds – when you move in and you never get that back. But that's the only money you have to pay except a nominal fee when your renewal comes up. That's once a year.'

'But how do you get away with paying no rent?'

'Well, the way Milton explains it, it's relatively simple. At first it sounds unbelievable. When you sign up he makes it all clear and I must say I was dubious because he looks so ... sinister. I didn't understand all the ins and outs but what he does apparently is invest the deposit money – one central fund for all of us. We're all stockholders. We have a meeting every three months – I'm told most people don't turn up, they just trust Milton to do the best for everyone. But we are given a statement about how much the fund has earned after expenses.'

'He never pays out anything that the investments make?'

'Heavens, no! Money's a dirty word around here.'

'But Barbara says all the property and possessions here are communal. If you leave you can't take any of your things with you once you've moved them in.'

'It's all spelled out in the contract you sign. I didn't read all the fine print but it didn't sound too ... radical to me.'

'But look at all this,' and I waved my arms around, indicating all the splendid furniture. 'Wouldn't you be sorry to lose all this?'

She gave me a winning smile. 'I'm sure there are ways I'll be able to get round the contract.' That smile would certainly help but Milton sounded too shifty a character to be taken in by it. Even her grace and charm would probably have no effect on him.

'Barbara mentioned there was also a barter system – I can't imagine you'd want to put any of your furniture up for barter. Just look at it – it's too ... tasteful.'

'Why, thank you. I don't think they make you join in the bartering.'

'I don't know. Maybe they'll exert some pressure.'

Lorna frowned – her frown gave a contemplative sternness to her face though it was still appealing to look at. Then she said very calmly, 'I think I'm capable of not giving in to pressure, of any kind.' Then she brightened. 'I don't expect any trouble like that. Things have been fine so far.'

We talked a little more. She told me about her interest in antiques and fine furniture, regretting that she couldn't buy more. 'A teacher's salary doesn't leave me much spare cash.' She asked me about my studies and I told her that I was looking forward to all the reading though there were certain aspects I was worried about. 'Oh, I can't see that anything you'll have to do will cause you much trouble. Barbara spoke very highly of you when she was here at lunch-time, even though she's only known you for a little while.'

I wondered just what Barbara had told her. Had they exchanged female confidences? I went on wondering what kind of secrets Lorna might have to reveal, especially as an ironically innocent smile appeared on her face again. 'After all, I know Gerry expects a lot from the young men who work for him, though of course my brother tells me the rewards are pretty good.' She was puzzling me a little. Was she leading me on? She had already indicated that she knew about the women Gerry kept on hand. 'In any case, what possible difficulties could there be in English studies?'

'Well, I've never had anything to with Anglo Saxon, and we have to do two years of that.'

'I'm sure you'll waltz through it.'

I could have gone on talking to her a lot longer but I tore myself away. She saw me to the door and said, 'I've enjoyed meeting you, Nick. Don't forget where I live.'

Then I surprised myself with my own audacity; at least it struck me afterwards as audacious. As she opened the door, she put her hand out to me. I took it and she let her slender fingers fold across mine with a small squeeze, leaving it there a little longer than was necessary. 'I'm glad you could come.'

'I was glad I could come as well.' Then after a very short pause I added, 'Perhaps you'd like to go to the theatre some evening.'

She looked directly at me, a smile hovering round her mouth. Her hand stayed in mine. 'I'd like that. Very much.' She let go my hand, went to a table, wrote something on a scrap of paper and handed it to me. 'I'm afraid I don't have a phone here. That's my school number. It's best to phone at lunch-time or straight after school's finished.'

'I'll phone you next week.'

She gave my hand another small squeeze. 'See you soon then.'

'I hope so,' I said as I stepped outside.

Things seemed to be falling into place: there was Barbara, Daisy was giving me some signs and now Lorna. The weather had recuperated after the rain earlier in the week and it was now a brisk, occasionally sunny day. I decided to walk back to my new place. After my meeting with Lorna, my steps were positively jaunty.

I started on my studies the following week and from then on I was kept busy. I found the reading, the lectures and the seminars exhilarating but, as I suspected, the classes in Anglo Saxon were difficult. Ron Burns was also bogged down. 'I wouldn't mind if she was worth looking at, but have you ever seen such a frumpy woman? I'd rather keep my eyes on the bloody Anglo-Saxon Chronicle than on her!'

He was referring to the lecturer in Anglo Saxon, Miss Hallam. I didn't think she was quite as bad as Ron made her out to be. She was certainly no raving beauty but then she did nothing to make herself in the slightest way attractive. It was really difficult to tell whether she could look reasonably appealing. She wore no make-up and kept her hair in a tight roll. She dressed in bulky sweaters and serviceable pleated skirts, flat shoes, even woollen stockings on occasions. She remained very much apart from us students, never saying anything remotely light or humorous.

Still, I felt like telling Ron that appearances could be deceptive. I could have told him about Barbara – granted, she always looked attractive even when she dressed as a businesswoman. But no one could guess just how splendidly outgoing she was, just what delight she took in being with a man. And that man, for the moment, was me. The more I saw her, the more I discovered about her sensuality.

She liked to play-act to tease me as I suspected she had done with the bracelet in the cinema. She obviously got a kick out of doing that, showing herself so amenable in public. I'm sure some of the people in the foyer of the cinema knew exactly what had been going on between us.

She liked using the darkness of the cinema to tease me, surrounded by people. Once I arranged to meet her outside a cinema and when she arrived I hardly recognized her. She looked dumpy with barge-like flat shoes, lisle stockings, a thick long skirt matted with ugly bobbles, a jacket far too big so that she seemed to have no shape and a high-necked blouse tightly buttoned. Her hair was scraped back against her skull and she had on a pair of glasses with fat lenses. Her face looked severe and she hardly spoke to me, a fierce scowl on her face.

But once we were sitting in one of the back seats, she took my hand and placed it under the voluminous folds of her skirt. She muttered in my ear, 'Looking at me, these people think I'm some miserable, drab woman, prim and proper. But I'm not. I'm as randy as hell.' And her fingers began to work on opening my flies, rooting inside my underpants as my hand slid up her thighs to discover she had nothing on underneath.

Then after the film at her place she unfastened her hair and let it lie wildly around her face, smeared heavy lipstick on, saying, 'I'm going to leave red marks all over your body.' She tore her clothes off and then started on me, pulling at my trousers, nibbling me, touching me, then making me sit to watch her model some of the lingerie Gerry had sent her recently. It was a teasingly raunchy performance which led to some acrobatic erotic acts, with her taking the lead.

If I had described this to Ron, it might have made him see Miss Hallam in a different light; he might have invented her into something more acceptable than the plain and sober personality she assumed in the classroom. I had been lucky in that most of the women I had known in London had been pretty open about their sexuality, always taking a delight in teasing me and leading me on. I had really never had to deal with a woman as sombre as Miss Hallam. Ron fidgeted through all the Anglo-Saxon classes, trying to concentrate but his eyes constantly shifted to the two or three pretty young women in the class. His behaviour disturbed me to some extent so both of us fell behind in our Anglo-Saxon studies.

Ron and I had become quite friendly and he used to drive me around to pubs and, once or twice, to some of the jazz clubs. He always imagined they would be filled with stunning women, eager to offer him delicious favours. He was usually disappointed, though I kept telling him that everyone was there to listen to the music. If he had shown any interest in it, then maybe the one or two women there on their own might have been more forward with him.

Eventually he stopped coming with me to those clubs. 'It's just noise to me, Nick,' he'd tell me. 'I won't find anyone there and you'll be better off on your own. These women will just see me as some morose idiot who doesn't get it and they'll lump you with me.'

Not that I was ever much interested in the women in the clubs because I was enjoying myself with Barbara. In fact, I'd found out about the clubs through her. She really liked jazz. It reminded her of Bill and I discovered that a visit to a jazz club often made her incredibly randy. And something of the atmosphere of those clubs reminded me of Gerry's private club in London and that's where I was involved in a lot of sexual action. I knew that if I took Barbara to a jazz club, I could rely on something exciting developing.

At first, in a club, she would sip at a gin-and-it, holding my hand, intent on watching the musicians play, her head nodding with the rhythm, not talking much, her fingers giving me lovely, enticing pats and strokes. She liked to lean against me, her thigh pressed against mine. Then after a time her fingers would move more suggestively, tickling at my palm, lacing her fingers with mine, nuzzling against me, a few little kisses speckled on my cheek, my ear.

Then she wanted to dance. If the group played a ballad or a slow blues (and jazz groups always got around to playing a slow blues sooner or later), she hauled me to my feet. She danced very close to me, sometimes whispering one of those song titles with the word 'dance' changed – 'Let's face the music and fuck,' she once said. We snuggled, Barbara moving sensually against me, smiling when she felt me stiffen, placing her cheek next to mine, her hand sliding down my back, eventually sneaking it down to my buttocks which she then pressed hard onto her, humming in my ear, urging me with little murmurs or a song title that particularly appealed to her.

After we'd danced for some time, without asking me, she'd take my hand and lead me out of the club. Driving home, if the traffic wasn't too heavy, one hand would lift from the steering wheel. She'd splay her fingers along my inner thigh, edging them upwards until her little finger eased between the buttons of my fly and I could feel it nudging to find the opening of my underpants. Sometimes she would place her hand on my crotch and squeeze my erection and mumble one of her titles, something like 'It Only Happens When I Fuck With You'. Once she said, 'I wish this damn car could drive itself so I could get both my hands on you. Just you wait.'

I often responded by running my hands under her coat, stroking her breasts or smoothing her skirt along her thighs. Usually, when we arrived at her place, both of us were excited and we would spend the next two or three hours together.

One particular evening our leisurely touches in the car must have made her feel even more sexy for as soon as she stepped inside her house, she went over to the gramophone to put on a record, a slow dreamy blues, and she began a languorous striptease. She strutted over to me, dropping her coat behind her, then leading me to an armchair, pushed me into it. 'Watch,' she whispered.

She unbuckled the belt of her dress, letting it slip through her fingers like a lazy snake before she dropped it. She reached round to her back, unzipped the dress and, with an enticing wiggle and shrug of her shoulders, she let it fall away, helping it with her hands at her waist, peeling it away and down her legs so she could step out of it. She stooped to pick it up and tossed it in my direction.

By now the record had finished so she simply repeated the same blues. She waltzed over to me in her bright red lingerie. She gently lifted, first at one shoulder, then at the other, the straps of the red slip, slid it round and down, smoothing her hands on the silkiness. She pulled it away from her breasts, slowly down, stopping to take it down her thighs and again stepping out of it, holding it up so that it fell in limp folds from her hands. She was smiling voluptuously and the sight of the lacy red slip which she had just skinned from her body was an incredibly lascivious vision. She came dancing to me and stroked the slip all round my head, leaving it draped around my shoulders, its gossamer softness still holding some of her warmth I felt on the back of my neck.

The music had stopped but this time she did not return to play it again. What happened next happened to the click and hiss of the needle at the centre of the record but all her movements seemed to fit exactly with the regular spinning.

She was now swaying in front of me in her usual garter belt and stockings. If anything, she was looking even more delectable than usual because of the red bra pushing up under her breasts, exposing her cleavage and outlining their smooth roundness. Together with the bra, she was wearing what we would eventually call a bikini. This was something I had never seen before – we were going through what was called an austerity period then so most things were dull and dour so to see something like that bikini, barely covering Barbara's Venus mound, was extravagantly sensual.

Barbara knew what the effect was on me and she took a delight in encouraging me even further. She stood closely and directly in front of me, hooking her fingers inside the waist of the bikini, moving them along the front, probing inside, the waistband pushed down a little so her pubic hair could be seen. Then she turned and thrust her buttocks towards me, bending down as her hands now came slowly up the backs of her thighs, back to the waist of her pants and she pulled the back part down.

With that, she sat on my lap, very deliberately placing herself so my cock, still in my trousers, was sticking up against her thighs.

She took one of my hands and let it fall on her crotch. She murmured, 'Take them off for me.' I needed no further invitation so I grasped the thin garment and gently pulled it away and down. She stretched her legs out to facilitate my hauling them down her legs and off. She took the red pants from my hands, stood up and leaned down to me, stroking the pants round my face. 'Taste them. I've creamed them.'

Barbara was not a one to talk much in that way – she liked the song-title game and occasionally she would let rip with something dirty and suggestive so when I heard her talking like that, I knew she must have been feeling especially hot. She pushed her fingers covered in the red silk into my mouth, making me suck it. Then she took it and fondled her mound of Venus, touching her clitoris briefly. By now my prick was chafing against my trousers so I made a move to undo my fly so I could unleash it.

But Barbara shook her head and said, 'No. Wait.' She walked seductively away to the gramophone and lifted the needle from the record. 'I'll help you with that. Unfasten your shirt and while I'm gone, rub my slip over your chest just to keep me in mind. Just wait till I call. Then, when I call, put this record on again. Just the right kind of moody music for me. You'll see.'

That was a long speech for Barbara at this stage of the game. She generally wanted action without much talking till she began to splutter with moans and yells. This time, I knew she had something special for me. I went along with her directions, unfastening my shirt buttons but not taking it off, slackened my belt, took off my shoes and socks and sat snuggling the back of my head against her slip, then drawing it lightly across my exposed chest. That felt delectably sexy.

Barbara had disappeared upstairs and after two or three minutes she called down to me, 'I'll need the music in about a minute.' I went over to the gramophone to be ready. I heard her coming down the stairs, then I saw her at the door.

She was dressed in a brilliantly blue robe which she then slowly opened, her arms stretched out wide, the material draping down like small wings. 'Music,' she said, and then in time to the dreamy blues, she moved sensuously to me but gesturing to send me back to my chair.

Under the robe was a nightgown, exquisitely lacy and low cut at her bosom, falling away in filmy folds that somehow suggested her figure under it. It seemed both to reveal and cover at the same time. She had so arranged the lights in the room that where she stood, the light shone on to her like a spotlight. As she raised her arms, the light spread under the robe, shining through the veils of the gown outlining her curves.

Knowing Barbara and the way she behaved, I suspected she had rehearsed this entrance, making sure the light was in exactly the right position to show her off to the best advantage. I imagined her posing in front of a mirror in the robe and gown, experimenting to find just the right angle. Whether she'd arranged it or not, the effect was devastatingly erotic.

She came over to my chair, leaned over me, her mouth searching out mine to place a delicious kiss on it, the soft inner tissues of her lips wet on my lips as her tongue slid inside. One hand was already working at my fly, her other hand shoving my shirt away. Her mouth began to travel onto my chin, tongue licking onto my chest, a trail of moistness across my stomach. And then, her hand firmly holding my cock so that it was standing hard and fat in her grip, she covered my stand with her mouth.

Barbara was unbelievably careful with her full soft mouth, lavishing an intensely creamy wetness along the whole length, doing a devastating nibble as she took my stiffness in. She began a delicate and sloppy suck. Sometimes her tongue traced the thick vein that was pulsing along the length of my cock. Sometimes the gentle tip of her tongue flicked at various parts before her lips ran down the length with little kisses till her mouth engulfed my balls. Her fingers laced themselves around my hardness, smoothing wetness all over it and tickling the head.

As she was doing this, she sprawled across my thighs so I was able to run my hands all over the robe and gown, then under, feeling the nylon like a light, soft skin on my hands. I reached for her quim, fully velvet and warm, my wet fingers sliding up to her breasts, nipping here and there, smoothing, falling to her waist where her skin flickered under my tickling till my hands played down her groin to reach back to her slippery slit. My finger started an in-and-out rhythm, her cunt wetter than ever, squirming round my finger as her mouth slathered my cock.

Barbara seemed to want to control the evening and I was enjoying myself hugely under her direction. After the delicious ministrations of her mouth, she stood up and went to the gramophone again, stopped the hissing needle and played that blues again. She held her arms out and, in the dim lighting, she was a wonderful vision, deep blue wings outstretched, her body beautifully outlined in filmy blue. 'Come to me, Nick,' she said huskily. Her voice almost sounded like the lyrics to the music. 'Room for both of us here.'

When I reached her, she folded her arms around me and the winged pieces of her robe felt silkily delectable on my back. Barbara pulled me hard against her so that my whole body was in a cocoon of soft nylon, my prick jammed into it, lying fat and hard against her quim. And we danced that way till the blues ended.

We did not move for a minute or two, entranced with the feeling of being closely entwined in softness and silk. Slowly I let my mouth move from hers, down to her breasts, pushing under the lace to suck a nipple, then further down, my head squashing gently against the folds of her gown.

I travelled down to her feet, found myself on my knees so that I began to lift up the hem as Barbara stroked my head. I lifted the two or three layers of nylon so that I could thrust my head inside. The nylon fell onto my shoulders and that gave me the idea to kneel inside those soft folds, be completely covered under there, my hands reaching up to touch Barbara's plush and creamy centre, my mouth following to kiss and lick those glistening wet lips, her trickling clitoris.

Barbara sensed what I was doing and opened her legs to make it easier for me. I was in a gauzy cave of blue, my kneeling body felt fluttering folds of softness encasing me, my hands and mouth sucking at warm moistness, Barbara stroking silkiness across my shoulders and soon we were heading towards a deliriously erotic climax.

We finished by Barbara languorously shedding her robe and gown while I lay stretched out on the floor. She spread them open on the floor, pulled me over onto them and then lay down on top of me. She began to move so that my prick touched her all over, her hands guiding my cock to touch every part she made available. She made me feel as if I was fucking every part of her, my cock on her breasts, sliding up into her hair. She rolled over, then lay on her stomach so that I could trace her spine with the tip of my prick, painting little oozes of jism. Then I slid my rod down to her arse, along the crack, circling the rim of her hole, down to her thighs and legs till I reached her feet where her toes did a little dancing tickle round my cock.

Soon the pace quickened and we began to push frantically against each other. Both of us now were puffing and panting, moaning, the hiss of the needle on the record nearly drowned out as we thrashed against each other. At last, with great outbreathings from both of us, my cock penetrated Barbara as she lay on top of me, a hard prodding as she kept her legs together and my prick fought to find its way home into the lush flow of her juices which were soon flooding round my prick, mixing with the gushes of come, both of us shuddering and shouting in immense relief.

That first year at university was made easier for me by Barbara. She made no demands on me and she enjoyed my company. She was always ready for sex and she was fun to be with. She knew just how to satisfy me and she was happy with my skills, whatever they were. I think I brought back memories of her days with Bill because she was always lavish in her attentions to me. I didn't know how to thank her enough for getting me adjusted to my new life. When I told her this, she just laughed and said, 'Your cock's thanks enough. You can come and dance with me any time. As the song says, "Ten Cents A Fuck"'. Then she smiled wickedly and added, 'And as far as I'm concerned, you can keep the ten cents!'

5. Blue Heaven

The end of term was approaching and I was very busy – final papers to prepare and an examination, fortunately only one examination but that was in the dreaded Anglo-Saxon. Miss Hallam, the lecturer, was riding us very hard and quite a few of us were struggling. Each time she met us, she lectured us on perseverance. 'You have to be stubborn with yourselves,' she said stridently. 'Persevere. What is required is discipline. Firm discipline.'

It was at this time that Ron began to refer to Miss Hallam as 'Gauleiter'. He explained why she should have the name. 'With all that talk about discipline, some day she'll come into class with leather boots up to her thighs, a peaked cap jammed on her head and a whip she'll keep whistling over us.'

We struggled on. I was helped by the relaxing evenings I was spending with Barbara. I was still interested in Lorna but nothing was happening with her. She phoned me a couple of times to invite me to afternoon tea again but on both occasions I had to refuse. I couldn't get out of prior commitments, much as I'd have liked to. I also phoned her and at last I managed to take her to the theatre.

It was a lovely evening. I met her at the theatre and she arrived stunningly dressed, her presence glowing so that she attracted approving glances from men and women alike. While I really liked being with her, I still had ambiguous feelings about her: it was as if she was too beautiful. I couldn't believe she really wanted to be with me. This made me very tentative with her – I didn't want to ruin my chances with her by being too pushy.

We enjoyed the play, we enjoyed an after-theatre drink and when I took her home, we exchanged deliciously sweet kisses at her door. She apologised for not inviting me in: her school work had piled up and she still had some to finish before morning. I half-suspected that this was a gentle way of letting me down and yet she was still warm and sounded genuinely appreciative about my taking her to the theatre. 'Phone me next term,' she said and her voice seemed to have an imploring ring to it. 'I can't see you again before Christmas. I'm going to spend the holiday with my mother. She lives in York and I'm going up there as soon as school's finished.'

I was disappointed, though my time was being swallowed up by studying. While I would have liked to see Lorna, I was being kept more than agreeably happy by Barbara. And my own Christmas holiday looked as if it would be interesting. Ron had invited me home with him for a few days and then I was heading for London. Teresa had told me the last time I'd seen her for a weekend that I could stay with her at Margo's. 'We can have a nice intimate Christmas dinner,' she said, 'and then Gerry usually throws this terrific New Year's party.'

I even hoped I could sneak in a quick visit to my aristocratic lady, Mrs Courtney, who had once hired me as a gardener and who used to offer all kinds of pleasures in her conservatory. Horticultural concerns were soon blossoming into other delicious delights.

But, for now, I was geared to sweating out my problems with Anglo-Saxon. If students didn't gain a passing grade in the Christmas examination, they were not allowed to continue but had to start again in Anglo-Saxon the following October, and that obviously delayed gaining a degree by another year. Ron and I studied together without making much headway. Both of us had almost decided that the niceties of Anglo-Saxon grammar would always elude us. Then one day Gauleiter Hallam surprised us all. She came in dressed in her usual dowdy manner: a bulky ill-fitting sweater, a plain long pleated skirt, flat shoes, thick woollen stockings, no make-up on her severe face and her hair done in its tight roll. So we didn't expect anything different from her but her announcement was totally unexpected.

'I tried an experiment last year with some of my first-year students who were having difficulties,' she said.

Ron leaned over to me and whispered, 'Something to do with electrodes, I bet.'

'It seemed to work for them,' she went on, and Ron added in his low voice, 'A thousand volts through your nuts will work wonders.'

'Sometimes, when you take teaching outside the formalities of the classroom, I find that some students really benefit.' Gauleiter Hallam paused. 'Seven or eight of you need extra help so I'm going to repeat what I did last year. I'll meet whoever needs help one evening next week, at my house. We can discuss the problems informally.' She waved a sheet of paper at us. 'Next Wednesday evening. I'll leave this paper on my desk here. Please sign it if you intend to come. It's meant primarily for those of you who are having trouble but of course anyone in the class is welcome. So please sign in.' She laid the paper on the desk and added: 'Next Monday I'll bring in a map to show you how to get to my house.'

'It's like "What's My Line?"' Ron muttered. 'Anglo-Saxon sadist, that's her line.'

After class Gauleiter Hallam's invitation was the sole topic of conversation. Of course we all expected that the two or three conscientious students, the 'swots', would go but I suggested to Ron that the two of us should attend. 'It might just pull us out of the hole,' I told him.

'Well, it might be interesting to see what kind of prison she keeps herself in,' Ron answered. 'I'll bet there's a big sign at the front door saying "Arbeit Macht Frei"!'

But her house turned out to be a rather ordinary small house, with ordinary furniture, bookshelves on three walls of the room we were in, straight-backed chairs arranged in a circle and a small easel. Though the chairs and the easel still gave a sense of the classroom, Miss Hallam herself had made a determined effort to dispel some of the prim aura she had in the classroom. Her hair was still scrunched in that tight roll but at least her clothes were an improvement: skirt and blouse in brown, still plain but fitting a little more snugly, nylon stockings and shoes with a small heel. It was surprising what the clothes did for her for we could now see she was not shapeless. She looked quite trim though her face, while unusually it had a little make-up, still kept its formidably stern look.

The nine of us who had turned up were a motley crew. Six of us were strugglers, together with three women who seemed destined to follow in Miss Hallam's footsteps, both in deportment and interests. The evening stuttered through two hours, with Miss Hallam waxing almost eloquent in explaining the finer points of syntax. Even Ron seemed to be getting something useful out of it, as I certainly was.

After about two hours Miss Hallam said, 'Let's take a break.' She looked at her watch. 'We'll be able to have another productive hour or so after that.'

I heard Ron groan softly as Miss Hallam came in from her kitchen with a tray with pieces of fruit and nuts on it. She put the tray down and clapped her hands in an attempt to be lively – and indeed, her face did seem to be a little brighter.

The three super-girls excused themselves. I suppose they had little time for physical sustenance; they had come only to slake their mental thirsts. After Miss Hallam had seen them out of the door, she came in from the kitchen carrying another tray with glasses and a large glass jug filled with a reddish-orange drink. 'Please help yourselves,' she said.

'No beer?' Ron complained quietly to me. But the fruit and nuts were very tasty and I ventured to sip at the liquid which I expected to taste something like a fruit punch. It did have that taste but it had something different about it. I almost caught the taste of something alcoholic, together with an indescribably exotic taste. It was very pleasant and I went back for some more.

'Ah, Mr Bancroft, I see you like it.' Miss Hallam was watching me as I poured myself a full glass.

'It's very ... interesting. Not like anything I've ever tasted before.'

'Something I learned to mix in India. A little cold tea, fruit juices, mangoes, passion fruit, bananas, a few spices and splashes of fermented kumquats and quinces. It's very refreshing.'

One or two others had heard her talking to me and someone asked her when she had been in India.

'I was in the Wrens at the end of the war. Just when I was about to get out, I heard they wanted people to go out with Lord Mountbatten to work on the problems they thought would crop up at the time of Indian independence. I applied to go. I'd studied sanskrit and while it isn't really the language that's used in diplomatic circles, they must have thought I'd know something about Indian culture. They gave me a two-year extension, so off I went to India.'

As she was recounting this, she became more animated than I had ever seen her. Her personality positively bloomed and I thought if only she could bring some of this to her teaching of Anglo-Saxon, most of us would have had no problems.

'Marvellous country!' she continued. 'I travelled about quite a bit. Spent some time studying Indian customs. The yogi I met were enormously helpful – I learned a great deal from them. The control they have over their minds and bodies is something that's unbelievable. Such discipline, and yet it isn't lacking in a fine-tuned ... passion.' She even laughed at this point. 'I expect you're all tired of hearing me babble on about discipline. That's where I got it from – India! Breathing and meditation to take control of mind-body. No differentiation.' She stopped a moment. 'It's quite surprising just what that kind of experience can do for one. It opens up remarkable possibilities.'

Ron had been listening to this and he sputtered in my ear, 'The bloody woman's a sacred cow!' Miss Hallam didn't hear this. Instead, she went on to explain how the mind can manipulate the body to overcome pain, to expand the frontiers of the mind itself when it is in tune with the body. There is a state, she maintained, where there is no distinction between mental states and bodily experience. 'Such a comprehensive blending goes beyond our wildest imaginings. It isn't intellect as we think of it. It's a far wide-ranging ... holistic vision. I mean, to be in the presence of one of these wise men in a yogic trance is ... well, if I hadn't seen it with my own eyes ... this elevation of both mind and body together...' She was looking almost dream-like.

Then she stopped. 'But I mustn't ramble on. Time to get back to our studies.' While the animation she had shown when she had been talking about India did not entirely leave her, she did reassume more of that severe side we were used to in the classroom. As the others moved back to their chairs, I filled my glass again – the drink's mellowness was just what I needed to get me through another hour of Anglo-Saxon.

We lasted fifty minutes before two students decided that they had to go – they had other work to do. As they were being shown off the premises, Ron came over to me and said, 'Listen, Nick. These two bints are ready to leave.' He nodded at two young women who were assembling their notes and books in readiness to go. I thought he was going to suggest we gave them a lift back in Ron's car but one of them was a little dumpy girl and I knew Ron had his eyes on the other one. I'm not necessarily against dumpy girls: sometimes they reveal interesting characteristics. But I wasn't certain I wanted anything to do with a student just then: perhaps I'd been spoiled by Barbara.

But Ron went on, 'The redhead seems interested but she can't bring herself to leave the other one. They came together so I'm giving then both a lift back. The other one lives in residence so I'll be able to drop her off first.

Then tally ho! You don't mind, do you? You can find your own way home, right?'

'Don't worry. I can catch a bus. I'm going to be leaving soon anyway. I don't want to be left here on my own.'

'Well, just let me get these two out of here. They'll just start asking awkward questions if they see you hanging about. Maybe they'll think I should be giving you a ride ... unless you want to join us, you know, the other one...'

'No. You go ahead. I'll give you five minutes to get going.'

'Thanks, pal.'

So I was left on my own with Miss Hallam. I attempted to make conversation with her but it limped along. She assured me that my skill with Anglo-Saxon was improving. 'There's still a lot to be done, Mr Bancroft. I think you have learned a little of the requisite discipline. If you keep it up, I'm sure you'll manage. Then next term you will find everything is plain sailing.'

The evening had not been as bad as I had expected it to be. I felt I had cleared up a few problems and Miss Hallam once or twice had shown herself to be not quite the ogress she seemed in the classroom. 'I hope you found the evening not entirely a waste,' she said.

I assured her it hadn't been, downing the last of my fruit drink and savouring the last drops. It was delicious and I suspected that those kumquats and quinces were responsible for the kick in it. 'It was very useful,' I told her. 'I just hope it will be enough to get me through.'

'I know sometimes Anglo-Saxon can be baffling. It still is for me at times. But as I've been stressing, a real effort, you know, a full involvement, a strict discipline, can give their own rewards.' She paused a moment. 'I learned that in India. At first I found the country a complete mystery. I was homesick but then I decided to get to know it, its customs, its ideas, its ... mysteries. And it became fascinating to me. I've never regretted doing that because it showed me a way to live.' She blushed a little. 'I'm sorry. I shouldn't go rattling on. I tend to get carried away when I talk about India.'

'That's alright, I really enjoyed listening to you. You convinced me that I should go there some day.'

'Really?' She nodded towards me as I put my glass down on the table. 'I have a little more of that left in the kitchen if you'd like to finish it off with me before you go. Whenever I drink it, I just get carried away. Reminds me of those years in India.'

She soon returned with two full glasses and after she had taken a hefty swig, she began to talk. And how she talked, almost as if she was making the most of having a captive audience. At first I was determined to drink up as fast as I could but I found the drink better in small doses. Miss Hallam's commentary was very interesting – she seemed to take on a very different personality. Her voice was softer, modulated into gentleness. Her face lit up and she sat relaxed in her chair. The minutes went by very quickly and I began to wonder whether I was being swayed by the drink or by the urgent wistfulness of her stories about India.

'I made friends with one of the old priests in the temple and after a time he let me watch some of the rites the dancers learned.' She stared as if she was watching those dancers. 'Some of those girls had been training since they were about eight. Amazing. Very graceful but all stylized. Part of their religious training of course but it took me some time to understand how something so...' She paused very briefly. '...sensual could also be so spiritual.' She drank again, then lifted her gaze to look directly at me. 'Like crossing the Kama Sutra with the Bible, if you know what I mean. It was part of that mind-body thing. They looked so spontaneous in their movements but it was all under control, every step planned but it looked so effortless. And some of them were still quite young, ten, eleven maybe. It took me some time to accept that these youngsters were simply learning the time-honoured rituals. Such small young girls dancing such extraordinary seductive dances.'

Her gaze was so intense that I took refuge by drinking again, then lowering my head, thinking about Barbara and her dances. When I looked up again, Miss Hallam had stood up and was swaying very sinuously, hips undulating, feet taking precise steps, her upper body gyrating slowly, her head moving from side to side. As she was moving, she was humming a strange tune (I thought of Barbara again). Miss Hallam's tune sounded Indian in its rhythms and half-noted drone but somehow it sounded almost familiar and in a strange way I kept thinking of Barbara, her song titles and what that had led to.

Suddenly Miss Hallam – Ron's Gauleiter name now seemed entirely inappropriate – stopped, looking a little embarrassed. 'Sorry,' she said. 'I got carried away. And I'm really not very good at it. Nothing like those young dancers, looking so innocent yet understanding the intricacies of their bodies.'

'You were very good,' I ventured. And I meant it, perhaps because she looked so startlingly different from the way she usually clumped around the classroom. 'That tune you were singing ... what is it?'

She blushed again. 'I'm not really singing it properly. It's an evening raga. I love it. I bought a record of it, nearly wore it out. Then it got broken when I shipped it home. I was heartbroken. Silly really to be so upset about a tune. I kept singing it, what I remembered of it. I don't suppose it sounds anything like it now.'

'It's almost as if I recognized it.'

'Oh well, maybe that's because of the way I try to remember it. I thought it was a bit like an old song my father used to sing to me when I was quite small. A bit of fluff really, just a popular song he liked.' She hummed a little of the raga. 'Recognize it now?'

I shook my head so she hummed it again. She stopped and giggled. 'Not really the same, of course, but it helps. It's a tune called "My Blue Heaven".'

'Oh now I recognise it. It's fairly close.' I said.

'D'you think so? It was a way for me to remember.' She started to sing again. At first a little falteringly, then with more confidence, she began dancing again. As she danced she talked. 'I suppose we remember things in that way, I mean, by thinking of something we know that reminds us.' She stopped dancing and stood right in front of me. I felt as if I was back in the classroom as she stood over me but her voice was much less harsh. 'Maybe that's why you find Anglo-Saxon so difficult because it's not like anything else you've ever done.'

She started to hum again, then interrupted the song. 'I try to keep my memories of India alive that way. I can relive them when I come home.' She was again looking very intensely at me but this time I returned her gaze. 'Would you like to see?'

'See? See what?'

'India. My India.'

I didn't really know what she was talking about but I

didn't see how I could refuse. Her voice was very persuasive – I would describe it as having almost a thrilling quality to it. She was so taken up with her memories of India, it would have been an insult to decline whatever it was she was offering to show me. 'There's a little more drink left,' she said. 'Come on.'

I followed her into the kitchen and she poured me more of that exotic drink. There was more than a little – she filled my glass and I couldn't keep out of my head the notion that she was trying to get me intoxicated. She moved past me, saying, 'Come along.' She went out of the kitchen, down a short corridor till she came to a door on her right. She turned to it, made a quick bow with her hands together as if in prayer, then turned to me. 'Shoes and socks off, please.'

'Pardon?'

'I keep this room as a sanctuary. Like the temple. The dancers. No scraps of the world outside must be allowed in, so visitors must have bare feet when they enter. I have my own special sandals.'

I stooped to take my shoes off. Miss Hallam went further down the corridor. 'Excuse me,' she said. 'I won't be a moment. I have to find my sandals.' As she turned into another room, she was already hiking her skirt up a little as if in readiness to remove her stockings. As she closed the door, she said, 'Please go in. Sit on the carpet. There are cushions. Make yourself comfortable.'

When I stepped into the room, I found myself in another world, alien from the one I'd always associated with Miss Hallam, a richly coloured world. A large carpet, a blaze of red, black and white in an intricate pattern, covered much of the floor. Scattered around on it were large, brocade cushions, plumply soft, in gold, green and blue, giving an almost garish rainbow of colours against the carpet. There was little furniture: two finely carved round tables, a pier glass bevelled inside a brass frame, two deep wicker chairs, a long low footstool upholstered in the same colours as the carpet. An ornate wooden overmantel held an array of brass ornaments – figurines, bells, candle-snuffers, small gongs – and around the room at regular intervals were tall brass candlesticks. It was flashily colourful but, in a mysterious way, the various shades did not clash.

The air in the room smelled pleasantly perfumed, slightly musty but also musky, a little smoky. I saw several slim vases, delicate china, thick pot, glass and brass, some with long reeds in, some with peacock feathers, some with sticks of incense in them. Small bowls on the tables and the overmantel were filled with potpourri.

I supposed this was Miss Hallam's way of memorializing her India. Many of the things in the room were Indian, though one or two were reminiscent of the British in India.

I didn't quite know what to do. I had the sense that I had been invited into a very private place and I didn't want to desecrate it. The cushions looked invitingly plump and arranged in ways that asked to be sprawled upon. But half-lying at length, especially in view of Miss Hallam's insistence on discipline, seemed incongruous. I perched myself in the middle of a set of cushions, sitting upright, though not very stiffly.

Another transformation occurred when the door opened and in walked Miss Hallam. There is the usual cliché in films when some ordinary secretary, wearing glasses, hair scraped back, in dowdy ill-fitting clothes, miraculously becomes a stunningly beautiful woman, surprising the hero who had never guessed she was so lovely. We in the audience know she is a beauty because she is a famous star so we are never as surprised as the hero.

Miss Hallam was dressed in a brilliantly coloured sari, the material like shot silk, with a glossy sheen to it. It was pulled tightly around her, one shoulder bare. It outlined her breasts and it was obvious she was wearing nothing underneath. The sari was a glistening deep blue woven with gold threads, fastened tightly at the waist, a large knot tied just below the waist. The skirt below fell away in a split that showed her legs as she stooped to place golden high-heeled sandals on her feet. She had unfastened her hair from its usual roll, shaken it out to fall onto her shoulders. She had made her eyes up with severe black outlines which made them appear larger and more sparkling. Her lips were daubed very precisely but fully with a fiery red colour.

As she moved around the room she lit the candles. She had dimmed the lights when she came in so the room was suffused with a warm glow. Soon the incense was burning, the room gradually made hazy with the spicy, perfumed smoke.

She lay down full length, obviously at ease. I was too staggered to speak at first. If I hadn't seen her in her serious guise in a classroom, I would have thought she was deliberately assuming a seductive pose.

'You don't look very comfortable, Mr Bancroft,' she said.

'Er . . . no,' I stammered. 'I was a bit taken by surprise by what I found in here.' I vaguely waved my arm around the room.

'It's part of my Indian past. It doesn't all fit together as I would like it to but this is such a small house, I have to cram it altogether in here. I can retire in here to meditate and sometimes I let friends in here, those who are interested. And you seemed interested, Mr Bancroft – especially taken with my concoction of fruit and spice. And after you'd heard all about the temple dancers and the yogi, I thought you might like to see this.'

'It's...' I was at a loss for words. 'It's ... lovely.'

'It's a place that gives me a lot of comfort. I often come in here when I'm feeling frazzled. The meditation techniques I learned from my guru are a great help.' She gazed at me with the faint suggestion of a smile. 'You look puzzled, Mr Bancroft.'

'Well, I always thought meditation was ... I mean, I don't know much about it ... but I thought it was removed from things, you know, nothing sensuous, nothing bright, everything pared down. No real comfort because they were happy with their inner peace ... that kind of thing. But these cushions, the colours, the atmosphere of perfume and...'

'What you're saying is true ... sometimes. They believe in simple clothing, a short loincloth maybe but that's because they believe in the beauty of the body itself. Of course, many of them believe that the body becomes even more beautiful when it is joined in full unity with the mind. It goes beyond mere beauty, mere sensuousness, though they never deny the real physicality, the sheer beauty of body. The adornment of the body gives way to a fuller self.' She paused and snuggled down into her cushions. 'You don't look very relaxed. It's difficult if we retain things from our normal lives. That's why I always change when I come in here.' She stroked the silk of her sari against her thighs. 'It puts me in the right mood. And lets me go with the mood. Take your jacket off if you like. Loosen your tie.'

Soon I was snuggling down into my cushions, feeling almost languid, taking in the shimmer of light and shadow cast by the candles, breathing in the incense and the subtle scents in the room. Miss Hallam was explaining in a very soothing voice some of the simpler ways of meditating that she had learned from her guru. 'I still try the more complicated controls and relaxations as well. I practise as much as I can. I can show you some of the beginning steps ... if you're interested, that is. I can't pass it on as my guru used to and I can't explain it but I can show you and you can try to follow. It's just a way of control and letting go, discipline and concentration in order to move to something more ... releasing. Would you like to try?'

I didn't think I could just stay lounging on the cushions – I might have just dozed off: maybe that was the effect of the drink and now with the soft light, the warmth of the colours, the perfumed air, I was in danger of dropping off. And I was still thinking that I shouldn't impose on Miss Hallam much longer. I'd just go through the routine of trying a bit of her Indian meditations (I had always been a little sceptical about them and didn't expect to gain much from them), then I could leave. So I nodded and said, 'I'm game for anything.'

'Good.' She stood up and arranged two cushions in the centre of the carpet. Then she looked at me and said, 'Just follow what I do.' So I moved two large cushions into the centre of the carpet as well. 'Closer,' she said. 'You'll find it easier if you're closer to me. Some of the movements are quite ... small so you'll find them difficult to catch if you're too far away.'

So I moved my cushions closer to hers until there was very little space between us as we sat facing each other. She folded herself carefully onto the cushions, squatting with her feet curled under her thighs. In the process the blue silk of her sari rode up her legs but that didn't bother her. She pulled at her feet till she was tightly curled in on herself. 'Pull your feet under, Mr Bancroft. You can do it. Really.' She smiled her slight smile again. 'That's it, Mr Bancroft.' She gave a short laugh. 'Listen to me – Mr Bancroft! Very formal. We're not going to be able to fall into our meditation on such formal terms. What's your name?'

'Nick.'

'Nick. A nice enough name. But not quite right for what we're doing. I'll give you an Indian name. I used to have a young guru I trained with. Kumar. I'll call you Kumar. It was quite common in India to be given a special name when you entered into the realm of meditation. They called me Vijaya. My name's really Veronica but it was too English for them, too much of a mouthful so they called me Vijaya.'

I sat as best I could but I felt somehow cramped. 'Relax, Kumar.'

'I don't seem to have quite got the hang of it, Miss Hallam.'

'Vijaya. You should call me Vijaya. Then we can work together.' She was staring straight at me, a wistful smile on her face. She didn't seem to be smiling at me, she seemed to be staring beyond me. 'Relax, Kumar. First, you must focus on something pleasant. Empty your mind and just focus on one thing. Imagine you are sending waves through your body down to all the extremities. Let the waves take you. Feel the vibrations. Feel your heart beating. Let it slow down. Slower. Slower. More slowly still. Relax. Relax into your beautiful thing. See it. Join it. Relax. Close your eyes if that helps. Shut the world out. Merge with it. It is beautiful. Relax.'

I didn't close my eyes – I was too fascinated by her, the way she was involved with what she was doing. Her eyes had opened really wide, her hands were slowly stroking the soles of her feet, her upper body was swaying slightly. Then her hands slid down her sari to her hips, her waist, then up, pulling the sari open a little so that it was not so tightly wrapped around her. I caught a glimpse of the first roundness of her breasts.

I found myself concentrating on an image of Lorna. I'd been told to fix on something beautiful so Lorna sprang to mind. I'm not sure that was the kind of beautiful thing Miss Hallam had in mind but, as I watched her hands smooth down her body, as I saw her sari open a little, I began to imagine Lorna dressed in this way, showing off a little of her breasts and legs as Miss Hallam was doing. Maybe that was not quite the concentration Miss Hallam wanted but it did put me into a warmly attentive mood. I felt myself slipping into a soft, blurry region.

'Try to be as loose as you can be. There can be no constraints.' She pulled her sari wider so the roundness of her breasts became more visible. She nodded at me that I should do the same thing. 'Please. Feel yourself let go. Make yourself free.' So I unfastened my shirt to my waist and pulled it loose a little. 'Good, Kumar.'

We sat gazing at each other and I was beginning to be hypnotized by the loose sway of her body. 'Concentrate. Visualize.' Then I closed my eyes and the image of Lorna became clearer. It was an ideal image – that remote quality she had underlined the way in which I had dressed her in a long flowing gown, only loosely floating round her body. It was a seductive picture in my mind and began to have an effect on me. I felt a first stirring at my centre, hot, thick, comfortable. Miss Hallam began to hum her raga, "My Blue Heaven", but strangely different, very slow, very Easternized.

We stayed in this state for about five minutes and by the time I opened my eyes, I discovered that she had pulled her sari wider. Almost the whole of her breasts were uncovered and her hands were on them. Her eyes were closed and she seemed to have dropped into a trance-like state. She began to run a finger round and round each nipple and then I noticed she had painted them with lipstick. They jutted out, hard and red and of course, my stirring grew more solid, more hard.

Her face had a soft shine to it. Eventually she opened her eyes. As she saw me watching her fingering her nipples, I dropped my gaze. She shook her head and again her stare seemed to go right through me, beyond me. She whispered, 'The vibrations of the body. Into the mind,' and her fingers became more insistently concentrated on her nipples. She reached across to me, brushed my shirt away and began the same finger-stroking on one of my nipples. Round and round her fingers went and I felt my nipples harden. 'Let the circles penetrate. Into your heart beat.' She kept her finger slowly motioning on me, a very slight touch but I had the strange sensation that she was reaching firmly into me, making me aware of my heartbeat. It was pounding, but not in excitement.

'You must follow the step,' she said in a dreamy voice. I was slow to realize what she meant. I reached across to circle her nipple with my fingers, first just one, and then, as she reached for my other nipple, I did the same to her. We sat stroking each other in that way, our fingers soon moving in exactly the same way. She started to sing again, interrupting herself on occasions to murmur words. 'Let the waves flow. Vibrations. Roll along the shore of your mind. Through your body. Feel. Feel. Discipline, Kumar.'

As she said 'Discipline' it seemed to me her eyes dropped to where my trousers were beginning to show a hard bulge. I was in such a pleasantly soothed mood, imagining the thick stand of my cock, poking against the rough material of my trousers.

'Discipline. Feel it spreading through your body. From your mind into your body.' And indeed, in a strange way, because I was thinking about my cock, it did feel if as its stiffness had been brought on by my thought. Somewhere in my mind was still the image of Lorna, bare to the waist like Miss Hallam. As I was stroking those nipples, I could see myself stroking Lorna in that way. And yet Miss Hallam was very obviously there. I felt both very conscious of the feel of her skin as my fingers touched the aureole, closed the hard nipple between two fingers, gently prodding at the very tip. And Vijaya (I was now thinking of her as Vijaya) was doing exactly the same thing to me. And her words were lulling me into a floating relaxation but also making me focus on my cock so obviously full and hard.

'Let it spread,' she murmured. 'Outwards. Upwards. Grow into it. I can feel it growing inside. Inside the mind. Growing outwards. Your body taking it up, it is growing. Feel it. Concentrate.'

By now I was very much concentrating on my straining erection. It was there between us. I felt that Vijaya was probably in full concentration on herself. I wondered if she was imagining my cock or whether she was experiencing a flow of juice within her, warm, creamy, like velvet. Whatever we were both thinking, the motions on our nipples were in tune. I had the distinct impression that our minds were also attuned, fully aware of the effects on our bodies. I felt we had arrived there in no conscious manner.

Eventually she let one of her hands trail from my nipple. She poked gently at my navel, circling, prodding a little. I did the same to her, my hand travelling under her sari and the material parted, fell away so that it was simply hanging loosely from her shoulders.

'Good, Kumar,' she crooned, though I didn't know whether she meant I was following her step correctly or whether she liked the way my fingers pressed a little into her navel, in and out in a slow, suggestive prod, then spreading it along her stomach, the top of her pubic hair scratching a little along my finger.

We stayed like that for two or three minutes. I had the impression that Vijaya was moving her body so that my hand seemed to be moving slightly lower across her stomach. In the same way I shifted as carefully as I could so that her hand moved down, a couple of fingers stroking against my warm skin, the tip of my cock poking up so hard that it was not far away from her fingers.

And in a chant-like voice she was slowly elaborating her feelings, that warmth that was suffusing us together. 'Your waves will move across. Into me. Big waves reaching up. Up and up. Ready to hold there. Holding but moving up. Rolling into me.' Her hand on my stomach was pushing in with a firm rhythm and each time she pressed, my prick reached up towards her hand, twitching. I was sure she sensed it there close to her touch. 'Discipline. Control. Concentration. Mindfulness. Feel it there.' And she gave my stomach an extra push then. 'Feel it. Feel.' And I seemed to sense a pulse running through my whole body, slowly but powerfully. I was sure she could feel it under her hand just as I could feel it beating up the whole length of my cock. Then her chant of "My Blue Heaven" began again, somehow in tune with that pulsing rhythm.

I could feel a regular pulse under my hand on her stomach but it was much more controlled, much slower. I wondered if she was really aware of the effect her hand was having. Yet my hand was spreading wider on her stomach, inching down till it was covering most of her pubic hair.

Her chant droned on, interspersed with spoken words that were almost musical. 'Open. More open. Flow. Flow out. Release. Let go.' Then the singing stopped as she pushed her hand very firmly into my stomach. 'Stand!' Though her voice was low, there was no doubt she was in charge. I was slow in understanding what she meant – at first, I was so transfixed by the sense of myself so stiff and hot that I thought she was referring to my erection. But her hand kept pushing and she repeated 'Stand!' so that it dawned on me she wanted me to stand up.

I pulled myself out of my squatting position and managed to get to my feet. Her hand remained in place so that as I stood, it slid over the length of my cock. She made no attempt to hold it – it was as if her hand was there on its own, not belonging to her body but as a separate part of her that simply lay against me.

'Good, Kumar. Let go.' Her hand crawled up my thighs, again across the length of my cock, fingers soon at my belt, tugging, unclipping the top, stole gently down unfastening my buttons. Somehow her hand had pulled at my underpants. They dropped with my trousers and I was standing with a very hard and long erection straining up level with her face.

Still she did not make a move to touch me. I thought we were still meditating. Perhaps I had taken the wrong attitude and in time all sensual thought would disappear; we would simply be together, one mind-body, not touching but somehow fully together, one unity.

She stood up. I watched her uncurl herself from her cross-legged position. She seemed to uncoil like a snake, a graceful, sinuous movement. We stayed standing, very close together, not touching. My cock seemed to be growing longer, wanting to close the gap between us, wanting to touch her. Her hands rose to my shoulders and, with the most delicate of fingertips, she slid them down the length of my arms, right to my fingertips, dropping them as she moved them inward, tickling on my thighs, meeting inside them, resting there, not quite touching my balls. While her hands and arms stayed in place, I pressed my fingertips along her arms, following where they reached across the small gap between us. Then I stretched my hands across to her so that my hands rested right at the top of her thighs, almost touching the folds of her slit.

'Breathe together. From the centre.' The way she said this was like breathing itself, exhaling slowly, then breathing in. I listened to the rhythm of that breathing, trying to match mine to hers. It was difficult at first for she was almost ineffably calm, taking deep inhalations, holding still, then following with slow, faintly hissing breaths out. She seemed able to fit words inside this rhythm and sometimes encouraged me with breathy words. 'Good, Kumar. We touch in air. Our warm breath. Merging. Warm. So warm. Let it fold round us.'

We breathed together for a while. Then she said, 'Close your eyes. Fall into emptiness. Breathe slowly.' And I began to feel strangely eased, yet still excited. My cock was at the centre of everything, its warmth, its length taking all of me over. Vijaya must have sensed that I was still not letting go into the empty space she wanted me to fall into. She said gently but still firmly, 'Discipline.'

As I drifted down into a kind of inner darkness, I was still holding on to the idea of how close we were. I could still feel her breath, still holding some of that taste from the drink. Somewhere within me (I couldn't say that it was really in my mind, or even in my consciousness, yet it was there) was the picture of her naked body, standing in the puddle of silk she had dropped when the sari fell from her shoulders. It was her body but in an odd way her body seemed to take on more shape, more curvaceous lines, more seductive charms. It was as if my whole body was travelling across the space between us at each breath I let out, as if my breath was like my arms reaching out to embrace her as I also felt her breath reaching to hold me. Yet we did not touch beyond leaving our hands in place between each other's thighs. I settled into a kind of warm trance, our breathing now absolutely simultaneous.

'One long breath out ... now!' Her voice was a long cooing sigh. I was surprised how my whole body seemed to be emptying itself completely so that as I reached the end, I gasped, and at that precise moment an incredibly soft flutter took the tip of my cock, lingered there, then tip-toed along its length on one side, circled the root, down and around the back of my scrotum, then up the other side of my cock back to the tip, resting on the slit, staying there a long, still minute before repeating the manoeuvre.

I felt myself no longer empty; everything in me was gathered around that gentle touch as it moved, then rested. It was as if all of me was open inside my cock and that touch was moving all over my body. I was quivering in anticipation of being brought into that sensitive fullness again. I still had my eyes closed but I knew it was Vijaya's fingers that were doing this fragile and exotic dance on me. After a time her fingers began their slow tour again and she cooed in a soothing voice, 'Control. Discipline.' She went on talking as her fingers continued their languid progress along my shaft.

She had told me about one of her gurus. 'Great control. Holding his emission.' The effect of her fingers being so slow in motion was again to make my cock feel enormously long. 'He knew he could hold it, control it with himself, his breath, his spirit. Find the rhythm and relax inside it. Feel his semen along the inside of himself. Brimming. Ready. But never spilling. Climax without spilling.'

I wanted to ask how she knew this. Had she learned her hand movements from him? Had he shown her when she had done this to him? And yet these questions weren't important. I didn't need the answers. The slow motions of her fingers were building me up, my cock stiffening more, and I knew this was come standing in a long column up my cock, gathering in my balls. Try as I might, breathing in time with Vijaya, concentrating when she said, 'Discipline,' my jism would not stay still inside. Every time Vijaya's finger came back to my slit, it touched a full drop of jism and as soon as the finger felt that warm drop of sticky cream, it traced that moistness all over my cock-head, around the drawn-back rim of skin. Then off it went again on its excruciating slow journey down my shaft, circling my scrotum, then up again to find another small surge of come at the slit.

I was simply standing there, concentrating, breathing, eyes closed, subjected to this long, marvellously precise stroking. I sensed that Vijaya must have been stimulated herself by this slight fingertip massage of my cock and yet she remained somehow remote, not holding me, her voice talking and chanting in a soothing drone. She showed no sign of excitement and yet she never wavered in her stroking. She seemed to have let her hand roam inside its own rhythm and that caused me to twitch, shiver, shudder, the drops of come steady, waiting for her finger to return to the slit. Gradually my whole length was covered in a thin slipperiness of jism. I felt her massage eventually must lead me to spill out but, incredibly, I didn't. There was just that slow ooze, a creamy lather brushed tantalizingly around the full length of my cock.

Some women by this stage would have wanted to feel that hardness against them, inside them. They would have wanted my hands to respond in the same way to their bodies, to slide fingers inside their moist centres. But Vijaya gave no indication that that was what she desired. She was content to do this extraordinary finger-exercise, in time to her breathing, her words, her singing. And I allowed myself simply to go with it, keeping my eyes closed as if I should remain in the dark – it seemed a true way to concentrate, my whole body wrapped in that thin creaminess, my whole body engulfed in softness, my hardness ready to burst.

'Grow into it,' Vijaya murmured, her fingers sending a great shuddering twitch along the whole length of my shaft, and as her finger returned to my slit, an extra spurt of come rose, leaking in a small stream along my cock-head.

'Discipline. Hold.' She scooped the extra cream on the end of her finger. My cock was beating against the inexorable slow rhythms of her fingers. I was enormously excited and yet I felt no desire to press myself onto Vijaya. I immersed myself in this immensely pleasurable touching as if it could continue indefinitely, my cock continuing to stiffen and fatten as it seemed to fill with more and more come. And somehow I had fallen into the state of believing that I would not spill out into her hand, my prick pulsing in time to her chanting of my name. 'Kumar. Kumar. Good. Hold. Control. Kumar. Good.'

As she continued I felt bathed in a warm wave spreading out from my engorged cock. Then her fingers seemed to almost stop moving, my stand throbbing and jumping under her touch which then slowly slid upwards, then off. Yet my whole length tingled as if she was still touching me. A few seconds later she whispered, 'Come back now. Eyes open.'

She was standing still in front of me, close, with her arms hanging loosely at her sides. She seemed removed from what she had just been doing. She turned, walked slowly to a line of cushions, stooped, then straddled them, lying full-length on her stomach. Lazily she signalled to me with one arm. 'Relax now. Lie down.' She motioned for me to join her so I lay down on the cushions next to her. As I was preparing to turn on my stomach, she shook her head. 'You lie on your back. We are yin and yang.'

I sank back, my cock a glistening wet pole sticking up, with Vijaya, her head on one side, gazing directly at it. Then her hand reached out and gripped me by the root, circling it with her finger and thumb, starting to press up and down, up and down, again almost imperceptibly although it felt as if her hand was extended along the whole length.

And again the oozing of jism began, a slow but steady stream of milky tears. She seemed to be totally involved in this, giving me the impression that the whole of her was concentrated in that finger and thumb. In turn my cock, bathed in its own warm juice, not only felt as if it was reaching up to plunge inside a moist quim but was also in a mysterious way reaching backwards into itself, extending back to some warm centre deep inside me.

'One. All one.' The words came as a low drone. At that precise moment I really felt as if I had an inkling of what she had told me about her guru controlling himself, willing himself not to spill out his semen, to retain it so that it flooded back into himself, though mine was still steadily trickling out. I was afraid I would soon be drained but still Vijaya drew me on and still the small spillings continued.

While I was trying to let my mind float inside this sensation, I couldn't help remembering Barbara and Daisy, Barbara with her bring-to-your-knees massage and Daisy's expert lesson in the various ways of stroking. Vijaya's handling of me bore little relation to the other two. Those fluttering fingertips were both immensely exciting and yet immensely relaxing to the point of almost transcending the physical. I was tremendously aware of my cock but at the same time I was somehow outside, thinking about that stiff stand and a sense of fulfillment suffused the length of my body. I wondered if this feeling was what Vijaya herself was experiencing, a mixture of remoteness and togetherness.

'I can feel your pulse,' she whispered, 'beating with mine.' Her finger and thumb were exerting pressure, pulling me over to her. My wet cock slid onto her buttocks so I moved myself as unobtrusively as I could onto her to cover her as that is what she seemed to want. She wriggled beneath me till I lay full length against her. Her hand was withdrawn and the length of my prick stretched fully along the crack of her arse, her cheeks slightly twitching against it. I was still leaking so it was juicily snug there. Her face was pressed into a cushion and her voice came to me as a mumble as she said, 'One. I am one.'

It was at that point that I had a very strong urge to be even closer to her though I was squashed on top of her. Her words sounded as if she too wanted that, her body sprawled to feel all of me on her. I began to struggle to release my cock, to slide it down a little, to let it find its way, to search out what it instinctively knew would be her juicy opening, one that would gently but relentlessly suck in my thickness so that I would ease fully inside her to reach some inner centre.

Vijaya was obviously feeling the way my cock was prodding and probing to her inviting centre. Somehow her small rolling motions appeared to be both a help and a hindrance, almost as if she wanted to hold that long penis in place along her arse and yet let it work its way along and down, finally to thrust inside the moist lips of her quim. She controlled that wetness so that I squirmed deliciously and slowly in, surging inside her, poking further and further in in a warm wash of juices.

All this time I was spurting out come in a steady stream. I expected that soon I would have nothing left. But I could sense my fat cock-head sinking into a slippery silkiness. I pushed a little harder and I seemed to break through to a soft openness, a valley of plushness that sent little tentacles of warmth around my cock, sucking and nudging, till I was going even deeper, moving in, sinking inside, Vijaya's legs holding me tight.

And then her cunt began an extraordinary motion,

similar to her fingertips, almost without moving and yet offering itself wholly along the fat length of my cock. I still kept leaking jism and I felt as if I was on the very edge of climax. And yet I knew I was also working to some greater bursting release. I did not need to move. Vijaya's moist centre moved on me and, as she wriggled so delectably, she began spasmodically to sing her raga, at first recognizably, then more brokenly, deeper in her throat, more drone-like as if the song was taking us over, leading us on, her juices now in a full warm flood, my cock quickening, her quim throbbing in tiny quivers that stroked velvet moistness along the thick length, as if she was making it longer, stretching it out and inside her further, her voice more strangled, sounding more Indian till, inside an exquisite final grasp from her, my prick seemed to break open in a large gush I thought it impossible for me to achieve and her voice rang out in an unearthly Indian tonality.

I don't know how long I lay there afterwards. I must have dropped into a deep well of darkness for I woke to find myself sprawled across cushions, Vijaya no longer in the room, the candles all extinguished, the incense sticks no longer burning. I shifted, stood up and began to dress myself, slightly bemused but remarkably at ease.

Then, as I had nearly finished dressing, Miss Hallam was standing just inside the room. She was no longer Vijaya, dressed now as she usually appeared in the classroom – bulky sweater, pleated skirt though she was in bare feet. 'I have taken the liberty of calling a taxi for you, Mr Bancroft,' she said in her usual brisk voice. 'The buses have stopped running by now. The taxi should be here in a minute or two.'

I have never figured out how she knew when I would be conscious, when I would be dressed and ready to go but I had no sooner finished the last of my dressing than we heard the taxi arriving outside. 'Ah, there it is, Mr Bancroft.'

We stopped at the front door and, before she opened it to let me out, she gave me what I thought was a flicker of a smile. Otherwise, she assumed her stern classroom look. 'I hope the evening has proved profitable for you, Mr Bancroft.' There was not even a trace of irony or humour in her tone. 'Perhaps some of your problems were solved. Maybe you will remember what I have been stressing about concentration and discipline.' And again there was absolutely no sly humour in her voice. 'I think that in all probability the examination shouldn't be too difficult for you now.' Then she opened the door. 'Goodnight, Mr Bancroft.'

'Goodnight, Vij...' but her head shook just a little. 'Miss Hallam,' I added.

When I sat the examination, I found my mind drifting off into a haze of memory about her Indian room. Nevertheless I came out convinced I had done well. From then on, Anglo-Saxon came more readily to me. Whether that was because, as time went on, I became more used to it or whether I had assimilated Miss Hallam's notions of discipline and concentration, I never knew. Whatever it was, that evening learning the steps in her Indian room was one of the most remarkable lessons I have ever been taught.

Throughout my studies over the following year and a half, I always saw the seductive presence of Vijaya beneath the serious, severe exterior of Miss Hallam. She never mentioned her Indian interests in class. She certainly never mentioned it to me again and never gave any indication that I had received her special attention. Ron kept referring to her as the Gauleiter and I never disillusioned him; I didn't consider it would be fair to Miss Hallam to tell him about how she indulged that Indian side of her life. She was obviously intent on keeping it a secret.

I heard that the following year she invited her first-year students to her house around examination time for individual help with their problems. I wondered if any student would be taken into her Indian secrets, though I didn't attempt to find out. I kept it as my secret, I didn't study any more Anglo-Saxon after my second year but, whenever I hear the song "My Blue Heaven" I think about Anglo-Saxon and how the figure of Vijaya emerged from the dour Miss Hallam to teach me her own particular lesson. Sometimes I hum the tune to myself – it always has the effect of cheering me up, even if I am sunk in a very blue mood.

6. Christmas Cheer

I was disappointed when I arrived at the Blue Lantern on Christmas Eve – no Teresa, no Margo, one or two nubile waitresses but they were bustling around, trying to finish so they could leave for their own Christmas celebrations.

I'd had a miserable train journey in a jam-packed carriage, everybody trying to get home for Christmas at the last minute. And the weather had turned nasty, cold with a heavy sleet falling. I was feeling very sorry for myself.

And Gerry was also rushing around. 'Good to see you again, old son,' he greeted me when I first walked in, slapping me on the shoulder. 'Have to excuse me, dashing about. Trying to get things sorted out so's I can let everyone go early. And I have to get off myself. Always spend Christmas with my old mum.'

He went off but before he did, he sat me down and served me a solid Christmas dinner, apologizing that Teresa and Margo were not there. 'Giving a party for a few businessmen at Margo's place before they head off back to the bosoms of their families, though I guess Margo's got them interested in other bosoms! Still, it should be all clear there by early evening.'

After I'd finished dinner, Gerry came back to me. 'I need to have a quick chat with you, Nick,' he said. 'Better do it now before you get yourself all worn out with Teresa.' When he was in a conspiratorial mood he became a little gangster-like, imitating the style he'd seen in films, even using some Americanisms he'd picked up from GIs he'd known. These always sounded strange coming from Gerry. He still spoke in a thick upper-class accent.

He leaned back in his chair in an extravagant sprawl. 'Things OK with you up in Manchester?'

I nodded. 'Barbara tells me you've settled right in.' He winked. 'Right in! With Barbara, I mean. Lovely lady, Barbara. And she thinks you're a bit of alright.' He paused. 'And I'm glad you're keeping an eye on things up there.'

'I haven't been keeping my eye on anything,' I protested.

'Except for Barbara. And Lorna, right? I knew she'd be a real smart cookie as soon as I saw her picture. Her brother showed me, said she'd be a help up in Manchester. I hope you're getting fixed up with her, kid.'

'I've taken her out a couple of times.'

'Well, that's what I want to talk to you about. Lorna. I want you to look out for her, Nick.' He leaned across the table and lowered his voice. 'She thinks she can take care of herself and I know she's a bright kid. But I'm worried about her. What I'm getting at is this – I feel sort of responsible for her because I got her to go and live at that place – what's it called? That funny name Barbara gives it?'

'Paradise Lost.'

'That's it. Well, Barbara didn't like it. She thought something odd was going on there and she didn't like the idea of putting Lorna in there. Tried to talk me out of it. She says this Stanley Milton guy is a crook. I've heard a scurried on, disappearing through another door at the end of the corridor.

I was anticipating that Teresa would soon be coming in to see me. After all, this was Christmas Eve and I thought I'd be in for a happy reunion with her. But the minutes passed and no one came. I began to feel uneasy and paced around the room, fingering some of Margo's Christmas ornaments. I looked at the Christmas tree in one corner of the room, a tall, bushy tree that spread out profusely with its branches evenly growing out from the bottom where a few boxes and packages in brightly coloured paper lay.

As I was stooping to look at these presents under the tree, Shirley came in. That startled me – did she think I was going to steal the presents?

Shirley was carrying a tray with a large crystal jug, filled with yellow liquid. There were three glasses on the tray as well, I noticed. She placed the tray on a low table, saying, 'Eggnog. You're to help yourself. They'll be in soon.' Then she left.

I've never been a one for eggnog but I drank some. I was feeling very disappointed – this was not the celebration I'd been expecting. I fidgetted in my chair, stood up, began to walk around, went over to peer out through the curtains into the darkness outside. It looked bleak and cold with small patches of fog drifting about – very dismal.

Eventually Margo walked in. She looked her usual splendid self in a form-fitting black cocktail dress, though she looked a little dishevelled, her coppery hair not so tidily arranged. She brushed a stray tress out of her eyes which were sparkling with their bright green.

'Nick! How good to see you again!' She came to me and placed a small kiss on my cheek. I put my hands on her waist and we stayed briefly holding each other till she moved away. 'You must think we're dreadful, leaving you on your own like this.'

She sat down and I was able to appreciate her finely shaped legs as she crossed them. 'We've had such a hectic time today,' she said. She lay back on the sofa. 'I'm quite done in. And poor Teresa. She's just finishing up in the kitchen. She's worn out.'

We talked in a desultory fashion, Margo asking me about my life as a student though she didn't seem too interested. We drank a little more eggnog and each time she came over to fill my glass, she touched me lingeringly on the cheek or gave me a fluttery short kiss.

She relaxed deeply into the sofa, her dress riding high so she was showing a lot of leg. It was all vaguely sexy without amounting to anything, a sultry and slightly seductive atmosphere. I almost forgot about wanting any particular action.

When Teresa eventually came in, she was a little flustered. She gave me a big hug, then flopped down at the other end of the sofa. She pulled me down next to her, sighing, 'I'm really tired. I'm glad they've all gone.'

Teresa curled against some cushions. She looked enticing though she too was a little untidy, wearing an old but obviously comfortable dressing gown. I was snuggled next to her and Margo was now half-supine, legs stretched out, propped on my lap. I felt pleasantly warm from their body heat. I convinced myself that soon the three of us would be enjoying ourselves in all kinds of seductive ways.

But nothing like that happened. Teresa gave me an occasional pat, a little smooch with her lips. Margo tweaked my hands on her legs every now and again when I ventured up above her knees, my hands resting under the hem of her dress. She didn't want my hands to travel any further.

Then she stifled a small yawn. 'You'll have to excuse me,' she said, moving her legs from me and sitting up. 'I'm really exhausted.' She stood up. 'I'm going to bed. Or I'll spoil Christmas Day for us.' She leaned down and kissed me gently, 'See you in the morning, Nick.' And with that she walked out of the room, which took me by surprise. Or had she gone simply to leave me alone with Teresa, I asked myself.

I put my arm around Teresa and pulled her closer to me. 'It's good to see you again, Teresa.' She leaned her head on my shoulder a moment, then raised her glass to her mouth just as I bent to kiss her. She gave her head a small shake. 'You wouldn't believe the day we've had!' She gave my knee an affectionate pat but she soon took her hand away. 'They made such a tip. The clearing up took ages.'

'What about Shirley? She's the maid.'

'She helped but it took the three of us hours.' She kissed me on the cheek. 'I'm really tired.' She gave me a quick smile. 'So I just don't feel up to anything right now.' She unfolded herself and stood up. 'You don't mind, do you, Nick?'

'No,' I lied. I'd expected a hotter reception. Here it was only about half past ten and both these women were going to bed – to sleep! I held on to a sneaking suspicion that this was an elaborate joke, that when I got upstairs, Margo and Teresa would be waiting for me to tumble me into a long bout of love-making.

Teresa gave me a final peck. 'See you in the morning.' And before I could make a move to hold her, she was gone.

After a few minutes I decided that there was not much point in my sitting up by myself so I went to my room. I half expected to be pounced on, hauled on, thrown onto the bed, smothered by their half-naked bodies as they struggled to get me out of my clothes.

But no such thing happened. I stood around in my bedroom for a few minutes, hoping Teresa or Margo or both of them would walk in, laughing at me for thinking they were going to leave me alone. Then I wondered if they really wanted me to visit them in their rooms but I decided against that.

I undressed and slid under the covers. I left the light on, nevertheless. At least they'd know I was waiting for them.

But half an hour or so later I was still on my own, frustrated, disappointed and a little peeved. I turned the light out, rolled over and after several minutes of tossing and turning I managed to fall asleep. Throughout the night, I was disturbed by very sexy dreams.

The next morning I was hauled out of those dreams by a persistent hammering at my door. 'Wakey, wakey, rise and shine.' It was Margo's voice. 'Come on. Up you get. No need to get dressed. We're not being formal this morning.'

I heard her moving away from the door, shouting, 'Merry Christmas, Nick,' she giggled. 'Hey, I just remembered – the other name for Father Christmas. Saint Nick. I hope you're not tired after doing your rounds last night. Anyhow, it's time for you to get your own present this morning. It's waiting for you under the tree.'

They usually cooked a special breakfast for me, so I guessed that was ready and waiting. I moved quickly out of the bedroom, happy now that the Christmas celebration was about to begin.

I took the stairs two at a time, flung open the living

room door but it was empty – no breakfast laid out, no Margo, no Teresa. Until I looked under the tree for my present...

Teresa was lounging there on plump cushions, dressed in a vivid blue ankle-length tea-gown, with high heels emerging beneath. She smiled up at me. 'Look who's come down my chimney,' she breathed.

I walked towards her. "Merry Christmas, Saint Nick.' She stretched her arm out and her hand found its way inside my pyjama trousers to fondle me. I stiffened immediately. She slid her fingers insidiously down the length, snaking round to trace fingers round my balls, the head of my cock resting against her palm.

'There's no mistletoe here but he deserves a kiss anyhow.' She raised herself, removed her hand and placed a lovely moist kiss on the slit of my shaft. I shifted my position slightly to accommodate her mouth, thrusting towards her. In response, her lips opened and she began a lingering wet slide down the length. I felt the little ridges on the top of the inside of her mouth play a fascinating scale around the head of my cock. She kept sucking me inside, a low moan coming from her throat as I sensed I was touching her tonsils.

By now she was kneeling in front of me and my hands were stroking her hair. She pulled her mouth along my prick till she was again nudging at the slit with her lips. She was very playful, using tiny, flickering kisses, circling her tongue around the fat head, then sucking wetly while her fingers trailed moisture along the length down to my balls.

As her mouth was busy on me, she took brief pauses to speak teasingly. 'Sorry about last night.' A finger probed, her tongue flicked. 'We were really tired.' Two fingers pulled at the slit of my cock to open it wide and the tip of her tongue darted inside. 'But you know Margo.' Fingers were fondling my balls, reaching underneath to slide up towards the crack of my arse. 'She thought it would be a nice tease.' Her words were almost swallowed as she drew me in. 'I wanted to grab you, even though I was tired.' The words bounced wetly at my cock-head. 'Margo said it would be better in the morning when we were fresh.' She grasped me hard.

Her stroking became slowly insistent. It was as if she wanted to pull the covering skin down, peeling me like a ripe banana, revealing a long, hard red cock. 'And now it's morning.' She rubbed the head of my cock enticingly round the inside of her lips. 'Time to open your present.' Her tongue lapped up and down the length of my shaft. 'D'you like what you found under the tree?' I nodded and mumbled a strangled 'Yes.'

'I think you'd better unwrap it then.' My prick was now sliding across her face and into her hair, her hands cupping my balls. 'You can find out what the juicy contents are under the wrapping.'

She rose to her feet, close to me, still holding my cock in both hands, warmly teasing me. I reached out and untied the belt of her blue satin robe. As it fell open, I caught a glimpse of red silk underneath. I placed my hands inside her robe, sliding them down her back, resting them on her round buttocks, feeling them covered by a slippery skin of soft fabric.

She let go of me, her hands hanging loosely at her sides, stepping to me so that the head of my prick nudged against the silkiness she was wearing. She moved herself slowly so that my cock rubbed delicately against her silky panties. My hands moved to slip the robe from her shoulders and with a slight shrug she let it fall down her body to her feet.

She stepped back a little so I could see her – she was wearing a flimsy red bra with very lacy matching panties. She twirled so I could see the way her waist dipped, accentuating the globes of her arse, her panties with a high slit at the sides, legs in filmy red stockings, the seam outlining their shapeliness down to slim ankles, made more deliciously slim by stiletto heels.

'This is just the best Christmas present,' I murmured.

She smiled mischievously. 'Now let's see what present you have for me.' Her fingers took the end of my pyjama cord and gave it a quick pull. The trousers fell and my cock sprang out into her hands. 'Just the present I wanted,' she whispered, leaning into me to give me an open-mouthed kiss, her tongue squirming inside my lips as my hands moved up to smooth her breasts. My cock found its way onto her panties, stiffened upwards and as we embraced, its hard length rested against her mound, poking upwards against her stomach, her hands on my arse pressing me against her. She somehow moved so that my cock slid down a little and was caught between her legs. She began to sway so that the thin band of her panties rubbed up and down my shaft. I could feel the thin soft silk begin to get wet.

'Remember when I wore these the first time? So I put them on this morning to make you want to fuck me just like you did then. I thought about putting your prick inside my panties because that makes me feel hot and juicy. When I slipped them on, I kept thinking how I'd take them off for you so you could fuck me. I just wanted to fuck. Just getting dressed made me all sticky. And I thought about your big hard cock sliding right inside all that juiciness.' I could hear that Teresa had lost none of her love of talking to urge me on.

I unhooked her bra and my hands massaged the

softness of her breasts, warm against my palms. Occasionally I tweaked her pointy nipples, and I felt them getting hard and jutting out. I stroked round the aureoles, then leaned down to lick, then suck those round nubs into my mouth, slavering moistly all over them, giving them little nibbles. All the while my cock was slithering along the juicy lips of her quim as she clenched her legs around my shaft, manipulating it so that sometimes it squirmed loose, lodging itself upright against the front of her panties, feeling the tickly fuzziness of her nest of hair through the filmy fabric.

Gradually she was waltzing me backwards to a long sofa, finally pushing me down, quickly stripping off my pyjama jacket. My cock by now had reached a full head, reaching up long and fat. I could see it as Teresa knelt between my legs, licking her way up from my ankles, placing delicate kisses on my legs, then on my inner thighs, licking her hand so that when she gently touched me, the wet stroking increased the slipperiness I was already bathed in. Her hands were so marvellously satiny – the wet palm circling my cock-head, a creamy tongue tracing the length down to my balls, taking them in her mouth while her fingers in an almost finicky way flickered around the rim of skin. All of this set my cock twitching and throbbing, even more when she leaned over me, her thick black hair falling across my stomach, then down, slowly, covering my shaft, swirling it over the length which she then let slide against her neck, her ear, across her cheek and finally deeply inside her persuasive mouth. She made this a repeating pattern – first her hair with its incredible tickling, the softness of her skin, her cheek, then the full swallowing of my prick, so deep that I could hear her sloppy gargle at the back of her throat where I was so sweetly lodged.

Eventually she spread her hair all around me, keeping me inside her mouth, moving up and down lingeringly, her tongue revolving, her fingers gripping the base of my cock, her fingertips smoothing around my balls. Then she stopped, a wickedly sly grin on her face as she looked down at me, wagging my cock as she said, 'Now I'm going to let you give me a nice big fuck.'

That invitation set my cock beating inside her hands till she let go and stood up at the side of the sofa. She turned her back, stretching the panties tight around her buttocks as she bent down. She hooked a thumb and forefinger in the waistband and very seductively slid them down her long legs, stepping out of them carefully, holding them in one hand. Then she pushed them onto my face, rubbing the softness on me, murmuring, 'Feel how wet you've made me.' And I could feel a slithery moistness mixed with the soft silkiness of the material.

'I'm all creamy for you,' she said as she pushed the panties against my mouth. 'Taste me. Smell me.' As she did this, I reached out my hands to fondle the curvaceous roundness of her arse, my fingers trailing down to flutter at her pink lips, caressing her long, squirmy clitoris. Teresa's breath sighed out, her hand holding the panties on my face as she rotated her body around my hands on her. 'Yes, yes. I want you in there. Come on in. I want your hot come splashing on me,' she gasped out huskily.

With that, I stood up. One of her hands snaked between her legs, pulling my cock so that she drew me to her creamy entrance, letting my cock-head roam around all the warmth and wetness, her other hand still holding the panties but now cushioning my balls till she could no longer resist leading my cock onto her quim-lips, the head pushing between slowly, then in, easing in more deeply, more and more deeply till I rested my whole length inside, my balls nestled tight against her creaminess, covered in the silk of her panties.

I stayed still, letting her flexible muscles inside twitch and tease around my cock till she eased away from me to let me slide slowly back. I was almost outside her as she shifted to let my prick play along those lips and clit again. I felt little drops of jism squeeze out and she sensed them; she shuddered and forced herself back onto my cock, starting a steady thrust, followed by a pulling back. I fitted into her rhythm and soon we were engrossed inside those motions, long thrusts, my cock deep, then throbbing right at her opening before she pressed back to take me inside again.

Our movements picked up speed and soon I was thrashing steadily, reaching as far as I could inside, her velvet juiciness covering my cock. She was so wet, I could feel her juices seeping into those panties she had rammed tight under my balls. She began to whimper and moan. I was almost growling as I pushed my cock all the way into that deep space that fluttered moistly around me.

And soon I felt that urge deep at the root of my cock, a gathering that wanted to shoot out though I was trying to hold it in. I pushed hard and fast into Teresa who was wriggling around me, her voice louder now, almost strangled till she must have felt that unstoppable throb beating up the length of my prick.

Her voice broke out, 'Drown me. Come.' And when I heard that, I could no longer hold on. I gave one final deep thrust, then as I slid myself almost out of her, a shower of jism spurted out onto the lips of her quim and onto her clit, Her fingers grasped me, slippery with come. Those syrupy hands began to stroke my cock, an almost unbearable sensation, soft and tingly, squirming, a delightful torture, tormenting me, her fingers insistent though I was yelling out with her exquisite teasing.

Her hands were soaked with my come and her own juices as she stroked my cock, pushing against her slippery lips, brushing my cock-head along the length of her slit, squirming on me, pumping at my prick till finally she pushed back so we flopped onto the sofa, curled together, lying there with gentle touches and soft kisses.

For most of the morning we seemed to have the house to ourselves. Though we wouldn't have Christmas dinner till evening, I expected that Margo would turn up at some point. There was no sign of her, however, till lunchtime. Afterwards I lounged around with both of them. We sat on the long sofa together, me in the middle, our arms round each other, their hands playing all around me so I was in a semi-aroused state, though neither of them went to extremes. It was a soft and sweet time, a little dozy and relaxed until Teresa stifled a yawn and announced that she was going for a snooze. I wondered whether this was a signal for me to go with her but as I shifted to stand up, she shook her head. 'No,' she said. 'You stay here with Margo.' Then she moved to the door. 'I'm sure Margo has some interesting things to talk about ... and show you.' There appeared on Teresa's face that mischievous grin of hers.

I glanced at Margo but her face gave nothing away. Her mouth hovered around a smile and her tongue slipped through her teeth to touch her lips briefly and wetly.

Teresa opened the door, raised her hand in a little

wave. 'See you later,' she said, and I was left alone with Margo. She was looking her usual attractive self. She never went in for elaborate dresses, keeping to straight sheaths, occasionally wearing a full skirt, though her blouses were usually form-fitting.

Margo's somewhat severe style of dressing belied the other side to her character. She was a ferociously passionate woman and part of her mysterious quality was the way she gave the impression she was always on the edge of an extraordinary sensuality even though her outward appearance made her look so strict. She managed to suggest, nevertheless, that she looked forward to revealing her sumptuous body, generally shown off in colourful, exotic lingerie. I always knew there was something enticing under that severity of dress.

This afternoon she was in an emerald blouse, with a deep V that accentuated her figure and full sleeves that suggested the slimness of her arms underneath. Her skirt, pencil slim, was black, short to her knees, with a pair of very high heels. She wore no jewellery but her coppery hair glinted with quick patterns of light, lustrously thick in soft waves falling to her shoulders.

I found it extremely pleasurable sitting with my arm around her, feeling the silky softness of her blouse while her long slender fingers wandering enticingly along my inner thigh. We sank into a very relaxed and warmly sensual mood as she moved closer to me and said, 'Well, Nick, how are you getting along at university?'

I began to tell her about my various escapades and I found myself filling in a lot of details, thinking that it would encourage her along sensual lines. I slouched down into a half-sprawl as Margo's hands moved delicately along my upper thighs. I made no attempt to hide my growing erection and I'm sure she noticed it, though her hands remained resolutely on my thighs. Occasionally she moved a hand to my face, and once one of her slim fingers played delicately along my lips even as I talked.

'I was a little worried about you, Nick. You're such a sensual person. I wondered if you'd be all hot and bothered when you came to stay with us, maybe starved for the kind of... attentions you always got around here.' One hand moved slightly higher on my thigh.

I moved my hand to her knee and let my fingers inch under her skirt, the feel of her stocking enticing me. I felt something soft and lacy there.

'I can see you haven't lost your touch, Nick.'

'You as well.'

She took my hand from her knee, touched her tongue on my fingertips, then drew one finger into her mouth, pulling it out slowly as her tongue licked it. 'You still taste good,' she murmured against my finger which she left against her lips as she spoke. Then she looked down and smiled, her tongue again sloppy along my finger. 'My, my!' she exclaimed, 'Something else looks as if it will be tasty as well.'

Then she stood up and I made an effort to stand up with her but she shook her head. 'Just sit still. Relax. Enjoy,' she said as she started to unfasten the buttons at her wrists, then the buttons down the front of her blouse. She parted the blouse and let it glide from her shoulders. The way she did this was both matter-of-fact and seductive. She did it as if it was a very ordinary, completely natural thing to do and yet there was about her an inviting sensuality. She knew the effect this revelation would have on me. 'We don't need to beat about the bush, do we, Nick?' she whispered, 'but we don't need to rush it either.'

My shaft stiffened more, pointing upwards, pulsing against my trousers. Margo stayed still. She was wearing what I can only describe as a half-bra which pushed her breasts up roundly, her nipples standing out just above the top. Then she placed a hand on each of my shoulders, letting her breasts play across my face, round, then along my mouth, so naturally I took first one, then the other nipple inside, my tongue flickering around.

Her hands slid down from my shoulders, one stopping at my groin, the other deftly unfastening a button at her own waist. Then both her hands latched at her waist, pulling that tight black skirt down, stepping out of it, all in that same matter-of-fact but seductive manner.

She smiled down at me. She was wearing a black half-slip, shiny, with a wide band of lace around the hem and a slit at the front. She pushed one knee forward and hiked the slip high so that it fell away to reveal a good deal of leg. She saw me ogling her and said, 'I see you haven't lost your taste for legs. University education hasn't spoiled you.'

Then she stepped back, reaching out her hand to me. 'Come with me, Nick,' she said. She pulled me up from the sofa so that I was standing close to her. She gave me a lovely wet kiss, her teeth nibbling softly along my lips, then her tongue flickering teasingly just inside my mouth. 'We have something new in the house. Let me show you.'

She kept hold of my hand and led me out of the room and up the stairs. At first I thought Margo would be showing me a new gown or an exotic set of lingerie. Instead we turned into the bathroom, an elegantly lavish affair but changed a little from what I remembered about it.

The big bath stretched along one wall. What was new

was that it was hung with a full curtain, printed in rich colours, with a large picture of nude native girls frolicking, long black hair decorated with large red flowers. It reminded me of a painting by Gauguin.

'Fancy living there with all those luscious girls dancing round you, their lovely tits bouncing up and down. You wouldn't be able to keep your hands to yourself, would you?' she said. 'You'd be walking around all day with just the biggest bone-hard horn you've ever had!' As if to illustrate what she had just said, she grabbed the front of my trousers and gave me an affectionate squeeze. 'And you're not doing so bad right now!' she added.

Then she reached to draw the curtain back. The tiles along the length of the bath were imprinted with a copy of a Japanese erotic picture: a lady on a swing, kimono open revealing a richly pink quim with neatly trimmed pubic hair, the swing obviously poised to move towards a man half reclining, his kimono also open and his enormous member sticking up, a full thick shaft waiting for the woman on the swing to float onto it.

Margo's hand again reached for my cock. 'I don't have a swing but I'm looking forward to swinging onto this,' she said throatily, giving my hard prick a tweak. 'Isn't that a nice thing to look at as you lie back in the bath, soaping yourself? I love to get my tits all slippery and sleek, looking at that giant cock.' Then she pointed at a pipe with a large spray on the end protruding from the wall. 'And it's good to stand in the shower while you look at this.'

For me showers were always associated with smelly changing rooms at school, cold water we had to stand under after gym, raucous dirty jokes and wet slapping on arses, yelps and anger, a very miserable experience. Not many houses had showers at that time and Margo's was entirely different from the ones I had known.

While I'd been gazing at these scenes, Margo had placed herself behind me. I could feel her nipples hard on my back through my shirt. Her arms had looped around, the fingers of one hand delving inside my trousers, nudging along my pubic hair, grasping the thickness of my cock at the root, her other hand busy at my belt buckle, then my trouser buttons. Her chin pushed onto my shoulder and her breath felt warm on my ear as she murmured, 'I think I need to give you a lovely hot shower, wash this big beauty, make it all soapy and slippery. We'll clean ourselves up! And anyhow, 'she added, 'this fat prong is already up,' freeing my prick from my underpants and holding it in both her hands.

She turned me around to get me out of my shirt. There was a lot of tantalising by-play as her hands kept dropping to touch and fondle. Sometimes she thrust against me so the tip of my cock prodded at her half-slip. Once she managed to draw my shaft inside her legs, pushing the silky slip there and letting my cock ride its length against it. She cooed, 'Oooh! You're so bone-hard. Just wait till I smother him in soft soap! Like this.' She let her fingertips play a maddeningly gentle flicker along the length, pulling my foreskin far back and rubbing her palm delicately across the slit, then squeezing my cock. 'You're such a big-headed boy. And I love to pull you out, roll back all that skin so I can feel your hot hard head.' And then her fingers began to pull my skin away from the head as if she'd roll it down the whole length. I thought my cock would emerge all raw and shiny and red, completely uncovered. 'I love uncircumcised cock,' Margo said. 'It feels so ... tempting, so ... vulnerable. It needs to be treated gently. She wrapped her slender fingers round me, sliding them slowly along the whole length.

'Just think of all those jungle girls waiting for you to rub themselves all over your naked body,' she whispered. Just like I'm waiting for you.' She squashed herself against me, her words coming through a sloppy licking and sucking at my ear. Somehow her hands were still folded round my cock. 'Now I'm going to pull you right down.' And incredibly it did feel as if she was peeling me, my cock firm and solid in her hands. 'Such a sweet banana,' she mumbled as she slid down. 'I need a large bite.'

Then she was rubbing my prick against her neck, trapping it below her jaw. Then she placed the head in her ear, sweeping her hair against it, moving it to let her eyelashes flicker along the length, stopping to look straight at it. 'I'm looking you straight in the eye,' she said. 'I wonder if you've got lots of those nice pearly drops all ready to spill out.'

Her mouth closed towards my cock almost as if the warm words were pouring over it. She kissed it all over, still sliding it along her cheeks, her neck, her hair, her throat till she finally opened her mouth wide and drew me in. It was exquisitely wet and warm. But then she let me slide out, holding my wet cock down against her breasts, pushing me down further, easing me under her slip between her legs, touching her moist quim gently, then down her thighs, along the grainy feel of her stockings till she let me rest, my cock along her thigh, the head just touching the moist lips.

'Such a firm ripe fruit,' she whispered. 'I'm looking forward to dipping it in my cream.' Then she slid it out, leading it across her stomach with one hand while the other unhooked her bra so my straining prick worked its way again onto her now-bare breasts, Margo pushing that silky plump skin against me. As I pushed up, her tongue snaked out to briefly touch the slit of my cock with a little wet slither. 'Very tasty,' she murmured. 'This is going to be a gourmet feast.' Her words were almost obliterated as she sucked me deeply into her mouth.

Margo had always surprised me with the way she could make me feel so extraordinarily randy. Even though I'd had a long bout of exquisite sex with Teresa that morning, here was Margo already leading me into an unbridled sexuality, careful, gentle, yet in charge, making me want her to lead me on, immersing myself in her exhilarating caresses.

Her mouth seemed to be full of me so it made my cock feel very big. And yet she was able to work with her tongue so that my prick was slathered in moisture. She let it slip out and down onto her breasts, holding me to press my cock-head first against one nipple, then the other, switching back and forth till she was very slippery all along her breasts. Finally she pressed my cock in between her breasts and slowly moved up and down.

After a few minutes of this sucking and stroking, she looked up at me, a smile hovering at her lips. 'I think it's time for us to get really wet,' she breathed. 'I want to give you a nice, soapy rub-down. Why don't you turn the shower on for us?'

I leaned through the curtain, bending to examine the taps and controls. I felt Margo's hands on me again, stroking my buttocks, moving her fingers along the crack of my arse. Her hand did a lazy dance up and down, sliding further down till two fingers probed in to stroke and pinch my balls.

The shower came on with a sudden surge. With Margo's hands performing their magic touches, that quick gush of water, the steady warmth streaming out, I was reminded of the way come spurts out in hot splashes. That set my cock throbbing and pulsing in Margo's hands almost as if she was coaxing jism out.

I was about to step into the shower when I felt Margo's hands gripping my length very hard. 'Wait! I'm not quite ready for the shower yet. Look.' And she turned me around as she then turned her back to me. Her hands began to lift her half-slip slowly up her legs. This gave me a full view of her long, elegant legs in sheer black stockings. She raised the hem until it was nearly at her waist. She was wearing no panties and so the firm round globes of her arse looked enticing in their smooth, slightly pink nakedness. Slowly she bent down, her legs slightly open so I could glimpse a little of her soft glistening lips.

If her previous undressing had been matter-of-fact, this was provocatively seductive. I was only too ready to prod my cock between those appealing buttocks but somehow her face, looking up at me from between her legs, suggested I should just stay watching.

Then gradually she let the satin-shiny slip fall back over her arse, though she stayed bending down. Her two hands stretched it tight so that it shaped those two delicious globes under it. 'Not bad for a thirty-eight-year-old lady, eh, Nick?'

'Any twenty-year-old would be happy to show a gorgeous arse like that.'

She looked round at me, winked lasciviously and murmured, 'I must say, you're good at compliments.'

'I mean it.'

'Well, what you've got there,' and she was staring directly at my cock, 'any man would be proud of.' That remark seemed an invitation of sorts. I pushed my stand where the fabric of her slip was a little loose and began to slide in and out in a gentle fucking motion. She hissed and gasped quietly when she felt that urgent prodding.

After a while she hooked her fingers inside the waist of her slip and, still bending down, teasingly drew it across her arse, revealing again that shapely roundness. She drew it down to her ankles, lifting first one high-heeled foot out, then the other. She straightened up, turned and threw the soft silky slip to land on my cock, though it slid away and finished on the floor.

'I'm glad it dropped off. Something that strong and hard shouldn't be covered up.' She smiled wickedly. 'Except by these.' She raised her hands. 'Or this.' She raised a hand to her mouth and sucked in one of her fingers.

'Step in the shower, Nick,' and I did. It was good to feel the jets of hot water hitting me. I stood facing the showerhead letting the water pound me. Margo climbed behind me, closing the curtain around us. Then she began a methodical soaping of my shoulders and back, her hands slippery with soap. She was particularly adept at letting her fingers stray down to my arse, lingering over my buttocks, inching into the crack, making it feel very greasy with soap.

When I was thoroughly covered in lather, she pressed against me, moving her body on my back. I could feel her hard nipples and the soft flesh of her breasts squashed on me. Her hands came round my waist to rest with a small bar of soap under my balls, her fingers pulling at my cock. Soon her hands were deliciously soapy and she lathered my cock and balls. It was an extraordinary sensation, my stiffness squirming inside her slippery hands, her fingers reaching under my balls.

We stayed like that for some time, her fingers working

at me, probing, prodding, circling, one hand urging my shaft to thicker stiffness, the skin of soap on it, a delectable touch, a finger skidding slowly around the head, now bulging even more fatly.

Then she turned me around. 'Now it's my turn,' she said, reaching to give me the soap she had placed in the holder on the wall. 'Make me soapy ... and sexy,' she crooned, letting her wet stomach rub against the end of my cock. 'All over. Make me sexy all over.'

So I started to soap her, a new sensation for me, feeling those plump breasts slide so effortlessly into my hands. I pinched the soap with my fingers and tweaked and stroked her nipples. They jutted out more, big, nubbly stands that I tickled with my palms as I soaped the full brown aureoles. Then I let my hand drop down to weigh them underneath, feeling their warm plumpness filling my palms. She gripped my prick, making it slide its length up her stomach, soaping herself there, my stand moving against her, her hands tight on it, fingering my balls as well.

'Doesn't it make you feel juicy?' she asked. 'It's so ... slippery. Slippery as a cunt sliding round a big long knob. All creamy and warm. Like come. It's like taking a shower in come.' She squeezed my cock. 'Not quite as good as the real thing. Those big splashes of wet cream squirting out. Doesn't it make you feel as if you want to let fly, watch all that cream come flying out?'

'Yes,' I groaned, stooping down to soap her thighs, my fingers occasionally flicking at her quim. She parted her legs to help me in my soaping, then pulled my prick between those silky thighs. We both let out a sigh as I probed deeply, the head of my cock forcing a way through so the head rested just at the edge of her arse-crack. I reached round and soaped along the crack, pushing my long dick along that slippery crack. Her hands were massaging my arse, holding me in place there, her mouth on mine, her tongue slipping inside my mouth, keeping time with my shaft's stroke along her arse-crack. She was also wriggling so that her soapy breasts squashed against my chest. The streams of water needled onto my back and I felt as if I was wrapped inside a whole thin film of skin, stroked and doused inside softness.

Occasionally Margo drew back so that she manoeuvred herself to let my cock-head sink just inside the lips of her cunt, as she slowly gyrated, promising to let it prod further in but never letting it go too deep. I certainly felt I wanted to thrust way inside but Margo was holding me in place, keeping control though she was squirming and squiggling and licking and sucking and gasping and snorting, her hands going faster all over me.

She reached behind me to turn the shower off, stepped out and took my hand, holding my cock with the other. 'I don't want you to shrink.' she said mischievously. She walked us across to the washbasin, set in a long counter with a large mirror running the length of the wall behind it. She dropped my hand, patted my cock and let go. Then, with her back to the mirror she put her hands on the counter to lever herself up to sit on the edge of the counter. She looked very voluptuous perching there, her skin slightly flushed from the water, beads of it sitting all over her body. Somehow she had kept her hair dry and now its coppery glints flashed as she shook it a little. She stretched out her hand to me and took hold of my shoulder. Her other hand pointed directly to my long fat cock.

'I want that in here,' she said, as then her hand pointed between her legs. 'Put that fine rod of iron inside me.'

I shuffled to her and she pressed my cock onto her as she moved to the very edge of the counter. She opened her legs and I gradually was able to slide into her. 'Drive him right in,' she urged. 'More. Stick it right inside.'

I found it a little awkward as the counter was low so I had to bend my knees. When Margo sensed this, she leaned back and, propped on her elbows, lifted herself off the counter. She pushed hard onto me and my whole length moved easily inside. She began to rotate herself, her slickly wet inner muscles holding me in place and yet I felt as if I could push further and further in.

Margo's head was flung back, her hair cascading down, a few guttural gasps breaking from her as I kept pressing my dick into her deeply. I could see myself in the mirror, rammed inside her. The sight of her naked body with head flung back, her hair so shiny and thick, made me even more horny, even more ready to fill her with my ever-fattening prick, especially as she suddenly yelled out, 'That's it. You've hit the spot! Fuck me!'

That plea to probe home did something to me. I had always considered Margo a very experienced woman, her appetite perhaps a little jaded in sexual matters. But here she was, seemingly letting go, asking to be fucked hard, thoroughly involved with me, a mere youngster – though I had learned a good deal over the last few months, occasionally in the hands of Margo herself. That yell drove me on to a faster pace, thrusting steadily in and out of her until we were both highly charged.

She was wriggling and pushing hard onto me, still up on her elbows. She was pressing so hard it was as if she wanted me to ram all of me inside her, not only my fat prick but my balls as well. Her quim was extraordinarily juicy. She was panting, she was shaking her head from side to side, she was squealing with delight. I was grunting with the intense pleasure that was riding on the fierce prodding of my cock inside Margo. Both of us together filled the bathroom with echoing cries and shouts, hoarsely yelling, 'Fuck! Fuck!'

But this couldn't last long though both of us would have liked to keep going. We were beginning to recognize the physical strain we were under. Margo was taking most of the weight on her elbows, her legs pointing up at the ceiling, resting on my shoulders. I was gripping the edge of the counter and that edge was digging painfully at my thighs as I bashed against it with my steady motions into Margo. My legs were starting to shake and I felt that I would soon collapse, though my cock was so hard it almost felt that it could hold us in place on its own.

Suddenly Margo eased herself down, her arse now on the counter, slowing me down so that my cock slipped back, a delectable slide out of her juiciness to lie just at the first soft entrance. 'Much as I liked that, Nick,' Margo whispered, 'I had to stop. Otherwise, I'd have been a candidate for the hospital and the services of an orthopedic surgeon!'

She smiled one of her intensely provocative smiles. 'But don't worry. I have some other plans for us.' She shrugged and my cock flopped out of her, still rigid against her. She patted it gently. 'More to come. And I do mean "come"!' With that she jumped down from the counter and said, 'Besides, it's time for us to dress for dinner.'

When she led me into her bedroom, I immediately looked across to the bed where Margo had first introduced me to deliciously exciting sexual pleasures. I half expected it would look inviting with silks and satins but all I could see laid out on it was an evening shirt, jacket and trousers and next to it what looked like a severe but elaborately fashioned gown. It had a long flowing skirt in black that resembled a pair of wide, bell-bottomed trousers though there was a long slit up one side. The top was white, plain but fully shaped, it reminded me of one of those shirts with billowy sleeves that fencing buccaneers wore in films. In all, it was very much the style of dress that Margo favoured.

'I thought we'd dress up a little for Christmas,' Margo said. She was behind me, her hand on my back at the waist and she steered me to the bed. 'I'm sure you'll look very ... attractive in the outfit I've chosen for you.' And she gave me a gentle push to the edge of the bed.

I reached out to pick up the evening shirt but Margo pulled my arm back. 'No,' she said quietly but firmly though a tone of mystery came through. 'The other.'

At first I didn't understand till she pushed me over to face the gown-like garment. 'I think I got the size right,' she almost chortled, a fetching grin on her face. 'I hope you don't mind. I just thought it might be ... interesting for you to experience some things ... from the other side as it were. You won't regret it. You'll look so attractive, I won't be able to keep my hands off you. I know how you men are when you get it into your head to seduce a lady.' She smiled ravishingly at me. 'Go on, Nick. No one else will see. It's just between you and me.' One of her hands strayed down to my cock, still in a state of semi-arousal.

She then moved over to pick up the shirt. 'I'll wear this. I think I'll look pretty suave. I'll bet you'll be ready to succumb when you see me all togged up like this.'

So Margo wanted to switch roles. She had evidently planned this very carefully for I discovered that, when I dressed myself in that gown-garment, I didn't feel too embarrassed. It still retained a kind of masculinity – it was not fussy and frilly and the skirt was cut severely, almost like a pair of trousers. Certainly the smooth feel of the material against my skin was lusciously soft so when it fell onto my cock, it responded by throbbing and swelling thickly.

I watched Margo put on the evening suit and it was obvious she must have had it especially designed, for it fitted snugly at her waist, the jacket trimmed to her shape, the cut emphasizing the firm outline of her breasts.

So, though we were now playing switched roles, Margo had cleverly manipulated the proceedings so that we still maintained something of our real selves. It was a game but not one that was designed to cause any embarrassment. I was certainly ready for action – my prick was making a tent at the front of the gown I was wearing and Margo made me stiffen more as she glanced down at me with an expression of open lust on her face. She licked her lips and her mouth then gleamed even more redly wet.

'Nick, you look ... exceptional. You make me feel very hot.' She spread her hands out in front of her. I was still a little fidgety simply because I was not sure just what was expected of me – not that I needed to be bothered by that. Margo knew exactly how to proceed.

She stepped over to me quite briskly, took my hand and led me to a small ottoman. 'Let's sit down here, shall we? We can relax together. Don't worry. Margo will make you feel quite comfortable, even ... loose.' She sat next to me, put an arm round my shoulders and gave me a penetratingly deep kiss, her tongue and teeth and lips meshed in an all-encompassing soft wetness, holding me close, one hand gliding all over my body, skating across my thighs, moving with a very brief pat on my cock, up to the top where she tweaked my nipples through the material. 'Isn't that what you young men do first of all, just to test the waters, just a touch on the titties?' Then her mouth was pulling my tongue in and out of her mouth as if she was sucking a tingly wet small cock. Her hands were stroking the satin fabric against me and her arm was so placed that her elbow was digging in gently where my prick was standing stiffly up.

'Such a naughty young man you are,' she whispered, her elbow circling against my stand. 'Can't control yourself. But it feels like a lovely big knob.' Her fingers were unfastening the buttons on the top and soon she had folded back the dress to expose my bare chest. She began a delicate stroking and pinching of my nipples, licking her fingers so that her fingers slid smoothly on me.

'Isn't this the next step you men take? Get your hands inside and fondle our tits. That's supposed to get us going, right, playing with our nips like this?' And her elbow was getting more insistent in its nudging against my prick. 'Is this getting you going?'

I decided to return the compliment. My hands moved to her shirt and I fondled her beautifully plump breasts and eventually I fiddled with her buttons so I could push my hands inside. Soon I'd uncovered her breasts and my hands stroked across her warm flesh there.

'The next step's to see what you have under your skirt,' she whispered. 'Are you ready? Are you hot enough now? You're not going to push my hand away, are you?' But her hand was already exploring under the skirt, brushing on my thighs as her hand moved through the slit of the skirt. 'I'll bet you're ready. Fancy wearing something like this, a wide slit so I can easily get my hand inside. It looks as if you really wanted me to do this.' And her hand was creeping higher and higher along my thigh till she touched my cock.

'By this time, if you've let a man go this far, you'll be sopping wet.' Her fingers reached to the slit of my dick. 'There! You're not wet yet. But I bet you soon will be if you let yourself go.' And her hand began a slow massage along the length. 'You might be surprised what you'll find under my trousers. Once we get here, a lady usually wants to get her hands inside the man's trousers.'

While she continued stroking, I let my fingers rest at her fly. I discovered she didn't have buttons there. 'A zipper makes it so much easier,' she murmured as I slid it down, probing my fingers inside to stretch them across her hair, one finger prodding down to her slit. It was really juicy.

'Look what you've done to me. It makes me want this beauty,' and she squeezed me hard as she said this. Then she leaned down, parted the skirt so my cock emerged in its long fatness. She placed a sweetly moist kiss on the slit and my cock twitched convulsively.

'There, there! Relax,' and I felt her breath hot around my cock-head. One of my fingers was now poking slowly in and out of Margo's quim and my other hand was still inside her shirt so that I could feel how hard her big nipples were.

'My! Look what a mess I've made!' I looked down at my engorged penis standing up hard and I saw a lipstick smear across the cock-head. Of course as soon as I saw that, my cock began a mad twitching. 'It's getting so excited,' Margo breathed over me. 'I'll have to calm it down and lick it clean.'

Her tongue then became an exquisite tool of pleasure, licking first the head, then the whole length, then letting warm, sticky saliva dribble onto it, letting it run down till her tongue scooped it up. I was fascinated as I watched those thin wet strands falling from her mouth and her hand tickling that shiny slipperiness round and round my cock. My stiff stand seemed to ease itself up through her hands and as the head poked out from them, her mouth took it in.

I was getting more and more aroused by these delicious attentions, so much so that my hand was now working more busily at Margo's moist centre. Her juices were flowing freely and my cock seemed to be thrusting up higher and bigger, sinking more deeply into her mouth. As I inserted two fingers slowly into Margo's quim, they slid easily inside in the warm and wet there. And as Margo felt my penetration, her mouth opened even more widely. She drew my prick deep into her mouth, a strangled cry, muffled by my hard cock, breaking from her throat.

Things were now getting feverish. My fingers were plunging steadily into her juicy valley, as warmly slick as my cock in her mouth. I felt I wanted to guzzle at her juices, lick her, flick my tongue to tease her clit but I was frustrated because she was too busily engaged in driving me crazy with her mouth. I had to be content with just pushing my fingers in and out of that sleek opening, my other hand pushing her trousers down, then thrusting my hand under her to fondle her arse.

'It's lovely to get my trousers off so you can touch me all over,' she mumbled, her words falling onto my cock. I was groaning with pleasure and Margo then let rip with muffled cries. She sounded greedy as if she wanted her mouth rammed full, as she guzzled away, making great slurping noises.

She then pulled away, turned her back to me, bending down so I got a full view of her full curvaceous arse which she thrust close to my face. I slopped my tongue along her arse-crack, and poked out my finger there to search out her arsehole. I prodded slowly in – it was tight and clenched around my finger as I pushed further in. She sighed and wriggled round my finger. I looped my other hand round to slide it onto her quim before pressing it inside. She yelped with delight as she felt my two fingers penetrating deeply as if they wanted to touch fingertips inside her.

Soon Margo lowered herself till she was on her knees. I crouched down so that she could guide my cock onto her. First she wanted it fully along the crack of her arse. Her fingers played delicately with my cock, letting it nudge at the rim of her hole, the head nestling there. I could feel its tightness begin to grip the head as Margo pushed back. Her hand snaked round to grab me, pull me down between her legs to lead my cock against her clit first, then slowly push it inside the lips. She did this at an excruciatingly slow pace and I felt the smooth oil of her slit take in my cock-head. Then Margo was pushing so that I slid slowly in, further and further in as she exercised the muscles inside against the hard stand. My cock felt harder and bigger as those muscles twitched and flirted with my whole length. The skin had rolled right back and my head was fully exposed, tingling with the delight of her moist insides.

I was stroking her clit at the same time. Margo kept moving herself so that my fingers on her clit gave her the maximum amount of pleasure while at the same time her motions were doing sleekly wet rolls around my prick. She controlled the sliding in and out of my shaft, easing it along her honey-canal, letting my cock rest with just the tip of the head held at her lips before she moved back to take it in again.

She began to quicken the pace, riding me though, with me banging at her from the rear, it was more like me riding her. So we rode together. She so moved that her cunt felt immeasurably long and that, of course, made my cock feel immeasurably large.

Soon I was ready to spurt out a flood of jism but Margo's experience came into play, stopping me at the very edge of coming, just a few drops dribbling out. She moved me so that my little jets of come fell onto the inside of her lips. It was all wet and oily and juicy and I was excited; it made me feel desperate to release a big deluge of come though Margo kept me still before she plunged back on me. But still she held me off from coming.

Then she unleashed a pounding ride, thrashing against me, sliding me out, rubbing her clit hard down the whole length of my prick, moving to let it stab inside again, deep down, then up, down and up and I fitted my thrusts to the jabs backwards she was pushing onto me. She kept on riding, my prick was pulsing and throbbing and I could no longer hold back. She yelled loud and I poured out inside her. She kept moving so come seemed to be flying inside her, then outside, on her lips and her clit, over my finger still stroking her clit, then plunging in as she rammed her arse against me. We seemed enveloped in a whole wash of stickiness and we were making wet, slapping noises as we banged against each other, riding to our explosive climax, our voices piercingly high and husky at the same time. I was sure everyone in the house must have heard us, must have known we were riding our way to a mutual orgasm.

A little later I was unutterably relaxed with Margo nestling close to me, scattering kisses all over my body, letting her fingers caress the sticky skin of my cock which was covered in a wash of our mixed juices.

We both eventually dozed off till Margo shook me softly. 'Nick, you were a lovely fuck. I'm glad you let me show you how it feels when a man is getting ready for you. But we did it right, didn't we? We remembered how we do it together. It was lovely.' She gave me a little peck. 'I think we'd both better have another shower though it's a pity to wash off all this sweet juice.' Her fingers slid along my half-limp cock, then she licked them. 'I'll remember this taste when we're eating Christmas dinner. So off you go. Into the shower with you. On your own this time. Then come down for dinner. About two hours from now. You'll have time for a rest. Recharge yourself. Then you'll get your appetite back. You might find some delicious treats at dinner.'

And the food at dinner was delicious – roast ham and turkey and a Christmas pudding flamed with brandy. While the meal itself was luxurious, I was surprised by the appearance of the women when they came to dinner. Both Margo and Teresa, as well as the blonde maid, Shirley, who had joined us for dinner, all arrived in the dining room dressed in the same way.

They all wore plainly simple dresses with severe lines, belted tightly at the waist to show off their slimness. But that was really the only concession to sexiness. Of course they were all good-looking women so any frock looked good on them but what they were wearing didn't seem particularly festive. If anything, it made them look rather stiff although all three of them usually moved in a lithe manner. These were straight dresses, Margo's in stripes of white on pale green, Teresa in plain yellow and Shirley in a muted red. And the design of all three frocks was the same. This was very surprising, for I always thought women detested being seen in a frock that another woman was wearing.

The frocks were smoothly fitted with a small V neck and white collar, the only concession to decoration. They were fastened by a row of white buttons down the front and each had a thin white belt at the waist.

We enjoyed ourselves eating our meal, the conversation pleasant enough with a few suggestive anecdotes and references to what we had been up to through the day. But every now and again I caught the three women suddenly smirking at each other, occasionally suppressing giggles, exchanging little winks. This didn't happen very often and I didn't really make much of it.

After long and leisurely coffees, and liqueurs, all of us lounging across the sofa and easy chairs, we were feeling very relaxed. I was enjoying looking at the three of them because they were careless about how they sprawled so they were all showing a good deal of leg. I was comfortably semi-aroused but, after my sessions with Teresa and Margo, I can't say I was especially randy. Of course, I was sure I'd be up to it if anything developed but the way things were going that didn't look likely, beyond this pleasantly smoochy atmosphere.

After a while Margo roused herself, stood and stretched. She did her patented slinky walk over to where I was snuggled up on the sofa next to Teresa, with Shirley nuzzled beside me.

Margo perched on the edge of the cushion next to me, ruffled my hair affectionately and said, 'How's it feel to be snuggled up with three ladies?' She smiled and smoothed the skirt of her dress so that it rode up high on her thigh.

'Did you notice how we're all dressed up for Christmas?' she continued. 'We wore these frocks especially for you, Nick. They're brand new. Gerry got them for us. Wanted us to try them out, see if they'll be something he'll want to deal in. D'you like them?'

By this time both Teresa and Shirley were stirring, Teresa's hand travelling around in fetching strokes, Shirley's tongue wriggling around my ear, Margo playing her hand along my thigh. They were giving me the idea they had some friskiness in hand but I couldn't figure out just what it was going to be and what it had to do with these dresses – perhaps they were going to give me a three-way strip, perhaps they'd want me to undo all those buttons on each dress so that they could step out of them.

Margo took my hand and placed it high up on her thigh but on top of her skirt. 'Feel this material,' so I stroked her. It felt stiff but it also felt a little flimsy. 'What d'you think it is?'

'Cotton?' I ventured.

Margo shook her head. I was still stroking Margo and my hand had got under her dress so I was flickering fingers across to touch both thighs. Shirley took my other hand. 'See how it feels on me,' she said and placed my hand so that it cupped her breast. 'We're all wearing the same,' she said, 'though what we've got underneath might feel a little different.' She moved to make my hand feel comfortable on her. The material was stiff on Shirley as well but in a strange way it made the soft weight of her breast under my fingers sort of appealing. And Shirley seemed to think so, for she sighed contentedly, her tongue still in my ear, licking wetly there, sliding along my cheek to place a moist kiss on my lips, then up to kiss an eye.

'Hey, let me in on this,' Teresa said and her hand moved to the inside of my thigh, one or two fingers nudging very close to my balls.

'So what kind of material is it?' Shirley asked.

'Linen?' I tried.

'Oh, tell him, Margo.' Teresa sounded a little peevish. She sounded as if she wanted to get on with whatever they had planned.

'It's a very new idea,' Margo explained. 'They're very cheap so you can wear 'em a few times, then just throw them away. Saves on laundry. And it'll look as if you're always in a new dress. Course, there'll be lots of different designs in time. Just think. You won't mind if you spill red wine on them because you can just throw them away.' She grinned. 'I bet men will like them. They'll be able to come all over them and nobody will know. Not that I've ever minded come spilled on me.' She smiled. 'It's nice watching that cream shooting out all over you.'

Teresa leaned close to me and said, 'Makes it easy to unwrap – you unwrapped me this morning. Well, this material's very easy to unwrap. You can just tear it off. Believe it or not, it's paper. Tough enough to stand up to some wear but it tears easily ... if you want it to.' She stood up in front of me close and lifted the hem. 'Go ahead. Try it.'

I grasped the hem and gave a sharp rip – and it tore easily. 'Oh, you can do better than that.' Teresa hauled me to my feet and took my hands to place them at her waist. 'See what you can do now.'

I must confess it was a very satisfying feeling as I bunched the material in my hands and pulled hard. The dress came away in my hands, opening, the buttons popping off. Teresa was standing there wearing nothing else but garter belt and stockings.

The other two women clapped and then Shirley stood up. 'It's my turn. You let him unwrap his present this morning, Teresa. And as for you, Margo, goodness only knows what you've been up to this afternoon. It sounded as if you two were murdering each other!'

'I can assure you it was a much more pleasant experience than murder,' Margo said.

'Well, anyhow,' Shirley went on. 'How about ripping me up, Nick?'

It was an invitation I couldn't refuse. I gripped Shirley's dress by the lapels and, after some resistance from the fabric, it suddenly gave way. There was a rustling, tearing noise as I pulled down, the buttons rattled open and Shirley was also revealed. She wasn't even wearing stockings, completely nude, the dress hanging limply down.

After that it developed into a kind of free-for-all. They raised their voices, squabbling in a joking way, each one demanding to be ripped apart, pushing each other out of the way, trying to put my hands on them to tear their clothing off them. Margo wanted to be first as I hadn't yet touched her but soon they were almost brawling and I was in the middle of them.

Shreds came away in my hands and soon the three women were in tatters. Then it was their turn to try and get me out of my clothes. It soon became scrappy, their hands all over me, knocked out of the way by other hands. Being fought over in this way greatly aroused me. Often their hands grabbed at my cock as I was tearing their dresses.

We were soon rolling around the floor, mouths slavering over each other, breasts flopping onto me, my hands ripping, then stroking. I was soon naked and I was wrestled around, hands and mouths all over me, sucking my cock, stroking, licking. I was feeling breasts, I was suddenly pulled to put my hands in quims, two at a time. My face was rubbed up against nipples I could suck on, I felt little bites on every part of my body. I was smothered by female flesh in a mad tumble, with squeals of delight, moans in sexy tones. I had no idea whose deliciously moist quim was smearing its juices across my face while another wet cunt slid itself onto my fingers.

My cock was throbbing, banging at breasts and thighs, grabbed and wanked before a mouth closed on it. We rolled around like this for a long time, all involved in the game, deliriously sexy until I could sense nothing but a flood of jism coming up the length of my cock. As it began to squirt out, the women went wilder, each one trying to catch the come, wanting to bathe their breasts, pushing a juicy cunt onto it, pulled off while another face came down on my cock as it pumped out this sticky cream.

We finished up in a heap on the floor, all giggling and laughing, still holding each other, almost stuck together with sweat and come and keeping ourselves warm in spite of the layer of jism starting to get cold.

We indulged in a little further tussling into the late evening. Margo was the first to leave. 'We older ladies need our beauty sleep, especially after a few rounds like that. And I'm off to see Gerry tomorrow. I'm sure these two youngsters will keep you pinned to the mat for the rest of the week, Nick. Goodnight.'

And those two did take care of me the rest of the week. That Christmas night went on into a series of gentle embracings, some slow fucking, my cock shared by two quims in turn. Shirley was very much a woman who loved her breasts to be stroked. At one point she lay me down flat and rubbed her breasts all over me. I saw Teresa looking down at us as Shirley took my cock finally, placed it firmly between her breasts and rocked me to a climax there. Teresa joined us on the floor and she moved Shirley to one side so she could straddle me, rubbing her quim, very juicy, from my stomach up, reaching my mouth to let me lick her as I felt Shirley's mouth close on my cock.

We were all pretty exhausted by the end of the evening and I went off to bed with Teresa. Nothing much happened that night. We slept deeply till we awoke late on Boxing day. Then Teresa took it upon herself to continue and expand the delights I'd experienced through Christmas Day.

In fact, in the days up to New Year's Eve Teresa and Shirley gave themselves up to a whole range of delectable encounters with me, singly and doubly. My holiday turned into a gloriously long sexual adventure and I was so pleasurably satiated that, by the time it came to go to Gerry's New Year's Eve party, it was all I could do to summon up my energy to go.

But go I did. Teresa introduced me to two other delightfully nubile ladies who managed to stretch my pleasure even further, until Teresa took me over for the whole of New Year's Day. You could say my holiday started at a ripping pace and so it carried on.

7. Out Of The Blue

I was almost glad to get back to university after the Christmas vacation; my senses had been so thoroughly satiated that it was quite a relief to buckle down to my studies again.

But I did still keep seeing Barbara regularly and she kept me in sexual trim. Ron was very envious of me in that regard, though he never let it get in the way of our friendship. In fact, he was so friendly that he insisted I should have the occasional use of his car. 'Sometimes you might need a change from Barbara. It impresses the hell out of women if you can take 'em around in a car. And the back seat's roomy enough for anything you might want to get up to.'

So I took driving lessons from him. Driving a car suited my purposes as well, beyond borrowing it for a few dates. A few weeks into the term Gerry sent word that he'd like me to do the odd delivery for him because he'd heard from Barbara that I could now get my hands on a car. He promised to provide extra petrol coupons and he knew I could probably use some cash.

I made an arrangement with Ron to take his car for some deliveries and in exchange I gave him the petrol coupons Gerry sent. Ron was generous in letting me use his car, often thrusting it on me, especially when I took the occasional woman student out. 'I tell you, Nick, you'll smell the sex as soon as you pick 'em up.'

But the car didn't work that well for Ron himself. He was always complaining about the women he took out. Whenever he went out on a date, I'd question him about him how it went. 'Did you get it in?' I'd ask.

His usual answer was a shake of his head. Once he said a little wistfully, 'You're a lucky dog, Bancroft, getting it in with Barbara whenever you feel like it. I wish I could find someone like that.' But he kept on trying.

As I kept on trying with Lorna. She became quite a project for me and I wasn't certain why. Barbara was certainly keeping me happy and perhaps I should have been satisfied with that. But, somehow, the enigmatic beauty of Lorna intrigued me. I wanted to see how she'd look and behave if we ever got into the throes of sexual passion.

I followed up on Gerry's idea of trying to find out whether Milton was involved in any operations that might interfere with the connections Gerry had in Manchester. And when I went to see Milton, I always used that as an excuse to go and see Lorna.

I pretended to Milton that I was looking for a place to live and talked to him three times about the organisation of Paradise Lost. He didn't say much beyond what I already knew from Barbara and Lorna, though once or twice he vaguely muttered something about the items that appeared on the 'bargaining board', as he called it. This was the board the residents used to list any possessions they no longer needed and were prepared to exchange.

'Some of that stuff is very ... rare,' he said with a

smirk on his face. 'You never know what you might get if you offered to take it off their hands. One or two bints here are only too happy to make interesting deals.' He was whispering conspiratorially as he continued. 'A bit of alright for a likely lad like you if you moved in here. Though I see you hanging about with a lovely bit of fluff in Number Three.'

I wasn't clear what he was getting at – was he running some kind of call-girl establishment, even a brothel, under the cover of renting out his houses? Was he making money out of the residents, especially the young women – I'd seen two or three when I visited Lorna. And even more mysterious, did he rent his houses out to women and then 'recruit' them for his operation? Did he blackmail them in some way? That made me wonder if at some point he would make a move on Lorna.

Once he told me that he might be able to provide certain items that were not listed on the board. He'd sell them to me and then I could advertise them on the board. 'You just don't know what might happen. I mean, you students don't have much ready cash. I can put you in the way of some good deals.' He leaned towards me confidentially. 'It must be pretty difficult for you to take a lady out for a treat and that's a pity. But it's easy for you to earn enough to treat a lady well. Who knows what you might get in return, eh?' He sniggered. 'I happen to know there's a few ladies here who find it difficult to make ends meet. I'm sure we could come to some ... arrangement.'

He was sounding more and more like some shady operator and I began to get an inkling of what Gerry suspected, the kind of thing he'd been relying on Lorna to find out. I didn't know how much she knew and, if she'd begun to ferret something out, I felt she might get herself in trouble with Milton.

He always acted charmingly with me in his own smarmy way but he never got down to specifics. His secretive nature came across as being untrustworthy, close-mouthed, always dropping hints but never revealing anything much. In spite of his charm, I got the impression that he was a nasty, even slimy character.

I mentioned this to Lorna one evening after I had dropped in to see her on one of my visits to Milton. These occasional visits were always delightful. I felt I was getting along famously with her. She was utterly charming and gracious, putting me completely at ease. Yet the very way she acted prevented me, in its own way, from attempting anything intimate with her, even though I was desperate to try.

While she was friendly with me, there remained a slight sense of aloofness, as if she didn't want to be disturbed, let alone frazzled, into disarray by anything remotely connected to sexual matters. And of course this sense of her being a little remote, almost untouchable, had the paradoxical effect of making me want to involve myself with her all the more, perhaps try to attempt something so that she might let herself go.

But she remained coolly elegant, serving me delicious, exotic teas or even single malt whisky, a drink I suspected Gerry supplied her with in some way. When she first offered me the whisky, I even thought it might make her a little looser but she drank very little, sipping very slowly. One drink lasted her an hour or so. And I was very circumspect about how much I drank. I didn't want to ruin my chances with this fabulously gorgeous woman by acting in a grossly drunken manner.

So we sipped the whisky decorously as I broached the subject of what Milton might be getting up to.

'I don't think he's so bad,' she said. I didn't know whether she really believed that. I hadn't told her I was making my enquiries on Gerry's behalf and she had never really indicated that she was any sort of spy for him beyond telling me that she had a vague connection with him and he had asked her to live at Paradise Lost.

'There must be something about him if Gerry's asked you to keep your eyes open.'

'Gerry's just playing it safe.'

'It's more than that.' Then I decided to tell her. 'I'm seeing Milton to find out what I can for Gerry.'

Lorna raised her eyebrows, then smiled. 'We're a couple of spies together, then. I must say I don't feel like Mata Hari.'

I felt like telling her she was certainly as ravishing but refrained, saying, 'Have you noticed anything fishy?'

'I must admit he's been coming over here more often. I don't know whether he suspects me or whether he's up to something else.'

'Such as?'

'Well, he sometimes looks at me in a way I can only call lascivious. And once he did make what sounded like an odd suggestion.'

'Odd?'

'As if he could provide me with some expensive antiques at a very reasonable price.'

'Nothing more than that?'

'He sort of croaked that I might be interested in them and he could arrange the right kind of exchange that wouldn't really cost me any money.' She smiled and shrugged. 'He never elaborated though he said he'd always be open to suggestions if I wanted to think about it.'

'There you are!'

'Maybe I just misunderstood what he was getting at.'

'I don't think so,' I said and then, after a pause I added, 'Mind you, I can well understand anyone giving you lascivious looks.' The remark didn't have any particular effect on her – she just waved her hand a little as if she was brushing the idea away as being ridiculous.

'All I can say is that you'd better watch out for him, Lorna. Are you sure you're alright living here?'

She nodded. 'Don't worry about me.' She grinned charmingly. 'After all, I'm a big girl. I know what I'm doing. I'm not likely to get myself into any awkward situation like that.'

I felt like saying that I wouldn't mind if she got into a situation like that with me, but I didn't. So we turned the conversation to other matters, but not those that kept nagging at me every time I saw her.

Halfway through the term I was almost swamped with work, having to stay in most evenings to write papers, read and study. I still went round to Barbara's but one evening I had a phone call from Lorna that really sparked my interest.

I was beginning to feel very down because of all the work. I found it difficult even to make time to see Barbara and the Manchester weather only added to my depressed mood: lots of rain, and a constant dampness that set into a real chill most days. When it wasn't raining, there was usually a dense, soupy fog.

So Lorna's voice on the other end of the phone – she rarely called me – cheered me up no end. After a few casual pleasantries, Lorna said, 'Milton surprised me this week.' I expected her to tell me that Milton had let something slip about his activities or that he had made a move on her and Lorna was calling me so I could pass the information on to Gerry, though I think she usually worked through Barbara.

But it wasn't anything like that at all. 'He's bought a television set that we can all share,' she told me.

Television was very much an expensive novelty in those days: very few people owned a set and the transmissions from the BBC were only on for a few hours a day.

'Where's he putting it?' I asked. I imagined he'd have to find a central place, unless he was going to put it in his own house and invite young ladies over to watch with him. I couldn't think of any other place he might be able to place it, for separate families lived in the other houses and the single people, like Lorna, lived in houses that had been converted into two large apartments. There was no central lounge, so far as I knew: the bulletin board for the bargaining notices was in a glassed-in case in front of Milton's house.

'It's for all of us, he says,' Lorna went on. 'I mean, we're allowed to borrow it. We just sign up on a list so we can have it for an evening. He'll even send someone round to connect it for us, and he's giving us each one of those rabbit-ears aerials.'

'What's got into him all of a sudden?'

'I don't know. Acted sort of treacly when he came round to tell me. Even creepy.'

'You'd better watch out for him.'

'He came round to tell me he'd like me to have it the first time, but that was mainly because they were going to show a Shakespeare play this week-end. Saturday night. I asked him why he'd thought of me, you know, it being Shakespeare.'

'What did he say?'

'He said he'd always considered me one of those intellectual types. He made it sound as if I was a woman involved in something sort of ... lecherous.' She laughed.

'Really?'

'He went on to say that he couldn't quite figure out why a charming young lady could be bothered with intellectual things when she could be doing something more ... worthwhile, I think he said. And that made it sound even worse.'

'He's acting like a real creep.'

'Anyhow, he said he knew I went to the theatre, though how he knew that, I don't know.'

'Sounds like he might be spying on you.' And I wondered then if Milton had worked out that maybe I was onto him and that Lorna was also in on it. 'I think you'd better go very carefully,' I cautioned her.

'Nothing to worry about.' She paused, then went on, 'Well, what I'm calling about is this. There's this performance of *Hamlet* on television this Saturday and Milton says I can have the set if I want it. So I thought about you, you being an English student, and you're doing a course in Shakespeare, I know. So how'd you like to come over and watch it? I could make dinner for us before it starts. I'm a very good cook. Then we'll watch the play.' She paused, then said somewhat hesitantly, 'Maybe you'd like to bring some other students over as well – though they're not invited to dinner. What d'you think?'

All of this came out in a rushed tumble of words as if it had taken her some time to make up her mind to invite me. It sounded almost rehearsed and she wanted to say it before she forgot it. Or she wanted to get it out before she changed her mind, as if she might be making a great mistake. It made her sound as if she was shy about inviting a man to spend Saturday night with her. Her embarrassment, if that is what it was, surprised me because she had always seemed so poised, so self-assured. But I just put it down to being part of her mystery, something I couldn't fathom, part of that atmosphere of aloofness surrounding her, even though she was always able to make me feel at ease whenever I visited her.

But I still persisted in thinking that she was unreachable beyond a certain point: she gave the impression that she might take it amiss if anyone tried anything with her. And yet she was so attractive that she must have known that most men would eventually want to try something.

So here she was, inviting me over for a Saturday evening for dinner. I decided not to let the opportunity slip, not that I would bring any other students with me – I looked forward to being with Lorna on my own. Admittedly, watching *Hamlet* did not seem to be the ideal set-up for any romantic overtures but maybe afterwards...

Still, I was game for the dinner and certainly I knew I'd enjoy watching *Hamlet*. 'Thanks very much for the invitation,' I said. 'I'd love to come over if it isn't too much trouble.'

I thought I detected a sigh of relief at the other end as if she was glad she'd managed to get the whole business out, though her voice sounded quite perky when she said, 'No trouble at all. I'm looking forward to it.'

'Me too.'

'See you Saturday then. Shall we say about half past five?

When I arrived at her place, Lorna was flustered and apologetic because she was still cooking and was wearing an apron. Yet to me, she seemed immaculately dressed, and even the few wisps of hair out of place and falling down at the side of her face seemed part of an effect she had planned. She brushed them away with a finicky touch of her fingers and said, 'Excuse me. I thought I'd have the dinner ready by the time you arrived. It'll just take me a few minutes more. Then I'll change and we'll be ready to eat.'

She disappeared into her small kitchen and I prowled around, again admiring her good taste – the furniture, the carpet and curtains were all exquisite. The only thing out of place was the clunky squareness of the television set, looking so heavy that I half-expected that the frail-looking table it was set on would splinter apart under the weight.

'It's terribly ugly, isn't it?' she said when she came out of the kitchen to join me.

She was wearing a rich peacock-blue full skirt made from fine-spun wool, with a long line of chunky buttons down the side and her blouse, full-lapelled with a plunging neckline, was in exactly the same colour. She even had on the same colour high-heeled shoes though her stockings were a filmy white. She looked gorgeous.

When I complimented her on the way she looked, she said, 'A friend of mine works in a very modern fashion store and she gets me tremendous discounts.' She stopped for a moment, then said very quickly, 'And of course Gerry helps me out with other things.' That was the first time she had mentioned anything that might be construed in a vaguely sexual way because I thought she was alluding to Gerry's imports of lingerie.

She flounced down next to me where I was sitting. It

was a small sofa, so small that we were close together, almost touching, and we stayed there cosily chatting for a few minutes until she served dinner.

The meal she'd prepared was delicious, very much in keeping with what I had expected from Lorna, very different from the food I normally ate. Some of it I didn't recognize. It had a slightly mysterious quality to it but richly tasty and beautifully served.

We lingered over coffee until she said, 'I suppose we'd better tune in. We don't want to miss any of it.' She went over to the set, turned it on and indicated as she fiddled with the controls that I should sit on that small sofa as it was conveniently placed for viewing. When she managed to tune in a clear picture, she came and sat next to me on the sofa. 'Comfy?' she asked.

I was more than comfy. She was sitting against me. I could feel the smoothness of her skirt on my hand I'd placed on my knee and we were surrounded by the sweet aura of her perfume. She had placed a chilled bottle of white wine on a small table at her side of the sofa so she poured some and handed me a glass. 'Cheers,' she said. 'I'm glad you could come.'

'I wouldn't have missed it,' I answered, 'even though *Hamlet* is not the most cheerful of plays for a Saturday night.'

'Well, we don't have to be as dismal as the play,' she said and touched her glass to mine. I thought I detected a mysterious glint in her eye as she looked at me over the top of her glass. She put it down on the table and sank back a little in the sofa. As she did so, she nudged against and joggled my hand that was holding my glass. 'Sorry,' she said, putting her hand on mine and letting it rest there a moment.

We settled down to watch the play. Gradually she

relaxed more, sinking into the cushions till eventually she curled up with her legs under her, spreading her skirt out, leaning into me. Her close presence was beginning to have its effect on me. Her perfume was like her, subtle but persistent. I slouched down a little and she moved herself against me.

Lorna seemed intent on the play but I found my attention wandering. I couldn't get my mind off the way she was leaning against me and of course I was aware of my burgeoning erection. So a few minutes later, I put my arm gently around her shoulder. She didn't acknowledge that I had done this, staring straight ahead at the TV screen, but after a minute or two, she slid down, laying her hand across my thighs, stretching her legs out along the sofa, shifting to make herself comfortable. There was not much room to push her legs out on the small sofa. And she did all this without taking her eyes off the TV.

We sat for a while till I became aware that her head was moving up my thighs, pushing further into my groin. At first I thought it was simply that she was trying to find the most comfortable position, rolling her head slowly so she could see properly. But then I thought that it was possible that she wanted to lean into my erection – there was no doubt in my mind that she was now fully aware of that fat stand pressing against her.

We nestled together like that for some minutes, neither of us talking, both of us seemingly intent on the play. I'm sure she felt my interest in her because of my firm cock against her and my hand smoothing along her leg on her skirt. I could feel that long row of buttons down the length of her skirt and almost nonchalantly I let my fingers play with each button as I stroked.

We remained watching the play though I sensed that Lorna was gently rolling her head against my cock as if she wanted to feel its length. So. again as casually I could without disturbing her, I let my fingers loosen one of her buttons on her skirt. A minute of two later I undid another, so there was a gap for me to push my hand through, though I didn't do that immediately. I waited to see if she reacted at all. But she didn't. She shifted a little when I unfastened the second button so that I imagined I could feel her warm breath across my groin even through my trousers.

I carefully moved my hand inside her skirt. She was wearing almost nothing underneath as far as I could judge with my hand, just a pair of panties which felt very soft and silky when my hand encountered them. I let my hand stay on the silk, then gently moved it down to feel the top of her stocking. I splayed my hand open on her thigh, some fingers moving on her stocking, my little finger just edging to the frilly lace on her panties. I thought she was going to interfere with things as they were developing because she raised her head a little; she seemed to be looking down, the first time she had taken her eyes from the play. I held my breath, hoping this was not the end.

But in fact she slid her other hand up to my waist, laid her head back on my lower stomach and quite deftly began to fiddle with my belt buckle. And still she hadn't spoken, still she hadn't stopped watching the play on the screen. I managed to slip my hand up, flitting a couple of fingers under her panties, not attempting anything as yet, just smoothing her skin with little circling tickles. She in turn had unfastened my buckle, unclasped my trousers, her hands very delicately, almost without brushing against my hard cock, undid my fly buttons. Then with an extraordinary quick movement, she had my trousers and underpants down to my knees, one hand at the front pushing in conjunction with the hand at my waistband behind me. Of course, without seeming to, I helped her by shifting my arse up to make it easier for her. She accomplished all this without saying anything to me. She lay there still with her head on my stomach, her breath now enveloping my hard long cock sticking up right in front of her face, perhaps though it didn't seem to disturb her view of the screen.

This was all totally unexpected. She hadn't as yet touched my cock but there was no way she could avoid seeing how thick and ready it was. Somehow this was all in character for her. She had done all this as if it wasn't really happening. My hand was slowly edging further up her leg — I even felt she moved her legs a little so they were opened slightly, perhaps to let my fingers move in more readily.

But I was still at a loss. I think most women, having committed themselves to this extent, would at least acknowledge what was happening. But Lorna was still aloof, had said nothing. She still watched the play though my cock was standing up so tall in front of her and my hand was stealing further inside her panties.

I decided to let things take their course. Perhaps Lorna wanted to take the initiative without seeming to. Over the past year or so I had been lucky enough to be involved with quite a few women, most of them a little older than me, who had been the initiators, though some were clever in letting it appear that, in fact, I was taking the lead. I had always found it difficult to judge just when I could move on with a woman — most of my early experiences had often turned embarrassing and unsatisfactory, and that is why I had never made a move with Lorna. For the time being, though, I was content to follow Lorna wherever she wanted to go. She was a woman, apparently, who retained a kind of remoteness, as if she wasn't involved. But at the same time that aloofness was sort of exciting – it kept me on edge, wondering what she would do next, how she would do it without appearing to be involved.

I nudged my hand up, two fingers inside her panties, the rest of my hand straying up to her slit to stroke her quim. I could feel already some moistness on the silk. We stayed like that for some time, my hand not moving. I hoped that she was feeling the hotness of my hand on her, and that it was making her wetter. She was breathing all over my cock, still not touching it but her hand had moved up my bare thigh, resting very closely to my scrotum.

I shifted a little so I could ease across her. With my other hand circling across I managed to unfasten the rest of the buttons on her skirt, laying it open to see my hand at her panties. They were delicately filmy, real silk, deeply maroon.

Then I felt her hand almost imperceptibly moving, up my thigh, one little finger touching my scrotum, then two or three tickling, my knob throbbing as her hand finally caressed my balls. I slid the hand on her thigh over to the inside and smoothed along her skin, progressing up to the other leg of her panties. Now both my hands were playing with the lace fashioned round the panties, with my fingers pressing at her slit. As I moved my hand, Lorna's hand moved as well, her fingers probing under my balls, to the back of my scrotum, prodding into my flesh as she wanted to feel where my cock started, the very root of it. And still she was seemingly enthralled by the play. For myself I was letting my gaze drift, from the screen to look at the enticing length of her legs and those maroon panties.

We had come a long way in the play – it was over halfway through. At this point Hamlet had just killed Polonius and was berating his mother for her sexual misdemeanours. I was trying to figure out just how this whole encounter with Lorna would go – would she somehow accomplish it within the limits of the play so she could retain that air of aloofness, as if we were just watching the play and doing nothing else? If the play ended, then she'd have to acknowledge that something else was happening because there would be nothing for us to watch on the screen.

But all those thoughts disappeared because Lorna began an exploratory journey with her fingers along my cock, up and down. Then her finger and thumb in a ring enclosed my thickness, sliding down the length, pushing hard but slowly, the skin uncurling from the head. I glanced down and the very sight of Lorna's hand stroking so firmly down made me feel even harder. She licked her other hand and placed her moist fingers on the head, skipping them and slithering round the peeled-back skin, flicking at that thin strand and holding it as if she were gently playing the string of an instrument. This double-handed stroking was driving me delirious for she got into a rhythm that was leading me inexorably to shoot out come. I didn't want this to happen just then but I also didn't want Lorna to stop. Some drops of jism oozed out and she smeared it round my cock-head with her wet fingers.

I moved the thin band of silk to one side and slid a finger softly to the lips of her quim. She was very wet and my finger easily moved inside that warm moistness. I tried to fix my movements in time with her hands on my cock. I reached my other hand over and quickly unfastened her blouse, opening it to reveal her breasts – she was wearing no bra. I glanced down, entranced by this gorgeous woman lying partially across me, her clothes open to reveal her terrific body, my hand sliding inside her panties, her legs open in their white stockings and her flimsy garter belt holding them in place. Her breasts were not particularly large but they were beautifully formed. I would have loved to push my cockhead onto her nipples, let her feel my length on both breasts but I didn't want to disturb her exquisite stroking of my prick.

I thought she was breathing a little heavier now as my hand went probing deeply inside her, my other hand roaming over her breasts, then back to slip inside that maroon silk, tickling her groin, edging under her arse. I am sure she was feeling very excited now but I still didn't know what I should do – did it all have to finish by the time the play finished?

Her hands were insistent, her breath seemed even hotter on my cock. Her hands kept on their artistry as I felt a lovely softness of moisture barely touching my cock-head. I looked down to see her open lips just at the tip of my cock. Her tongue darted out every now and again, her lips slowly opened, moving down slowly and gently, her hands still working on me as her mouth moved down. Her tongue was flickering around the length as I went deeper into her mouth. As far as I could tell, even as she sucked me so entrancingly, somehow she still was watching the play almost as if she was pursuing a climax for us as the play reached its climax.

Her teeth were fluttering round my stretched skin,

her tongue rolling and licking, biting quite hard but not to hurt me, sucking upwards until my cock-head was again slippery against her inner lips. My fingers were working steadily at her quim, and she was now flowing juicily. I think she moved herself against my hand though it was difficult to tell. She certainly let out a small whimper every now and again, the first sounds she had uttered during this whole encounter.

As her hands encased my cock, her mouth moved hard onto me, opening wide to suck my balls, first one, then other until she pulled them inside her mouth together. They felt tight and swollen and my cock was about to burst. It all gave me the distinct impression that Lorna's subtle but definite strokes and urgings were passing along my whole body, as if I had become one enormous cock and somehow Lorna could take all of me inside her. That led my hands to move more rhythmically into her, so much so that I let my other pull at her panties, stopping briefly to untangle them and slide them down her legs. She seemed to approve of this move because her legs moved to let me get them off and she was able to open her legs wider. I took that as a signal to push my fingers deep inside her, letting them slide out, circle the lips, roll around her clit before plunging in again.

Hamlet's tragic predicament was now only a shadow in my mind though strangely I still had the impression that Lorna was watching as the play drew to its close. I sensed that Lorna was orchestrating all this to coincide with the end of the play and I was fascinated as to how she would accomplish this.

Her mouth was deliciously sloppy all over my cock, her fingers pressing and pulling, her wet sloppiness covering the whole of my cock. She removed one of her hands to take the panties I had peeled from her. She took them and rammed their silkiness under my balls, letting the frills snake across my thighs. I was reminded of where they had been and how my hands had managed to get inside them. I think I could feel a little of the wetness of her juice that had leaked onto her panties. This in turn drove me to excite her even further by poking my fingers in and out of her quim, faster and faster until her whimpers became louder.

Her muted cries by no means disturbed the closing scene of *Hamlet*. It added almost naturally to the rather funereal music that was just beginning to play. Her hands on my cock and her mouth's slow sucking kept in time with that steady marching rhythm. I was still pumping my fingers into her, my other hand now under her arse, pushing it upwards. Her whimpering continued and it was obvious that both of us were moving into an inevitable orgasm. I was ready to explode, she was running juicily, wriggling around my hand now. And then came the final line of the play, 'Go. Bid the soldiers shoot.' And that's what I did, a great surge brimming out of my cock.

I had a very brief moment when I wondered if I should somehow try to point my cock somewhere so that my jism wouldn't spew out onto her tasteful furniture but I didn't quite know how to do that. In any case that feeling of release took over and I just lay back to let it fly where it would. Lorna's whole body was juddering and shivering, her legs spasming slightly as her quim overflowed.

The play's closing music was that rather mournful funeral march and Lorna's hands and mouth making their slavering noise round my prick fitted in. And my worry about my come jetting out was of no consequence for as Lorna sensed that big throb pulsing up my cock, she touched her lips just at the slit. She seemed as intent on that spurting cream as she had been on the play. She let it fly across her lips, dribbling onto her chin, sucking at it so that my juice flew inside her lips. Then she made my cock withdraw while it was still surging cream, her fingers trickling across the head and at the slit, rubbing come into her hands and onto my cock, then pushing my stand against her neck where I leaked more. She finally pulled my prick up, slid her mouth completely along the length, her saliva mixing with the thin slipperiness of come all over my cock. She left my cock inside her warm mouth, her hands now scrunching slightly at my balls and I could feel how wet with come her hands were. As she lay against me, my cock still in her mouth, I saw how her mouth was really wet – her moistness and my come had covered her chin. I could see little oozings of come at the corners of her mouth as she settled back, still sucking and licking me as the music continued till we saw on the screen the words 'The End'.

But it was not quite the end for Lorna and me. She was reluctant to move, listening to the music and the final credits of the play. Then the screen turned to speckled black but she rested comfortably, her head on my lower stomach, her hands gently on my cock, my hand softly placed on her pubic mound. She pulled the panties away from under my balls and held them up – there were a few dark stains on them, from her own juices when I had stroked her while she was still wearing them and from my splashes of come that had dribbled down from her mouth and neck. As she held them up, she looked at me and smiled, not sexily but just a sweet, almost innocent smile.

She then rose and stood in front of me, her skirt still

held at her waist, open as her blouse was. As if the maroon silk were a delicate lacy handkerchief, she patted it at her lips, gently wiping at the wetness which glistened around her mouth and chin. Then she stepped into her panties, pulled them up and smoothed them into place, smoothing the moist patches till they stuck against her skin. She turned and slowly walked away, disappearing into her bedroom. I didn't know whether to follow her but decided against it. She hadn't spoken a word and I didn't feel I could go to her without some sense of an invitation. In fact, I stood up and adjusted my clothing so that when she came back I was sitting on the sofa, dressed as I was when I first came.

She also was dressed the same way, her skirt and blouse now fastened. Of course I presumed she was wearing the panties underneath and imagined she was feeling their wet patches against her. But she showed no outward signs of what had happened. Her hair was immaculately in place, her skirt and blouse didn't appear to be wrinkled much, her face was freshly made up.

She went over to put some music on. I expected she would put on some low, moody music but what it was was some sprightly classical music, Mozart or Haydn. Then she came back to the sofa and poured out the last of the wine for us. She raised her glass and we both drank.

'I thought it was very good, didn't you?' she said.

'Just marvellous,' I replied. I thought she was talking about our experience on the sofa but when she went on to talk a little about the performances it dawned on me she was talking about the play. She made absolutely no allusion to anything else except to say later, 'I've had a lovely evening. Thank you for coming over.'

Again she gave the impression of being aloof and yet I

was sure that she was remembering with pleasure her own excitement, her marvellously sensual offering of herself, her infinitely subtle hands, her delectable mouth on me.

When I was leaving, she gave me an enticing kiss, very wet with her open mouth which still held that musky, sea-wet taste of come. 'We must do this again sometime,' she said without a trace of humour. It was impossible to know whether she meant us to be together or whether I was simply to come over when she next had the television set.

I hoped that, whatever the programme was, we would both watch and enjoy the performance, both on the screen and on the sofa.

8. Picnic Time

Spring that year was very wet but the weather was not really getting me down. My work was going well, I was still seeing Barbara on a regular basis and I had a few dates with students which, though I only got as far as some tentative gropings, I enjoyed.

Soon after Easter my general cheerfulness was added to immensely by a letter:

My dear Nicholas (*it read*),
I was so sorry it was impossible to see you during your Christmas vacation but since then I have been trying fervently to find some free time to come to see you.

I'm pleased to say that I have schemed to arrange a long week-end in two weeks' time. We'll be able to celebrate Spring – all the flowers blooming, and you know how much I love flowers!

Charles will drive me up there on the Friday and I don't have to leave till Sunday lunchtime. Perhaps we'll have a nice picnic together. I know how adept you are at coaxing the flowers to grow. I remember our little *tête-à-têtes* among the flowers with great fondness.

My father used to travel to Manchester some week-ends – goodness only knows what he got up to there! But he always said that the service and the discretion at the Midland was superb – unobtrusively dependable was the way he expressed it and that sounds as if the Midland would suit our purposes admirably.

I have already written to the manager to tell him that a Mr Nicholas Bancroft will be making the suite comfortable for me before I arrive so he will give you the key.

I will bring all the supplies for the picnic. You have to do nothing else but *be there*. Please send me a short note if this is entirely too inconvenient for you though I am hoping that is not the case. I think you know that I will try my best to compensate you for any inconvenience I may cause you.

My dearest Nicholas, I am looking forward to spending time with you again, especially as I know we can arrange our own Spring festivities to our mutual satisfactions.

Till then,
Phillipa

Phillipa was Mrs Courtney, a ravishingly charming lady I had met when I delivered packages to her from Gerry. Later, I worked for several weeks as her gardener. We usually had two or three meetings a week in her conservatory, at first to discuss horticultural matters but also to enjoy tea and pastries together, followed by the very different tasty sweets she offered me with her body.

So I knew just what she meant with her references to picnics and flowers. She always behaved with aristocratic charm, but she readily sloughed it as she slipped out of her clothes. Her stylish manners and impeccably refined accent remained in place even though she indulged in marvellously erotic manoeuvres. Occasionally she would let out with particularly seductive phrases and because she kept her precise accent they always seemed to me to be tremendously exciting.

Naturally enough, I made sure I had cleared away whatever work I had on hand so that I could be free for that week-end. And I was especially looking forward to spending it with her at the Midland Hotel which had the reputation of being the classiest hotel in Manchester. I had often stared through its bright glass doors, seeing the smart people in the foyer, recognizing even then that they lived in a completely different world from the one I lived in, more luxurious and sensuous. I never believed that I could ever be a part of their world as I gazed in on those immaculate people till the commissionaire, splendid in his deep crimson overcoat with shiny buttons, moved me on.

So I was really looking forward to spending a week-end in that lap of luxury – and in the lap of Mrs Courtney!

The desk clerk looked askance at me when I asked for the key to Mrs Courtney's suite. He excused himself, disappearing into an inner office. Two or three minutes later, he reappeared a little shame-faced, following an imposingly tall man in a smart morning suit. He was holding a letter in his hand, peering at it over the top of his heavy, black-framed glasses. He poked them back onto the bridge of his nose as if he wanted to inspect me closely, making me feel like an insignificant insect under the hard scrutiny of an authoritative scientist.

'Bancroft? Mr Nicholas Bancroft?'

'Yes,' I mumbled.

'Could I see your identity card please?'

Most of us still carried our wartime identity cards, though we rarely had to show them anymore. Fortunately I had mine with me though it was a little rumpled and creased. The manager – I presumed this bespectacled, morning-suited person was the manager – took it from me gingerly, almost as if he might catch some monstrous infection from it. He stared at it for a long time and then made a grating noise in his throat like a note of disbelief, evidently suspicious that my card was a forgery and I was really an anarchist intent on planting a bomb in his palatial hotel.

But I was not carrying a bomb. In fact, I had no luggage of any kind, just a bunch of roses. I realized that I must have seemed very out-of-place and that made me uncomfortable. My discomfort obviously made the manager even more suspicious of me.

He held onto my card as he pushed a large book towards me. It was the hotel register. The desk clerk handed me a pen and the manager said somewhat disdainfully, 'This is all highly irregular but I'm sure Mrs Courtney knows what she is doing. You had better sign.'

He gave me a distinctly frosty smile as I signed. He pulled the register round to inspect my signature, checking it against the one on my identity card. 'Hm!' he said. 'It seems to be in order,' though the tone of his voice suggested that he thought things were definitely not in order. He slapped my card down on the counter and slid it across to me. He turned and gave a curt nod to the clerk, then strode away self-importantly into his office.

'There you are ... sir,' the clerk whispered as he handed me the key. 'Fourth floor,' he added, his voice even lower. It was as if we were in collusion, part of a treacherous plot against the manager.

Then he gave me a broad grin and I briefly wondered if Mrs Courtney had done this before, inviting young men to spend a week-end with her at the hotel. Or did the clerk know that this was the place where the most dissolute upper-class women came for their assignations?

I shuffled awkwardly across to the lift. The liftman stared at the roses I was carrying though I tried to make them inconspicuous by letting them hang down the side of my leg. But he smiled extravagantly and he may even have winked as he slid the gate shut, moving the handle into place with a dramatic flourish, asking, 'Floor, sir?'

'Oh ... er ...' I was flustered and couldn't remember.

'Room, sir? What room?' He sounded sharply impatient.

Of course I didn't know the room number and had to fumble the key out of my pocket, dropping the roses in the process. The liftman sighed.

'Er ... 412,' I muttered.

'Ah!' he said jovially. 'Then 412 it is!'

When the lift stopped he drew the gate back with a squealing clang. 'Here we are, sir!' I wasn't sure but I thought I detected a smirk on his face. And something else. I don't know whether it was deliberate but he had stopped the lift so that it was an inch or two below the level of the floor.

As I stooped to pick up the roses, he said, 'Watch your step, sir,' the peremptory tone seeming to suggest a moral admonition rather than a simple warning. It was as if I was a miserable, jumped-up little squirt who had no right at all to be in this hotel. His attitude seemed to suggest I would be completely out of my depth in the company of the splendid people who stayed in the hotel, and even inferior to those who worked there.

I convinced myself that I was being paranoid. After all, how would the liftman know that I was meeting Mrs Courtney for a sexual assignation? Yet it was possible, I told myself, that she had done this before. The hotel staff were in the know, the clerk, the manager, even the liftman secretly laughing at me, doing their best to make me feel as uncomfortable as possible.

I tried to rid myself of these thoughts as I walked along the corridor on the thick, plush carpet, though I was still convinced the liftman's eyes were boring into my back. I hadn't heard him close the lift-gate and I didn't dare turn round to stare back at him.

I was even further convinced that a plot was developing against me when I opened the door of the suite to discover the chambermaid smoothing down the counterpane on the bed. She was quite pretty and as she leaned across the bed, she showed a lot of nicely shaped leg. I momentarily wondered if I was supposed to seduce her, only to be found in a compromising position with her by the manager. He could then order me out of the hotel in a suitably imperious manner, comforting the maid as she whimpered on his shoulder.

But without a word and with scarcely a glance at me, the chambermaid took the roses from me, arranged them prettily in a vase, bobbed a little curtsey at me, all in a shy way, and almost ran out of the room, muttering, 'Beg pardon, sir,' as she left.

All my paranoia and discomfort disappeared, however, as soon as Mrs Courtney arrived. I had spent nearly three restless hours in the suite, trying to read, pacing about, debating whether I would have the nerve to go down for a beer in the hotel bar but deciding against it in case Mrs Courtney arrived while I was out.

She didn't get there till about 4:30, striding in with a

beautifully gracious motion, to plant a quick kiss on my cheek, whispering, 'Nicholas, darling! How nice to see you.' Her hand briefly stroked my face, not lingering, dropping to hold her fur coat tight at her neck. She smiled and it was a slightly crooked, lascivious smile. That was quite enough to put me at ease.

She had been followed in by two of the hotel boys, one carrying two large cases, the other a bucket with the neck of a bottle of champagne sticking out of it. He then turned to bring in a large picnic basket and placed it just inside the door.

Mrs Courtney waved her hand at the boy as he deposited the two cases in the bedroom. 'I couldn't decide what the weather was going to be like so I just packed for all eventualities.' Her voice was reassuringly soft and lilting and yet had a tinge of seductive suggestion in it.

She smiled again. 'It's such a damp, cold city, though, isn't it?' She paused. 'But I'm sure everything will be ... agreeable in here, whatever the weather is like.'

She was holding her coat close against her as she struggled to open her purse to tip the two boys. I had made sure the heat was turned up so I couldn't understand why Phillipa was feeling the chill so much.

She ushered the boys out of the door, standing with her back to it, still clutching her coat tightly at the neck. 'Will you be an absolute darling, Nicholas, and open the champagne? I thought it would be just the thing to start our week-end on the right note, a bottle of champers. Don't you think so, my pet?'

She was still leaning with her back at the door, her arms loosely embracing herself as she seemed to nestle inside the fur. She shook out her long coppery hair – a deeper colour than Margo's and exquisitely waved. Then she took one step forward and I could see her long legs pushing out from the coat, her ankles very trim in black stockings and high heels.

I managed to open the champagne, the bubbly foam gushing out. 'My, my!' Phillipa giggled. 'I think you did that deliberately, Nicholas, you naughty boy! I do believe you're just trying to get me all excited.'

'How?' I asked.

'All those creamy bubbles squirting out like that. You just knew it would remind me of something else creamy and wet squirting out!' I was a little surprised that Mrs Courtney was making suggestive remarks so early on. It usually took her some time to lose her inhibitions about mentioning things like that.

She must have noticed a puzzled look on my face for she went on, 'Have I said something I shouldn't?'

'Oh, no, not at all. It sounds very ... intriguing,' I replied.

'You'll find two glasses in the picnic basket.'

I went over to the basket and took out the glasses. I carried them over to a small table so I could pour the champagne. When I turned round I discovered that Mrs Courtney had moved further into the room, her purse on a chair but her arms still clinging onto her coat. I was uncertain whether I should take her glass to her as she obviously seemed to be feeling the cold. Maybe she wanted to sit down and wrap the coat around her.

She was grinning mischievously at me as she nodded to the table where I had put the glasses. 'I think we should have a toast, Nicholas.' I moved to pick up the glasses but she stopped me by saying, 'Just leave mine there for a moment.' I left the glasses on the table. 'Oh, I didn't mean to stop you, Nicholas. You can certainly raise your glass. Don't you want to toast me?'

I raised my glass in a toast. She broke into a wicked laugh and dramatically pulled her coat wide open. She was wearing almost nothing underneath. She swirled around, her coat floating out even wider. 'Am I worth toasting? D'you like it, my sweet? I did this especially for you. I've been sitting in the car like this for the last part of the drive and it's made me quite extraordinarily ... what shall I say? Randy, is that the word?'

I nodded and smiled at her. She looked delectable, wearing just a garter belt, stockings and high heels. That was why she had kept the coat tightly wrapped around her – nobody could guess just how little she was wearing under it.

She had also decorated herself in a very clever way. Around each breast she had somehow fashioned a small wreath of blue flowers. And just below her navel was a trail of exotic pink blossoms that seemed to bloom out of her pubic hair.

'D'you like it?' she repeated, dancing round again.

'It's wonderful,' I stammered.

'Does it remind you of our meetings in the conservatory?' I nodded, dumbstruck by this vision of Mrs Courtney, so extravagantly forward for her. 'I was afraid I'd crush them under my coat but they've managed to survive quite well, haven't they?'

'I think they would find it easy to survive, snuggling up against such beautifully warm places,' I said.

'Why, what a charming thing to say, you dear boy!' She was trailing her fingers along the petals of the flowers near one of her breasts, her hand straying to touch herself there. 'Oh, my! I can feel something else growing a little here.'

I could see she was circling her nipple with her fingertip and then her other hand snaked down the trail of flowers near her crotch. 'These flowers are opening out beautifully, aren't they?' She raised one gently in her fingers. 'I think they must have blossomed so much because of the special treatment they are having there – so warm ... even hot.'

Then she slowly swayed towards me, making sure her coat was hanging loosely open. This was, in a way, a new Mrs Courtney. She had always been very sexually forward once she got under way but here she was taking the initiative in a more striking manner than she normally did. She was usually excessively polite, almost gracious in her approaches to me.

I handed her a glass and we raised our glasses to each other. 'Here's to a week-end festival of flowers,' she said and we both sipped. Then she looked at me. 'You have one or two enticing little bubbles. I'd like to taste them.'

She leaned across to me and the tip of her tongue slid daintily around my lips, prodding just a little inside my mouth. 'Still as delicious as ever.'

I returned the compliment by tasting the champagne on her lips, my tongue slipping inside to touch hers, our mouths open. When we pulled apart, she stepped back and smiled somewhat shyly.

'I don't know what got into me,' she said.

'Oh, don't apologise. It's delightful.'

She opened her coat wide and showed herself off. 'I didn't know just what you'd make of this.'

'It's beautiful,' I said.

'You don't think I've been too forward? I was thinking about you all the way here. Such a long drive and by the time I was just a few miles away, I'd got myself into ... quite a state. And I wanted to give you a nice surprise.'

She was now obviously in the mood she had been nervous about establishing. She strutted about the room, swaggering, floating the fur coat out, circling round me, a slightly lecherous smile hovering at her mouth. She came to rest by a chair where she raised a leg, propping her elbow on her knee, making sure the coat fell open to reveal the full shapeliness of her leg.

'D'you like this surprise, Nicholas?' That impeccable accent and precise pronunciation somehow made her sexy pose even more sexy, especially when she added, 'All the time I was sitting in the car, I was thinking of you ... what a big boy you were ... I was remembering just how big you had grown.' Her hand went to her mouth briefly as if she shouldn't have been saying anything like this.

'But you're not a boy, are you, Nicholas? Even though you are so big. What a big boy you are!' and she began to swagger slowly towards me. 'That's all I could think off on the way here. Just how big a boy you were.'

She was now standing close to me and her long fingers were slipping gently along my thighs. 'I wonder if Charles knew what was going on in my head while he was driving.' Charles was her chauffeur. 'I made him stop at a small hotel once we were getting close. I told him I needed to stop. I took my vanity case in with me.' She paused. 'I'd put these flowers in there.'

She touched the flowers delicately with one hand while her other hand pushed closer to the bulge in my trousers. 'I went into the Ladies' and undressed. I had some sticky stuff to glue the flowers on. I put my clothes in the case and I sat in the back of the car, just thinking of you, Nicholas,' and her hand was now nudging between my thighs, brushing against my balls. 'Thinking of showing you, thinking of doing this,' and she squeezed my balls, 'thinking of putting my hands all over you.'

No wonder Mrs Courtney had started so soon after she had arrived. She had been working herself up all the way from her house in St Albans.

'I wondered whether the flowers would stay in place. Well, they did ... and it doesn't matter now if they fall off.' She very carefully lifted the flowers away from her breasts, throwing them to one side, then pulling at the line of flowers lower down. 'There!' she said,

'I've sent Charles away, told him not to come to pick me up till Sunday lunchtime. So we have the whole weekend to ourselves.' One of her hands was now caressing my erect cock. 'And we don't have to go out at all. We can have our picnic in here.' She grinned mischievously. 'And if you want to pick flowers, there are some right here for you.' As her fingers began to work on my fly buttons, I placed my hand on her pubic mound, fingering the flowers and letting my fingertips touch her hair, poking a little lower to the moist opening.

'We'll be able to have a veritable feast, not just a picnic,' she said as her fingers wandered inside my underpants to root out my cock. 'There's going to be enough for a banquet.'

She was busy pushing down my trousers and my underpants. Both her hands were now fondling and coaxing me, taking my cock to touch it against the flowers. She held me there with one hand while her other unfastened my shirt.

I pushed the fur coat away from her shoulders and she let it fall away. She led my prick between her legs to rub it at the creamy moistness there. Then she breathed in my ear, 'Doesn't that remind you of a long piece of fruit bathing in a nice, sweet, thick syrup?' She moved herself backwards and forwards gently and wetly along the length of my shaft.

We stayed like that for a few minutes, her mouth nibbling at my ear, her tongue sliding inside my mouth as I bent to her breasts where I caught heady whiffs of the perfume left by the flowers. I licked and sucked her breasts, and her nipples hardened, jutting out as she pushed them into my mouth.

My cock was juicily stiff, moving easily along that lubricated slit, poking every now and again past to nudge at her arsehole and that soon became slippery too. I pushed in harder to let my shaft lie along the crack of her arse and Phillipa was quite content to feel that stiffness there, occasionally pulling back so that I was able to probe briefly at the moist and fleshy lips of her quim, riding up to circle her clit before pushing back along her wet slit, prodding in to touch the rim of her hole before my prick again nestled along the crack. When she felt my length there, she twitched her buttocks, holding them gently clenched to hold my prick in place.

Eventually she whispered, 'This is all very lovely but I think it's time to picnic, my sweet. The things they must have been teaching you here! You're a very good student. I've been thinking of you studying all that poetry. How to rhyme words – Nick rhymes with thick.' Then she laughed a little nervously. 'And prick, of course.' She paused as her arse moved caressingly on my shaft before holding it tight in the crack. 'Lock it in there,' she said. 'Lock ... cock.'

'I remember that poem that says something about a loaf of bread, a jug of wine and thou beside me in the wilderness,' she said, tugging hard at my cock. 'I shall have to call this "thou" and put it not just beside me but inside me. Deep inside me.'

She led me over to the bed so that I stretched out. She bent over me and spread her thick hair across my stomach, her mouth so close to my cock that I could feel her breath sending hot streams along the length, tickling warmly round the swollen head.

Then she sat up, leaving one of her hands weighing my balls. 'You just wait there,' she said as she slid off the bed.

'I don't intend to go anywhere,' I said.

'I'm going to give you something to whet your appetite. Oh, there's another word, "whet". I know my appetite is very wet. Maybe I can make yours wet too.' She was standing at the side of the bed looking down deliberately at my cock which was standing up fat and long. Then she turned away, walking slowly with a very salacious sway to her walk.

'Where are you going?' I asked.

'For the picnic. My basket's full of tasty morsels.' She was still wearing her garter belt and black stockings and as she strutted away, she let the flowers at her crotch fall.

She slid the picnic basket along the floor to the bed, raising the lid and pulling out a large oval fruit, mostly red, with a little green and yellow.

'What's that?' I asked.

'This is a lovely exotic fruit. A mango. Very juicy and sweet. Very soft flesh. Haven't you ever seen one before?'

I shook my head. Mangoes I had heard of but they had never figured in my life though I dimly remembered that Miss Hallam had mentioned mangoes as one of the ingredients of her drink.

'Well, well, my pet, you're in for a real taste treat.' She had a sharp knife and was paring the mango and I could see the juice dripping onto her fingers. She cut the fruit in two, removing the stone. She held up the two halves, then placed them carefully on a wad of serviettes she had placed on the bed. She licked her fingers lasciviously.

'So sweet and juicy,' she mumbled as she licked and sucked her fingers into her mouth, letting the juice run around her lips so that her mouth looked enticingly open and wet. She arranged herself on the bed next to me and said, 'Would you like a taste?' I nodded and she leaned over me, rubbing one of the halves of mango across my lips so that the juice dribbled down. Her mouth came to mine and she licked my lips, her tongue teasing my mouth open. As she did this, she was making soft, whispering noises till she fastened her open mouth on mine.

It was a strange kiss, our lips almost glued together with juice and yet not really stickily. It was sweet and slippery as Phillipa moved her soft lips all around mine. Then she said, 'Isn't that the most delicious thing you've ever tasted?'

She then sat up. 'Maybe I can make the taste even more delicious.' She lifted the other half and placed the two halves on her breasts, circling them around. I could see thin streams of juice running down. 'You'll like the taste even more,' she muttered and she leaned down so that I could lick the juice. My tongue followed the trails of juice and Phillipa lifted the mango halves away so that my face was buried between her breasts, the juice smearing me, sweet and a little sticky, my mouth searching out her nipples, my tongue circling them. Then I opened my mouth to guzzle at the juicy taste spread over her breasts. My mouth made slurping noises that joined with Phillipa's sighing and soft gasping. 'Eat it all up, Nicholas,' she sighed.

Somehow she moved herself around and slid down the bed a little, making sure I could still nuzzle at her. Then I felt a cool, wet sensation encase my balls. I knew then that she had placed a half mango so that my scrotum nestled softly in the spongy moist texture, feeling at home resting in the hole where the stone had been.

A few minutes later she began to wipe the other half down the length of my prick, covering the head with juice, letting it prod into the hole, squeezing it against me, the juice running slowly down my length. My cock responded with quick twitches and throbs, beating into the mango half, Phillipa felt that – it seemed to excite her for she moved the mango on me more and more sensually so that I began to shift to probe my cock into the soft flesh of the fruit. It felt as soft and yielding as a quim.

'Don't spill your juice, darling,' Phillipa said throatily. 'That's the sweetest juice of all. And I want you to save it all for me.' Her hands kept working with slippery strokes, my face still squashed in the sticky juice of her breasts.

Eventually she laid one of the pieces of mango, by now pulpy and a little shredded, on the serviettes. Her gluey fingertips began exquisite touches along my cock. She leaned down, saying, 'Time for a little nibble, a succulent taste.' Her moist mouth came down to cover my cock-head, and then slowly she pulled me deeply into her mouth. I could feel her tongue flickering at the slit of my cock and it was all I could do to stop myself from letting fly with gushes of jism.

Her mouth kept sliding further down till I experienced this strange mixture of her warm mouth and the stickiness of mango juice, for her other hand was still squeezing the other half of mango against my balls. She moved round to straddle me and every now and again she let my prick slide from her mouth to slither its hard fatness over her breasts and in between them. The flood of juice there made it feel as if I was probing inside her honey-sweet cunt. Sometimes she would dangle my cock-head at a nipple, tickling herself with it, shuddering with delight, then pushing it back so that once again she could enclose it inside her mouth.

One of her hands fumbled along the bed trying to find the other piece of mango she'd placed on the serviettes. When she closed her hand on it, she moved it between her legs. Her mouth and tongue were still playing with my cock-head so her words were oddly mumbled. 'Press it there for me. Make me more juicy. Then you can taste all the juice.'

I took the mango from her hand and pressed it gently along the lips of her quim. Her mouth came down the length of my shaft, gulping around the fatness, then slowly drawing upwards. As her lips played with my cock-head, she muttered, 'It's time for you to eat up your dessert, darling Nicholas.'

I squashed the half of mango against her. Its soft pulp broke apart and spread along her quim. I laid her on her back and knelt between her legs. My mouth reached in to nibble at the slippery spongy pieces of fruit which slid in juicy bits along the lips. My mouth was partly full of mango but I managed to suck at her cunt, flicking my tongue inside, tasting a mysterious flavour of mushy saltiness and sweetness.

Phillipa was reaching down, squiggling herself around

to squash the other piece of mango around my cock. She had moved so that she could get her mouth on my prick again and I felt little nips from her teeth as she sucked small pieces of mango into her mouth, biting on my hardness as she did. I was just able to decipher what she was saying: 'It's so soft and hard at the same time.' Her lips were sloppy with mango juice, slippery-sweet along the length of my shaft.

We stayed eating and licking till finally we had both swallowed the pieces of mango. We kept guzzling at each other, my cock feeling harder than ever, bathed as it was with Phillipa's juicy, sticky mouth. Her quim was slithery-wet, syrupy and salty. She kept pushing herself hard against my mouth, my nose buried in her pubic hair, my tongue lapping at her.

It was Phillipa who called a halt. I was a little disappointed when her mouth made its last, long, lingering sticky trail up my cock, her tongue flickering at the slit to give it a teasing tickle. She stayed with her mouth hovering there as she said, 'We've been very naughty. We had dessert first. Let me give you something a little more ... substantial.'

I really wanted her to continue sucking me. My cock was hot and stiff, filled with a long tube of come ready to shoot out. I wanted her to continue till I spurted out a great deluge of come as she led me there with her mouth and hands. I knew she liked to do that because once, when she had been particularly uninhibited, she told me she loved to watch jism squirting out in high jets. 'All that lovely cream shooting out. It spews out so high and it's me that's made it squirt up like that. My mouth and my hands did it.' So that's why I thought she'd do that to me now, her hands and mouth so insistently stroking and tickling. I knew she would be feeling the big vein swollen along the length of my cock, feel the blood pumping in it. And then she'd see the first tentative drops of come spill out. She would pump her hand faster to coax the rest out, as if the faster and more caressingly she stroked, the higher my jism would fly.

But this time she stopped, though my cock was certainly at the ready, aching at the verge of release, my balls wrapped inside her hand big and tight. 'Phillipa, please. Please make me come,' I urged her.

'My dear young man, have a little patience! You must savour a meal to the utmost.' Her voice sounded both humorous and tempting at the same time. Then, matter-of-factly, she began to feed me small sandwiches she lifted out of the picnic basket, touching my cock now and again. Sometimes she let a sandwich rest at the edge of her mouth and I had to reach up to nibble it down till our lips met and her tongue fished inside my mouth, lolling and licking there.

Once she delicately entwined my cock with thin strips of smoked salmon. Her teeth very carefully chewed it away without her mouth touching my cock though it sent my shaft into delirious twitches. She then placed some strips around her breasts and said, 'Tit for tat.' She laughed. 'Tit,' she said. 'I've had tat so it's your turn for tit.' I let my tongue slide around her nipples, liking the vague smoky taste that lingered there when I sucked her after eating the salmon.

She ladled a thick blob of whipped cream onto my cock-head, placing a glacé cherry on top of it. 'Cream for your cream,' she whispered. 'And a lovely red cherry.' She bent to take the cherry in her teeth, then pushed her mouth at me so that the cherry rested between us and we both nibbled at it. She lay back and watched the heat from my prick slowly melt the cream so that it began to drip down the length. She leaned over and licked it, her tongue-tip travelling up the length, her lips sucking the cock-head inside.

Whatever she did to me, she then did to herself, ladling cream onto her breasts, a big spoonful on her pubic hair, waiting for me to guzzle it down. And all the while I couldn't erase from my mind the impression that in a vaguely eccentric way, she was playing the role of charming hostess. Her remarks, while full of politeness, were full of lecherous suggestions so I was almost continually being brought to the edge of showering her with jism. This strange mixture of impeccable manners and wanton language and sexual ploys, her fastidious handling of food and highly lascivious use of hands and mouth, all conspired to keep me in a state of feverish excitement.

As she gobbled and nibbled at the hard fat muscle of my cock, I couldn't keep out of my head an image of her presiding over some social event at home. I couldn't imagine her friends engaging her in chit-chat without knowing that behind that gracious façade was a highly sexed woman who let loose on a young man a whole barrage of sexual tricks that she enjoyed wildly. Once she got in the mood of things, she was wholly extravagant in indulging herself in all kinds of enticing ways.

I suppose that was part of her attraction for me – I flattered myself that she could release this enormous variety of teases and touches, lickings and suckings, without in any way losing her inbred aristocratic mien. Of course, eventually she tended to lose control of her poise, shouting out in great hoarse pleasure, though the words came out immaculately phrased and beautifully pronounced. And I think she drove herself to high ecstasy because she knew that in some way, with my working-class background, she was offering me upper-class sexual gifts while she also felt I in turn could offer her something more raw and rough, something almost vulgar that she couldn't experience in any other way in her class. She seemed to like to be that haughty duchess type that succumbed under the delights of sex to the lecherous whims of a working-class young man.

'Back to dessert,' she said after a while, carefully opening a tin. She speared a fork inside the tin and on its tines out came a half-peach, dripping with heavy syrup. 'Not quite as good as fresh peach but this syrup adds an interesting touch.'

She let the piece of peach slide along my lips, then circled it round my cock-head, where it felt delectably smooth. She leaned down to lick the syrup from my cock as she put the peach between her legs. She then pulled me over so that my mouth was down there and again I had that smell and taste of slippery, salty sweetness in my mouth.

'Is that tasty?' she asked softly, a hostess making sure that her serving of food to a guest was to his liking. I mumbled my assent. She emptied the whole tin of peaches, probing each piece into tempting areas of her body, sliding them over me, each of us chewing the pieces down till finally she dribbled the heavy syrup left in the can in a gentle trickle so that it flowed down the length of my cock while she lapped it up. Her mouth was warm and sweet as she slavered all over my cock and, again, I was taken right to the edge of explosion.

She stopped when she saw a pearl of jism emerge from the slit of my cock. She ever so slowly touched her fingertip to it, letting it spread over my cock-head. This tripped some switch in her after her prolonged nibbling and licking. Still retaining that charming mellowness, she smiled down at me, then drawled in mellifluous tones, 'And now, you hard, throbbing man, you, we are all ready to have a super fuck.'

I was lying on my back on the bed, my body covered in sweat and juice. A pervasive smell of heady musk was hanging round us as she straddled me, her cunt invitingly moist and just resting at my swollen cockhead. Once again, her face was lit up with that lascivious smile of hers and out came rough words in that perfectly modulated voice. 'I am going to fuck the living daylights out of you, so soft and hot that you'll see shooting stars.'

She pushed down meticulously carefully, drawing me up inside her in a teasingly languid way, throbbing her inner muscles, gripping me in that juicy grasp inside. Down and further down she came, gasping as she felt how my fat prick filled her. I felt she was never going to stop pulling me in and it made my cock feel inordinately long. Her velvet moist clench made me push hard into her. And yet I had at the same time the sensation that my aching stiffness was floating in a calm, warm pool, with a trickling waterfall dropping a warm stream onto my cock-head, then splashing slowly down its length.

At last, after what seemed like an interminable sinking down onto me, Phillipa came to rest, her pelvis now pressing fully onto me. She stayed very still, though I felt fluttery pinches all along the length of my cock. She leaned down and pushed her sticky breasts onto my face. My mouth and tongue sought to suck and lick, my hands stroked her buttocks, pulling her further onto me.

So began the slowest fuck I have ever experienced. Phillipa took control, riding me with an inexorable stroke, pulling up my length till I rested at her moist quim-lips where she turned very slowly, the slipperiness circling my cock before she started to suck me in again, marvellously languorous but with an agony of little twitches and muscular spasms playing round my cock.

She was obviously enjoying this maddening motion for she let escape from her lips long whooshing sighs that seemed to empty her lungs, for they lasted the length of her plunges down on my prick. She was almost out of breath as she began to pull up on the long stroke along my shaft. She breathed in a long intake of air, again in time with her up-stroke, so soon she was gasping and spilling out air. I could feel her heart pounding, my mouth washing wetly over her breasts, her buttocks pressing back into my hands till I accommodated myself to her movements, an excruciating rhythmic pulse, pushing her down then slowly up, then down, on and on.

Soon I was also gasping, exhaling great drafts of air into the valley between her breasts. I didn't think I could keep this up much longer and yet Phillipa kept riding so slowly that I seemed to reach a plateau where come was threatening to burst out without it actually ever doing so.

I hovered in that ecstatic state for what seemed long minutes. I could tell that Phillipa had also reached the same peak, for her whole body was juddering and quivering. Then I had this weird sensation of pins and needles along my cock, almost as if hundreds of moist fingertips were drumming along it. I was sure the inside of Phillipa's quim was experiencing a similar sensation for she was whimpering and quaking.

Eventually that sensation became the signal for Phillipa to pick up the pace. Later I was puzzled by the fact that, though we had both been at the edge of release, the breakthrough into higher orgiastic pleasure would normally have wanted a fast thrash to drive us over the edge. But somehow Phillipa managed to make it all go on, lingering on that exquisite verge, her pace only increasing gradually, building towards an impossible crescendo, impossible because I still don't know why I didn't let go. The flood gathered in my cock seemed unstoppable but I did hold it in.

Phillipa sensed that I was at that high frantic moment. We were now moving steadily, still with those long, controlled strokes, metronomic in intensity, quickening a little as the moments passed. I was ready to come, with Phillipa's creamy flow all around me. I wanted to come, I needed to come, for the stiffness of my prick was almost unbearable.

Then she twisted a little, her hand trailing down behind her to grasp my balls really tightly. Then her other hand made a ring round the root of my shaft so that, when she pulled herself up so far along the length of my cock that I was almost out of her quim, the ring of her finger and thumb steadied me in place. And her hands, both so tight on my balls and cock, made it seem as if the whole outer layer of my prick was stretched to its limit.

I could no longer wait. Nor could Phillipa. She began to pound away faster and faster on me. Incredibly, that fierce grasp on me was like a barrier holding back a vast whirlpool of come that was threatening to swirl up into a big spout in waves of orgasm.

And then the floodgates broke open, our voices strangling in strange yells, Phillipa now tall above me, bouncing ferociously as if she wanted to pull a whole stream of jism from some bottomless well inside me. She had released successive pools of moisture that ran all over me, soaking the sheet beneath us. She finished by letting my semi-flaccid prick flop out of her, as she moved up my body, leaving a damp trail on my stomach, then my chest till she perched where she could smear her wet quim against my mouth. And I swear that in spite of the gushing flood of her own juices that had flowed and the moist squelch of my come oozing out, in that wash of salty moisture I still could taste hints of mango and peach.

Nothing quite lived up to that first long drawn-out encounter, though the rest of the weekend was a real feast of sensual thrills, at one point edging into taboo or at least almost forbidden territory. I stayed naked the whole week-end, only covering myself under the sheets when we had our meals sent up.

Phillipa was entrancing. She made a special effort to indulge me, inventing all kinds of niceties of touch with her hands and mouth, tempting me with tidbits of sex, fast gushes of jism covering her breasts or spraying onto the lips of her quim. She was fond of trapping my cock tightly in the crack of her arse, making me move in a grip that was almost painful but nevertheless capable of bringing me to a full spurt by simply touching my cockhead at the end of each stroke along the crack. She was leading me in a direction that had not occurred to me and I was surprised that she wanted to go that way.

She never lost her bright, clear, speaking tones. But as the weekend progressed, she slipped more and more into more blatant talk, the raw words coming out in that meticulous voice. And I think she knew that was calculated to egg me on into more excitement.

She had other ways to egg me on. While she rarely was fully dressed during the week-end, she wore a set of dazzlingly colourful panties. It was a special treat from Gerry, she said, for he knew she was coming to see me. The panties were in a bright floral pattern – maybe she had told Gerry about our escapades in the conservatory. So she strutted about in those panties, just those and high heels.

Once, when a waiter brought up lunch, she stood behind him as he pottered and fussed around his cart arranging and serving food. She opened her dressing gown to show me her flowered panties, just as she had flung her fur coat open when she had first arrived. She sucked a finger into her mouth very suggestively and then she flicked it down to the lacy opening, pulled it back so I got a glimpse of her hair, even a quick flash of pink lips. After the waiter had left, of course, the food went stone cold!

On the Saturday evening, after we had eaten dinner I came out of the bathroom to find she had dressed herself in a full-skirted light blue chiffon dress that floated around her as she swirled it out. Underneath it she had on a richly floral slip. 'I thought you'd like to be reminded of flowers, Nicholas,' she said. 'We've always both enjoyed flowers, haven't we? They have a way of leading us into all kinds of ... interesting ideas.'

She kept swirling around to show off her legs, with the slip also floating out. 'This dress is so lightweight, it's almost like not wearing a dress. Just feel how finely gauzy it is. Very frail and flimsy. Almost as if I'm not covered up at all. Unprotected. A poor defenceless woman. Here, feel it.' And she held the skirt out for me to feel, the many folds of the dress showing as she pulled it wide.

I moved closer to her and she draped it on my upstanding prick. 'Just look how big and strong you are, and me a poor and weak woman. What are you going to do to me with that big long stick of yours?'

I pushed inside the skirt to let my length stretch against her silky slip, prodding at her quim under it, probing at her panties. 'That's such an impudent stick. The way you wield it. So masterful. It makes me want to surrender to it totally.'

Then she turned round, letting the skirt fall back in place, but walking so that it swayed seductively. She moved behind a couch and leaned against it on her elbows so that her arse was sticking out and up, the chiffon falling away so that the roundness of her arse was shaped under the chiffon. She pressed her hands on her skirt so the material tightened and her arse looked gorgeously shaped.

She was half bent over and she glanced back at me over her shoulder. 'The skirt's so full but I love to press it against me. It makes me feel I have an extraordinarily fine arse – or is that too impertinent of me to say so? What do you think, Nicholas? Do I have an extraordinary arse?' She paused but before I could compliment her on her arse, she went on, 'Isn't that lovely word to say – arse?' She lingered over the sound of it, drawing it out in a drawling way but still in her upper-class accent. 'I'd love to shock some of my friends over tea by standing up and bending over and asking them to stare at my extraordinary arse.'

Instead of telling her how gorgeous her arse was, I walked over to her and touched my cock to her where the tight fabric dipped to fold over her crack. 'Actions speak louder than words,' I said.

When she felt me there, she let out a short gasp. 'Nicholas! You are such a masterful man! Like a teacher with his cane. Or a thick stick. Perhaps you are going to beat me with it.' She giggled. 'I feel so unprotected bending over like this. What on earth are you going to do to me with that big stick? And this frock is so light and flimsy.'

I didn't really know where she was heading though I suspected that she wanted to be taken somewhat roughly from behind, just as if I was almost attacking her. 'It's so frail, so... useless. It can't keep anything out and that stick is so hard, so powerful.' I grasped the hem of her dress and the material felt like a veil, like gauze, almost see-through. 'No weight to it at all. Lift it up higher, Nicholas. That's it. Higher still. Fold it back.'

I did as I was told. I gently lifted the skirt of her dress higher, raising it so I could fold it over, placing its layers carefully over her back. She was now bent over so that her floral slip stretched tightly around her arse. I stepped to her again and placed my prick on her crack again, the silkiness of her slip delectable against my cock-head.

'You just love to use that stick of yours, don't you, Nicholas?' She sighed as I moved it along the crack. 'It feels so close to me, it's getting bigger next to me. I can feel it growing.' If anything, her voice, though huskily sexy, was sounding even more thickly aristocratic. For a fleeting moment, I must confess I felt a real twinge of satisfaction in the fact that I, a working class young man, was getting such a marvellous look and feel at a finely refined woman. I knew she was glad to be thrusting her wonderful arse at me, letting me pull her clothing up to reveal herself bent over in a very vulnerable position.

Then she invited me to peel back her slip. I gripped the lacy hem and she said, 'You're so demanding, Nicholas.' I didn't want to point out to her that I hadn't demanded this – she had been taking all the initiative. But if that was what she wanted, I didn't want to disturb the flow of her plan.

'That's it. Pull it right up. Higher. Now fold it over. Yes. You are so forthright.' She shivered ecstatically. 'I just become putty in your hands. You put your hands on me and I'm like soft jelly. And now I suppose you want to play with my soft jelly.'

Her talk was making me feel very randy, especially as now she was bent over, her clothing folded over onto her back. She had shifted to thrust her arse a little higher and I gazed at those perfectly round globes now just covered by her panties. She was wearing no stockings and her long legs looked ravishing in high heels, altogether a fascinating sight I couldn't resist. I stepped to her and placed my erection just at the edge of her panties, pushed a little and my cock made its way inside her panties, probing in under the silkiness – it was a lovely feeling, the silk so smooth on my prick as it pressed into the soft yielding flesh of her arse. I pushed in harder till my length was nestled along the crack of her arse. Phillipa clenched me, letting her crack move gently, holding, then relaxing her grip on my hard stand. It was very exciting and it obviously had a similar effect on her for she let out a strange noise, a half hiss, a half whistle.

She began to rotate her arse slowly, settling herself on top of my prick, clenching and relaxing still, pushing down on me a little. I wondered if this was all she wanted to do, move on me like this till I spilled out. But after two or three minutes of this rapturous movement on my cock, she looked directly at me over her shoulder. 'I just know you are thinking about pulling down my last shred of protection. Such flimsy things, aren't they?

It's a wonder they don't fall off by themselves. I suppose you want to help. Slide them down, Nicholas. Uncover my spectacular arse.'

Again I did as I was told. I pulled the panties down her legs. When I was stooping to loose them from her ankles, she lifted first one foot, then the other so I could pull them away. As I did that, she planted her feet a little wider – it seemed a preliminary for me to thrust my cock into her quim from behind for she also settled her stance more firmly.

I decided to probe my prick carefully between her legs, let the head feel the flow of her juices because I was sure she would by now be very wet. I gently prodded my cock onto her. As she felt my hardness, she let out an involuntary sigh and added to it, 'Oh, no.' I took that to be merely a polite but ultimately meaningless refusal but in fact she meant it, for she went on, 'My arse.' It seemed as if she had fallen in love with the word for she let it drawl in a long soft aaah sound, almost like a sighing invitation.

So I took care to let the whole length of my shaft lie along the crack and then pressed it firmly in. She began her clenching and relaxing motions again. I stood still and let her find her own rhythm. Each time she clenched she made a little noise, a soft moan that sounded like an endearment.

This was exciting – a marvellously intimate embrace that she enjoyed performing. I simply stood and let her continue till I began to push in further with little thrusts upwards so my stiffness was moving along her arse-crack. Her moans became a little louder, her movements a little quicker. I felt she was moving towards that moment when she wanted to feel me inside her so I withdrew my cock till the head was resting at the bottom of her crack. One firm thrust would send me deep into her quim from there.

She realised what I was doing and said in a whisper, 'Wait.' She leaned further down, still circling herself on my cock. Her arms dipped over the edge of the couch – she looked as if she was trying to find something. And suddenly I felt her snake back and my cock was covered by her warm hand, slathered in an oily cream. She gently rubbed that smooth oil all over my cock – it was exhilarating and I began to twitch. When she felt that, she grabbed me hard and stopped her stroking. 'Wait,' she said again.

Her hand let me go and my cock lay between her legs. 'Move back, my sweet,' she murmured. I wasn't sure quite what she wanted from me for we seemed to be on the verge of some deep embrace. I watched as her hand came back, not to grip my cock again but to stroke her own arse. Her hand was liberally full of that oily grease and she layered it along the crack. I could see it glistening there and gazed as her finger circled her arse-hole, one finger reaching inside, then two, in and out till that small hole was oiled. 'There!' she said.

I thought she was simply saying that because she had completed what she wanted to do, and that was greasing her arse-crack. I surmised that she wanted my cock to slide into that oily crack so that I would spurt my jism there. But she wanted more than that. I moved in to let my stand press along the crack, and soon I was moving in a softly lubricated slipperiness. Phillipa was helping me, making sure I pressed deeply in till she gently moved herself away. Then she breathed out almost inaudibly, 'In.'

At first I couldn't tell what she was saying, so I simply continued with that greasy slide. Then her voice came more sharply to me. 'Inside. Put it inside.' I made a move to let my cock slide away so I could press between her legs but she clenched me. 'Inside. There.'

I knew what she wanted. I knew now why she had covered herself with oil, why her fingers had probed inside. She wanted me to push my cock inside her arsehole. I was staggered by this. I had never done this. I had always presumed that to push my prick in there was in some way humiliating to a woman, though I had heard that for some it was a heightened experience, even more exciting than any other way. But it had never occurred to me that Mrs Courtney would want that. But here she was, insisting, moving her arse so that the head of my cock was now resting at the rim of her hole.

'You can push in,' she muttered. 'Slowly. I want to feel it going in. Thick. Gentle.' I began to think that this was some ultimate experience for her. It was part of what we were: she an upper-class charmer laying herself open to be taken roughly from behind by a working-class man, pushing his hard cock (and by now I was tremendously hard) inside her arse. I think she knew that would excite me enormously, not only because it was something that was rare, even taboo, but because she knew that within me was still this notion of being made to feel inferior by upper-class people. It was a kind of revenge. The blood rushed to my cock to make it feel bigger and stiffer, perhaps too fat to probe its way into that tiny orifice.

But what Mrs Courtney was doing was not simply for me but for herself as well. All her tricks led her to be more and more explicit and it seemed that now she had found a way to experience something she wanted to try, something that perhaps she could never experience with anyone else. Here in this hotel room, unknown to anyone else except me whom she would not see again that often, she could attempt this. And she knew she could rely on me to fulfill this desire. She had obviously had it in mind. She had worked it out, had left the tube of oil on the couch so that she could reach it as she was bending over.

All this ran through my head in the few seconds after she had asked me to prod my prick into her there. That quietened my qualms about the act and how humiliating she might have found it – after all, she was offering herself in this way, I was not forcing her. 'There, now, there,' she repeated breathlessly. 'Push it in. I want you to fill me up.'

With a slowness that I found difficult to control because I was thoroughly excited, I let my cock-head nudge at the hole. She whimpered and gave a little yelp so I stopped, thinking it was painful for her. 'Go on,' she sighed, shifting her stance to accommodate me so I moved on ... and in.

It felt remarkably tight, almost impossible to move, my cock gripped so hard that it was somewhat painful. And yet somehow I had a sense that if I moved further in, all the pain would diminish. Something would break open without pain and without damage, Phillipa would take me towards some excruciatingly ecstatic moments that she herself would also experience, as if we would be fused more closely than we had ever been.

So I pressed on. Her whimpering became steady and I was afraid that we would have to stop. I stood without pushing and I felt a firm muscular grip on me, my cock-head just inside.

One of Phillipa's hands had come between her legs and was squeezing my balls. I had looped a hand round to stroke her quim which was freely and juicily flowing. She was moving her body on me and that enabled me to prod in further. She drew in a hissing breath as she felt my stiff prick enter her further. She began to push back on me, wanting me deeper and I kept moving in slowly. Each time I went further in, she groaned from the back of her throat, an almost unearthly cry that made me wonder whether I should stop.

But she didn't cry out to ask me to stop. My cock was working its way in, feeling enormously swollen because it was so tightly held. Progress in was very slow and Phillipa was pushing back carefully on me but drawing me in, a throbbing grip holding me. I was tremendously excited by this but strangely I did not feel I was moving to a climax, though I surmised that my climax when it came would be a real burst.

Phillipa was still clenching me. It was still very difficult to move. She was groaning and I was panting and grunting. In a strange way I almost forgot what I was doing. I knew I was fucking, of course, but it no longer mattered to me where my cock was. I was consumed with the notion of moving on because I sensed that something vital would happen.

And it did happen. Suddenly Phillipa's quim seemed to unleash a veritable spasm of juice which made me push harder and then there was a letting go, a beautiful relaxation as if we had achieved some inevitable opening. My cock finally seemed to be able to move at will, Phillipa was loose though she said between moans, 'I'm full. You fill me up.'

I was now entirely inside her and began to move steadily in slow thrusts. Phillipa's groans now were large sighs of excitement. Her quim was bathing a free flow of juice over my fingers. Her hand was stroking my balls, pushing them against her arse, as if she needed more inside her.

Then there was no stopping us. My thrusts quickened and Phillipa pressed back onto me till I felt I was as deep as I could go. A whole bevy of pulses throbbed along my cock, Phillipa's juice was flooding out, her strangled cries were now very loud, interspersed with cries of 'Fill me!' and 'Yes! Yes!' And my cock-head began to swell and there came out of my slit a surge of jism, unlike other surges for in that confined space it splashed back all over the head and I thrust on, an excruciating experience, almost unbearable.

Phillipa felt my cream inside her and that made her judder fast against me, driving me on and driving herself into an ecstasy of quick pressures. It was as if she wanted my jism to spurt so hard that it would break through to her quim She was wriggling very fast so that my fingers on her quim did not have to move – she was pressing them into herself.

And this seemed to last longer, my cock seemed to remain harder and even when eventually I lost some of my stiffness, it remained snugly inside Phillipa. And we stood together a long time till finally we both were aware of ourselves, where we were, what we had done.

Phillipa led me to the bed. She never mentioned what we had done but the way she treated me afterwards, her mouth seeming to wander into every nook and cranny of my body, indicated that she was grateful to me, that she had wanted this and had found it more compelling than even she had imagined. She told me all this, not by words but by her attentions to my body. And later she gave me a deeply satisfying fuck that was straightforward, with almost no frills but a real concentration on lingering, unhurrying, letting me feel completely close to her.

And on the Sunday morning, our last time together,

she was still attentive. Again she did not mention what we had done but eventually she had to move away from her sexual ventures to get herself ready to go. But she interrupted her dressing and her packing with little touches and random caresses till we drifted away from each other. Both of us were tired and I for one was quite sore.

'Thank you for such a lovely weekend,' she purred while Charles had gone to supervise the loading of her cases in the car. 'I especially enjoyed our picnic.' Then she added in a quiet and vaguely mysterious voice, 'And I'll especially remember our Saturday night.' She laughed a tinkly laugh as if to dismiss her thought. 'I hope we can do it again sometime.' I didn't know whether she meant another weekend or just that exciting Saturday experience. 'I'd love to see you more often, my dear Nicholas, but I'm finding it more and more difficult to get away on my own.'

She gave me a warm. open-mouthed kiss. 'Perhaps I'll have an opportunity to invite you down to see me. And ring me when you're next in London. Maybe I'll be able to get away to see you.'

Charles came in to report everything was ready. She gave me a quick hug and as she pressed her cheek next to me I thought I heard her breathe out into my ear. I may have been mistaken but it sounded like a long 'aaah!' and it reminded me of her lingering over the word "arse". And when she took her arms down, there was a slightly wicked smile on her face.

Charles began to move out of the room and Phillipa stepped slowly back. 'I'd love to stay,' she whispered, 'but I'm afraid I wouldn't survive.'

At the door she turned to give me a little wave. 'I've paid for the room for this evening, Nicholas. I won't be here but perhaps you'd like to stay. You can relax . . . but spend a few minutes thinking about me.' She smiled again. 'I won't be dressed quite the same way on the way back but at least you can sit here and remember!' And with that she swept out.

I did manage to dash through London in the early summer on my way down to Devon where I was going to work in the kitchen of a hotel in Torquay for the summer. I didn't have enough time to see Mrs Courtney though she sounded as if she would have liked to rush down to Torquay at some point. But she never did.

Still, I told myself, there would be other times to see her. At least, I hoped so. I had grown to like her horticultural delights, her banquets, her forbidden fruits. She was the most marvellously hospitable hostess I have ever known: she always made a great effort to put herself out to entertain me in tremendously appetising, tempting and exotic ways.

9. Dance To The Lady

My first university year was moving to its close and I was preparing for final examinations and writing essays in my various courses. I was working very hard but I was still managing to find time to spend an evening or two a week with Barbara. That seemed to suit her – she didn't want any committed relationship with anyone and she was happy with our mutually satisfying escapades.

I seemed to make very little headway with Lorna even after our interesting encounter with the television and *Hamlet*. She was always busy with schoolwork and we never found convenient times to get together, though I wondered if she really just wanted to avoid any further elaborations with me. If we spoke on the phone, she sounded shy whenever I edged the conversation towards that evening. Finally I stopped mentioning the subject.

Occasionally Daisy phoned me and our talk often veered deliciously into lascivious innuendo. She was a great talker: her voice floated to me with a whispery huskiness, peppered with little laughs, invitingly affectionate but without wavering from her resolve though she always apologised. 'I'm sure we'd have a good time together, Nick,' she said once, 'but you understand, don't you? I have to keep to my decision, stick to my guns.' Then she laughed and added, 'though I'd really like to let you stick your gun at me!' After another laugh, she went on, 'It'd be a real pleasure to make your gun sticky!'

Sometimes she talked in a very enticing way, trying to break me down to give in to her. 'Save your spare cash, Nick. It's value for money.' And though cash was never a problem for me (Gerry was still being very generous), I simply decided that maybe Daisy would break down before me.

Once every four or five weeks I'd meet her for lunch. She always looked so fresh, acted so openly, I was sometimes tempted. She'd touch my hand, stroke it a little though I don't think she really set out to make me succumb. Still, it was obvious that Daisy was one of those women who exuded a subtly, extravagant sultriness, not vampy, not simply teasing. And she was terrific to look at. While she was eager to save her money, she didn't let that stop her from dressing herself with a tasty sexiness. She attracted admiring glances wherever we were and sometimes when she leaned across the table to whisper something especially sexy, (I sometimes thought she was deliberately letting any men sitting near overhear her remarks) I know the men in the place were all envious of me.

She often reminded me of her decision to save money so that, by the time she was twenty-five, she'd have a nest-egg that would allow her to choose what she really wanted to do. 'After all, it's only just over another two years,' she would say. 'Just about the time you'll be finishing university. So I'll be graduating at the same time as you. That calls for some kind of celebration, don't you think? And I know the kind of celebration you'd like! Me too!'

When she made a promise like that I wasn't quite sure she meant it. I tended to take it as part of this sexy game she liked to play with me though she did keep referring to her 'retirement' and how I was going to be a part of her celebration. And there wasn't an ounce of deception in her when she talked to me and she did seem to enjoy being with me. So I held onto my money and I held onto that promise she kept making, hoping that one day she would fulfill it.

Ron and I had remained friends though we led our separate lives. Once or twice a week, when we'd had enough of studying, we'd go out for a couple of pints and while we might chat up any women hanging around the bar, we never pushed them with any real interest. Ron was, by now, enjoying a much better love life; a lot of women students found his jovial, almost devil-may-care approach to university life attractive.

Most Saturdays Ron and I went to the Student Union dances which, we discovered were attended by many young women on the look-out for a good time – not just students, but nurses, secretaries, office workers and so on. Quite a few of them were very interested in fixing themselves up with a man at the end of the dance though not all of them would end up sleeping with their partner for the night. Still, a fair number of them would and it soon became almost common knowledge which women were the most amenable. Of course this knowledge was not always correct, as Ron and I sometimes found out.

But we enjoyed our evenings there, scouting around, drinking, pursuing various partners through the course of the evening. As we danced, we'd let our talk drift towards their situation and what they might be doing at the end of the dance. In the process we'd try to discover if they wanted a ride home, hoping they had a flat to themselves. Sometimes we ventured to suggest that they might like to come back to my place or to Ron's.

It became a kind of game. Towards the end of the dance, Ron and I would confer about our chances, each egging the other on to make a serious play for some woman so we could keep the evening going together. After all, we had an ace up our sleeves – Ron had a car, still a rarity at that time. Women liked the idea of getting a ride and Ron always gave me a lift with whatever woman I had in tow.

Obviously we tended to go after those women with a reputation for always being ready for action. But they were often besieged by other men who knew about them, so Ron and I were not always successful. Not that we worried that much if we failed – Barbara was always happy to see me and these days Ron didn't lack for partners among the students. We kept our Saturdays at the level of a game, laughing about it afterwards, enjoying it when we succeeded.

This may all sound a little callous but I'm convinced that most of the women we met at the dances also saw it as a game, playing off one man against another, promising but leaving things tentative, trying to make the best 'deal' they could. It was certainly not as free as those times in the 1960s, that period of sexual liberation, but those dances were about as free as anyone could find at the time.

And over the months I did manage to hook up with three or four women who lived up to expectations, perhaps not immediately on that first night after the dance but revealing enough about themselves to suggest they would be worth pursuing.

I remember particularly a blonde called Sylvia who had looked startlingly attractive in a skin-tight purple dress. Early the next week I took her out for dinner and as I was waiting for the waitress to bring the bill, she said in the most innocent of voices. 'I've just moved into a new flat. The landlady's so nice. She doesn't mind me having visitors at all just so long as we don't make any noise. And she decorated it really nicely. Would you like to come and see it?' I thought I knew what that invitation meant so of course I accepted.

As soon as she let me in she took off her coat and then began to take her dress off. She indicated I should do the same. 'Don't drop your shoes on the floor.' She scattered her clothing in a trail across the floor leading to the bedroom and by the time we both were in there, we were naked.

I spent a very hectic night with her though she insisted I creep downstairs at five in the morning in spite of how 'nice' the landlady was about visitors. 'I don't think she'd take kindly to overnight visitors,' she said as she kissed me and pushed me gently out of the door.

Then there was Judith, a petite, dark-skinned, black-haired Jewish woman who had clung very closely to me when we danced, giving me all kinds of ideas. However, I was a little disappointed when we went back to Ron's place. Ron soon made himself scarce in his bedroom with the woman he'd brought and that left the living room to me and Judith. But she remained aloof, more often than not shrugging me away after a few little embraces and touches. She seemed more interested in raiding Ron's pantry for food though she complained that most of it was not kosher. She scoffed cheese and crackers by the ton and sipped continually at Ron's best sherry.

She was an engaging personality but I soon resigned myself to just having conversation with her. She was bright and companionable but I couldn't make any moves on her. She drew away, began eating or drinking and started new conversations whenever I tried to put my arms around her.

Eventually Ron emerged from his bedroom to suggest it was perhaps time for me to take Judith home. I wasn't too unhappy. I calculated that I was getting nowhere so the best thing to do would be to take her home and for me to get a good night's sleep.

Ron was prepared to drive us, though I knew he had plans in mind for himself. It turned out that the woman he was with, though very interested in Ron, was a little embarrassed to proceed while there were other people about, even though they were in another room. While Judith was in the bathroom, Ron said, 'You understand, old chap. She's warmed up in there. I'd like to bring her to the boil but I can't while you two are in here. She's a bit shy,' and he winked.

I fully expected that I'd simply get Ron to drive us to Judith's place where I'd drop her off after exchanging a few casual goodnight kisses. Then Ron would take me to my place and he'd be back in bed with his partner soon enough.

Judith was a very charming and attractive woman but I was reconciled to some quiet, uneventful moments with her to end the evening. She certainly didn't seem a prime candidate for any kind of sexual ploy.

We were sitting in the back of Ron's car and Ron was driving in his dashing manner – he obviously was in a hurry to get back to bed. It was about one in the morning and the streets were almost deserted so Ron was not taking any chances with his fast driving. If anything, Judith was faster!

Her appetite for food now was transformed into a different appetite. It took me completely by surprise. She squashed up tightly against me on that back seat, took my hand and gave me a sloppy lick across my palm, then placed my hand on her breast. Her face came to me, her mouth open and her kiss was almost voracious. She began to suck at my tongue, pulling it deeply into her mouth, her hand opening her coat so that my hand slid along the silk of her dress. She moved so that my hand was stroking her breast without my having to move it.

That was only a beginning, and soon she had climbed across me. Her hands were expert in getting my cock out of my trousers. Almost as quickly I had all the buttons on her dress undone, my hands sliding under her slip, inside her panties. As soon as I touched her, I felt how moist she was and when she felt my hand there, her own hands started a furious jerking and pulling on my prick.

Soon she flopped back and pulled me on top of her and in a flurry of hiked skirt and slip, I was tearing her panties down – she herself was so rough, she had got me in the mood of acting a little tough with her and she seemed to enjoy that.

I couldn't figure out why she had changed so radically. Maybe she liked the roughness, the cramped groping and stroking in the car. She was one of those women who wanted things to develop quickly and she didn't mind how uncomfortable it became. And maybe she found the discomfort added to her excitement for soon she was lying right back, her legs way up high, her dress and slip pushed up to her waist.

She reminded me a little of Lorna. She had started as

the same kind of aloof woman but now she was panting for me to push my cock inside her, grabbing at my shaft, letting it slide all around her pubic area in her effort to stick it inside her. Lorna hadn't gone to these lengths, of course, but when she did get it on she acted as if she didn't acknowledge it.

Judith was different. She was muttering breathlessly in my ear, things like, 'Get it in. Right in. Push hard. Do it! Do it to me!' I still didn't know what had triggered Judith into being so sexually active so suddenly. I remembered that Saturday was the Jewish sabbath so I was wondering if she had religious scruples but it had been after midnight when we'd arrived at Ron's. Maybe one o'clock was the turning point for Judith – was that because of Daylight Saving Time? Anyhow, I gave up on trying to discover what made her this way. The way she was behaving had had its effect on me and I was only too willing to oblige her.

She was not constrained by the limited space in the car for she soon had pushed my trousers down so I could move more easily into her. Once she felt my cock touching her quim, she began an exhausting thrashing, bashing herself against me, squiggling so that I could probe into her. Then she ran me ragged with her quick pressings, her twitchings. She clasped her legs tightly round my head and pushed against me hard so it was not long before I was gushing out all over her. My cock was so slippery with come I came slipping out of her so I shot her with jism inside, on her stomach, some shooting up to drench her slip and dress.

I think she was trying not to make too much noise so as not to disturb Ron's driving, but her voice kept breaking out with strangled cries and deep, long hisses, intakes of breath as she drove herself on. I was surprised that the sound from behind Ron – cries, yelps, the rustle of clothing, the heavy breathing, the slap of flesh against flesh, the wet slurping – didn't make him too distracted in his driving.

She sat up straight afterwards, winked at me when she saw the wet spots on her dress, patted my cock, even pulled up my trousers and with a firm grip rammed my cock back inside my underpants. We had a smoochy cuddle for a few minutes till finally, in a very sultry voice, she gave final directions to Ron and we arrived at her place.

She was still living at home so there was no way I could go in with her. We stood at her door for those few kisses I had expected. But they were not as casual as I had expected earlier. She took my hand and placed it on her dress so I felt my still-wet come on her dress. She pushed hard against my hand and gave me one of her ferocious tongue-sucking kisses. Then she went in.

Ron was grinning at me when I got back in the car. I was feeling thoroughly depleted after Judith's furious sexual ploys so I didn't say much and Ron was too concerned about getting back to join his partner. So he simply said, 'Looks like she lived up to her reputation.' We had heard that she was a very amenable woman, though her behaviour always seemed quite demure at the dances and certainly to begin with I thought her reputation was untrue.

I saw her a few times after that first meeting and once or twice she repeated that hectic sexuality. I took her to my place once but she was in her mood of remoteness and nothing much happened. But at other times she was very forthcoming. In the cinema she would drive me wild with her quick grabbing and hauling on my cock. Once she even struggled herself out of her panties. I wondered what she was doing – I had my arm round her and she was wriggling fast and furious, bending down. I thought she had dropped something but when she straightened up, she held something white in her hand. She rammed the material in my trousers pocket, whispering, 'I won't be needing these for the rest of the evening.'

Another time she was quiet in the cinema but afterwards she led me into a back alley and literally pounced on me. While she was a very exciting woman in many ways I found myself too nervous with her. I never knew what she was going to be like and occasionally she manhandled me so roughly I was sore for two or three days afterwards. So I gave up seeing her.

There were one or two others with reputations like Judith's and Sylvia's and during my time at university I managed to see most of them. Sometimes I found that their reputations had been exaggerated, sometimes they lived up to them, sometimes discovered that, while they were amenable, they were only ordinary in their sexuality. As I was involved with Barbara, ordinariness was always a let-down.

But there was one name that always kept cropping up in any discussions about the 'talent' at the dances. That was Noreen. She was a nurse and a little older than the usual run of women at the dances, probably in her late twenties. As I had had nothing but fascinating experiences with older women, I became intrigued by the idea of cottoning onto Noreen at some point. I danced with her sometimes on several Saturdays but got nowhere. The reputation she had meant that she was difficult to lead on: it was common knowledge that she was 'hot stuff'. After all, she was a nurse and the general consensus about nurses was that they dealt with the intricate workings of the body as part of their daily duties so physical things were no problem for them. We all believed that nurses were free and easy though, in my attempts with two or three nurses, I discovered that that was not always the case.

Still, the rumour persisted that Noreen was an experienced and extravagantly co-operative partner. That meant she was besieged every Saturday night by men who fancied their chances with her. An added bonus to her reputation was that she had been married and as Ron reminded me, 'Once they're married, they're getting it on a regular basis. They get to like it a lot. It's a habit with them and most of them find it hard to break it.'

Obviously we all thought that anyone lucky enough to persuade Noreen to let him take her back to the nurses' residence was bound to have a great time with her. Because she was constantly pursued at the dances by a whole gaggle of men, it was very hard even to get to dance with her, and even when a man got lucky, he would have only three short songs to try to set something up with her before he had to hand her over to her next dancing partner. So he knew he had to move fast and, of course, Noreen revelled in keeping men dangling. She enjoyed all the attention she got and men stayed buzzing around her on the off-chance.

Noreen always left the dance early for nurses were supposed to be in by midnight. Most nurses broke their curfew and I don't think they really got into trouble. Besides, they could always use the fact that they had to be in by midnight to get rid of any man who was making himself a nuisance with them.

But Noreen appparently didn't like to take the chance of getting into trouble – she kept to the rules. However, the rumour was that by eleven thirty she was usually so hot to get her hands on a man that she would have left early with him so she could get him inside before midnight. Once he was inside with her, Noreen would never be discovered bringing a man in – the nurse on duty at the door never seemed to take account of how many men were inside the residence, though I was never able to understand that for I heard that usually on a Saturday night it was a dragon-matron who was on door duty.

Anyhow, all these rumours about Noreen made her into a woman always on the look-out for sex, a woman who would smuggle a man in before midnight so he could spend an agreeable amount of time with her. She was not like some of the other nurses at the dances who were into just a quick poke before dashing into the residence. It seemed that Noreen needed more than a fast prod before midnight. So anyone wanting to fix himself up with Noreen needed to make his move early on in the evening, keep hustling, keep trying to dance a second and a third time with her. If he got to that stage he was well on his way with her.

I had been trying to get Noreen's attention for several weeks and she had become a kind of obsession with me. I danced with her on separate occasions and she was very snug against me. She got into a dreamy state during slow dances and the faster ones were an opportunity for her to fling herself out so that her partner pulled her back to nestle close to him. Almost everything Noreen did suggested shivers of excitement; her body fitted neatly against her partner, she pressed close, she breathed warmly into his ear, some of her remarks could be taken as offering suggestive hints.

One Saturday I got lucky. I had arrived at the dance

early on my own – Ron had arranged a date for himself. I didn't think much would be happening at the dance. I had decided that I'd just go into the bar and have a pint or two, I was sure I would meet someone I knew there so I'd pass an hour or so talking and drinking. The bar at that time was open only for men and it was a regular hang-out, not only for men going into the dance but other students and gatecrashers as well.

But as it happened, I knew nobody in the bar so after I'd downed my pint I decided to go and see what talent had arrived at the dance, even though it was still relatively early.

Only a few couples were shuffling around the floor and none of the women standing at the side of the floor waiting to be asked to dance looked especially striking. I was sure that soon the dance would be crowded and lots of more enticing women would be there, so I was about to head back to the bar when, off in a corner, I spotted Noreen dancing with a short and skinny man, somewhat unprepossessing though I could see that he was a very fancy dancer. He was using his brilliant steps to try to fascinate Noreen, perhaps hopeful that he could set himself up with her. But while Noreen was showing that she could follow his steps and was seemingly enjoying the dance, it was apparent from the look on her face that she was not particularly interested in the man.

Noreen was not what one would call a raving beauty. She was tall and slim but her face was almost plain. Her wide mouth looked a little too wide (though the rumour was that she made excellent use of her mouth! Someone even suggested that it had become so wide because of what she put in it!). Her teeth were big and protruded slightly and that gave her mouth a kind of fullness that was somehow appealing. She made the most of her mouth by shaping her lips with a lusciously dark lipstick. Her eyes were brown and large and she was one of the few women at that time who took care to emphasize them with make-up. She used mascara and eyeliner to make the most of those deep brown eyes. Her black hair was unfashionably long, curled sensuously below her shoulders. She usually wore dark dresses and this particular evening she was wearing a black sleeveless frock, showing off her slim arms. The bodice had a daringly plunging opening at the front which finished at the point of a V almost at her waist. Her legs looked exquisite in black stockings with seams immaculately straight along the length of their enticing shapeliness.

I could tell she was slightly bored for she was staring over the shoulder of her partner distractedly in spite of the fact that she was moving gracefully to the music. And then as she made a quick elegant swirl around, I thought at that point she had taken the lead and whisked her partner around before he could stop her. She looked in my direction and a mere wisp of a smile crossed her lips. She raised one finger from her partner's shoulder as a small wave – after all, she had danced with me and she did know me slightly – so I took the smile and the brief waggle of her finger as a signal. I took it as a plea to rescue her so I moved as nonchalantly as I could – I didn't want to draw attention to myself in case the few men who were standing about also were eyeing Noreen. Once the music had stopped, I was in the right position to step quickly onto the floor and, before she could even walk away from her partner, I moved in and asked her for the next dance.

She looked at me with that slight smile on her face, her eyes seeming to assess me. 'My! You are keen, aren't you? You must really want to dance.' There was a mischievous emphasis on the word "dance", I thought, though I was so obsessed by Noreen and her reputation, maybe I was seeing signs that weren't really there. The way she spoke to me gave no indication that she had smiled or waved her finger at me.

'Well, provided it isn't a tango or one of those new-fangled conga things, yes, I'd like to dance with you. I can't get the hang of some of these new dances. I guess I'm just old-fashioned. You get used to the things you like to do and you just go on doing them.' And again I started to read all kinds of innuendos in her words.

When the band started to play for the next set of dances, I took her hand immediately and then took her in my arms. And so the dance began, with me already determined that this would be my evening to keep Noreen for myself.

I am not a very good dancer but luckily the band was playing a slow waltz. Noreen made me feel as if I was much more skilful than I really was, though in her own way I think she was really taking the lead. She felt light in my arms and her waist under my hand moved sinuously. I had a real sense of holding an elegant slimness and after we had circled the floor for a minute or two she somehow positioned herself snugly against me. We were taking slow, small steps, sliding our feet, our legs moving together. She was swaying against me and I felt the beginnings of a warm stiffness growing. I remembered Barbara's game with the words of songs, substituting the word "fuck" for the word "dance".

I presumed Noreen could feel that I was semi-erect but she made no move to pull away from me. If anything, I thought that perhaps she was nestling her body so that she could feel it more firmly. And by the end of the third song in that set, she was holding me tightly and her cheek was brushing against mine.

I decided I would try to hold onto her for the next series of dances. I had already made a few tentative remarks about the possibilities of seeing her home but she shrugged them off. 'It's still early in the evening to think about going home.'

'Well, I don't mean we should go right now. Later on. The end of the evening. Whenever you're ready to go.'

'We'll see,' she said teasingly. She gave me what I thought was a small squeeze of encouragement at my waist, so I made up my mind that I would pursue her for the rest of the evening. I was sure I stood a real chance with her.

'Whenever you feel you want to leave, just let me know. I'll be ready when you are.'

We were dancing closely and she pulled away from me briefly. I thought I'd perhaps overstepped the mark. But she said, 'Oh, I'll know when I'm ready.' She stared at me with her big eyes, then grinned, pulling herself back against me. Her cheek was against mine and her voice breathed out softly, 'We're not in any rush, are we? I always enjoy taking things easy. Making them last. Plenty of time yet. Let's just dance for now.'

She put such an emphasis on the words "for now" that she seemed to be suggesting she'd like to change that word "dance" to the other word Barbara loved to sing. I took this as confirmation that I was doing well with her. She made it even clearer by squeezing very close to me, her chin on my shoulder, slowing down her steps so that we were almost not moving at all. She whispered in my ear in a dreamy voice, 'I love this song. Every time I hear it you wouldn't believe what it does to me. It gives me ... goose pimples.' She sighed and then, in a voice that was almost inaudible, she said, 'At least that's what I'm feeling now.' She ground her chin further into my shoulder, and added, 'Maybe it's not just the song.'

I thought I was making good progress with Noreen for over the next hour or so she danced with me a couple more times. One was a set of medium fox-trots and she swayed even more sinuously against me. I asked her again if I could see her home at the end of the dance, 'Save the last waltz for me,' I said.

'Oh, I never stay till the end. I have to be back before twelve.' She pressed closely to me. 'I might turn into a pumpkin or something.' She paused. 'And I wouldn't want to lose my shoe or anything else ... here.'

'Well, I'll be ready when you are,' I insisted.

This time she stepped further back from me though she continued to sway, her hand still holding mine. 'Oh.' She was giving me a very quizzical look and her mouth formed a perfect open circle before it spread into a smile. 'Will you?'

'Will I what?'

'Be ready.'

'Absolutely.'

I knew this set of dances was nearly at an end and I still hadn't got a definite answer from her. 'What d'you say?' I persisted.

'I say lots of things. There's lots of things I like to say.' This verbal fencing was getting to me though I was hoping to snare her finally. She slowed our dancing down again and breathed into my ear, 'Lots of things I like to do as well.'

I took this as a positive response. 'So where will I meet you?' By now we were both moving so sensually against each other, it was obvious to both of us that we were more interested in moving the dancing into other directions. I had a firm hard-on and Noreen was pushing herself against it as we danced. Even so I was a little surprised when she said, 'I'll have to see.'

By now I was beginning to feel that I was being teased. I had almost decided that I might as well give up, though it had never been a part of Noreen's reputation that she was simply a cockteaser.

'Oh come on, say yes,' I said a bit peevishly.

'You'd like me to say yes?'

'I certainly would.'

The music was winding its way to the end as she said, 'I'm here with a couple of friends.' For a moment I was convinced she had been leading me on – maybe all this time she had fixed herself up with some other man. But she went on, 'I invited them to the dance. Two nurses. They've only been here two weeks or so. They don't know the ropes so I brought them and I don't see how I can leave them in the lurch.'

'Oh, I'm sure they won't mind. They've probably met someone. They'll be able to take care of themselves.'

She gave me that quizzical look again. 'Can you look after yourself? You keep going on as if you want me to look after you.'

'That would be nice.'

'I'm not sure I can handle you as well as look after the other two.'

The music came to an end but Noreen stayed glued close to me for some time, moving ever so gently onto my erection. Then she said, 'Come on. I'll introduce you. Maybe we can work something out.'

Her two friends, Pam and Eileen, were quite attractive, especially Pam; I was surprised no one had latched onto them. I didn't remember seeing them before when I'd first come into the dance. Maybe they'd gone to the

Ladies or were dancing. I began to wish that Ron was with me – I'm sure he'd have been very willing to take one of these two off Noreen's hands.

We stood chatting for a while and then the music started again. I didn't quite know what to do. I was thinking of asking Noreen to dance again but somebody came and whisked her away before I had a chance to ask her. So quickly I asked Pam to dance.

She felt very different to hold from Noreen. She was of average height, a blonde, very vivacious but something of a quick stepper when she danced. Still, she was soon nestling close to me. She was not nuzzling to press against my erection which had quietened down after I had danced with Noreen but she pushed her plump breasts onto my chest. I even felt that her nipples were big and firm.

I began to explain that I was with Noreen and would like to walk her back to the residence. I was hoping Pam would understand what I was suggesting. I even tentatively suggested that Pam and Eileen could avail themselves of the company of some men at the dance if they were interested.

Pam shook her head slowly. 'I'm new here. I don't think I'm ready just yet to ... well, you know how it is.' She paused. 'With men.' Another pause. 'After a dance.' She smiled. 'I just don't want to ... start anything just now.' She squeezed my hand as we danced. 'I don't want you to get the idea that I'm a ... wet blanket.' She laughed. 'It's just that ... I'm new in the residence. I don't want matron to get the wrong idea about me early on.'

That didn't sound too encouraging, though the way Pam danced with me certainly didn't give the impression that she would be a wet blanket. In fact, if I hadn't been doing so well with Noreen, I might have tried my luck with Pam. And as she clung closely to me, I surmised that she might be quite interested in me.

So I was in something of a bind. Still, if I stayed with Pam at the end of the dance I was sure that Noreen would come back to be with her two new friends.

And that's what happened. When Noreen came back she surprised me by linking me, rubbing up closely to me, looking straight at Pam. 'I saw you two smooching round the floor. Nice ... but I saw him first.'

'I could get used to coming to dances if there's men like him around,' Pam said.

Noreen laughed. 'You can almost count on it. You'll soon find out.'

'And I really love to dance,' Pam went on.

'Me too,' Noreen added and they both laughed. I think they were playing a little game between them, something to do with that substitution of the word "dance".

I danced with Noreen again, moving languorously. It wasn't long before my erection returned in full vigour. Noreen's hands gradually wandered down my spine, resting just below my waist, exerting pressure to push me against her. She began a slow rhythmic pressure that was like pushing my cock into her. Then she suddenly said, 'I think Pam and Eileen are alright. I don't think they'll mind. And Pam thinks I'll be in good hands. I think she likes you.'

'What time then?'

'I'd better stay around just in case they don't know what happens at the end of these dances, you know, all that mad scuffling and chasing around. So all being well, I'll see you about half-past eleven at the door.'

'Isn't that a bit late? I mean, you have to be in before midnight.'

Noreen laughed. 'Not to worry. I'll be in before midnight,' then with a very broad grin on her face she added, 'Then I'll get you in even if it isn't before midnight.'

That sounded like a direct invitation and it may well have been but she followed it by saying, 'I tell you what, Just to be on the safe side, I'll stay on with Pam and Eileen here and the three of us will walk back to the residence together. Then I won't feel badly about them.'

I was beginning to feel my opportunity was slipping through my fingers. 'But ... d'you want me to come along with ... Won't it look awkward, the four of us, all going in together, and so late, near midnight?' I was confused about Noreen's plan.

'It'll be OK. We'll head out about eleven fifteen or so. You can go and have a last pint if you want.' She crushed me against her and went on, 'I'll be waiting for you.' She paused. 'In my room.'

'I can't just walk into the residence on my own ... and after midnight.'

'It's not a problem. You can climb in through my window. I'm on the ground floor.'

'Somebody told me that they've locked all the windows tight.'

'Not really. They've just screwed in blocks of wood to stop us raising the windows too high.' She squeezed me again. 'I loosened the screws. I leave them in place in case there's an inspection but it's simple for me to lift them out. And then it's up we go!' She made it sound very sexual, especially when she continued, 'I'm a dab hand with a screw.'

She explained how I was to count the windows along the ground floor. 'I'm the fourth one along. Count carefully. I wouldn't want you climbing in the wrong window. That'd be a waste of the evening for me. And I'll have the window all ready for you. You can just slide it up and get in.' The band had just stopped but she leaned provocatively against me, saying, 'As the actress said to the bishop.'

There was no doubt in my mind now that Noreen was definitely fixed on a sexual track. She gave my hand a loving stroke as she moved away. 'See you later,' she said.

I had a couple more beers, drank them slowly, went back to the dance, and to my surprise I saw that Noreen and her two friends were still there. They were having a good time together, so it seemed, huddling in a conspiratorial group, laughing, giggling, nudging each other. Then Noreen saw me and waved and Pam and Eileen also waved to me. Noreen leaned and whispered something in Pam's ear who laughed and then whispered something to Eileen. The three of them went on laughing together. Then they all waved at me again.

That made me feel a little paranoid. In the past I'd been the victim of some practical jokes played on me by women. I'd been set up but their jokes had always developed into intriguing and exciting sexual escapades. I knew Noreen's reputation so I was not sure she was trying to set me up. All her remarks had been geared towards sexual meaning. Her body had been pushing at my erection and she seemed genuine when she had talked about my climbing into her room. Eventually I was able to convince myself that everything would work out fine.

As it was only about a twenty-minute walk to the nurses' residence, I took my time, waiting around a little. The bar had closed but a few acquaintances were standing around, waiting for their women, joking with me when they discovered I wasn't waiting for anyone. I didn't tell them about Noreen.

The night air had cooled down after a pleasantly balmy late spring day. Cloud cover had moved in so it was quite a dark night. That would make it easy for me to slip through the grounds of the residence without being seen. A few lights were still shining out of some windows but the curtains were drawn. I looked at my watch, just after twelve thirty, safe enough for me to make my move into Noreen's room.

I counted the windows carefully to decide which was Noreen's. I had a brief flash of discomfort again – suppose Noreen had set me up to climb into the supervising nurse's room? But then I told myself that the supervisor would keep her window securely locked so I wouldn't be able to climb in. It would just mean I wouldn't know just which room Noreen was in.

I counted the windows again and scuttled across to the one I figured was Noreen's. I knocked quietly on the glass – no answer. I knocked again – still no answer. I decided to try the window. At first it wouldn't budge, then suddenly it gave way and went up fast, making a harsh squeal. A female voice came, 'Sh! Keep it down.' Then after a pause the voice said, 'No. On second thoughts, keep it up!' That was followed by subdued and muffled snorting and laughter.

I climbed in. The voice came again, 'Close the curtains.' It sounded like Noreen's voice.

'I can't see a damn thing in here. It's very dark.'

'I don't want to put the light on in case you haven't closed the curtains properly.' There was a moment of silence. 'Well?' Noreen said.

'Well what?' I asked.

'What are you waiting for?'

'I can't see a thing in here. I don't know where you are. I might trip over things.'

'Feel your way over.' That snuffling snort broke out again. 'Over here. Follow the sound of my voice. I'm in bed. Feel in front of you. You never know what your hands might get hold of. Mine too when you get over here. Get your clothes off and you can get straight into bed. You won't catch cold. And I'll keep you warm.'

I didn't need a second invitation. It was definitely Noreen who was talking so I was prepared to stumble my way across the room to find her bed. I was throwing my clothes off, just dropping them on the floor. My eyes were getting a little accustomed to the darkness; the curtains must have been made from very heavy material because no light came in from outside and in any case it was a dark night.

'Where are you, Noreen?'

'Over here. The bed's right opposite the window. Just walk a straight line. There's nothing in the way. And I bet you've got some probe sticking out in front of you.' And again I heard the snort and snuffle and laugh.

As it happens, I was starting to grow stiff, not a full erection but substantial as Noreen's remarks, her nononsense jokiness, and the thought of her lying in bed waiting for me was enough stimulus. 'Get over here,' Noreen muttered in a husky voice. 'My hands are really warm for you.' I gave a sudden lurch when I thought I had managed to move across the room. I just hoped I wouldn't bang into anything. My cock had now sprung further into life when Noreen had spoken.

Then there was a sudden flash as the light came on. Pam and Eileen were standing at the foot of Noreen's bed, looking right at me, laughing. Noreen was sitting up in bed, the sheets pulled around her.

'Sorry, Nick. We couldn't resist it!'

'It was Pam's idea!' Eileen mumbled.

'Well, I certainly couldn't resist that!' Pam said pointing at my cock, still hard though it had shrivelled a little from being in the spotlight.

Pam took a step forward, her hands out in front of her. 'The poor thing! It's getting cold. Let me warm it up for you.'

'Hold on!' Noreen growled as she started to get out of bed.

'Share and share alike. What are friends for?' Pam said as she moved to grab me with her outstretched hands.

Noreen gripped Pam and held her away. 'No. No. We agreed. You only get to look. That was the agreement. Just a joke.' Noreen then flung herself on me. My cock had stiffened again – it was kind of flattering to think that two of these women were almost fighting over who should touch my prick. And then Noreen was holding me tight and I stiffened even more. She began to haul me to her bed, saying, 'That's enough for you two for now.' I must admit that I thought we were in for a foursome though how we'd have managed it, I didn't know. Noreen's bed was very narrow.

'That's not fair,' Pam said in a pouty, sultry manner but I think she was just carrying on with the joke. Eileen had moved to the door. 'Come on, Pam,' she said. 'Don't spoil Noreen's fun.'

'Just let me have a little touch, Noreen,' Pam sulked. 'Don't be a spoilsport!'

'It's you who's being a spoilsport now. Remember, I said, no touching. You've had a good look.'

'Alright then,' Pam muttered. As Eileen opened the door to leave, Pam scuttled around the room scooping up some of the clothes I had dropped and before I knew it she was at the door. I tried to struggle away from Noreen so I could retrieve my clothes from Pam but it was difficult as Noreen had a firm hold on my cock.

'Oh, no. You're not going anywhere,' Noreen insisted. 'She's just trying to get you to follow her.'

Pam by now had pushed Eileen outside into the corridor. 'Then you'll have to come and get them for yourself,' Pam said. 'I'm just two doors down, this way.' She pointed down the corridor.

'Out you go!' Noreen hissed hoarsely. 'and turn the light out as you go.' So then we were in the dark again, tumbling onto Noreen's bed. She flopped on top of me, mumbling how she thought it was a joke I wouldn't mind having played on me. 'But the joking's over,' she said. 'It's serious business now.'

Her long body completely covered mine and she was pressing down hard on me. My stiff prick was squashed up against her and she was licking and sucking and kissing all over my face, my neck, my chest. As her mouth was busy she was saying rambunctiously, 'Fat chance there'll be anything left for her after I've finished with you.' She squiggled a hand between our bodies till her fingers found my cock, 'You might be a strong piece of rope now but you'll be no more use than a piece of chewed string soon.'

She was as good as her word. At first I thought she was going to be one of those strong, domineering types who like to take charge. She had hauled me onto the bed, she had kicked Pam out of her room and she had clamped herself on top of me. Then her fingers somehow got my shaft loose to poke through her legs and her other hand looped back to tickle my cock-head deliciously.

She kept her slippery mouth working on me but gabbling away as well. 'I hope you didn't mind us getting a good sken at you. We all thought you'd be worth looking at ... and we were right! Got me going to see you sticking up like that!' She was sucking at my ears, licking her tongue round my eyes, sliding it down my nose and into my mouth with quick darts. Her fingertips were devastatingly soft and supple, peeling my foreskin back from the head and touching me with little nibbling flicks so I was twitching mightily between her legs.

I was content to let her continue with her feelings and kisses while my hands began to stroke the round firmness of her arse, sliding up to her waist, then endeavouring to grope through to her breasts squashed against me. She moved off me a little so my hands had more room to stroke. I let my palms rest gently on the top of each nipple and slowly I felt them grow hard. I circled the aureoles with my fingertips, occasionally grabbing at the nipples.

It was then she began to melt, let go of her slightly domineering attitude. She sighed and slowed down her own movements on me to savour my stroking. 'I told you we didn't need any light. It's better to feel our way.' Her fingers were doing a tantalising flutter along my cock. I squeezed her breasts gently.

'I'd still like to see more of you. After all, you've seen me!'

'Wait a minute then.' She clambered off me. 'You stay right there.' I saw her vague shape go to the window. She pulled the curtains back. A little light drifted in, just enough for me to see the outline of her long, slim body. It had an immediate response from me – my dick sprang up fatter and stiffer.

'There!' she said. 'I hope no one's prowling about out there, peering in here to watch what's going on.' She walked slowly back to me. 'But who cares? They'll get a kick out of it ... but not as much of a kick as I'm going to get! Just look at you, you fat horny man, you!'

She shivered a little. 'Hey! You left the window open.' She turned back to squeal it down and scurried over to me. 'I need to be warmed up.' She leapt into bed. It was so narrow that we were tightly crushed together side by side. I could feel that she was in a way, not unpleasantly, going limp, relaxing against me, giving me the message that she was ready for me to take over.

I pushed her away and then shoved her to lie on her back. I raised myself on an elbow, gripped my cock and waggled it at her. 'I have a red hot poker here that'll warm you up. Just make you sizzle.' I moved up and placed my cock on one of her nipples, let it rotate before I pressed it down into the yielding flesh of her breast. She moaned a little and her hand reached to stroke me, pushing it harder onto her breast.

'I know just the place to quench that red hot poker,' she whispered. 'I've got a wet place to stick it in and soon you'll be hosing yourself down.'

'I'm going to let it burn all around you first,' I told her.

'My titties feel so good. You're scorching them up.' I slid across her so that my prick was free to move easily from one breast to the other and she kept her hands in place to do a delicate finger-dance along the length of my shaft, one fingertip lingering at the rolled-back foreskin, flickering in a teasing tickle round and round. Then she licked her fingers and smoothed them round the swollen head. My slippery cock was sliding effortlessly over her breasts, banging against her nipples, stiffer and harder now.

One of her hands had grabbed my balls. Her palm felt very soft on them. I moved again so that my balls could hang more freely and Noreen murmured 'Mmm!' as her hand found more to hold onto. She weighed my balls in her hand and her fingers rode up to flick at the root of my cock.

Then she began an even stroke, one wet hand rolling back the skin from my cock-head, the other circling the root, gripping it firmly, pushing down so that she was constantly nudging at my balls. I was still sliding my shaft against her breasts and her hands helped to push it where she wanted to press it onto her. We did this without a word, without a sound, both of us deeply inside this mixture of touching and stroking. I could tell she was involved in her stroking and I was certainly concentrating on my stiff prick, enjoying its prodding and probing at her breasts and nipples, feeling the soft warmth of her flesh.

Finally I moved over her, kneeling across her. She grasped my cock, licking the palms of both hands so that my cock seemed to be moving inside a slick oil. She carefully placed my length between her breasts, pushing the lovely swell of them against me. I started to shove deeply down and inside her breasts so that with each thrust my prick touched under her chin, my balls banging gently at the lower rounded firmness of her breasts. She was pressing her breasts firmly against my cock, so that the channel between them was tight but the flesh was yielding. I moved so that my strokes between her breasts were long and hard, up to press at her throat, down so that the head rested at the plump underside before moving up again.

She pushed her hands even harder, somehow folding her nipples closer to where my dick was moving. I was trying to let my whole shaft throb against her and she was determined that her nipples would touch my hard length as it buried itself inside her breasts.

I rode above her that way for several minutes. My cock was quivering, fattening and it was like a hard, steel rod though her flesh was soft and warm. I imagined that somehow it would melt my stiffness in a deluge of jism. I kept on, hovering at the rim of a flood, stiff and ready to spill onto her breasts.

But I convinced myself that I wanted to thrust into Noreen where she was juicy and creamy. This was a wonderful slow ride but I felt a great urge to touch her quim, to slide inside that juicy slit. I wanted my fingers to trail round those lips, to roll round her clit, to slide a finger inside, deep and long like my cock, pushing in and out, slippery on those lips before prodding inside again.

And as if she was reading my mind, she raised her head slightly so that when my cock emerged at the top of her breasts, her mouth encountered the head. Her lips were sloppy on me, her tongue making little swirls against that tightly rolled-back skin. I stayed there as she worked her mouth, as oily and wet as her quim, I was sure. In a way I wanted to probe my long cock into her mouth deeply, fill her with a hot stiffness, so she could savour the hardness, taste the hotness but we were jammed together too tightly for me to move any further. In any case, her lips and tongue were lapping and licking so exquisitely. She was so generously moist, her teeth so urgently nibbling till she sucked the little jabs of pain away in a gulping slither of lips, I decided to stay with that, my balls resting against her breasts, her mouth guzzling at my cock-head.

I gazed down at her. I would have liked to watch her

mouth as it sucked in the fat head, then see it emerge glistening with her wetness, looking slippery and stiff but the room was too dark. In spite of how much I was enjoying Noreen's tender moistness, I eventually pulled back. As my cock withdrew from her mouth, she whispered, 'No. Come back, love. Bring it back to me.' I could just vaguely see that her mouth was sloppily open, dribbling wetness, her lips red and moist, the wetness covering a whole area around her mouth.

'I want to see your mouth on me. Can I turn the light on?'

'I don't like too much light. It inhibits me. I'll make up for it by doing some more sucky things to you.'

'But I want to watch.'

'Well, you can open the curtains as far back as they'll go.'

I tried to scramble off her but she was still ravenous for my cock. She gripped my buttocks and pushed me hard into her mouth, slavering all over it, covering it with a rich wet ooze.

'You'll make me shoot off doing that!'

She mumbled against my cock-head at her lips, 'No. Not yet. Don't you dare.'

Finally I managed to struggle off her and threw the curtains further back. Not much more light came in but as I moved back to Noreen, I saw the shape of her breasts, high and firm, with her nipples looking huge and stiff. Though, because she was lying down, the flesh had spread a little, somehow her breasts seemed to keep their shapeliness.

She reached an arm out, raised herself a little, touched my cock before bending across to cover my cock-head with her mouth. She slurped at it, her inner lips like moist silk stroked around all my swollen hardness.

She was a true expert at sucking, different from other women whose mouths had also been expert. Her ministrations were making my prick feel as if the head would split open, with a great flood of come spurting down her throat, so much that I imagined white stickiness drooling out of her mouth, dribbling down her chin. I could see how she would wipe it away with her hand, the glue of jism sticky on her fingers as she stroked them against my trembling cock.

Even then Noreen seemed to want to feel my cock all over her face. She let it slide from her mouth, nudged my cock at her chin, took it in her delicate fingers to press it along her nose, hold it to stare at it, tickle her eyelids against it, handle it at her ear before returning to swallow it deeply, sucking hard till it thrust out and up to bang against her nostrils as if she wanted to fill them with come.

This incredible massage of my cock on all the parts of her face gave me the sense that Noreen would like me to push my dick into every part of her body but I didn't know if I'd have the patience or the strength to do that.

Eventually she moved me back to her mouth, sucking me so sloppily that her saliva dribbled down the length before she pushed my wet shaft between her breasts again.

As she was doing all this I was still standing at the side of her bed. I stroked my hands along her stomach, slowly edging them down onto her thick pubic hair. When she sensed the movements of my hands, she spread her legs wider and as my fingers probed down to encounter her clit, she let out a whistling sigh before she drew my cock back into her mouth and thrust her pelvis up to let my finger press and rotate around her clit.

And so we went on, my fingers washed with a warm juiciness. She was very wet, so much so that it was running in trickles down her thighs. I would have liked to spread it all over her thighs with my tongue – I was sure that quim-juice would be sweetly tasty, salty, musky, heady, but her mouth was too involved with my cock that I didn't want to lean down to lick her. So I just let my fingers bathe themselves in the creamy flow, one hand holding her so that her quim-lips were wide open and my other fingers could skid and probe at will.

She wriggled under my hands, still pushing her pelvis up to take my fingers further inside her, pushing up, pulling back as if she wanted my fingers to fuck her, as if my fingers were acting like a fat cock. I looked down to see her whole area of pelvis and thighs sloppy with juice. Her motions and my hands disappearing inside her made me uncontrollably randy, especially as her mouth now felt even more hotly oily on me. It was then I decided that I would have to stop. Now was the time to fuck before we collapsed in orgiastic frenzy.

I moved so that my cock slid out of her mouth but she kept her hands on me, yanking at me to swallow me again. But I resisted. She thought I was moving right away as she said, 'Where are you going?'

'I'm not going anywhere but I'll be coming soon.' I was clambering back onto the bed by now, edging my fat cock along her thigh, sliding it towards her quim.

'Wait, Nick!'

'You don't expect me to wait now!'

'Have you got something to put on that?'

'What?

'You know. A Durex.'

'You're joking!' I could see her shaking her head but I

went on, 'But you're a nurse, Noreen. You nurses know all about that, know what to do.' But she still shook her head.

'We see too many young girls coming in to us who've been screwing without taking precautions. And there they are, pregnant. Not for me, thanks.'

In all my sexual encounters over the past two years I'd never had to do anything at all about contraception. I suppose I was lucky – it was the time when diaphragms were popular so I imagine the women I'd known had one of them fitted. I always carried French letters with me but I'd never had to use one. Of course I suppose one or two of the women I'd known didn't bother with anything so I might have been taking a chance: I couldn't really imagine someone like Judith, for instance, having a diaphragm. But then she hadn't expected me to wear anything, so who knows? But I could almost guarantee that Barbara had one. So I was surprised that Noreen was not equipped in the same way.

My cock was resting high up on Noreen's thigh but she was squirming to prevent me from moving into her. She even began to gently beat at me with her fists. 'Really, Nick. I want to do this and I'm sure you do, but I'm not going to do it without you putting something on.' She sounded breathless, panting her words out. It flashed through my mind that if I persisted, she'd come round. I didn't really want to stop – I was already on a strung-out edge. If I wasn't careful, I'd shoot my load, especially as Noreen's squiggling about was pressing at my cock. The last thing I wanted to do was fumble about with a Durex. Noreen was obviously hot so I debated whether I should continue. But then I thought that would be unfair. I don't like to force myself on someone who has shown some unwillingness.

In any case Noreen was showing some determination. She was holding her legs tightly clenched. 'I'm serious, Nick.' She held my cock hard. 'I want to feel this inside me but you have to put something on it! I hope you've got something. Find it quick!'

I struggled off Noreen and then I remembered that Pam had taken most of my clothes. Just my luck! I grovelled around on the floor where I'd dropped my clothes but she seemed to have taken everything. Damn!

Then I thought back to when I'd first climbed through the window. I'd flung my jacket to one side. But where? Had Pam scooped that up too?

The room was still pretty dark. I stood up to peer around hoping I'd see my jacket somewhere. 'Jesus, Nick! Just look at you!' I was standing by the window so even in the dark I suppose I was outlined. 'You're bigger than I thought you were. Find something quick and get your big prick over here.'

That was further incentive for me to search. 'I'm looking, I'm looking!'

'Hurry!'

Then I found my jacket over in a corner. I was so hot for Noreen I could hardly wait so of course I fumbled around in the pockets trying to find my wallet. 'It's in here somewhere.'

'For God's sake, what are you doing?'

'I'm coming.'

'Not yet, I hope!'

'No, I mean . . .'

'Have you got one?'

'Yes.'

'Good. Then get over here and let me help you put it on.'

'I can do it.' I staggered over to her, thrusting my cock out in front of me, but I was so excited at the prospect of fucking Noreen, I couldn't even fit the Durex on my cock, couldn't unroll it.

'Come here. Give it to me.' She snatched it away from me, her mouth coming over my cock again while her fingers were trying to start the unrolling a little so that it might slip on more easily.

'Put it on me. Now!' I was almost yelling.

Her mouth came away and she said, 'Don't come yet! I can feel you're beginning to leak!' She had made me so wet with her mouth that the Durex kept slipping off. She'd get it poised on the head but just the touch of her fingers there set me twitching and she was trying to hold me steady to roll it on. But then feeling her hands on me was no better.

Then she nearly dropped it. She was trying desperately to roll it on. My cock was really wet and I had spilled the first drops of come as well. All her fiddling and fumbling was making me feel randier than ever. 'Put the damn thing on!' I growled.

'It's hard. Like your cock. It's so big, maybe it won't fit.'

'Of course it will!'

'It's all slippery. You have to stay still.'

'How can I when your hands are all over me? Hurry up! I'm ready. Right now!'

'Hold it in. Just let me do this!'

'You shouldn't have made me so wet.'

'You liked it.'

'I know, I know.'

'And I liked sucking you. And now it's making you come. Stop it!' She kept on fumbling and I was nearly bursting. 'This is making me wetter than ever. Just the feel of this big fat thing makes me want to ram it inside me.'

'Do it then. Do it!'

When I said that, it excited her and her hands gave my cock a smooth squeeze. 'Noreen,' I said, 'stop that if you don't want me to have an accident.' The squeeze had the effect of drawing out more drops of come and that made it wetter and even more difficult to control the Durex.

'You're coming! Don't spoil it!'

'I'm not! Not really. But I soon will be.'

'Don't you spill anymore, you randy bastard.' She sounded really exasperated. 'Not till I've got this thing on and got you inside.'

'This is ridiculous. Come on, Noreen, forget it.'

'This damn thing's so squelchy, it's wriggling around like an eel.' Her hands were slippery all over my cock. 'Get me another one.'

'I don't know where I've put my wallet now. Besides, I think that's the only one I have.'

Noreen was muttering and cursing under her breath. 'Maybe if I put the light on, you'd be able to see what you're doing,' I said.

'Oh, that's right, isn't it? And someone out there will see me with this thing in my fingers and you with your big knob sticking into my face. That's just what I need! Someone's boyfriend on his way home looking in here and seeing this. It'd be all over the residence tomorrow!'

'Well, just get it on and let's get on with it!'

'It's so wet, I don't think it's ever going to get on. Can't you stop dribbling for a second?'

'You're the one who made it all wet!'

'What's all this sticky stuff?'

'This is ridiculous.'

'Wait. I've got it ... I think. Hold still.' Noreen held my cock steady but that caused another dribble of come to ooze out. We were both losing our patience and I knew we might both of us lose our interest. I thrust my cock right up to Noreen but it was too close. She had no idea just how much the Durex had unrolled – perhaps it had become too slack, too much unrolled so that it was simply impossible to fit on.

After one final slide of it around my prick, Noreen took it away and said, 'To hell with it!' She flung it across the room. 'Come here. It's such a long time since I've had raw dick, just get that thing of yours in!'

And that's what I did. I didn't care by then and neither did Noreen. I didn't know if she was at a crucial time of the month and it no longer seemed to matter to her. She pulled my cock hard so that I fell onto the bed on top of her. With her finger and thumb holding my cock she jammed it between the lips of her quim, thrust up her body as I pressed down.

Immediately I felt all that juiciness round my cock, I leaked out some more come. Noreen felt it leaking inside her so she began to hold my buttocks steady. 'Careful!' she murmured. Her juices were lavish so that my whole length of cock was bathed in a warm wetness. I pulled out slowly – I didn't want to come just then, letting my head play around her quim-lips as a little more come spilled out.

When Noreen felt that again, she said through gritted teeth. 'If you're as ready as that, you'd better give me a good fuck now. Hard. If you're going to come, stuff it up me. Give it to me.' So I thrust deeply into her and began to pound away steadily. Her mouth was open under mine and she sucked in my tongue, taking it in as if it was another slippery cock. She moved her legs wider, raising them, hooking them onto my shoulders, wriggling and squirming on me, her pelvis bucking.

I increased the pace until I felt as if I was going a mile a minute. My cock felt very long as Noreen kept me clamped inside, forcing me inside more deeply and I could feel very inch of my prick sliding inside that juicy tunnel. While I was thrashing away, it still seemed as if I was experiencing a slowly heightened sense of a cock longer than ever.

And as I kept on fucking, my come kept dribbling out, not in spurts but in a slow steady dribble. It got so that I believed that I'd be drained away like that, no final surge, just this slipping and sliding along a channel of warm come.

Noreen seemed to be as open as she could be, her quim miraculously oily and wet. As I pounded against her, we were making squishy, slapping noises so it sounded as if we were both splashing with our juices mingling together. Sweat was pouring off me, Noreen was grunting hard, banging against me. Her grunts turned to hoarse shouts of 'Fuck! Fuck!' And incredibly it was as if she had turned some inner tap on for her quim-juice flooded even more around me. I could feel it flowing all over my thighs as I quickened my pace, even though I thought I'd already got up as much steam as I could. The feel of all that juiciness steadily flowing, spreading all around my thighs, slathering all over my cock was enough to stop the come dribbling out. It stopped and for a moment my prick was bashing away till suddenly the slit of my cock opened wide and I drenched Noreen while I was still pounding at her. My cock was squirming inside, then sliding outside, jism flying into her, outside her quim, dripping down her thighs while I was trying to probe my way back into her. Noreen slid her legs down and closed them tight so that my cock couldn't fall out of her even though it soon was wilting after its exertions till finally it slid out, resting in the liquid warmth of Noreen's quim-lips.

We lay back, panting, close together in that narrow bed. 'Chewed string,' I said.

'What?'

'That's what you said I'd be like. Chewed string.'

Her fingers strayed down my stomach to touch my semi-erect cock. 'Still a little ropey.' Her fingers began to move as if she was trying to conjure more life down there. 'Well, you sure know how to hose down a fire. I'm dowsed but there's still something burning. I'll keep it kindled while you go and look for that Durex I threw away.'

'You don't mean we've got to go through all that again? You've done it once in the raw so what's the point?'

'No. You just have to find it. They send a cleaner round on Sundays. Some of them are real tattle-tales and I'd hate one of them to find a Durex in here – and all scrumped up with your come. That'd get me in a whole lot of trouble and think of the jokes they'd be making about me. So off you pop and find it.'

I didn't feel like leaving her bed, especially as she'd sort of promised a repeat performance. Her fingers were coaxing my cock as well but when she felt some signs of life, she let go and dug me in the ribs. 'Don't want to give you any fancy ideas just yet. Not till you've found that thing anyhow.'

I hopped out of bed and went towards the light switch. 'Don't put the light on! The curtains are open.'

'Nobody'll be out there. D'you think the matron has spies patrolling the grounds?'

'Who knows? Best not to take any chances.'

'Are you serious?'

'Well, at least draw the curtains first. And open the window, would you? You've made me break out in a sweat.'

I spent a good ten minutes looking around, Noreen egging me on, promising me all kinds of delights as soon as I'd found the Durex, Then she started cajoling, saying it was all my fault, 'That dick of yours. Too big.'

'And who d'you think made it that big?'

'And all that come.'

I finished up on my hands and knees, crawling slowly round the floor but there was still no sign of it. Then Noreen clambered out of bed to help me. 'Where the hell is it? It must be somewhere,' she said in exasperation.

It was a little too much for me to watch Noreen on all fours, her arse inviting in its roundness. 'We're like a couple of dogs sniffing around,' I said. Her buttocks looked bewitching so I crawled to her and put my face on her buttocks, reaching under a little and flicking my tongue out to lick her quim. It was still wet and juicy. She looked over her shoulder at me and though she said, 'You dirty dog, you,' she didn't move away. I rolled over onto my back, moved my head between her legs and began to lick her in earnest. I took hold of my cock and waggled it. 'Look how happy I am to see you. I'm wagging my tail.'

She turned around, settled herself so that my mouth could reach her more. Then she bent over me and started her wonderful ministrations again, persuading my cock to stiffen again. It wasn't long before we'd completely forgotten about the Durex. We were too interested in slurping sloppily over each other until, finally, she straddled me there on the floor, pumping away. There was no nonsense about a Durex this time. Of course we drove each other longer and harder till we finished by my humping her doggy-style, spilling myself again into her gloriously honeyed and creamy cunt.

Soon we were lying relaxed in bed again. I'd turned the light out and I was thinking that maybe I'd just drop off to sleep. Maybe Pam would relent and bring my clothes back for me the next morning and I'd be able to sneak out of the window. I was feeling pretty dozy after my activities with Noreen and she looked as if she too was tired. I thought she was already drifting off to sleep till I heard her mumble, 'You've still got to find that Durex.'

'Oh, come on. If the two of us can't find it, I'm sure the cleaner won't. And why me? You were the one who insisted on my putting it on and you couldn't do it.'

'That was you. I can't help if you're sloppy with your come. In any case, you couldn't put it on yourself.' She paused, then sat up in bed. 'You know what? I threw it over there.' She pointed towards the window. 'I bet it landed outside.'

'I don't think we had the window open then. And if it's outside, there's no problem. The cleaner won't find it.'

'No. It's worse. I don't want the man who does the grounds to find it. He's sure to report it. And right outside my window. And a lot of the nurses walk that way to the hospital. What if they see that slippery Durex lying outside my window? What'll that make me look like?'

I wasn't sure if that would make much difference, especially if Noreen's reputation was known by the nurses as well it was around the dances. But she insisted. 'Go and find it for me.'

'You're joking.'

'I'm not.'

It's cold out there. I'll have to go and get my clothes from Pam first.' I sat up in bed and started to push the sheets back. Noreen grabbed me. 'Oh, no, you don't. I know her. She won't let you come back here once she's got you in her room. And you're such a randy devil, you'll be into her before she knows it.'

'I won't, I promise.'

I slid my feet onto the floor but Noreen held onto me. 'Just step out there. You'll soon find it, I'm sure.'

'I'll freeze to death.'

'Don't be so nesh.'

There was no getting round Noreen so I went over to the window, threw the curtains back and began to search for the elusive Durex, leaning out. 'No sign of it,' I said.

'You can't see from there. Get out there and look properly.'

'I'll freeze my balls off.'

'I'll warm them up for you afterwards.'

I climbed over the sill and just for a moment I thought maybe I was being set up for another so-called joke. Once I was out there, would Noreen quickly close the windows and put the blocks back so that I couldn't raise the window and I'd be stuck out there naked?

I scrabbled around in the dirt and the grass but there was no Durex. 'Haven't you got a torch or something?' I asked.

'Keep your voice down, for God sake. And no, I don't have a torch.'

I went on looking but I didn't want to stray too far from the window. I tried to convince myself that there was only a very remote chance that Noreen had arranged all this as a joke. And if I saw Noreen move towards the window, I'd soon be able to jump into the room again. Still, you never know.

I was getting colder by the minute and so stood at the window looking in. 'You're not giving up?' Noreen asked me.

'It's freezing out here and I'm never going to find it.' I climbed in, pushed the window down with one hand while I rapidly drew the curtains with the other, walking over to the bed, pulling the sheet back to slide in beside Noreen.

'Hey! Stop that! You've brought all the cold in with you.' She huddled herself deep under the covers.

'So much for warming my balls!'

'They've had a pretty good warming over for one night. And I'm on early rounds in the morning.'

'Well, at least let me get warm in here for a bit.'

'Go and get your clothes from Pam. Then you can go and get warm in your own bed.' She turned over, her back to me. She was obviously fully satisfied and would drop off to sleep immediately.

I picked up my jacket and slipped it on. It made me feel a little warmer. I decided I'd peer out of the door and try my luck down the corridor, find Pam's room, get my clothes and go home. By now I was feeling so cold I had no thoughts of trying anything with Pam. Maybe I wasn't exactly chewed string but I was feeling pretty ragged.

Then again I began to think I was the victim of a whole series of practical jokes. Maybe the three of them had worked all this out, an elaborate scheme. Suppose Pam had gone off to sleep and her door was locked? I thought maybe I could prop Noreen's door open so I could get back in her room if that was the case. But suppose Noreen locked her door behind me and I couldn't get back in? Then I'd be trapped in the residence virtually naked. What about all those nurses waking up to find a naked man roaming around the corridors? Maybe in different circumstances, they'd enjoy it, at least some of them. But I'd be in deep trouble.

I was feeling cold and miserable. I peered out of Noreen's door – the corridor was empty and quiet. After all, it was about half past two in the morning. So I decided to take the chance. I'd leave Noreen's door open, scuttle along the corridor to Pam's room, knock, get my clothes and vamoose.

As I tiptoed along the corridor, I heard Noreen's door click shut. Damn! I hoped it wasn't self-locking. I stopped at the second door and tapped gently. No answer. I knocked more loudly. A drawly voice said, 'Who is it?'

'A chewed piece of string out here.' I felt Pam would know who that was. If it was someone else's room, the occupant wouldn't have the vaguest notion what I was talking about.

'Wait a minute. I'll open it for you.'

It was just as dark inside Pam's room as it was in Noreen's but I stumbled inside. An arm steadied me, a hand rested on my arm, then slid down to encounter my bare leg. There was a giggle.

'You feel cold,' Pam said. 'Let me get you warm.' Her hands came up to my shoulders and pushed my jacket off and then gave a lingering stroke all over my back. She took my hand and soon she had reached her bed. She lay down and invited me under the covers. 'Just to get warm,' she said.

I lay on my back and then I felt her leg thrown over mine. 'Why, you poor piece of chewed string. I'll have to untie some of your knots. You have got yourself into a state. Weren't you ever in the Boy Scouts? Never mind. I know all about knots. I was in the girl guides. You know, it's amazing what badges you can earn in the girl guides. That was one of my best. I'm good with my hands. And you know what they say – boy scouts, girl guides.'

She lifted one of my hands and she placed it on her breast. Then her hands began to stray all over my body. I was soon warm again, and it was true that Pam certainly loosened me. I soon forgot all my thoughts about the practical jokes I had imagined they were playing. She was very gentle with me, taking her time, encouraging me, coaxing me, egging me on, urging me.

'Sometimes I find some knots are very difficult to unfasten. But you just have to persevere.' I think she was really talking about me and how I might be a little depleted after spending the time with Noreen. But Pam was persistent. By now her hands were weaving around my cock and balls and I was already coming to life there. 'You know what they say. When a rope is all frayed, you sometimes have to grease it so the knot slides easily open.'

She burrowed under the sheets and found my upstanding prick. Her muffled voice floated up to me. 'My! You must have been in the Boy Scouts. You know how to pitch a tent. Just look at this tent-pole here. It's a lovely strong tent-pole.'

I was happy to let Pam take me over after my strenuous time with Noreen. She surmised correctly that I couldn't be hurried but soon she began to see that her urgings were getting good results. I was stirring and I was already exploring her body. I wasn't too sure if I'd have enough spunk left in me but I was willing to give it a try, though I did mention to her that perhaps she shouldn't expect too much.

'Not to worry. I'm a very brave girl guide. I'll be spunky enough for both of us. You just relax and let me guide you.' She took my hand and placed it on her pubic mound and that was enough for me. I moved so that my finger began to touch her. I realised I was finding the right places for her for she started to moan.

I didn't remember too much about that session with Pam except that it stuck in my mind as intensely warm and embracing. Pam seemed to take a delight in ministering to me, all my needs, waiting for me, helping me along. All that remains in my mind is a sense of long, gentle cuddling, a tantalising exploration of all of my body, lots of warm embraces, a very fluid feeling, slippery and smoochy, a slow penetration, snuggling close till I shuddered to a climax, somehow summoning up a shower of jism that Pam let me sprinkle all over her.

'Oh, my! Who would have thought it? Your tent-pole has sprung a leak! But it's such a lovely leak. You must have been a Boy Scout. I'll bet you've earned plenty of badges. One for erecting tents.' She giggled. 'Well, erecting something!'

She let me sleep a little, woke me in time to get dressed and climb out of her window. I told her I'd be looking out for her at the dances. 'Maybe I won't be at the end of my rope the next time,' I added And I did spend a couple of great evenings with her. I discovered that it was her nature to be very soft, and yet strangely she liked to lead me on into various softnesses, fluid, charming, cuddly.

In fact, I saw her the following week at the dance. It was late in the evening and unfortunately she was already fixed up. 'I don't know whether he's a Boy Scout, though. Hey, but don't forget. I think we could work on earning a few more badges together, don't you?'

Pam was there with Noreen and of course Noreen was in her usual situation of being chased all evening by men who wanted to finish up where I had the previous week.

She was just about to leave when I finally found an opportunity to talk to her. She was the first to speak. 'You'll never guess what.'

'What?'

'That "thing" we were looking for.' She laughed.

'The gardener found it?'

She shook her head. 'Sounds like a mystery story, doesn't it? You know, the butler did it.' She patted my arm, and laughed again. 'In our case it was the English student who did it! And without a thing on him! And the gardener didn't find it.'

'The cleaner then.'

'No. We should have realised.'

'Realised what?' I asked her.

'Well, I threw it in the direction of the window, right?'

'Yes. But I never found it there.'

'I know. And you'd closed the window, remember?'

'Yes. So it couldn't have been outside.'

'No. But I found it. Two days later.'

'It took you that long?'

'Well, you see. When I'm on day shifts I leave my curtains closed. Then when I'm off duty, I want to sleep so I keep them closed.'

'So?'

'Well, it just so happened there was a warm sunny day last week so I decided to let a little sun in. So I drew the curtains back and guess what?'

'I've no idea.'

'There it was,' she said and laughed. 'In plain sight for those two days. Two whole days when everybody knew. Except me. Of course nobody told me. They thought the joke was on me so they kept it to themselves. I'm sure everybody was told about it and I bet they all came to gawk at it.'

'What d'you mean?'

'I mean, there it was, stuck on the window. I must have thought the window was open and I'd thrown it out. That's why I asked you to look for it outside. But the window was closed.'

She leaned closer to me and whispered, 'You with your leaky dick. Sticky as glue so the damn thing stuck on the glass. And of course you raised the window so we didn't see it stuck there. So there it was, plastered on the window for everybody to see and it was obvious to everyone just what I'd been up to.' She shrugged her shoulders. 'I'll take a bit more care next time.' She laughed again. 'I wish there was some kind of test I could run on men. Something simple to check whether they're leaky. By the time you find out, it's too late.'

A tall man came to join us and Noreen looked him up and down, then at me. 'What d'you think?' The man looked a little puzzled, wondering what we had been talking about.

She linked arms with the man and walked slowly away. I watched them for a moment, then I shouted softly after them, 'Watch your aim this time, Noreen!'

10. Pairing Off

The end of term came at me in something of a rush. Suddenly I found myself in the middle of examinations and most of my time was taken up with studying.

I still managed to see Barbara for an occasional relaxing evening and I met one or two interesting women at the Saturday dances. I was figuring out a way to go to London at the end of term to pick up with Teresa for a brief fling before I headed off to Torquay to work at my summer job. I thought I would also see Gerry again though he had not asked me to do anything very much for him while I'd been in Manchester. He kept in touch with Barbara and she sometimes gave me money Gerry had sent. I used to complain that I was being paid for doing nothing and tried to make Barbara keep the money instead.

'I can't do that,' she protested. 'Gerry sent it for you.'

'I haven't done anything for him.'

'I'm sure something will crop up. In any case you've done a few deliveries, talked to Milton, and looked after Lorna. And you know how Gerry is when he cottons on to somebody. He does that with me and it's over two years since I've seen him. I suppose it's just that he knows you're here and you'll do what's necessary when the time comes. I know he keeps asking me about what

Milton is up to with his Paradise Lost thing. Gerry thinks it's a front for something.'

'Front for what?'

Barbara shrugged. 'You know Gerry. Keeps his mouth shut.' She paused. 'D'you hear anything about Milton?'

I shook my head. 'Why should I?'

'You go and see Lorna there, don't you?'

'Not too often.'

She raised her eyebrows. 'I thought you two were getting along famously. That's what Lorna says. She's always going on about you.' Then she went on. 'Talks a blue streak about your going round there. Something about you two watching television.' She smiled. 'Must say didn't sound too exciting ... at first!' She smiled again, then continued. 'I think she's on the look-out for something. With Milton. Gerry suggested she should.' She paused. 'She's such a sweet thing, maybe she's in over her head. We'd better watch out for her.'

'I haven't seen her in weeks.' I was still feeling out of my depth with Lorna. She was an enigma to me, but still so elegantly herself, I was still uncertain how to deal with her. I'd seen her only once after the television episode. We went to the cinema and afterwards she invited me in for coffee. And that's all it was. I couldn't summon up my courage to make a move – we had a fumbling quick cuddle at the door as I was leaving but it didn't amount to anything.

So this conversation with Barbara came as a surprise to me. It made me see Lorna in a different light. I vowed to myself to make myself more 'available' to her. All this business about Milton and Gerry's suspicions convinced me that I should be more concerned about her.

But I was so busy preparing for examinations that I

didn't get a chance to go to see Lorna. I rang her up and she was her usual charming self on the phone, very apologetic about not having contacted me recently. 'You know how it is at the end of the school year,' she said. 'It's very hectic.'

'Same for me.' And because she sounded busy and because I was sweating over my Anglo-Saxon for the examination, I didn't ask her to go out, though I did call her before I was due in London. There was no answer. That made me worried so I phoned Barbara who told me she'd rushed off to York because her mother was ill. Lorna was going to spend the summer looking after her.

Things were not quite the same when I went back to the Blue Lantern. I spent some time with Teresa but she seemed a little abstracted. I should have expected that, I suppose, as I hadn't seen her for weeks and I knew she wouldn't wait around for me.

So I went off to the hotel in Torquay. It was not a bad place to spend the summer, I thought at first. There were plenty of gash women on holiday looking for a good time, and indeed I did meet two or three. But nothing worked out. They were free through the day and of course I was working. I also met a show-girl who was dancing in the show on the pier but that was no good because again she was free through the day and I wasn't.

Barbara cheered me up considerably by coming to spend a couple of weekends with me. She told me she had heard from Lorna. Her mother was still ill so it didn't look as if she'd be able to take a holiday, 'though she said she'd love to come down to Torquay to see you,' Barbara said with a mischievous wink. 'She'll be back in Manchester at the end of August,' Barbara went on. 'Said she hoped you'd get in touch with her as soon as you got back in town. She'll still be at Paradise Lost. I hope she'll be alright there.'

So I phoned Lorna as soon as I got back. She wasn't her usual assured self on the phone. She sounded jumpy, a little odd, and strangely she was stammering, sometimes even at a loss for words. I tentatively suggested that I'd like to go round to see her but she put me off abruptly. I was momentarily disappointed until, rather breathlessly and sounding a little conspiratorial, she agreed to meet me the next day for lunch.

She was already at the restaurant when I arrived and as soon as I sat down, she reached across and laid a hand on mine. 'Sorry to have put you off yesterday. I didn't think it was wise to have you come round.' This sounded ominous. 'But I do need your help.'

Over lunch she explained what she meant. Her explanation was not entirely clear – she still seemed nervous, glancing round the restaurant every now and again as if she fancied someone was spying on her. 'It's that Paradise place. Milton. I think he's on to me.'

'On to you? In what way?'

'Well, I think there's a couple of houses there that are clearing places ... for stolen goods. Imports as well, probably. And I'm not sure but I think there's something to do with drugs going on. Maybe he's keeping a supply there. I just happened to be walking past one day and I saw something suspicious.'

'What?'

'A couple of bruisers carrying some cases and one spilled open – there were bags of some white stuff in it. I tried to look as if I hadn't seen anything but I don't think I fooled them. So I think Milton's on to me.'

'What makes you think he suspects you?'

'He keeps coming around. On the feeblest excuses. It's

like he's snooping. Poking his nose in, looking for clues. At first I thought he was going to make a pass.' She smiled wryly. 'Sort of as if ... well, I half expected him to ask if I'd be interested in being ... one of those ladies. Offered me a bigger house. Mumbled something about entertaining his business associates.'

'You'd better get out of there. Who knows if he'll try to persuade you, you know. Maybe he'll send a couple of thugs round, those bruisers you saw.'

'Barbara's already found me another place.'

'That's good.'

'But you know the rules there. Anything you take in, you have to leave.'

'You can't leave all those nice things you've bought!'

'Oh, I don't intend to. I've been smuggling some of the small things out to my new place. It's the furniture and carpets that are the problem.' She stopped and smiled at me winningly. 'I hope you don't mind. You're the only person I could think of who'd be able to move the things out. I can't get any furniture movers in. Milton would stop me. I signed the lease agreeing to the rules.

'So how can I help?'

'Barbara knows a man who works fitting carpets. I'm going to tell Milton that he's coming round to measure and he'll be coming round in the evening because I'm at work through the day. I'll have him park at the side of the house so no one can see much.' Then she laughed almost as if she was enjoying this. 'Then I'll do a moonlight flit.'

'I don't mind helping. But isn't it a bit risky?'

Lorna giggled but I couldn't tell whether that was from fright or whether she was looking forward to the escapade. 'I don't mind losing my deposit but I'm not going to leave my treasures in Milton's filthy hands.'

She looked straight at me in an appealing way. 'Will you do it?'

'I'll be glad to.'

'Is next Friday alright?'

'I think so.'

'Barbara's going to go round and tackle Milton.'

'She's not going to say anything that'll get him riled up?'

'Oh, no. She's going to talk to him about tenants, about her real estate dealings with him.' She looked directly at me again. 'She'll turn the charm on ... and you know what Barbara's like when she's being charming.' Lorna smiled again. And that made me wonder just how much Lorna knew about Barbara and me.

So that Friday Barbara picked me up and drove me to meet the man with the furniture van. We waited till it was dusk. Fortunately there was a little of that Manchester pea-soup fog in the air. We gave Barbara time to settle in with Milton before we made our way to Lorna's. The van-man, whose name was Len, parked his van on the grass by Lorna's side-door. He seemed unperturbed and very organized, so much so that I wondered if he too was one of Gerry's men – maybe he picked up any goods that Gerry was 'importing' through the Manchester docks.

Lorna was fluttering around. She looked both nervous and excited, her face a little flushed, panting a little, flashing great smiles at both of us as we carried the furniture out. She supervised how we stacked the items in the truck. I was surprised how she took her time arranging everything in the van. Len and I were working as fast as we could but she kept reminding us to be careful, to take it easy and that made Len exasperated.

Lorna had wrapped her small vases and ornaments and she was responsible for carrying them out to the van. Once I was left there to move a chair where she wanted it. When I had finished, she stopped me, leaned up to touch my cheek with a gentle kiss. She laid her hand invitingly on my arm and whispered. 'You're so sweet to do this for me. I don't know how I'll be able to repay you.' I was certainly thinking of one way she could repay me! 'Maybe I can return the favour soon.'

We soon had all the furniture and carpets packed in the van without a hitch. Lorna kept a look-out for Milton — I think she had some system worked out with Barbara who would give us some kind of warning if Milton made any unexpected moves. But nothing like that transpired.

We had to leave the curtains there — too much light would have shone out if we'd taken them down. Lorna was sorry to leave them. 'I hate leaving stuff for that terrible man. It's bad enough he gets my money.'

'Does he know where you're moving to? Don't you think he might come after you? I mean, I suppose that lease is legally binding.'

Lorna shook her head. 'I don't think he'll want to draw attention to himself. And I think Barbara would make a stink about it and the last thing Milton wants is publicity. And he'll never get out of Barbara just where I'm staying.'

Finally we were ready to move. I clambered into the back of the van and Lorna sat up front with Len to direct him to her new place. Len beeped the horn as we left. I suppose that was a signal to Barbara who was due to join us at Lorna's place.

We unpacked Lorna's things, Len laying the carpets while I positioned the chairs and settee in roughly the places Lorna wanted. 'That'll do,' she said. She looked radiant, a little more unkempt and flustered than I'd seen her before but still very attractive. In fact, the evening's adventure had given her a kind of special glow. 'We don't want to spend the rest of the evening arranging furniture. I need a drink ... and I want to buy you two whatever you feel like drinking. I can't thank you enough. As soon as Barbara gets here, we'll find a nice pub and celebrate.'

And that's what we did. We were a merry group – I think we'd all got an adrenaline high from our evening's work. While we didn't drink a great deal, we were all pretty cheerful after about an hour or so. Len had to leave and Lorna thanked him profusely again. 'Nice guy,' she said after he had gone. I was a little surprised, for Lorna didn't usually use a word like 'guy'.

Then she turned to me, leaning close to me and murmured, 'But not as nice a guy as you!' We had another couple of drinks, then Barbara said, 'I don't know about you two but I've had enough. In fact I'm feeling quite tiddly.' She fished her car-keys out of her purse and handed them to me. 'How about you drive me home?' She was looking at me in an openly lascivious manner so I supposed that this was one of her invitations to finish off the evening with a bout of sex. But I was surprised when she turned to Lorna and said, 'You don't want to go back to your place. I'll bet it's a tip. And you can't put that bed of yours together by yourself.' When I heard that, I was about to offer my services to Lorna – after all, if we put the bed up together, what would be more natural that the pair of us using it?

But I was foiled, for Barbara went on to Lorna, 'You'd better spend the night with me. I've a spare bed, it's quite comfy.' She turned to me and said, 'You can ask

Nick. He's spent some time lying on it.' By that, I realised, she was probably talking about the divan-like bed she used for massage. 'And tomorrow's Saturday,' she went on. 'You don't have to work. You can sort out your furniture tomorrow.'

So that's how the three of us found ourselves in Barbara's car, with me driving, Lorna in the front seat next to me and Barbara in the back seat behind me. I felt good – I'd had a few drinks so I was feeling mellow and the inside of the car was warm and full of sweet-smelling perfume from the two ladies, who were both huddling fairly close to me. Barbara was leaning forward from her back seat, her arms resting on the back of my seat. Lorna had turned slightly sideways to lean a little against me and in the process her skirt had ridden up over her knees. I let my eyes stray to look at them every now and again and I'm sure Lorna was conscious of my looks, though she did nothing to cover herself.

Barbara's hand began to massage my neck soothingly, her fingers stroking into my hair. I could feel the warmth of her breath as she hunched forward a little further. 'So, how are you feeling, Nick?' Barbara asked me.

'Good. Very good, in fact.'

'I'm glad everything went well,' Lorna said. 'I was a little nervous. You know, in case Milton found out.'

'You needn't have worried,' Barbara continued. 'I kept batting my eyelids at him, crossing my legs. I thought his eyes were going to pop right out of his head.'

'You're such a naughty lady,' Lorna said with a laugh.

'Naughty! I can be a lot naughtier than that!' Barbara's other hand had crept over my shoulder to loosen my tie, her fingers sliding inside my shirt. 'Nick knows just how naughty I can be, don't you, love?' She had moved right up against my seat and both her hands were warm against my skin now, as she had been able to unfasten my shirt buttons. 'And anyhow, Lorna, a little bird told me you can be quite the naughty one when you want to be.'

Lorna's giggle sounded like a cover-up for her embarrassment. Barbara was licking and sucking at one of my earlobes, whispering in a smoochy voice, 'You've got lovely, warm skin, Nick.' I was trying to concentrate on driving but Barbara's smooth hands and mouth on me were beginning to have a telling effect. And Lorna seemed to be taking quick glances at me as if she was checking me out.

'Just feel how warm he is, Lorna.'

Lorna laid her long fingers along the inside of my thigh. 'It must be all the excitement tonight,' she muttered, her fingers moving gently. 'And I must say, I found it exciting. I'm feeling in something of a to-do.'

'Oh, ho!' Barbara's chin was on my shoulder and I thought she was looking down at Lorna's hand on me. 'I think Nick's getting into something of a to-do, if I'm not mistaken. I bet he's even warmer near your hand.'

I was enjoying this stroking, this jocular kidding, these small embraces egging me on. But I wasn't quite sure just how far Lorna would go at this point, even though her fingers closed on my thigh as Barbara talked about how warm I was.

'I'm beginning to feel quite hot,' I mumbled.

'Well, we don't want you catching cold, getting out of a warm car into the chilly night,' Barbara huskily croaked. 'Perhaps you should let him get a little air, Lorna.'

Lorna giggled again. 'He's all wrapped up in these

clothes. Making him sweat. D'you think I should let the air in?' I thought for a moment Lorna was going to open a window but her hand on my thigh inched across to squeeze me as she encountered my firm erection. 'There's something here that's really burning a hole in his trousers,' she said, turning to look at Barbara and laughing a little.

'Give it some air then, before he burns right up!'

Lorna's hands moved to my belt, tugged to loosen it. She pulled and my fly was soon open. My cock was straining stiffly inside my underpants but Lorna did not push her hands there. She turned round more fully in her seat and both her arms went round my waist, pulling at my trousers. Her head was on my chest and her voice floated softly up to me. 'You'll have to lift up a little so you can get the full benefit.'

As I did so, she deftly yanked my trousers and underpants free, pulling them down so they finished bunched up just above my knees. My prick was standing up very straight.

'Look there! Nick! You must be a magician. I bet that wand can help you do all kinds of tricks!' Barbara's hands were moving further down as she said this. But Lorna stopped her by saying, 'Naughty, naughty, Barbara! I'm the magician's assistant.' She licked her fingertips and pressed their wetness around the head of my cock. 'He's really burning up. Red hot. We will have to spend a long time putting his fire out.' Her fingers were roving up and down my length now and I was finding it very difficult to drive, especially as I was finding this new and different Lorna exceptionally exciting.

Barbara's hands slid up my chest as Lorna continued her lingering caresses along my cock. In a minute I felt a silky softness against my cheek. It was Barbara. She had unbuttoned her blouse, moved her slip down, unhooked her bra and her firm round breast was sliding against my cheek. I turned my face a little and touched the tip of my tongue to her nipple. She sighed.

'I'm hot enough to do that,' Lorna whispered, 'but my hands are too busy.'

'Let me.' And Barbara leaned across to Lorna and unfastened her blouse buttons. As she was doing this, she was murmuring to me, 'I suppose you didn't think Lorna was like this, eh? She's been wanting to do this ever since I told her about us. For some reason she didn't think you wanted to do this. She'd got the idea you were ... unapproachable. How she decided that, I have no idea.'

'That's what I thought about her,' I stammered.

'Well, I am a little ... circumspect ... at first.'

'She likes to be in the right mood, I suppose,' Barbara said. 'She tells me that that new-fangled television has a really soothing effect on her.'

Soon Lorna's breasts were free and she bent down to brush my cock against them. It was all I could do to keep the car on the road. 'Well, it does make me feel all cosy,' she whispered as she worked her breasts across my shaft, letting the head prod at her nipples, her hands fondling my balls.

This sexy playfulness went on all the way as I drove to Barbara's. I wanted to drive faster so we could get there and I could participate more fully, though I really enjoyed all these gentle caresses. Once Barbara stopped and I could hear a quick rustle behind me. Then I felt soft silky material trailed along the back of my neck, then round across my face, smoothed enticingly around, under my chin, then up just beneath my eyes.

'Can you smell me?' Barbara asked quietly in my ear. 'You're not the only one burning up. I was so hot, I gushed out. I'm all wet.' She pushed her panties onto me across my mouth. 'Can you feel how wet I am?' She wrapped her finger inside the nylon and pushed it into my mouth. 'A little tasty snack before you get the big feast.'

Lorna's movements around my cock and balls were driving me crazy and I was desperately trying to hold myself in. We were now quite close to Barbara's so I pressed the pedal a little harder.

'I bet his hose is already full, isn't it, Lorna? Ready to squirt out and cool us down.' Lorna nodded her head as she kept on with her careful and sure stroking.

At last I managed to park the car in Barbara's driveway. I struggled out of the car, clutching my trousers. Barbara had hurried ahead, scrabbling in her purse for her house-key. I turned to watch Lorna following me, her coat open, and as she got closer I saw her perfect globes with jutting nipples.

In Barbara's living room, I flopped into an armchair while Lorna quickly divested me of my trousers, roughly pulling them down and off, my shoes and socks with them. Soon I was sprawled full length with my shirt fully open and my cock ramrod-stiff.

Both of them were of course already half-dressed. Lorna had dropped her coat by the door and was standing in front of me with her blouse open, her bra loose and her slip peeled off her shoulders. Barbara had already flung her blouse and bra away and her slip was folded at her waist.

Then both of them treated me to an elegant striptease. In my time working for Gerry I had seen a lot of stripping. At the Blue Lantern one evening a week was devoted to strippers, doing a full strip which could only be done in private clubs at that time in England. These were professional strippers and they were very good. But they were well organized, that is, their clothing was specially designed to come off easily with secret zippers, easy hooks-and-eyes, cunningly placed studs to unclip quickly, all very seductive. But in a way it's more seductive to watch a woman stripping for you when she is wearing her ordinary clothes, though I must say there was never anything ordinary about Barbara's clothes. She obviously had a good stock of Gerry's special French lingerie – and I discovered that that was true of Lorna as well.

There is something very sexy about seeing a woman half-dressed. They look a little untidy, dishevelled even, their hair loosened but you know that they really mean what they're doing. It's not just entertainment like the strippers. They are doing this specifically for you and you know what is going to happen when all their clothes are off. That gives their stripping an extra edge. That's one of the reasons I'm so fascinated by lingerie – I always find it makes me very randy thinking about what a woman I'm with has on underneath her coat and dress, especially if that outer clothing is sort of severe. I imagine all kinds of silky, sexy things and wonder if, when she was putting them on, she was expecting to show them off or not.

I knew Barbara was one of those women who took a delight in wearing really sexy slips and panties but I didn't really know just how Lorna was in this regard. She always dressed in elegant, fashionable clothes and because she had a connection with Gerry I suspected she would have some delicious lingerie. And that turned out to be true.

I lay back in the armchair, ready to enjoy the sight of these two delectable women. Barbara was standing in front of me, one hip jutting out. Her skirt had ridden up a little and one leg was slightly forward. She had a teasing, raunchy look on her face as she twirled her hand around slowly with her panties hanging from it. With a quick flip she tossed them at me – they landed on my stomach before they slithered off to the side.

I wondered how Lorna was going to behave, having got to this stage. I had no idea but to begin with she seemed to be following Barbara's example. She stood quite still, her bare breasts jutting out, firm and round. She was wearing a camisole, not a slip, which she had folded down to her waist, a lovely piece of green silk with black laced edging. She was looking directly at me with her face a strange mixture of shyness and forthright sexiness. She smoothed her two hands down her skirt along her thighs, then up to unfasten the button at her waist, slowly drawing the skirt down to reveal a short half slip matching the camisole. She stepped out of her skirt and laid it carefully across the back of a nearby chair.

As she took a step or two towards me she said, 'I've been wanting to do this for you for some time.' She reached out her hand to place it just at the tip of my cock. 'I just loved to touch you here,' reminding me of that time she had swallowed my jism, and then her fingers squeezed and pulled down, 'but I just couldn't go any further that night.' She blushed a little. 'But now that I've talked to Barbara...'

'Oh. Don't blame it all on me. After what you did that television night. You've had it on your brain for some time. You didn't need me to push you into it.'

Lorna laughed and said, 'Well, it's nice to know I'm

not the only one who gets these ideas.' Her hand began to slide slowly up and down.

Barbara was now swaying her hips as she too slid her skirt down and as she already had her panties off, she was soon standing in just sheer stockings, no garter belt as they were the elasticated kind. Once her skirt was off, she peeled her red slip down and laid it across my chest. 'Lorna told me about your television "adventure" so I told her about our little get-togethers. We decided that perhaps tonight we would both run you a little ragged.'

She leaned over to put her open mouth on mine while her hand smoothed the soft nylon across my chest, down to my stomach while Lorna's hand kept on with its delicate stroking. Barbara was an extraordinary kisser – her mouth was beautifully moist and warm. She took in my tongue gently, sucking, flicking her own tongue round it till she forced it between my lips, its lovely slippery length pushing in. It was incredibly sexy and my cock twitched strongly. Lorna felt that under her hand and sighed, 'You're being a very naughty girl again, Barbara, I can tell.'

'Mmmmm!' Barbara replied, her mouth still on mine, sliding around a little, her lips back so that I could feel that inner softness. All this together with her hand stroking her slip on me and Lorna's hand doing unbelievably gentle strokes on my prick was making me feel very excited.

Barbara raised her mouth from mine, slid the slip up onto my face, smoothing it round before flinging it away, then bending down so her breasts brushed onto my face. 'Watch me, Nick,' I heard Lorna say. I moved slightly without disturbing Barbara's soft plumpness. Lorna stood close to me at the side and drew her camisole over her head, dropping it onto my cock, shaking her head so that her hair fluffed out. She then hooked her fingers in the elastic waist of her slip and her face assumed a kind of lasciviously innocent look. She drew the half-slip down and off and I was surprised to see that she was wearing no panties, just a garter belt holding up her black nylons. She smiled at me. 'You see. I've been waiting all evening for you with no panties. I wanted to take your hand in the pub and push it under my skirt so you would feel how I was ready for you. I wanted to feel your hand sliding up my leg, under my skirt, under my slip, higher and higher till it touched me here.' Her hand strayed down to her pubic hair and fanned out across it. 'But I'm not as forward as Barbara.'

'I don't know about that,' Barbara mumbled against my mouth.

'You can touch me now,' Lorna said, standing directly at the side of the chair I was sprawling in.

'Who's being naughty now?' Barbara muttered. I let my hand tease round Lorna's tight and compact arse, my fingers poking to the inside of her thighs. She opened her legs wider and I felt for the first time the sweet moistness of her slit, edging my finger up to stroke her clit. She shivered and said, 'It's Nick that's being naughty now ... and I love it.' Somehow she eased herself so that two fingers moved slowly into her. She was slippery and juicy and she moved against my fingers.

So there I was, Barbara's breasts rubbing all over my face, my mouth and tongue slathering them, her nipples big and hard. I had one hand circling round the curves of Barbara's buttocks, slinking it along the crack of her arse sometimes, even pushing a fingertip gently into her arsehole, rimming it round and round. My other hand had taken up a steady thrust in and out of Lorna's slithery quim as she again began to massage my cock, first drawing off in a long lingering way that green half-slip she had put there. I was feeling immeasurably raunchy and I could tell the two women were also becoming more and more engrossed in what they were doing. They were evidently enjoying making me feel I was putty in their hands, wanting to continue till I was ready to burst out in showers of come. As for myself of course, I was fighting to keep in control so that this luxurious attention they were giving me would go on.

They too seemed to want to let things go on happening in this way. Lorna was sumptuously moist and by now Barbara was also slippery and wet. My hand reached between her legs to stroke along the soft surface of the lips of her quim.

My hands were swimming in juicy cream, moving in and out, with soft but firm curvaceously plump flesh pressed on my face. I was entranced by these two women. One was obviously the older woman who knew many tricks. The other was equally adept, though I knew her only as a charming, elegant companion who now was revealed as a thoroughly sexy spirit. She was more randy than I ever thought she could be.

Then they must have signalled to each other because they switched and it was Lorna who now squashed her breasts onto me, taking her hand from my cock to hold one breast and point the nipple into my mouth. Barbara's hand clutched my shaft and started a steady pumping, her other hand tickling me around my cock-head. She accommodated herself onto my hand inside her so that I could probe more deeply and firmly. I sucked at Lorna's nipple and felt it jut out more stiffly, a long, pointy nipple. Her hands were sliding along my chest, reaching down until her fingers joined Barbara's around my cock. Together they made me stiffer still until I leaked a little jism. When that happened, I felt both of them touch the creamy stickiness with their fingers, sighing and moaning as they both moved their juicy cunts on my hands.

As usual I was desperately trying to hold onto myself. I really liked having my cock stroked by these two experts. Their hands were especially good at what they were doing, by turns extremely gentle as if the skin of their fingers were made of the most incredible velvet, then extremely rough, gripping my length in a hard grasp, pulling the skin further away from the head till one of them licked her hands and wiped soft saliva all over the shaft.

Then somehow they were both bending down, on their knees at the side of my chair. Their arses looked ravishing and I managed to get my hands over both of them, sliding my fingers down their arse-cracks, past their holes till I poked inside their creamy quims. As I was doing this, Barbara had taken my balls into her mouth, letting them jiggle inside, sucking as her fingers pressed down under them. Lorna's mouth came down along my shaft and again it was exactly as I had imagined it would be. She even sucked my cock in an elegant fashion, so gently but so exquisitely warm and wet. My cock pulsed quickly as I felt her take me deeply inside her mouth. It was as if she wanted both to be infinitely patient with my stiffness but also hungry to swallow me so that my cock went through a variety of suckings and lickings, her hands rubbing slippery, gluey wetness all over it.

Their mouths were fantastically sensual – my cock and balls inside slithery warmth, in the grip of delicate fingers and hard clenches till I was absolutely lost to anything but their attentions. And then they both began to talk, quick phrases before their mouths went on with their work again. This had an added effect because it made me want their mouths back on me but it made me even more excited when their words wafted up to me. Sometimes it wasn't possible for me to know just who was saying what but it didn't matter because all three of us were working together, the two of them getting wetter and wetter under my hands and my cock slathered in creaminess, jism dripping out, licked and tongued around my cock-head.

'Look at him all wet!'
'So hard!'
'Tastes so good!'
'Yummy yum!'
'Just look how red it is!'
'That big vein beating away!'
'Oooh! He's dripping!'
'Lick it up!'
'Mmmm!'
'I want some.'
'Here it comes again!'
'Lovely hot cream!'
'Shall we let him squirt?'
'He'll hit the ceiling!'
'I love to see that.'
'Hot come.'
'It feels full.'
'He's got lots. You'll see.'
'I know. He flooded my panties.'
'We'll make him come and then you'll see how he lets fly.'
'Yes. I'd like to do that.'
'Me too. Especially when I've been sucking at it.'

'Yes, yes. Spraying right up.'

'A big stream of come.'

So they talked and my prick seemed to be oozing come all the time till I wondered whether I'd have any left for the big surge that I knew was going to spurt up my shaft.

And yet, of course, I also wanted to put my cock inside their quims where my hands were still juicily stroking. The two women seemed to read my mind.

'Is he going to come?'

'Soon.'

'I'd like to let him push inside me.'

'You want to fuck?'

'Yes, yes!'

'Let's do it this way first. Then we'll fuck him.'

'Will he be able to do that? I want to feel him. He's so big.'

'You will. Nick's good at coming round.'

'You know, don't you?'

'I certainly do. He's very good.'

'I'll suck it out of him then.'

And with that their two mouths, their four hands pulled, pushed, grasped, slid, sloppy and slippery. My prick bulged and reached up stiff and long, my balls swollen, jism gathered down at the root of my cock and the two women teased it up until I couldn't stop and out it shot.

'Look at it go!'

'Mmmm!'

'It's steaming hot!'

'Sticky hot glue.'

'Good for the complexion.'

And as I released that whole flood, some of it I could sense covered their hands and streamed onto their faces for they didn't let go. My prick was extraordinarily sensitive but still they kept on, rubbing and stroking, slapping my length on their cheeks, wet and sticky, prodding it at their necks, then down, its sticky length pressed, onto their breasts. My hands kept working on them until they both began to yelp and cry, moving faster on me, creaming my hands, my cock sucked again till we all seemed to merge in a wet stickiness of hands, mouths and tongues.

Afterwards we all relaxed together, Lorna and Barbara lying back on each side of me on the floor so I could gaze down and see their slim-waisted bodies, both still wearing their nylons. My cock had wilted by then though it still retained a kind of limp fatness. Every now and then Barbara looked me over, easing up onto her elbow.

'It still looks nice, you know.'

'Really?' I said.

'Mind you, I prefer it in its other state!'

'Me too,' Lorna said. Her head was resting on her hands clasped beneath her head. 'I can't wait for you. Here.' She lifted one hand away from her head and walked her fingers across her breasts, down to touch her quim. 'Isn't he ready yet, Barbara?' she asked.

'Give me a few more minutes,' I answered. I certainly wasn't going to let this evening end when I had Lorna in this mood and I always enjoyed the way Barbara bounced around on my prick.

'Maybe we should help him a little,' Barbara countered. 'I'm game,' said Lorna, standing over me.

'Take it easy, Lorna. Don't touch him just yet. He might spill out too soon. I know what he likes.' Barbara went over to her gramophone. She had just got one of the new so-called 'black boxes' for long-playing records. She put one on – soft, moody jazz, and she began to dance in a very sensual way, drifting towards me. Lorna watched her, then stepped a little away from my chair towards Barbara, I lay back and watched these two almost naked ladies perform a very erotic dance for me, swaying nearer, trailing fingers through my hair, down my arms, circling my stomach, almost but not quite touching my dick which certainly took the hint by twitching a little.

'Did you see that?' Barbara said.

'I think there's life in the old dog yet!' Lorna added.

'Old dog! No. Young dick we should call him.'

'Yes. Young dick. I like that.' And as if to prove how much she liked it, she said it again and again. 'Young dick. Young dick.'

Soon it became a chorus as first Lorna, then Barbara chanted out phrases – 'young dick, big prick, fat roger, long dong, sweeter peter,' until they both chanted together, 'cock, cock, cock,' and Barbara broke into a strange Scottish reel, singing against the moody jazz, 'Oh, he's the cock of the North.'

Lorna then began a slow, deliberate slink to my chair, perching on the arm and undid the clasp on her garter belt. She smoothed her hand leisurely down her leg, along her black stocking to her ankle, then up. She began to roll her stocking down, lifting her leg high so I could admire its shapeliness.

Barbara joined her by sitting on the other arm and she too started to roll first one, then her other stocking, holding one high by the toe so that it was hanging down in its filmy length. She let the top drop in a circle round my prick. That had the desired effect for my length roused itself a little, by no means a full erection but noticeably stiffer.

Lorna looked down from her perch, her leg still high in the air. She pulled off her stocking. 'Maybe if I get my stocking a little oily, it'll slide on more easily' and she dropped her stocking there as well. Then she took my hand as she lifted her other leg, still with its stocking on, and placed it on her ankle. 'Maybe you'd like to take my other stocking off, Nick.'

'I don't want to put a ladder in it.'

'Oh, I don't mind. Anyhow, it'll make it better for you to climb up!'

I sat up a little and rolled the stocking down, finally drawing it off. 'There! Clever boy! Not a ladder. Not a scratch.'

Barbara reached down and pulled the stockings away from my cock, making sure they lingered around it so that again there was a series of twitches from it. She threw the stockings away and took my cock gently between two fingers. At their touch, my length thrust up some more and her fingers pried the skin back from the head. It felt delicious.

'There! Didn't I tell you, Lorna? You can soon get Nick's attention!'

'Me first then!' Lorna yelled, getting off her perch, positioning herself over my cock. Barbara was still holding it and she directed it towards Lorna who moved down and sighed. 'I can feel it. It's beautiful.' And then she eased herself onto me, her legs shooting up high, not hooking onto my shoulders but resting against them. I sat very still, enjoying being enveloped in the soft plushness of Lorna's quim. She was wriggling a little, keeping me deep inside her though. She arched her body back, reaching her arms above her head so that they fell onto the carpet. She was now stretched full length against me.

I began a very deliberate rhythm with my pelvis, moving very slowly. There wasn't much movement but it made me feel the end of my cock touching some deep softness, lush and sweet, inside Lorna. She pushed against me more as she began to pant a little.

Barbara opened her mouth on mine as Lorna stretched one arm up to tickle my balls. Then Barbara somehow climbed up onto the chair, planted her two feet on the arms and lowered herself towards my mouth. Her quim glistened with moistness and I flicked my tongue out to taste it. Barbara shuddered and whispered down to Lorna, 'He's licking me. It's delicious.'

Then began a special double motion. Lorna quickened the hold she had on my prick inside, a slippery, slithery hold, squeezing my cock out a little, then pushing firmly down, each time her hand tightening, then loosening on my balls. I occasionally pushed my shaft further in but mostly it was Lorna delighting herself, manipulating my cock, throbbing against it, her inner muscles pulsing, her voice now a wordless kind of song in tune with the jazz still playing.

And Barbara was holding onto the headrest of the chair to steady herself as she rode up and down. She was incredibly juicy and each time she pushed herself onto my mouth, I slid my tongue along the lips before rolling it onto her clit, then slipping it down and in, letting my inner lips kiss the softness of her quim. My hands were holding her buttocks, stroking, poking a finger inside her hole. I remembered how unbelievably sexy that had felt that first time she had massaged me.

I'm surprised that the chair was able to take the weight of the three of us. There were some ominous creaks as we swayed against each other and the pace quickened. But we were all so involved that I don't think it would have mattered if the chair had fallen to pieces. We'd have gone on sucking, stroking and fucking in the middle of the debris as we carried ourselves further and further along that exquisite ride, prodding and poking, licking and touching, rocking and pushing, each of us reaching out towards our own climax.

I was hoping we would all reach that high point together but I didn't believe it would be possible. But what happened was something near to that. Lorna began to urge herself on, hard against me, murmuring 'In, Nick, in!' then hoarsely shouting up to Barbara, 'I can see his finger doing it to you. In, Nick, in.'

When Barbara heard Lorna shout, that seemed to egg her on. She pushed her slathery slit hard against my mouth and at the same time somehow moved her arse so that my finger probed deeply inside her arsehole. She closed her crack around my hand, holding it tight there, squirming on it. Above me I heard her groaning quietly.

And my cock began to feel more engorged, fattening, brushing inside Lorna against those pulsing muscles. And that drove her even wilder and she thrashed against me. That seemed to make our whole position precarious and I think we all sensed we should finish before we did ourselves some serious damage.

From the floor I heard Lorna moaning loud, panting hard, her pelvis thrusting fast against me. 'Cream me!' she yelled.

'Oh, yes, Nick, do it! Do it!' Barbara groaned loudly. Somewhere at the back of my throat a strong croak filled my mouth, muffled in the damp velvet of Barbara's quim. Suddenly Lorna let go. Her whole body quivered against me, her voice soared into a high register and I sensed a great surge of sticky moistness cover my cock. This triggered me to spill out, not a great flood of jism but what seemed like thick spurts which sent Lorna into further paroxysms and higher screeches.

When Barbara felt my cries against her wet lips, she began to rub herself furiously onto my mouth, bucking herself by pulling herself up and down. The chair was in danger of tipping over as she heaved and strained until she finally yelled, 'Oh, God. Here I come!'

We somehow disentangled ourselves and we finished up in a tumbled embrace, the two women snuggled against me, letting their hands slide all over me. It was a marvellously sexy feeling but without any attempt by any of us to start again. I had my arms around them as we all lay sprawled in the chair. Their hands propped my limp cock up and, occasionally one or the other would lean down to place a gentle kiss on it. My hands were fondling their breasts and nipples and time passed in that relaxed way until, almost without knowing it, I felt my cock stiffen a little.

Lorna was the first to notice and quite matter-of-factly she said, 'Barbara, why don't you see if Nick can manage it with you? I'd like to watch.'

'Only watch?' Barbara asked.

'Well, maybe I'll join in.'

'What d'you think, Nick?' I was feeling exhausted but I'd had some great evenings with Barbara. The final fuck with her had been so excruciatingly long and slow that I always experienced an intense release. I was too tired to say anything but I nodded my head.

Barbara wriggled across me and on the way her mouth took in my half-erect cock. That had the effect of making it more than half-erect. Barbara positioned herself in front of the chair and bent down. The globes of her arse looked very enticing so I stood holding my cock so that it stuck out in front of me as I manoeuvred it into her quim from behind.

Immediately Barbara began to rock backwards and forwards. I began to push as deeply as I could as she moved back onto me. Then she let herself lean down further, my cock squiggling just to the lips of her quim. She waggled around the head of my cock with those slippery lips before pushing back to take it in again. I responded by plunging as far in as I could, holding myself there, gripping Barbara so that she could move to slide me out. I let my cock rest there for I could feel it throbbing. I knew that Barbara loved to feel a throbbing prick inside her.

We stayed like that for a moment or two until I felt a gentle touch enclose my balls. It was Lorna's hand, I knew, because I felt those pointy nipples of hers prodding on my back. My arms were reaching in front of me to stroke Barbara's breasts but I pulled away so I could reach round to put my hand on Lorna's buttocks. She shifted a little and it became obvious to me that she had seen me fingering Barbara's arsehole and wanted me to do the same to her. And so I obliged, sliding my way into her tight arse as she gripped me firmly.

The three of us were jammed together in this way for some time until I felt the need to shoot off whatever I had left. I began to move fast in and out of Barbara's warm and moist cunt. She was battering herself against me every time I thrust. Lorna was pressing even closer against my back as she also bent her knees to take my finger further into her. We each fitted into what we were doing and it wasn't long before I sensed that familiar full rod swelling up the length of my prick and from the last of my supply I spurted my jism inside Barbara. That was enough for her to go off into shivers and jerks and that seemed to communicate itself to Lorna, for she pushed hard onto my fingers and let out a long whistling croak. As one, we all tumbled onto the carpet, the record on the gramophone long finished. Only then did we notice that the music had stopped and the room was filled with the swish and click of the needle at the centre of the record.

It was a mood we never again reached. We got close a couple of times, though we didn't have a threesome very often. It wasn't quite the same, enjoyable, yes, but we soon discovered that we each enjoyed each other more when we were separate. So I would spend an evening with Barbara on her own, and then Lorna. And that's what we did all through the rest of my time at the university.

Lorna remained her elegant self and, at first, when I went to her new place, I was still my reticent self. She just seemed too lovely, too charming to be the woman I had seen become so raunchy on that first evening with the three of us. Lorna herself still played the decorous hostess and while, eventually, we did manage to make love on our evenings together, I think we were both too bound up with the way our relationship had started in the first place.

I don't know what it was. My evenings with Barbara were still terrific but then we had got off on the right foot to begin with. It was always good to be with Lorna and though those times we tried the threesome together were certainly fun, eventually we gave up because we were never able to recapture the fire of that first time. Maybe it was because we had been through an exploit that had some element of danger, maybe we expected some consequences because we were involved in something which in a way was criminal, maybe we simply outdid ourselves sexually because we were so delighted by the fact that we'd got away with our moonlight flit, that we'd put one over on Milton. But the fact is that after two months or so, while I still kept on seeing Lorna and Barbara on their own, we never again paired off in that devastatingly exciting way we had done that October evening when we rescued Lorna from Paradise Lost. Still, for that one night, we did find another kind of paradise.

11. A Bicycle Built For Two

I heard nothing more about the moonlight flit we did for Lorna until Barbara phoned me three or four days later. She soon got onto the subject of Milton.

'He's a real sod, that one!' It was unusual for Barbara to use bad language though she liked to drop suggestive hints to me in the course of conversations. So when she called Milton a sod, I knew she was steamed up about him.

'You wouldn't believe the way he talked the other night! I couldn't shut him up. I gave him the prim and proper treatment but it wouldn't do. He kept coming at me till finally I had to play along. Very creepy. I'm surprised I was able to keep him at a distance. He kept giving me these dirty looks, fluttering his hands about, and his lips were all wet. He looked as if he was drooling over a particularly juicy piece of steak.'

'Maybe I should go and give him a piece of my mind,' I offered.

'You stay away from there, Nick. He'll know you were in on Lorna's flit. He was fuming when he phoned me the next day. Accused me of betraying him. I ought to have known what a nasty piece of work Lorna was, he said. Nothing short of a tart, according to him. Yet when he was talking to me that night, I got the impression he was trying to set up some kind of operation in those houses, running a high-priced gambling place and brothel. He implied he was going to start with Lorna. He even seemed to be offering me a partnership in it. God! Just think what a partnership with Milton would get you into! No wonder Gerry's interested in what he's doing, especially if Lorna's right and he's into drug dealing.'

'But I didn't think Gerry had anything to do with drugs,' I said.

'No, he doesn't. But he's afraid things will get too hot at the docks if the police start investigating Milton for drugs. They'll be checking every cargo that comes in and that means they'd be checking Gerry's stuff more carefully.

'At one point that night,' Barbara went on, 'I almost thought the game was up. A big bruiser came in and whispered something to him. Milton's eyebrows shot up so high I thought they'd fly right off his face. He stared at me and got up from his chair as if he was coming over to me. Then he stopped and told his thug to leave it to him. I could see this other geezer wanted to do something else but Milton wasn't listening. Finally the thug shrugged his shoulders and left the room. Then Milton turned his stare back on me. And he kept on staring without saying a word.'

'What d'you think it was?'

'I think the thug was suspicious of something. Who knows? Maybe he'd been prowling around the grounds. Anyhow, I gave him the works.'

'The works?'

'Put on my sultry look, sidled up to him, let my fingers slide along his arm, sat down, crossed my legs so he got a good sken at them.'

'I know what that does to a man!'

'Well, I don't mind doing it for you... and more! But it gives me the willies doing it for Milton. I got out of there as fast as I could, soon as I heard the van beeping its horn. And he told me he found out about Lorna being gone about an hour after I left. He phoned me, he said, but my phone was engaged every time he called.' She stopped and laughed. 'I'd taken it off the hook, you remember, Nick. I didn't want us to be disturbed!' She laughed again.

'You'd better warn Lorna. I wouldn't put it past him to try something really nasty.'

'Don't worry. I've found her a very nice, safe flat. He'll never find it.'

'He could find out where she teaches, and pick her up on the way home.'

'She's put in for a transfer, and she thinks she'll get it in a few days. It's you I'm worried about.'

'Me? Why me?'

'He's seen you round at Lorna's. He was asking me about you.' That had me a little worried but Barbara assured me that he had no idea where I lived. She certainly wasn't going to tell Milton anything about me.

'Just watch your step,' were her parting words. For two or three days I kept glancing over my shoulder to see if anyone was following me but I didn't notice anyone. Still, I kept pretty well in a group with friends, went out with Ron, didn't go round to see Lorna, though I would have liked to, and I kept away from Barbara in case Milton was keeping an eye on her. I felt as if I was skulking around but after a few days I lost my nervousness. Lost it, that is, till Daisy phoned me.

She started in her usual cheery, sexy way. 'Hello

there, Nick. How's it going? Been keeping your hand in . . . not only your hand, I bet! But don't forget! Only just a few months to go!'

She was reminding me that she'd soon be twenty-five and she'd be giving up the game. I'd be graduating at the same time so she was planning a double celebration. 'I'm going to double you up, but not with a fist in your stomach. I'm thinking of something you'll really enjoy.' I thought all of this was a tease. I liked being with Daisy – she was really attractive, bubbly, fresh, full of sexy come-ons, always cheerful but she was resolute in not giving up on her vow to stay only in the game with men. So I knew I'd never get anywhere with her. I thought she was just egging me on, teasing, though she always had a real twinkle in her eye when she talked her sexy talk with me.

This time, though, she didn't go on with any innuendo. 'Someone was asking after you yesterday.'

'Is that right?'

'A couple of fellers, as a matter of fact. I heard 'em banging at the door downstairs. I thought they were paying a call on Liz – that's the woman who lives downstairs, you know, the place you lived in at first. But I haven't seen her around for a few days so I called down to tell 'em she wasn't in. You should have seen the size of them! Right then I thought they were after Liz – she likes a bit of the rough trade, she does. But I didn't like the looks of them. And they weren't looking for Liz anyhow. Asked about you, whether you still lived there, though they didn't know your name.'

'What did you tell them?'

'I didn't know what to say but they looked so shifty I played it cagey. "Is it Big Sid you're looking for?" I said. Well, they wanted to know a bit more and I thought to myself that you'd got yourself in a bit of trouble so I decided to lead 'em on.'

'What did you say?'

'"Oooh! Big Sid!" I said. "You've got to watch out for him. The Terror of Moss Side, they call him. I've never seen a man as big as him. The muscles on him!" I was exaggerating a bit though I must say I could have said the muscle on him. I mean, I know just what a muscle you've got, Nick.'

She was thinking about that first evening we'd met when she'd 'instructed' me on the different ways men liked to be stroked. And she went on, 'I got sort of carried away. You know me. I like to have a bit of fun so I told them you were really huge. And your muscles! I showed 'em how thick you were with my hands. And how hard you were. I could see they were getting a bit worried so I laid it on – well, not really, Nick. You do have a very nice hard "muscle"!'

'So what happened?'

'I convinced them they'd better stay out of your way. I tell you, by the time I'd finished telling them how big and strong and hard you were, I'd got myself all worked up! But I knew it'd be no good asking you to come over.'

'I'm a penniless student, Daisy.'

'Well, I've only a few months to go.'

'You still sticking to that?'

'I certainly am. Twenty-five and that's the end of it for me. Are we still on for our celebration?'

'Looking forward to it.'

'You hard-muscled man, you!'

'So did those men go away?'

'Scooted out and haven't been back.'

I imagined these men were two of Milton's thugs looking for me. I was a little frightened by the idea, expecting get beaten up at any time, especially after I had a close shave one evening.

I'd been staying away from Barbara just in case Milton was having her watched but she convinced me one night to go to the cinema with her. She was looking absolutely stunning when she turned up – stiletto heels showing off her great legs, a short skirt with a row of buttons up the side – 'easy to unfasten,' she whispered to me as we walked into the dark of the cinema. She led me along the back row and immediately snuggled next to me, taking my hand and placing it high on her thighs. I started to unfasten the buttons on her skirt but she stopped me.

'Just a minute,' she cooed. 'I have to go to the Ladies.' She was soon back and I noticed she'd left three of the buttons on her skirt undone so I slid my hand underneath and let my hand begin to slide upwards. She eased herself against me to make it easier for me. Then she rummaged in her handbag and pulled something out. 'Well, look what I've found!' She was holding a pair of filmy panties. 'Silly me! I must have forgotten to put them back on when I went to the ladies.'

She lolled against me as my fingers began to play slowly with her under her skirt. She was already wet and my fingers slid inside her and around her slit in a creamy way. She soon had my fly buttons undone and we stayed like that for an hour or so into the film, both of us feeling hotter and hotter by the minute until she suddenly stood up and pulled me out of my seat. My cock was sticking out of my trousers and I clutched it to try to push it back inside. Barbara's hand gave it a final squeeze as she said, 'Come on! Let's go to my place. Milton's given up on us by now, I'm sure,' and she hurried me out of the cinema.

She went to get the car which she had parked round the corner and I waited for her outside the cinema. After about a minute I felt a hand on my shoulder, a hard grip that forced me to turn round. I was face to face with an ugly-looking brute. 'Hello, sonny. Fancy meeting you here. Think you're going to get a nice big fuck, right? Well, what you're really going to get is a nice big fist in your gob. By the time I've finished with you, that lady friend of yours will have no use for your balls. She won't get fucked because you'll be all fucked up! Come on!'

I was really scared. I was no match for him though I did try to stay put as he tried to yank me away. I somehow thought if I stayed near the cinema, there'd be too many lights for him to start anything there. But he began to manhandle me – he drove a big fist into my gut and I felt I was going to vomit. I doubled over and that made it easier for him to move me. But in a way it saved me. He thought I was too weak so he relaxed his hold a little. When Barbara drove around and saw what was happening, she leaned over quickly, opened the door of the car, yelled 'Run!' Somehow I wrenched myself away and flung myself into the car. Barbara revved hard and I sank down into the seat. The last I saw of the thug was through the rear window of the car. He was shaking his fist, his mouth opening as he shouted obscenities, though we couldn't hear him above the roar of the engine.

'That settles it,' Barbara said through gritted teeth. I didn't really know what she meant and I was afraid that if they had traced us to the cinema, Milton had probably got a man watching Barbara's house. All thoughts of the delectable evening I was going to spend with Barbara had disappeared but strangely this hadn't dampened

Barbara's ardour. One of her hands was kneading my crotch and I was surprised that I could still manage an erection.

We were obviously driving back to Barbara's house and I said to her, 'Don't you think they'll have someone waiting for us at your place?'

She shook her head. 'No. They think they're such tough nuts. Milton sent that creep to deal with you. He'd expect him to take care of you. So not to worry. Barbara's going to take care of you tonight. And speaking of nuts...', and her hand rooted around to fondle my balls. 'I prefer these nuts,' she said, then followed that by giving my cock a hard squeeze. 'And I'll fix that Milton once and for all.'

'How you going to do that?'

'Just you sit back and enjoy yourself.' Her fingers had unfastened my fly buttons and she was massaging the head of my prick gently with her fingertips. 'There you go. Just you forget about that nasty man. Nobody's going to touch you ... except me! And from now on, Milton's had it!'

When she parked the car in her driveway, she moved out quickly and ran round to my side of the car almost before I was out of it. She grabbed my stiff cock. 'Come on, big boy!' and pulled me towards the side door of the house, only letting go of me to find the key. I was still thinking that at any moment someone was going to loom out of the shadows and start to punch the pair of us. But we got inside safely, and Barbara began to struggle out of her skirt and blouse. 'Get your clothes off, Nick,' she whispered and she moved into her living room, shedding her clothes as she went. 'Just one quick call, then I'll be with you, sweetie. Why don't you go upstairs and get the bed warm?'

I did as I was told so I didn't hear whom she phoned. I suspect it was Gerry for from then on none of us had any more trouble with Milton and his thugs. And the evening became a delight. I was surprised for I never thought that, after the scare I'd had, I'd be able to get myself interested. But the sense of danger seemed to have the opposite effect on Barbara and that communicated itself to me – we went at it as if the hounds of hell were after us and then proceeded to spend long hours in lingering embraces, slow strokings, deep probings and proddings till we both fell asleep absolutely exhausted.

Things went along pretty smoothly after that. I spent most of my time with Barbara though I didn't have a lot to spare. My final examinations weren't too far away so I had to concentrate on my studies. I saw Lorna only once more. She had transferred to another school and she was busy adjusting to that.

The evening I spent with her was very pleasant but she was back in her elegantly removed mood. She was beautifully sexy but in a kind of aloof way, not the way she had been with Barbara and me. She was sweet and gentle and she was very attentive to me but she never let herself go. Still, it was a differently erotic happening for me – her quiet elegance made me work harder, made me want to unleash her passionate nature she kept closely guarded but she kept a firm hold on it.

I was more and more determined to break through with her because once before I had experienced her hot excesses of raw passion and I looked forward to finding that again with her. But she went home to her mother's that Christmas and then wrote to me to tell me she was staying in York. She had found a teaching job there and it would be easier for her to look after her mother. Her letter was nicely affectionate but it was obvious from the tone that she didn't want to continue anything with me.

So I was thrown back on Barbara – nothing wrong with that, for she enjoyed being with me and we indulged ourselves in all kinds of different ways. Occasionally I still went to the Saturday night dances and I met a couple of interesting women there but neither of them had the erotic know-how of Barbara.

And I was still seeing Daisy, but only in our usual way. I'd take her out to lunch about every ten days or so and she was always really sensual. She dressed especially for me, she said, in dresses that clung to her figure like a second skin. Sometimes she would turn up in a looser dress and explain why. She'd lean across the table and in her incredibly sexy voice say, 'I wanted to wear this for you. D'you like it? It feels really smooth and silky.' She'd take my hand and place it on the dress just where it folded over her knee. Then she'd push her leg forward so that my hand slid the dress up a little. 'Doesn't that feel nice? I love to feel it against my skin. So soft. And that's when I want to feel something hard against me. I go all juicy just thinking about hard, hard things all hot on me. And when it hangs loose like this, you'd be surprised what kind of things there's room for under it.' Then she'd smile in a mischievous way.

'Do you like to think about soft and juicy things? Makes me warm and soft all over. I'll bet you get hot and hard, not warm and soft.' Sometimes she'd place her hand on my knee, then grip my thigh tightly. 'You'd be surprised just what I'm wearing underneath this dress. It's lovely. It's just waiting for something to come along and pry inside. Right inside.' And then her hand would move a little higher and grip my thigh even tighter.

'Would you like to come along? And I do mean *come*

along? Wouldn't you like to come?' And she'd give me an encouraging pat. I don't want to give the impression that Daisy was simply a prickteaser. She did all this in a very good-humoured way and I must say I liked it, though I think she was trying to entice me back to her place. But of course she had made up her mind that she was not going to indulge anybody without paying. I'm sure she would have been unbelievably sexy with me and that twinkle in her eye, her infectious laugh and her lecherous smile tempted me a good deal. But we kept it as a game.

And that's what I thought we were doing whenever she mentioned how she was stopping at the age of twenty-five. It was all a game and I went along with it. So when she mentioned the celebration we would share – she for her birthday and her giving up of her 'profession' and me for my graduation – I always told her that I had it marked down in my diary.

'What day?' she once asked me.

'Oh, any day will do.'

'Oh no, it won't. It's a special day. My birthday. And my free day. And you'll be the first.'

'First for what?'

'You know what I mean! I'm setting myself free.' She laughed. 'Freedom. What did they call it when they set the slaves free in America?'

'Emancipation.'

'Right. Put it down in your diary. June the seventh. Daisy's Emancipation Day – and aren't I just going to kick up my heels ... and anything else! And it's not kicking I'll be thinking of!'

I didn't have a diary but that date of June the seventh stayed in my mind because Daisy kept reminding me of it.

'What are you going to do afterwards?'

'I don't know for now and I don't care! But just watch me on Emancipation Day.' Her hand rapidly flew up my thigh and patted my crotch briefly. 'You'll really want to watch me then! That's the day for both of us, isn't it?'

I must have looked quizzical because she leaned across the table and gazed at me with her gorgeously big brown eyes. 'I mean it. You're invited.' She clasped my hand. 'Give me your answer, do.'

'You're not going to burst into song, are you?' And I started to sing, 'Daisy, Daisy,' and then she joined in and we both sang the words.

'So what's your answer, Daisy?' I asked her, laughing.

'Haven't I been telling you all these weeks? On June the seventh, the answer is yes, Nick. Oh my! Yes. Just you wait and see, Nick. Yes, yes. Of course it's yes for you too. Yes, yes, yes. And yes again!' Her hand moved from mine and it snaked under the tablecloth and rested on my crotch. She began a very slow stroke – that was the most open touch she had given me, apart from that lesson in stroking she had given me the first night I had met her. As her hand moved on me, she half-said, half-sang, 'You will look sweet, you know, upon the seat of a bicycle built for two.'

She could feel that her hand was rousing me and she smiled at me. 'It isn't a bicycle that'll be taking us for a ride but it will be a terrific ride, believe me.' She squeezed me and said, 'And I'll find something much more comfortable for this . . .' and another squeeze, 'than some old, cracked leather saddle. Something plush and soft you can sink into.' Then another squeeze and a slow stroke along my shaft before she drew her hand away. 'You'll see. Emancipation Day.'

While this seemed more definite than she had been before, she was still approaching the idea in a kind of jokey way. Examinations were underway so I was very busy but I still found time to see Daisy. And she still talked about her Emancipation Day. 'Check your calendar,' she always reminded me. 'I'm counting the days. Get yourself in shape for the best bike ride of your life.' Then came her enticingly lascivious smile. 'The two of us. Our bicycle built for two.'

I was beginning to sense that Daisy was really serious about this celebration in spite of the fact that she kept our conversations on the light and suggestive side. Her touches had become a little more explicit so, each time I met her, I became randier and randier.

My randiness found a release with Barbara and she occasionally remarked on my more than usual sexiness. 'Has somebody been feeding you Spanish fly? Or maybe you've been practising fly fishing because your rod's really ready to reel in anything you can get your hands on!'

'Not just anything – I just want to get hooked into you.' And that's all I was doing then, though I was thinking about the promise of Daisy. And that promise seemed to be materialising because soon after I had finished my examinations at the end of May, I received a card by post. It was handwritten in exquisite calligraphy. It read:

Daisy requests (insists on) the company of Nick, champion cyclist, for an evening of racing pleasure (and I do mean pleasure!). Food and drink will be plentiful but not in quantities sufficient to reduce the athletic skill required for a full round of events featuring a bicycle built for two (and I do mean two:

Daisy and Nick celebrating the end of term and freedom!)

June 7   Emancipation Day   7 p.m.

I was always amazed by Daisy. Though she was not formally educated, she had done a lot of reading. Her vocabulary was very good and I suppose that's one of the reasons I liked the conversations I had with her. She could talk suggestively dirty but she loved to make it humorous and always laced it with formally correct language. The suggestiveness took on an additional sexiness when it was expressed in such a meticulous way. So naturally this card made me even more randy. I could hardly wait for the days to pass before I went to Daisy's to celebrate her emancipation.

When she opened the door to me, I was bowled over. She looked sensational. Daisy always dressed well and I imagined she made a special effort when she came out to lunch with me. But this evening she had surpassed herself.

I may not have done justice to Daisy when I've mentioned her before. She was petite, a little over five feet tall but she dressed to make herself appear a little taller than that. She wore tall high heels and her skirts were never much below her knees so her legs seemed long and that gave the impression of tallness as well. Her figure was slender, a very small waist and her breasts were in proportion, not too large but very shapely and firm. Her hair fell in natural waves to her shoulders and she had a habit of letting it fall across her cheek, then lifting it gently away with her slim fingers. That gesture used to get to me – her hair was so lustrous and thick and her fingers so careful but so sure of pushing her hair back, I'm certain that any man watching her wanted to be touched in all the right places by her fingers, thinking about the feel of her hair under his hands or falling across his skin anywhere.

Her face was oval with very clear and bright skin. She had large brown eyes that could almost melt you when she turned them on you in a sultry look. She didn't wear a lot of make-up but it was always put on with a real sense of highlighting her best features: her eyes, her cheekbones and her full lips.

She greeted me with a dazzling smile. 'Come in, Nick. I hope you brought your cycling suit!' I followed her into the room wishing her many happy returns of the day. Without turning to look at me, she said, 'Well, as it's my birthday, I guess I won't wear my cycling suit. It'll soon be time for me to wear my birthday suit instead.'

'I like the suit you're wearing right now.' She had on a form-fitting red dress, an off-the-shoulder number with no sleeves. It looked as if her body was captured inside it but was somehow trying to escape. It was so smooth on her, I couldn't imagine her wearing anything underneath it. And when I thought that, I felt a pleasant warm swelling as my cock responded in its usual way.

Her living room didn't look quite as garish and brash as I had thought it was the first time I had been in it almost three years before. It was still decorated in blues and greens but somehow the colours seemed to be more subdued – maybe it was because the lighting was low and diffused a warm glow.

Daisy saw me looking around. 'Not really my choice,' She said. 'I like my colours a little more ... dramatic and the geezer who lived here before me obviously was a poufter.' She laughed. 'You know, didn't want to admit it but anyone coming in here with him would get the idea.' She flapped her wrist limply. 'Just look at me in here,' she said in a twee voice. 'I'm such a naughty boy. These vibrant colours but I keep them ... muted so's no one will guess.' Then she giggled.

She moved over to a side window and drew her hand along the arm of quite the longest sofa I had ever seen. It looked very plush and soft as if you might disappear into it when you sat on it. 'I bought this. I love to stretch out on it and relax. Lovely and comfy.' She waved her hand at me. 'Why don't you try it?'

As I sank into it and the soft material seemed almost to embrace me gently, inviting me in, I thought what a very apt piece of furniture it was for a woman like Daisy.

By now she had gone into the kitchen and after a moment or two she came out carrying a large bottle of champagne. 'I don't often drink this. It goes to my head ... and other parts of my anatomy!' She laughed.

'Shall I open that for you?' I asked pointing at the bottle.

'I can do it myself. It's my Emancipation Day!' And with that she untwisted the wire around the cork, then covering it with a cloth, she began to yank it out. 'Got to be careful the damn thing doesn't shoot out and hit someone in the eye.' She lowered the bottle so that it was pointing at my crotch. 'Let it go now and you'd be speaking in a high voice!' She then pointed it upright. 'And that's the last thing I'd want to happen to you!'

With one last twist, the cork came loose and champagne frothed out of the neck. 'What does that remind you of?' She laughed. 'No wonder they say champagne makes women go weak at the knees. It's not just the taste and the bubbles. It's what must go through their heads when they see all that creamy froth spurt out like that. And I bet it's not just their knees that go weak!'

She poured two large glasses, gave one to me and sat close to me on the couch, leaning into me. She raised her glass and touched it to mine. 'Cheers! Drink it down like a good boy.' We both drank and when she had taken a hefty swig, she looked straight at me. 'Your lips are all bubbly.' She reached her hand out and placed her fingertips on my mouth. She ran them around and then pressed two fingers so that my lips opened and she slid them inside. 'Hmmm!' she murmured. 'Lovely, lovely.' She sipped at her glass, still giving me her sweetly salacious smile. 'It's lovely to feel something slide inside like that, isn't it?'

Her fingers in my mouth were certainly giving me ideas. I rolled my tongue around the tips and encountered the pointed shape of her nails. She pressed them onto my tongue but very carefully so that she added a little sharpness to the feel of them against my tongue. She raised her glass again and she licked up to the rim. 'Spilt a little. Don't want to waste any.' There was a little flicker of a wink as she went on, 'And I don't want to waste anything tonight.' She leaned up to me, her tongue still peeping from her lips. Her mouth came to mine as she slid her fingers out. Then her warm, slippery tongue flicked slowly between my lips, sliding not very deeply in, just a soft touch circling around the inside of my lips, then a quick dab at the tip of my tongue. I began to respond, trying to push my tongue into her mouth but she drew back.

'Just a little touchy-feely, Nick,' she said in her wickedly low and sexy voice. 'We don't want to lose our appetite too soon. I've spent the whole day looking forward to a feast.' She raised her glass again. 'Here's to our freedom feast!'

We stayed on the couch, sipping our champagne and each other for some time. I was already stiff but I relaxed into the couch and gave myself up to a succession of little fluttery kisses and pats from Daisy. She was very close to me, my arm was around her and I was rubbing across her back; the feel of the silkiness of her dress was very enticing. And it certainly felt as if she was wearing nothing underneath it, though she was wearing stockings. I imagined some small and flimsy garter belt was holding them up but, for now, my hand simply stayed above her waist, venturing briefly every now and again towards the first swell of her breasts without actually placing my hand on them.

While we were indulging ourselves in this way she talked about her plans. She was thinking about going down to London, she said, doing some secretarial work maybe, or being a receptionist. 'Perhaps even take some night courses.' I was interested to hear this because I was thinking of going to London that summer and I'd lost touch with Teresa. I felt it was probably time for me to make a break with Gerry so I'd reconciled myself to leaving Barbara, living in London until I could find a teaching job somewhere. The summer looked as if it would be terrific if Daisy was going to be there.

She went on to tell me about the way she had lived these past three years though she said very little about the men who came to visit her. It seemed she had been very choosy about her clients, as most of them sounded professional, some well-educated, a few very rich who seemed to give her presents as well as money. 'They liked it here. More colourful than their homes. And very discreet. No one to spy on us. The poufter must have been dead scared of being bombed. He put up these heavy dark curtains, then plush velvet as well. No light got out – he must have thought the bombers were looking for his lights so they'd drop the bombs just on him! But it makes it very cosy in here. Like you're sealed off from the world. You wouldn't think anyone was in here from the outside. And you can turn the lights down really low in here. Very smoochy.' And she leaned over to me, one finger probing inside my mouth next to her tongue which was squirming inside as well.

She had prepared a delicious meal and it was made more delicious by her quick fondles and touches while we ate. I was reminded a little of Mrs Courtney and her picnic but Daisy was not outrageous – everything was done gently and subtly. Once she reminded me of our first meeting. 'I was tempted. It was such a rainy night outside and I almost convinced myself that it would be nice to cuddle up to you for the night.'

'Well, I enjoyed myself anyhow.'

'And I learned a lot about you then.'

'What d'you mean?'

'I was feeling you out.' She laughed – she really seemed to be enjoying herself and while she was still being something of a tease, I had the feeling that tonight the tease would lead into something more. 'I could tell what you'd be like and the way you'd like it. You'll see.'

We lingered over the meal. I think both of us were perhaps a little shy because we knew what was going to happen. We were both looking forward to spending the whole evening together and we wanted to savour it to the full.

Finally she brought the coffee pot in. I was back in that deep and plush sofa and she handed me a cup. 'I'm not giving you any cognac just yet,' she said. 'I'm just a little tiddly myself so I don't think we need any more just yet. No more to drink, I mean. That's lots of other tasty things to sample.' And she walked round the room turning the lights even lower.

'I won't be able to see you soon.'

'Oh, but I'll be here, believe me.'

'I think it's time to taste those other things.'

She turned to me with a very serious look on her face. For a very brief moment I wondered if Daisy was really nothing more than a tease. I'd been through this with other women but I ought to have known, for the women I'd known had teased me but they had not left it at that.

'I have just the thing in mind. Very tasty.' She was walking towards the kitchen.

'What is it?'

'What's a birthday without a cake?'

That wasn't what I was thinking but if she had made a birthday cake for herself, I'd certainly like to taste it. The meal she'd cooked had been scrumptious.

After a moment or two she came out of the kitchen carrying a cake with candles flaming on it, a cream confection piled with white fluffiness. She placed it on the small table by the couch and sat down in the big armchair opposite me.

'There! What d'you think?'

'It looks delicious. But first you have to blow out the candles and make a wish.'

'Well, I know my wish is going to come true tonight!' she whispered sexily. 'I've been saving it up for over two years till I knew it would come true.' Then she was up again, going round the room, turning all the lights off.

'Candlelight's so romantic. I thought it would get us in the right mood.'

She was soon back in her chair, her face a soft glow in the light of the candles. She looked stunning, as she had done all evening. I felt like telling her that I didn't need candlelight – I was already in the mood.

She was holding the cake-slice in her hand and I expected her to cut into the cake and hand me a piece. But she leaned forward and blew the candles out. We were in pitch blackness and, though she was only a couple of yards away from me, I couldn't see her. I knew she was still there because she was chuckling a little.

'Know what I wished?'

'You're not supposed to tell anyone. Otherwise, your wish won't come true.'

'Oh, I don't think it matters tonight.' She let out a very fruity laugh. 'I wished for a big, fat cock, something I want in the raw after those that I've always had to cover up with a French letter.' She chuckled again. 'I think you've probably brought one for me as a present, haven't you, Nick? I mean, a cock of course, not a French letter!'

I had actually brought her a present, a whole set of lingerie I'd asked Gerry to send me, a camisole, half slip, panties and a long, flowing gown in the sheerest red silk. It was strangely almost the same shade as the dress Daisy was wearing. I had not given the present to her – I was saving it for an opportune moment, a time when I could watch her trying the outfit on so that I could also help her out of it. I had hidden the package behind the couch when I had first come in but now, in the dark room, I couldn't have found it if I had tried.

I was really at a loss as to what to do. I expected after a minute or two that I would be able to make out a vague shape or two in the darkness as my eyes got used to it but that wasn't the case. It was absolute blackness inside the room.

I thought about venturing up from the couch, sidling round that small table to try to find Daisy but I didn't want to stumble into, perhaps fall into the cake, make myself messy and spoil everything. So I waited.

Daisy made the first move. I sensed it rather than heard her moving. She knew where everything was in the flat so she could find her way around though I couldn't see a thing. Then I felt her sit next to me on the couch and soon her fingers touched my mouth.

'Eat up, Nick.' Her voice was right at my ear as her fingers wiped against my lips. She had scooped some of the cream from the cake and I tasted the slippery creaminess on her fingers as she slid them slowly into my mouth. Those fingers moved delicately against my tongue, stroking the cream around till my mouth felt deliciously wet. Her fingers began to move in and out of my mouth. She obviously stooped to the table to take up more cream because her fingers came back to my mouth with that thick slipperiness.

A moment or two later her fingers left my mouth and I heard her make a small slurping sound. 'Very tasty. Your cream is very tasty. I know you are a very creamy boy, Nick. I remember how it poured out of you. This reminds me of it. And your mouth. How juicy it is. Reminds me how juicy I get sometimes. Right now I can feel myself getting juicy.'

That seemed almost like an invitation so I slowly reached my hand out to where I thought she was sitting but again I sensed she had moved. I heard her sit down in the chair opposite me and I didn't know if she expected me to follow her.

'I'm just wiping that juice off my fingers. A pity because it feels lovely, all sticky and sweet. But I don't want to leave any on my dress because you know what I'm going to do, Nick?'

'Whatever it is, I'm sure it's going to be great.'

'I'm going to take my dress off so I'll be nice and comfortable.'

'I'd like to see you do that, even help you.'

'You're such a sweet, helpful man, Nick, but you just sit and relax and think about it. If you listen carefully, you'll hear me taking it off and you can imagine just what I look like, sitting here, no dress on, feeling juicy, and thinking about you over there with that big fat present you've brought me. You know, sometimes it's better just to let your imagination dream up things, makes you feel really randy, a half-naked woman just stripping off for you.'

'I'd like to see you. My imagination couldn't dream you up as well as I know you are.'

'Why, thank you. But just sit back. Listen carefully. Here I go. There's a row of buttons down the back. I'm reaching round ... one, two ... That's better. A little looser. There. I feel a little freer already. Emancipation Day. I'm slipping it off my shoulders now. There! Ooh! My titties feel so nice and free now. Can you hear my dress sliding down? I'm wiggling my arse so I can get it off.'

I don't know whether I really heard the dress being pulled down but I sensed a faint rustle. Of course my mind was running on ahead as I imagined Daisy pushing it down and baring the delicious curves of her buttocks.

'That's it. It's off.' I heard the sound of what I suppose was her dress being laid across the arm of her chair. The thought of Daisy over there in that state was driving me wild. I had a very stiff hard-on, pushing out against my trousers. As if she was reading my thoughts, Daisy said, 'I bet that big, fat present of yours is dying to be unwrapped.'

'Why don't you come and unwrap it for yourself? After all, it is your present.'

'That would be lovely, but it's your present as well in a way. You're free now. All those examinations finished. So you go ahead and unwrap it.'

So I did. I delved into my flies, ripping the buttons open and drew out my prick. As I did, Daisy murmured, 'I remember what a long, thick cock you have. Such a lovely smooth head. All that skin pulled back.'

Daisy's voice made my shaft twitch. I lay back deeper into the couch so that it stood up stiff and hard. 'I'd love to warm my hands on him,' she went on.

'Why don't you come over and do it then?'

'Oh, I don't think I could find my way over there just yet.'

'Turn the lights back on then.'

'You mustn't be impatient, Nick. Emancipation Day is a very long day, so we'll make the most of it. And I have some other things to do just yet. Are you ready?'

'I'm ready for anything.'

'Well, I'm sitting in my chair, lying back a little. I'm lifting one leg straight up and my hands are just unclipping the stocking at the top. Ooh! It feels so warm up there. I wouldn't mind someone else warming his hands there.'

'Yes please!'

'I'm rolling the stocking down. Very slowly. They're such beautifully silky stockings, sheer, can you hear the thin nylon sliding down my leg? Now I'm pulling it off my toes, dangling it from my fingers. Maybe I should let it drop onto your present, all silky to wrap it again but it's such a big present I'm not sure there'd be enough to cover it.'

My eyes had grown a little used to the darkness but Daisy was just too far across from me for me to see her. 'It's a little unfair,' Daisy continued. 'I've got almost nothing on – one stocking, a very flimsy garter belt and the teeniest pair of panties.' I was surprised to hear that so had to adjust the picture of her I had in my head for that dress had looked so tight, I couldn't believe she was wearing anything at all underneath it.

'I think you should join me,' she suggested.

'Coming right over,' I almost shouted as I struggled to get up from the couch.

'No. Stay there. I meant you should join me taking your clothes off. I'd like to hear you taking your shirt off, your trousers, your underpants, everything. I don't want anything in the way of that hard and strong present you brought for me. I'd like to listen to your clothes coming off, Do it slowly. Entice me. I have very sensitive ears. In fact, I'm sensitive all over. Just the sound of you uncovering all your muscles will start making me tingle. Ooh! Delicious!'

I began to do what she had asked. 'Tell me! Tell me what you're doing!'

I felt a little embarrassed but I described how I pulled my trousers off, my cock banging against my arm as I did it. 'Oh, the poor thing!' Daisy cooed. 'Always getting in the way. We'll have to keep it out of harm's way, find a place for it to tuck itself into. Warm and juicy. I know the very place. And I know he'll just love to find his way in there.'

Soon I was lying back on the couch with nothing on

and my cock beating a steady tattoo. I really wanted to find my way over to Daisy but the sound of her voice kept me in place as she described how she was rolling down her other stocking. She had rubbed her hand all along the length of her leg and I heard that faint swishy scratchy sound and I imagined my own hand sliding up that leg, reaching up to those panties, pushing the material aside with my fingers, feeling her slippery quim, stroking her there, making her push down to take my fingers deeper into her. But for the moment I had just to lie back and listen to her.

'Now I'm standing up ... and I know something else that's standing up! There goes my garter belt. All I have left is these teeny weeny panties, just covering me. Do I dare to pull them down for you? I'm really a very shy person. Still, I've come this far. Might as well go the whole hog. Shall I do it, Nick?'

'Yes, yes, please, yes!' I groaned. I was amazed just how randy I was feeling. I had always liked women to talk to me in sexy terms but normally it was not in the dark. But now Daisy was driving me crazy with her talk. She was good at talking, insinuating things. She rarely used the obvious words so she seemed subtle as well as sexy and this striptease in the dark was a really hot happening for me, and though it was a tease, I was now convinced that Daisy was enjoying doing this. But this time she was going to follow through.

'Here I am, all bare naked. And I think I want my present now.'

'I'll bring it right over.'

'No. You stay right there. I don't want you hurting yourself bumping into furniture. I'll turn the lights back on and then you'll be able to see me.'

I heard her move and then a small table lamp was

switched on. At first I didn't see her. I thought she was playing a little trick on me, hiding so that I'd have to find her. I managed to get out of the chair and peer around the room. The lamp didn't shed much light but my eyes circled the room. I turned a complete circle and when I had come round to looking across the back of the couch, there she was. And surprise, surprise! Daisy was still dressed, still in that bright red dress, smiling at me. And I was feeling a little foolish because my cock was sticking right out in front of me, pointing straight at her.

'I couldn't resist doing that,' she said through her giggles, 'just telling you I was stripping. But I didn't think you'd mind.' Then she pointed. 'At least a certain part of you seems to have enjoyed it. And to tell you the truth, so did I. And a certain part of me is more than ready to play with that present of yours.'

It was not the first time I had been duped in this way but Daisy was making it clear that this was only a preliminary. So I grinned at her and she grinned back. 'After what you said, maybe you'd like to help me do it all over.' She began to walk very slowly over to me and I also moved towards her. We met just at the end of the couch. She leaned to me, very careful not to let her body touch the long stiffness poking out in front of me.

This time the kiss she gave me was a deep one. It started like the others, a gentle, moist placing of her lips on mine, her tongue wriggling in, the tip curled a little, licking into the inner lips, feeling its way right to the corners, sliding along, then gradually she moved it into my mouth, testing it against the tip of my tongue, pushing it in, moving my tongue to the side, going further in as she brought herself to touch just the head of my cock against her stomach. Slowly her body circled very gently against my cock, her tongue making the same circling motions inside my mouth.

Then I felt her hand reach right under my balls and begin to stroke upwards, lingering. Sometimes separate fingers traced a slow trail around, sometimes her hands gripped the shaft, sometimes letting the whole length nestle on her palm. My prick was pointing straight up by now, pressed against my stomach. She brought her body close to mine as her tongue seemed to be even longer and deeper inside my mouth. We stayed that way, she grinding gently against me so that she could feel the hot shaft pressing hard against her, me feeling my knob rammed against my stomach, warm and titivated by the silky material of Daisy's dress.

Then she lifted one leg and hooked it round me, her heel resting just above the back of my knee. She exerted pressure so that I was squashed as close as I could be against her. Her mouth was working a little faster now with her tongue sliding in and out as I moved my body in slow motion against her. My cock felt huge as she made her body move with mine. My hands were round her pulling her close to me. I let them drop lower, smoothing over the dip of her waist, down, the curve of her arse under my palms. Her dress was so closely moulded to her that I was sure there was nothing underneath and that excited me for I knew that if I slid my hands under her dress I would soon be touching that sweetly soft and moist opening.

So after a little while I dropped my hands further till they reached the hem of her dress. Her hooked leg pressed more strongly as she felt my hands slowly drawing her skirt up. I soon encountered the tops of her stockings, the flesh there soft and warm. And I had been right. In spite of the fact that she had talked about pulling her panties down when she had described how she was undressing in the dark, she wasn't wearing any, just stockings and a garter belt under that skin-tight dress.

As she felt my fingers splay across the top of her thighs ready to probe further up and then in, somehow her mouth seemed to open even more. We were both now very excited, salivating around each other, our bodies swaying together, her hands now holding my arse tightly, as if she wanted me even closer. As one of my fingers reached in to touch the wet slit, she shuddered and moaned, 'Help me take it off. Now. Freedom. I want to be free. Get me out of it now.'

The sound of Daisy's husky order made me terrifically horny. Just the way she demanded to be undressed was enough to set my cock beating hard against her. My hands began to search for those buttons down the back of her dress that she had mentioned when she had been pretending to be stripping off. I started at the top where the dress was in a half-scoop across her back. The first button was tight – I suppose that was because the dress was so firmly skinned around her.

Daisy's wide-open mouth was slavering all over my face, her tongue lapping at me, sliding inside my mouth and she was letting out strangled words. 'Hurry! For God's sake, hurry!' she croaked, her wet lips skidding and sucking at my neck. The leg hooked on me was pushing at my own with an insistent rhythm so that my prick was ramming at her stomach. It was enormously exciting and I was having to control myself from spilling out all over her dress.

At last I got that first button undone. The second one was easier but it wasn't quick enough for Daisy. 'Faster! Faster!' she growled. Then she went on, 'Wait! I'll make it easier for you.' And she turned around with her back to me. I still had one hand under her skirt and she was careful to move so that my hand slid round so that I could fondle the firm globes of her arse. I could feel my cock touching her, prodding at the crack, the material stretched tight, shaping her arse so that the length of my shaft rode comfortably along that slim soft place between her buttocks.

Daisy by this time was doing a wriggling circle with her arse, moving it up and down so she could sample the full long stroke of my cock. She was obviously well tuned in to what we were doing. I suppose that act she had put on of stripping for me had had an effect on her as well. Now she was very steamed up.

I was still wrestling with her buttons. 'Wait a minute,' she said. She balanced herself against the arm of the couch and bent over. 'Now you can get at them better,' she whispered. I glanced down and saw this delectable set of buttocks outlined by the red silk of her dress. 'Get on with it!' she almost shouted.

As she was leaning over. I pressed my cock against her arse. She wriggled and opened her legs so that my cock slid in between. One of her hands hiked up her skirt and reached round to me, grabbing my cock, letting out a big, sexy sigh as she touched it for the first time. She pulled it quite roughly between her legs, letting the head sweep along her arse-crack, then probing in so that my shaft lay snugly along her slit. She was dripping wet and her hand soon became well moist with her juices. She held my cock in place there, smoothing her quim along my length, her hand still holding and stroking her moistness along it and down to my balls.

Again I was desperately near shooting off so I concentrated on the buttons and finally had them all undone. I peeled the dress away from her shoulders, folding it down at the waist. Then I reached my arms round and placed my hands on her breasts.

I'd always liked to see the way her breasts curved so firmly under the blouses and sweaters she wore. I was looking forward to touching them. They felt beautifully round and fitted into my hands perfectly. I tickled her nipples with my fingertips – they were already stiff but as I played with them they seemed to jut out even further.

Daisy was groaning and moaning, rubbing at my cock, dribbling wetly, her hand amazingly subtle in the way she was fondling the head, trailing fingers down the length, shoving it hard against her quim, teasing me a little by letting the head nudge just a little inside.

'I want to sit on this,' she murmured as she gave my prick a squeeze. 'It's a beautiful saddle. We're going for a lovely ride.' I was content to let things stay like this and Daisy was happy feeling my cock squirm along her slit, edging onto her clit, then back, prodding carefully and slowly along the creamy crack, back, with a gentle touch near her arse before pushing along the slit again. She was now so finely balanced that she could take her other hand and circle it round my arse, searching out the root of my balls, pinching them a little, holding them in her palm, her fingers gripping round the base of my cock hard, her other hand peeling back skin to expose more of my cock-head as it bathed in the warm flood between her legs.

I still hadn't managed to pull her dress completely off. It was bunched at her waist where we had pushed it as our hands worked at each other under it. I had, of course, rolled it off her shoulders and while I couldn't really see her, I had this picture in my mind of her bent over, legs wide apart, hands busy under the red silk which was all bunched together at the waist. I think most men get heated by picturing a woman with a dress half off, with its skirt pushed high and hands invisible under it. And it's especially exciting when the woman is helping in this. I suspect women also are excited when they imagine what it must look like, showing a whole length of leg when the dress is up high and they can feel a man's cock under there and they can't keep their hands off it.

I was certainly feeling tremendously worked up and it felt as if Daisy was too. I knew I would have to stop soon or I'd be gone, flooding her with a great spout of jism. I really wanted to fuck her and she'd made it obvious that that was her plan as well, part of her day of freedom.

It was if we were both thinking along the same lines because she straightened up, turned round to me, grabbed at my prick again, and said, 'You are a slowcoach! You haven't taken my dress off yet.' I reached for her and it was a struggle to peel it away from her waist. She stepped out of it when it was at her ankles and, still holding my cock, she manoeuvred me to the couch. 'Take the weight off your feet,' she breathed.

She literally arranged me on the couch, making me lie full-length – it was a long couch so there was room for her to kneel where my feet were. She held my ankles and pushed them apart. Then she bent down so that she was looking up at me with my cock directly in line with her eyes. She grinned and lowered her head so that her hair brushed against my ankles. Her hair was shoulder-length and thick – it felt soft on my flesh. She started to shake her head from side to side and her hair was spread across my legs. She slowly drew her head up my legs, letting her hair tumble across them, shaking from side to side.

Of course I sensed her rising up my legs as I watched her head moving across me. That feeling of her hair slowly rising towards my thighs gave me a real sense of urgency. My prick was standing very straight, waiting for her mouth. I knew this was going to happen but her progress up my legs seemed incredibly slow. I really wanted her mouth on me – I wanted her to swallow my cock. She was giving me little fluttery kisses along my legs and on the inside of my thighs but she was still not touching my cock. Her hands were stroking my thighs, her hair was trailed across my skin, my cock was twitching as it waited for her. In one sense I didn't want her to stop this sensuous massage with her hands and hair. I lay back and enjoyed this lavish attention. My shaft was straining up as I thought about how incredibly moist she was. I knew her mouth would be sweetly warm on me. I wanted to feel her take in my cock but I also wanted her to put it off for a little while so that I could enjoy thinking about it, imagining how she would rub her inner lips along its length, how her tongue would lap it, the tip a wet tickle on its length. The anticipation was a delight and my prick was pulsing, seemed to be growing stiffer and longer.

But the anticipation was as nothing to the way she rose to me, her hair covering my cock with thick tresses, One hand sneaked along my upper thigh, snaked under my balls, two fingers stretching up to grasp the base of my thickness. Her other hand gathered some hair and wrapped it along my length and stroked it lingeringly up, tickling the head with a little wisp or two of hair.

She lay like that for a minute or two. I was sighing

with sheer delight, waiting for that lovely slippery mouth to descend onto me. Instead she kept on with this smooth stroking – I could feel her nipples against my thighs. I tried to reach down to touch her breasts but she was now lying across me. I couldn't get my hands on her, so I just lay back and let her massage me, She was unbelievably gentle and slow. And still her mouth did not suck at me.

She moved over me upwards a little more until I felt my cock sliding along her face, her neck, down until it was lying along that valley between her breasts. Her tongue was now licking at my nipples while her two hands held her breasts softly on my cock and gradually I began to move in that warm space. The flesh of her breasts was hot and smooth, slightly sweaty, so that my cock was free to slide up and down there.

I began to stroke her hair across my chest and she reached her mouth up and took in two fingers of mine. She began to suck them deeply in, letting them slide out to her lips, her tongue flickering along their length before she sucked them inside again. This slow sucking of my fingers made me think how her mouth would be on my prick. I could feel my shaft hard and rhythmically slippery between her breasts, an intensely hot immersion in softness, the breasts tight against me, moving the skin down so that the head of my cock was exposed. I leaked a drop or two of come.

When Daisy felt that cream on her breasts, she took the fingers from her mouth and slid them onto my cock. Her fingertips played round the head and it was so fantastically sexy that it made me want her mouth on my cock. But at the same time I was feeling so deliciously relaxed that I just wanted her to continue what she was doing.

She slid further up my body, moving a little to the side, sucking at my nipples, moving herself till she was astride me and I was gazing at her glistening slit, moist with a frothy, bubbly flood. It was then that I felt her mouth descend onto my cock.

I took that as a signal for me to reach out my tongue and dab it gently onto that warm froth. I licked my tongue-tip along the slit, lingering at her clit, closing my lips on it. Her mouth was gulping in my length, her tongue circling the fatness, the head touching her back teeth and the soft flesh at the side of her mouth. She kept her mouth still while her tongue began to play. I kept my lips on her clit and let my tongue slide around it. She began to move her pelvis and it seemed as if she wanted my tongue to fuck her so I slid it into those wet, pink lips. At the same time her mouth began to work on my cock in the same way and she fucked my cock with her mouth.

While our mouths were so busy, of course, neither of us could speak. We were both making short grunting noises in the backs of our throat and once or twice I thought Daisy's mouth had taken me in so deeply that her vocal cords were buzzing against the head of my cock. I felt an incredible tingle that shivered along the whole length.

Her sucking was very controlled. She let her hair fall in a shower of soft swishes against my balls and her hands moved on my cock as she let it in and out of her mouth. She enjoyed what she was doing, I could tell, by the way her quim seemed to open under my tongue so that I could place it well inside. She tasted a little salty but she was so wet and warm my tongue was washed by a bath of sweetness as well. Her moistness seemed to flow all over my lips, gathering along the inner surfaces, my own saliva mixed along my gums with this oozy salt-sweetness.

Daisy was able to judge just how she was bringing me towards spilling out. She took her mouth away and let my cock nuzzle at her neck, pulling it up close to her eyes. I felt a spattering of jism ease out of the slit. When she saw it, she fingered it delicately, rubbing the juice across the head of my cock before she then licked at it with her tongue. And then she continued with those long lingering sucks along the length, in and out of her mouth, her hands doing unbelievable touches on my balls, slightly pinching them, then letting go to touch them deliberately, drawing her fingers around each ball as if she was measuring them, then feeling their weight in her palm.

Finally, after one long-drawn-out suck up the length of my cock, she breathed against the head with her warm voice seeming to cover me, 'I'm going to ride you!' I gave her one last, long lick along her slit as she moved herself across me, round and down. Holding the base of my prick delicately, she straddled me on her haunches, looking down to watch as she guided my cock inside her.

It sank into an ineffable slipperiness, a plushly warm moist velvet, the head probing in deeply as she lowered herself onto me. Somehow she had stretched her legs up to my shoulders so she was sitting on my cock. It gave her the chance to press down on me as if she wanted my cock to go as far inside her as possible.

We were so closely together, she pressed down on me hard, her legs firm on my shoulders, me lying with my cock rammed right inside her, that I thought we would just have to stay still. It seemed impossible to move. We stayed like that for some time as Daisy manipulated her inner muscles very gently along my prick. It felt like a lot of tiny fingers pulsing against my length, playing with the fat head. Somehow it seemed as if my shaft was sinking ever more deeply inside her.

Then gradually both of us slowly, even gingerly, experimented with moving. She leaned back, and that sent my cock wild because it made it rub against a different part inside her. She put her hands on the couch outside my legs and gently nudged them closer together. That made the grip of her quim on me even tighter and she obviously felt my rod stiffen more inside her, for she shuddered and groaned. Then she levered herself up on my cock by pushing on her hands. Her pelvis moved up until the head of my cock was resting just at her inner lips and she managed to remain there.

I dug my elbows into the soft cushions of the couch so that I raised my pelvis a little. Daisy was so wet and open that my cock slid in effortlessly, even though Daisy had closed her legs. I didn't think that we could keep this up but we both fitted together, she pushing up on her hands till I slid out to her frothy, creamy lips, then me pushing up my pelvis till my cock rose into her, deep and steady. And we kept that motion up till we both wanted more pace, more pressure and soon we became an incredible fucking machine, geared together, lubricated by lust.

Whether she thought about it at the same time as I did, I don't know but all of a sudden we both burst out into mad laughter. I was laughing because in a strange way I got this mental image of us on a bike with me in the saddle. My cock was the crossbar and Daisy was sitting astride it. We were both pedalling like mad. Daisy told me afterwards that she too remembered the idea of the bicycle. She was imagining a saddle with a great fat prong sticking up from it and, as she sat down on it and pedalled, the prong moved inside her. Whatever we were thinking, our fucking brought to both of us the idea of a bicycle built for two!

For a few minutes we kept those motions going, Daisy levering up to let my cock squirm right at the entrance to her quim, me wanting to plunge it upwards so that it probed deeply inside her. Of course it couldn't last very long. My prick seemed to gather itself into an immense stiffness, swollen more fatly, bursting with come. Daisy was unleashing fast rhythms on me and she too seemed to open herself wider till, balancing on only one hand while her other hand gripped my balls, she raised herself up. Just as my cock-head rested at her lips, the first gush of come spurted out. Daisy gasped as she felt the hot liquid wash across her slit and I pushed upwards so that the rest of my jism spouted out inside her. She told me she felt my cock throb each time a spurt came out. 'It was like a big, foamy wave breaking inside me,' she told me later as she lay across me, her fingers still sliding up and down my sticky prick as I let my fingers stroke around her quim, now more wet than ever with her bubbly froth. 'Just like champagne!' she said when I told her how frothy she was, mixed with my full burst of come.

We lay together for a time, caressing each other without returning to full arousal. Both of us were still intrigued by our 'ride', talking about it, and the talk kept us firmly fixed on the idea of repeating it.

After a time I struggled out of Daisy's arms and wandered round to the back of the couch to find the present I had for her. She exploded with shouts of approval when she saw the set of lingerie, holding the red panties against her. The sheer deep red had long insets of lace where the leg split high on her thighs.

'These are terrific!' she told me. She stroked the silk against herself. 'So soft. I bet you wouldn't be surprised to know that it puts me right back in the mood!' She leaned over me and let the silk smooth over my face and neck, then down to flicker against my cock which was already half-erect.

'I can see something else that's getting in the mood!' She held the panties up by one finger. 'Whenever I wear these, I'll remember tonight. They'll be my emancipation panties. You know what we used to call these? Not panties. French knickers. So I'm right in the French Revolution. Or part of the free French! I tell you what – you didn't see me before so this time I'll give you a chance to watch. Wait right there!'

She disappeared into her bedroom and after a while she called to me, 'Why don't you come in here?' And I found her there, standing by her bed wearing the red French knickers and camisole. Over the top she had wrapped the long robe though it was hanging open a little at the front. She looked delicious in the sheer red ensemble.

'Why don't you join me?' she invited so I walked to her, my cock already poking out in front of me. She folded me to her, wrapping the soft robe around me with her arms and planting a luscious kiss on my mouth. She smoothed the silk along my back, whispering in my ear, 'I can feel something that's trying to barge its way inside my free Frenchies!' And it was true. My cock had somehow got in a position to be nudging at the edges of the lace gusset on her thigh, throbbing against the silk as if it was knocking to go inside.

We stayed like that for a minute or two and we both became hot, beginning to feel anxious about tumbling onto the bed to mount our 'bicycle built for two' again.

The silk I felt against me reminded me of how slippery-soft Daisy's quim had been when I probed into it and I remembered her moist mouth on my cock. And of course that made me all the more aroused.

Finally Daisy pushed me down on the bed. 'Just sit there and watch. You're not in the dark this time.' She swayed back a little from me, holding out her arms so the sleeves of the robe were hanging down loosely. Slowly she peeled the robe down from her shoulders, keeping it in her fingers till it was quite low on her arms. She dropped her arms so that the robe slid down her body in a shimmer of red and there she was just in her free Frenchies, as she'd called them, her camisole and her black fishnet stockings she still had on. They blended in with her red outfit because there was a lace trim in black as well as the thin, filmy red silk.

'I can't do this really gracefully,' she said, her voice muffled as she pulled the camisole over her head, 'but here we are.' She threw the camisole at me when she pulled it all off and it landed across my thighs. 'Good shot!' she shouted. 'After all, I don't want to cover you up too much. I can see you're all at attention watching.' Then she placed her fingers in the waistband of those red panties and exquisitely slowly she pulled them away from her waist, down to uncover the hair above her quim, then further, stopping at the top of her thighs as the red went lower to reveal everything.

She acted the coy maiden then, one hand at her mouth, her eyes wide open staring at me, her other hand fiddling with the black lace. 'Oh, what must you think of me, showing you this?'

'I think it's terrific,' I said.

'They're so lovely,' she cooed as she let her hand stretch the elastic of the waistband, drawing the material further down till she stepped out of them. 'Is that better than keeping you in the dark?'

'It certainly is!'

She came towards me and laid her hand on my shoulder to push me back on the bed. She stooped to lift my legs on as well, resting the silk camisole across my stomach where my cock reached up, the head every now and again beating against the soft material. 'You wouldn't believe how soft these feel on me,' she said, looking down deliberately at my prick throbbing, and holding the red silk free Frenchies over me. 'Makes me randy as hell!'

She clambered onto the bed next to me. Her head nestled in the crook of my neck and her very low voice came to me clearly, 'I'm going to fuck you again!' Her hand holding the panties was stroking across my chest gradually moving down towards my cock. 'I'm going to make you as randy as I feel!'

'I'm already feeling randy!' I answered.

'Oh, but just like me,' she went on. She drew the panties down further, as she scrambled round, straddling me with her head now directly over my beating, straining cock. Her hand moved the panties across my length, lingering over my balls, then down my thighs. She moved a little further down to flatten herself against me, her breasts now brushing onto my prick. She swayed from side to side, and I felt her hard nipples banging gently, first one, then the other, against my cock-head.

Both her hands were now at my feet, and she was straightening the panties. 'I think these will just fit you. A bit tight but you'll like to feel them snug against you. Then you'll know just how it feels to be wearing them. You'll find out how randy they can make you feel.' And then she began to push my feet inside the free Frenchies.

When I realized what she was doing, I expected to feel embarrassed but I didn't feel that way. The red silk covered my feet and ankles in a cool slipperiness that rose up my legs. I had always loved to feel a woman's lingerie but usually with my cock pushing under skirts and against whatever was being worn underneath. That always made my cock warmly snug. I had never had a pair of panties actually on me in the way Daisy was doing it. With Teresa once, I had found myself somehow inside a half-slip she had been wearing but this dressing me in panties was a first. I have to confess I found the delicate fabric was really having the right effect on me as Daisy slid it very slowly up my legs.

And she was right. It made me more randy and I reached my mouth up to suck at Daisy's quim which was nicely placed in reach just above me. The smooth tickle of the red silk had now reached my thighs and my cock was anticipating how it would soon be covered with that soft material. 'I'll have to be careful. Mustn't snag it on this big fat dick here,' she said, and she carefully lifted the waistband out to accommodate my cock. Then she let the elastic fall and I felt my cock encased in silkiness.

All kinds of thoughts were rushing through my head at this point. My tongue was massaging those wet, pink lips of Daisy's and I recognized that she was becoming more steamed up. I think that seeing my cock bulging under her panties, tight around my length, was having a very sexy effect on her. She began to stroke the silk up and down on me, finally sneaking a hand under the silk to grasp and pull at my cock.

This was driving me crazy and so I was slurping very

wetly at Daisy and of course this made her hotter still. She tucked my cock back inside the silk, giving it a little pat before lowering her head to take it into her mouth wrapped in the silk. She seemed to be dropping lots of saliva down there and in between her deep sucks she murmured, 'I'm making my panties all wet as well. As wet as they get when I think about fucking. When I think about a cock riding up there. As wet as I am now. As wet as your cock.'

This playfulness with the silk and our mouths continued for a time. I reached down and placed the camisole across her arse as I kept licking her. Her mouth was now going great guns and I briefly thought her panties would soon be wet through with my jism. She pulled my cock out and sucked it incredibly deep into her mouth till suddenly she lunged away and yanked the panties free from my cock, pulling them down and off. 'Get rid of them!' she gasped, lifted herself away from me, turned round and unceremoniously, fast and almost roughly she sat herself on my cock.

And then began another ride on our patented 'bicycle'. This time it was a fast and furious ride, Daisy thrashing away above me. Normally this would have caused me to shoot off fast but of course it was still not so long since we had had our first ride. While I was really ready, feeling thick and long and stiff, I was able to keep going and match Daisy's speed.

She seemed to pick up the pace even more and I was thrusting upwards with my pelvis. Each time I thrust up, she yelled and then raised herself very high over me so that the tip of my cock was just lying along her frothing lips. She slid back and forward so that my whole shaft banged along her slit, prodding at her clit, nudging at the rim of her arsehole, then back and forward again until she wanted me inside her and she plunged onto me again.

And of course I responded by thrusting up into her. So we went on and, though we were both holding back, though we were both in that state when it would take us time to come, we managed it. Sometimes, when that moment comes, there is a such a sense of release and relief that I tend to slow down a little as if to make things last, to savour those moments to the full. Most women, especially those who can keep on having climax after climax, tend to grind away even faster, push cock into themselves even deeper and that's what Daisy did. She was yelling and groaning above, her head shaking from side to side, her quim brimming with juices. When she felt my come gushing out, that drove her even more wild and she was humping like mad. Normally I become quite depleted but Daisy was determined to keep going. For a while my cock kept some of its stiffness but eventually it was impossible to stay in place and Daisy rolled away and we lay quietly together. We may even have dozed off a little but soon I felt Daisy covering me with her long red robe, then lying full length on top of me, moving the material on me till I began to be aroused again. She grasped my cock and rammed it into herself, murmuring to me as she did it, 'What a Big Sid you are! The Terror of Moss Side! Well, I feel all mossy and moist,' and again we began another of our rides.

That went on through the night in some different variations. Daisy was an expert in trying out new positions, teasing me, flirting, rough sometimes, exceptionally gentle at other times and the night passed in a complete immersion in stroking, poking, prodding, gentle and mad.

We woke up the next morning tangled in Daisy's

bedsheets which had somehow also become entangled with her red silks. What woke me was Daisy's playing with me by wrapping me tightly first in the robe, then in the bedsheets, touching her hands all over me, always coming back to my cock till I couldn't stand it any longer. I wanted her hands on me free of all coverings so I rolled around till I'd got myself free. I pushed her back and rode my cock inside her and off we went again.

It was a glorious Emancipation Day ... and Night ... and Early Morning. Both Daisy and I agreed that it had been a marvellous celebration of freedom. 'I think we ought to celebrate our freedom for the whole week ... or the month ... or the year!' Daisy said, and I took that as an invitation, staying with her for several days, neither of us going out, just having an orgy of fucking with bouts of deep sleep in between.

In a way I was sorry that I hadn't been with Daisy before that night. On the other hand, the wait made it all the more sensational – a real marathon of a bicycle ride!

Epilogue

Barbara was lying across me, stroking my diminishing cock against her juicy quim, letting her hands rub our mixed juices and make the sleek moistness run along my length. She loved to have her hands sticky with come, so that they slid easily over my stiffness though I was wilting – she had suggested we go straight to bed after she had finished work. She picked me up and began to run her hands all over me as she drove with one hand on the steering wheel. She was full of laughter and happiness as she told me that a good business deal had fallen into her lap.

'Well, it didn't really fall into my lap. Let's say it was steered there. But anyhow, it's cause for celebration so the first thing is for me to steer this, and she gave my prick a very persuasive squeeze, 'into my lap as soon as we get home.'

And that's what we did. The delights of Barbara had not lessened in the three years I had known her. She was unbelievably open, full of surprises, full of affectionate tricks, an enormously talented bed companion. And this celebration of her business deal was also to be our last night together for some time. I was going off to my summer job in Torquay though that was going to be my last year there.

I had got my degree and I had been applying for

various jobs, mainly in teaching. I had stumbled into a position that I thought I was lucky to have found. I was starting to teach English at a private school out in Cheshire near Knutsford, the heart of the county set, the kind of environment that Mrs Courtney was part of, though she lived in the south in Hertfordshire.

I was at first dubious about accepting the job. After all, I was raised in the working class and I had always frowned on that Cheshire county set, 'All plus fours and kidneys for breakfast' was the phrase that had always stuck in my mind to describe it. But then Ron and his family were a part of that same set and I could never forget just what Mrs Courtney was like. I suppose these last three years had revised my opinion about the high-faluting snobbery and superiority I had always associated with county people.

The school seemed admirably orderly and serious about its students' education when I went for the interview. I immediately felt at home there; the teachers I met were mostly friendly and I must confess there were a couple of women teachers that took my eye. And of course I was surrounded by a whole bevy of nubile schoolgirls, inexperienced maybe but looking mature – I suspect that they had learned proper social behaviour in their families so acted like confident and graceful young women.

But it was really because the buildings, several rather stately buildings and a couple of old manor houses, looked so secure, so comfortable. I would be teaching small classes and, though a junior member of the staff, they were going to give me some of the upper school classes to teach. It looked to be an ideal opportunity.

Of course I would miss my friends in Manchester but,

as Barbara pointed out, 'You won't be that far away. You'll be able to tootle in to see me quite often – I'll keep my weekends free.' I imagined I would buy myself a car after a few weeks so I wouldn't be stranded out in the wilds of Cheshire.

I was not sure just where I would live – Barbara promised to help me find a place though, at first, I thought I might keep my place in Manchester and simply commute. But that would have made for long days and Barbara was insistent that I not wear myself out. 'I want you fresh as a daisy at the weekends,' she told me.

And Daisy? She had moved to London. I'd put her in touch with Gerry who had found her a cushy job in a solicitor's office. As far as I knew, she hadn't joined in with the other activities that developed around Gerry but I was sure that if she felt the urge, she'd be more than welcome in that company of women. I wouldn't have time to call in on her on my way to Torquay but she was going to come down to see me there during the summer – as was Barbara.

So my moving out to Cheshire was essentially not going to disturb my life considerably. I was looking forward to seeing whether there were any Mrs Courtneys connected with the school. I suspected that some of the parents might be socially (and sexually) active. And while I knew that as a teacher, I would have to be very careful about my dealings with the older girls, some of them might have older sisters who had been to the same school. Who knows? They might return to visit it on days when there were social events there.

So, all in all, I was very contented with my immediate future. This last evening I was spending with Barbara had started delightfully, promising to be a marathon of sexual exploits. So it was a double celebration – for my job and for Barbara's new business success.

I didn't want to bring business matters up while she was still busy caressing me with her slippery fingers, her mouth travelling around my body, her legs sprawling against me. But eventually I wilted down to limpness so I broached the subject of her deal.

'Well, I've been given carte blanche with the houses of Paradise Lost.' She grinned at me. 'Milton didn't survive so, with a bit of dickering, some notice of foreclosures, he took whatever money he could save from the shambles and ran.'

Since Lorna's moonlight flit and her going to live in York, we had had very little to do with Milton. I know Barbara had reported everything to Gerry and I suspect that Gerry moved in certain ways to clamp down on Milton.

Barbara went on to explain just how Milton had collapsed. 'I don't know how he did it but Gerry got certain people he knew up here to start to put financial pressure on Milton's investments. He had to keep moving them around and in the process he kept losing money. Gerry did it very subtly and very slowly and Milton, I'm sure, never knew this was a plot against him. He just thought it was the pressures of the market and he was having a run of bad luck. Then over the last few weeks Gerry began to put a lot of extra pressure on him and Milton had to make some quick decisions. He started to take out mortgages on Paradise Lost to cover his losses, he thought, then found he couldn't meet all the payments. So he decided to sell off quickly and get out. That meant Gerry simply passed the houses over to me to deal with. I can sell them for him or rent them and I get loads of commission.'

She leaned over and gave me a big kiss. 'How's it feel to make love to a rich woman, Nick?'

'The money doesn't matter,' I said. 'You're as good as gold at fucking.'

'You're such a charming boy and you have such a lovely way of expressing yourself. Those schoolgirls don't know how lucky they are to have you as a teacher.'

'I've been lucky enough to find the right kind of teachers over the last four years or so,' I said.

'Oh, I didn't mean you were going to teach them all *those* things!' Her hands were now working on me as there were distinct signs of revival. 'I've still got a lot of lessons to teach you,' she murmured as she leaned down, her mouth opening to bathe my cock in her soft sweetness.

'Well, after all,' I said, 'I will be teaching English and that means that I'll have to give them a few lessons in oral expression.'

'Like this,' Barbara breathed. Her mouth descended and covered me with a silky slide.

Headline Delta Erotic Survey

In order to provide the kind of books you like to read - and to qualify for a free erotic novel of the Editor's choice - we would appreciate it if you would complete the following survey and send your answers, together with any further comments, to:

> Headline Book Publishing
> FREEPOST (WD 4984)
> London
> NW1 0YR

1. Are you male or female?
2. Age? Under 20 / 20 to 30 / 30 to 40 / 40 to 50 / 50 to 60 / 60 to 70 / over
3. At what age did you leave full-time education?
4. Where do you live? (Main geographical area)
5. Are you a regular erotic book buyer / a regular book buyer in general / both?
6. How much approximately do you spend a year on erotic books / on books in general?
7. How did you come by this book?
7a. If you bought it, did you purchase from: a national bookchain / a high street store / a newsagent / a motorway station / an airport / a railway station / other........
8. Do you find erotic books easy / hard to come by?
8a. Do you find Headline Delta erotic books easy / hard to come by?
9. Which are the best / worst erotic books you have ever read?
9a. Which are the best / worst Headline Delta erotic books you have ever read?
10. Within the erotic genre there are many periods, subjects and literary styles. Which of the following do you prefer:
10a. (period) historical / Victorian / C20th / contemporary / future?
10b. (subject) nuns / whores & whorehouses / Continental frolics / s&m / vampires / modern realism / escapist fantasy / science fiction?

10c. (styles) hardboiled / humorous / hardcore / ironic / romantic / realistic?

10d. Are there any other ingredients that particularly appeal to you?

11. We try to create a cover appearance that is suitable for each title. Do you consider them to be successful?

12. Would you prefer them to be less explicit / more explicit?

13. We would be interested to hear of your other reading habits. What other types of books do you read?

14. Who are your favourite authors?

15. Which newspapers do you read?

16. Which magazines?

17. Do you have any other comments or suggestions to make?

If you would like to receive a free erotic novel of the Editor's choice (available only to UK residents), together with an up-to-date listing of Headline Delta titles, please supply your name and address. Please allow 28 days for delivery.

Name..

Address..

....

....

A selection of Erotica from Headline

SCANDAL IN PARADISE	Anonymous	£4.99 ☐
UNDER ORDERS	Nick Aymes	£4.99 ☐
RECKLESS LIAISONS	Anonymous	£4.99 ☐
GROUPIES II	Johnny Angelo	£4.99 ☐
TOTAL ABANDON	Anonymous	£4.99 ☐
AMOUR ENCORE	Marie-Claire Villefranche	£4.99 ☐
COMPULSION	Maria Caprio	£4.99 ☐
INDECENT	Felice Ash	£4.99 ☐
AMATEUR DAYS	Becky Bell	£4.99 ☐
EROS IN SPRINGTIME	Anonymous	£4.99 ☐
GOOD VIBRATIONS	Jeff Charles	£4.99 ☐
CITIZEN JULIETTE	Louise Aragon	£4.99 ☐

All Headline books are available at your local bookshop or newsagent, or can be ordered direct from the publisher. Just tick the titles you want and fill in the form below. Prices and availability subject to change without notice.

Headline Book Publishing, Cash Sales Department, Bookpoint, 39 Milton Park, Abingdon, OXON, OX14 4TD, UK. If you have a credit card you may order by telephone – 0235 400400.

Please enclose a cheque or postal order made payable to Bookpoint Ltd to the value of the cover price and allow the following for postage and packing:
UK & BFPO: £1.00 for the first book, 50p for the second book and 30p for each additional book ordered up to a maximum charge of £3.00.
OVERSEAS & EIRE: £2.00 for the first book, £1.00 for the second book and 50p for each additional book.

Name ....

Address ....

....

....

If you would prefer to pay by credit card, please complete:
Please debit my Visa/Access/Diner's Card/American Express (delete as applicable) card no:

Signature .... Expiry Date ....